GOING HOME

HARRIET EVANS

Going Home

HarperCollins*Publishers*

HarperCollins*Publishers*
77–85 Fulham Palace Road,
Hammersmith, London W6 8JB

www.harpercollins.co.uk

Published by HarperCollins*Publishers* 2005
1 3 5 7 9 8 6 4 2

A catalogue record for this book
is available from the British Library

ISBN 0 00 719843 4

Typeset in Sabon by Palimpsest Book Production Limited,
Polmont, Stirlingshire

Printed and bound in Great Britain by
Clays Ltd, St Ives plc

*To Rebecca and Pippa, with love
and thanks for everything*

'But I think she would have been happy with
Fabrice,' I said. 'He was the great
love of her life, you know.'
'Oh dulling,' said my mother sadly. 'One
always thinks that. Every, every time.'

Nancy Mitford, *The Pursuit of Love*

Christmas

ONE

The bus ground its way slowly up the Edgware Road as I sat, like a mad old bag lady, gripping my last-minute Christmas shopping between my legs and on my lap, casting angry glances at those who tried to sit anywhere near me. It was Christmas Eve and I'd only just got round to buying my presents. With the depressing predictability of riots on May Day, rain at Wimbledon, and stories in August about hamsters who can play the kazoo, I promise myself every year that I will have bought and wrapped all my presents by 15 December, and every year I end up in Boots with an hour to go, buying my father a small, slanting glass toothpick-holder, my mother a furry hot-water-bottle cover endorsed by the Tweenies, and my sister Jess a gilt-edged notelet set that says, 'Happy Christmas!'.

I jumped off at the lights, closed my eyes and ran across the road, praying that this would not be how I met my death. I had half an hour before Tom, my cousin, and Jess arrived to pick me up. We were going home, *home* home, in one of thousands of cars setting forth from London, after their occupants had put in a half-day at work, bags hastily packed, driving into the twilight. It was only three p.m., but dusk already seemed to be descending over the city.

My flat is just off the Edgware Road, behind an odd assortment of dilapidated shops that are a constant source of delight to me. There are the usual cut-price off-licences ('Bacardi Breezer's at 75p!') and poky newsagents, neither of which ever stock Twiglets but promise they'll have some next time I come in. There's also an undertaker, a computer shop selling ancient Amstrads, a joke shop called Cheap laffs – handy when you're in urgent need of a pair of fake comedy breasts – and Arthur's Bargains, which, incongruously, sells pianos and keyboards. I would not personally spend my hard-earned cash on a musical instrument from a place called Arthur's Bargains but *chacun à son gout*, as the French say. Off a tiny alley, so nondescript I have frequently noticed people not noticing it, away from the roar of the cars and lorries that thunder up and down the Edgware Road day and night, is a small cobbled street with tall, spindly houses, one of which is mine. Well, one of the shoebox flats on the top floor is mine.

The noise of traffic faded as I turned into my street. I could even hear the faint rumble of a tube beneath me, full of passengers escaping from work to enjoy the usual bout of indigestion, seasonal belligerence and disappointing new episodes of *Only Fools and Horses*. The flowers I'd bought for Mum, fiery red and orange ranunculas, crackled in their brown-paper wrapping as I grappled with the temperamental locks on the front door. I hauled myself up the stairs, struggled with my own front door, nudged it open with my bottom and lowered my bags on to the floor.

I headed into my tiny bedroom, which I love despite its size, sloping roof and lack of light. The view isn't uniformly picturesque, unless you call Wormwood Scrubs picturesque. But it's my flat, my view, so while other people look out of the window and say, 'Oh, my God – is that a dead body in your street?' I say, 'You can see Little Venice from here, if you stand on that chair and use a periscope.'

The packing I'd been so smug about at one o'clock this morning was not at the advanced stage I'd imagined when I rushed out of the door, hung-over and dishevelled, a handful of hours later. I'd packed all my socks but no shoes, seven pairs of trousers and no jumpers, and had obviously been in a nostalgic mood because Lizzy the drunk had seen fit to pack three teddies (bears, not lingerie), a collection of *Just William* stories, and just one pair of knickers.

Expecting to hear the beep of Tom's car horn at any minute, I rushed around the flat, plucking Sellotape and knickers out of drawers, contact-lens solution and moisturizers from the bathroom cupboard, shoving one plastic bag of presents inside another, watering plants picking up the papers and magazines that lay strewn across the floor and dumping them beside the sofa. The flat had a dusty, neglected air. Christmas cards had fallen over and not been picked up, videos and CDs lay out of cases, and there was a collection of unopened, unthought-of statements from BT, the bank, my mobile phone company. I loved my flat. I'd bought it two years ago from the old lady I used to rent it from. It had been painted by me, the pictures and photos were put up by me, and the hole in the plaster by the front door had been made by me kicking the wall when I was cross. It was my home. But it was at times like this, as I dashed around, longing to get away, that I knew it wasn't really a home, not in the way Keeper House always had been, since long before I was born.

As I was cramming some old newspapers into the wastepaper basket, I heard a car horn and leaned out of the sitting-room window. Tom and Jess were waving up at me.

'I've got fags!' Tom shouted.

'And I've got mags!' Jess chorused.

'I'm coming!' I yelled down at them, and scooped up my suitcase and bags, pausing at the door as I spotted the answer-phone flashing. Like a cross between a *t'ai chi* instructor and a Russian weightlifter, I bent my knees slowly and elbowed the play button.

'You have two messages,' said the machine, as Tom leaned on his horn.

'Well, come on, then,' I said, in frustration to the machine.

'Message One. Hi, Lizzy, it's Ash here. I'm just ringing to say you left your chequebook at work. Anyway, happy Christmas and have a lovely time at home and I'll speak to you when you get back. Oh, and I forgot to tell you this today and it will really annoy you but you know Sally? Press-department Sally? Well, she saw Jaden on Sunday and he told her you still haven't told him whether you'll go out with him or not and he thinks you don't like him any more. He also thinks you're not over your ex and you're holding on to negativity in your life and all women have these flaws and essentially hate men, which is why their menstrual cycles club together when they live in the same house, to exclude men from the life of their women. But he also said he'd still like to sleep with you and that you have great boobs. I agree. 'Bye.'

'Oh, God,' I said.

'Message Two. Lizzy, it's Tom. I've got this week's *heat*, so don't buy it. Also, can you bring some CDs? I've got a new streaming system in the car and you can play about fourteen or something at the same time. Also, I just spoke to Jess and she spoke to your mum and last they heard Uncle Mike said he couldn't come back. He's been out of town and has to work in a couple of days. Bye then.'

I clenched my teeth at the first message and moaned at the second. Jaden. Oh, Jaden. He was a scriptwriter and I met him at work. He lived in LA and was bloody gorgeous but totally insane, ringing me at seven on a Sunday morning to tell me that the wheat I ate was clinging to my lower intestine and poisoning my bowels, which was why my liver was wet and I felt drained all the time. When I later explained I felt drained because I kept going out and getting drunk by mistake, then waking up in the middle of the night lying on my sofa fully clothed, he simply shook his head. I'd reserve judgement about whether to see him again till the hell of New Year's Eve was over. And as for not being over my ex, well . . . ha.

And it was gutting about Uncle Mike. Even though we'd all known he probably wouldn't be able to get the time off, Christmas wouldn't be the same without him. Uncle Mike is one of those people who makes everything brilliant the moment he walks into a room.

The horn beeped long and loud, and I roared, 'Coming – flipping heck!' waved goodbye to my poor neglected flat and locked the door on my London life. My heels clattered on the cobbles as I slung my bags into the boot, kissed Tom and Jess, then flung myself into the back seat.

After a heated discussion about which radio station to listen to, and having plumped for Capital, we argued about what time we'd get home and whether or not we were late. Then, once we'd reached the motorway, we argued about Jess's request to go to the loo. I pointed out that, while she was my younger sister, she was twenty-five now and should have learned to control her bladder for the duration of a two-hour journey. Tom pointed out that it was his car and if she peed on the seat he would personally skin her alive, so we stopped at the first service station we came across.

By this time it was dark, nearing five o'clock, and a light drizzle was falling. Capital had long since gone out of range,

7

and we were listening to a CD of carols Jess had produced 'to get us in the mood'. Tom and I called her tragic for buying it, then sang along for the rest of the motorway, quarrelled again, then played Shoot Shag Marry, yelling rudely at each other's choices.

'OK, OK, OK!' Jess shouted, as we passed the last exit before ours. 'Tom, this is one for you. OK. Janet Street-Porter, Esther Rantzen, Lily Savage. Shoot, shag or marry?'

'Good one, Jess,' I said. 'Tom, that's easy, I know who I'd pick.'

'But you're weird,' said Tom. 'Right. I'd shoot Esther Rantzen. I'd shag Janet Street-Porter. And I'd marry Lily Savage.'

'Are you mad?' I shrieked. 'You'd marry Lily Savage over Janet Street-Porter? No way! She'd eat you for breakfast. And she'd be off with Dale Winton and Cilla Black all day long. You'd be a grass widow.'

'Hm,' said Tom. 'I'll take a chance. Better than Street-Porter jawing on all day.'

'No, I like her. She's into hill-walking and stuff. You'd be able to have great chats. And are you gay? Lily Savage is a man in drag.'

'Like you'd be able to tell. And since when have you been into hill-walking?' Tom sneered.

'That's not the point. You've picked the wrong one, that's all.'

'You're a fine one to talk,' Tom snapped.

There was an awkward silence.

'I meant in the game, not in real life,' he said, after a moment.

'I know you did,' I said.

Jess cleared her throat. 'Lizzy, your turn. OK, this is good. Right – Jonny Wilkinson, David Beckham, Mike Atherton.'

'Easy,' I said. 'I'd shoot David Beckham, because I think

he's a bit of a wally. I'd shag Mike Atherton, because he seems nice. And I'd definitely marry Jonny Wilkinson – I'd live on a rugby field if he asked me.'

Tom slapped his forehead. 'God, oh, my God,' he moaned. 'Are you two serious? For a start, *Mike Atherton*? Why include him?'

'He's the cricket captain,' said Jess, looking surprised. 'You know, for England.'

'No, he's not, you mallet! He hasn't been for ages! Jesus . . . And, Lizzy, even if he was, are you saying you'd shoot David Beckham and shag Atherton instead? I mean, seriously?'

'Yes,' I said firmly, knowing I'd made a bit of an error. I mean, David Beckham may speak like a six-year-old girl but look at him! However, I couldn't let Tom know I agreed with him. 'I'm telling the truth,' I said.

'You're lying,' Tom said crossly.

'So are you,' I said automatically.

Tom frowned. 'What do you mean?' he said.

'You always do this! You always pick them to annoy me, then lie about who you like best. You never tell the truth about it.'

'I didn't pick them,' Tom said. 'It's only a game.'

'But I'm taking it seriously and you're not,' I said.

'Well, I don't know what to say. You're a terrible picker. And I won't say what's on the tip of my tongue because you'll get upset.'

'What?' I asked, then realised he was going to say something mean about David. My David, not David Beckham. My ex-David. 'Oh, right. Forget it.'

Even though Jess, Tom and I all lived in London, we saw each other less frequently than we would have liked. Jess is doing an art foundation course and living in a crummy flat in South Clapham with three schoolfriends. I love my sister,

9

but she can't even draw a circle, let alone a 3D object, so I'm not quite sure what she does all day.

Tom is a high-powered lawyer. He works terribly hard and lives in trendy Clerkenwell where, in his infrequent leisure time, he surrounds himself with gossip magazines and indulges his obsession for high-tech gadgets. Aside from my parents and sister, Tom is my favourite person in the world. We speak often, usually when he's still in the office at eleven p.m. and I'm in a pub, drooling into my phone and slurring, 'Comehere! Youneedadrink!' Tom is terribly nice-looking. His hair does lovely floppy things without seeming outrageously Huge Grunt-ish, he's always tanned, and he's very smiley, which masks the fact that he is the most sardonic, annoying person in the world.

The only person Tom really loves, I'm sure, is his mother Kate, who lives near my parents. When we were both three his father, Tony, had a heart-attack and died. He was only twenty-eight, the next in age to my dad. Tom can hardly remember him now, although he can picture lying beside him in the long grass of the meadow opposite Keeper House one summer and being tickled so much he was sick. I always think that's a rather unfortunate last memory to have of your dad, but Tom always says no, because it's complete; he can remember what he was wearing, how he felt, what his dad looked like, and how hot it was. Tom doesn't talk much about Tony, in fact none of us does. But our house is full of reminders of him, from a little cricket trophy he won when he was twelve to his huge collection of opera programmes, and I think Tom likes looking at them secretly when he goes there. And being in the house where his father grew up.

As we headed deeper into the countryside, the roads became thinner and darker, the trees arching over us. The car wove its way through the old familiar places, the scenes of our childhood that I always forgot about until I came back. We were getting closer and closer to home.

Past the meadow we used to own when my aunt Kate still rode and kept a pony there, and where as children we used to play Funerals for Pets, a rather ghoulish game involving the re-enactment of the various ceremonies we'd held for recently deceased dogs, cats, hamsters, gerbils and guinea-pigs. Along by the river that had an island at its centre, then skirting the edge of a small wood, where Tom once got lost, gave up on civilian life and determined to be a child of the forest until our other aunt, Chin, found him there. The road sloped gently down the side of the valley and now I could just make out Wareham village, a mile away – it was the same view as the one from my bedroom. Now we were driving past the house where sweet Mrs Favell lived: she had made a pet of me when I was small and rewarded me with old copies of the *Radio Times*, a glamorous luxury to Jess and me because it was banned in our house as a waste of money. Last time I was home I found an old copy and was disappointed to see that its most exciting feature was on the new series of *Ever Decreasing Circles*.

We passed the track that led down to the ivy-covered tunnel of the long-neglected railway, along which the steam trains had ferried my father and his brothers to school, and my grandparents to town. It had been closed down long before I was born, and replaced with belching, unreliable buses, crowded and sticky, especially in summer, and thoroughly unsatisfactory.

'Nearly there,' said Tom, as he swung off the main road, the sound of wet leaves mulching beneath the car. 'Can't believe it. I thought I'd die of alcohol poisoning before I made it to Christmas Eve.'

I knew what he meant. I find the lead-up to Christmas so

11

exhausting that it's sometimes a struggle to preserve some energy for the holiday. Some of the stores on Oxford Street put their Christmas lights up two weeks before Hallowe'en. It's ridiculous. I remembered the slanting glass toothpick-holder and shuddered, resolving that next year I really would do my shopping before Bonfire Night.

'So, who's going to be there when we arrive?' Jess asked.

'Mum will, because we're staying at yours,' Tom said. Kate lived in a cottage down the road from my parents.

'And Mike's definitely not coming?' I asked.

'Mum spoke to him a week ago. He's obviously knackered, and he has to be back in the office on, like, the twenty-seventh to finish some deal.'

'What if he's just lying, doing an Uncle Mike joke?' Jess said hopefully.

'Don't get your hopes up,' Tom said. 'He's not coming, and that's that.'

Mike was Dad's eldest brother and everyone's favourite. He's the funniest man I've ever met. He did a lot of the work necessary to earn that title when I was about five years old and fairly easy to impress, but he somehow knows exactly what will please you most, or cheer you up when you need it. Who else would forget his godson Tom's tenth birthday, then arrange, a week later, for a pair of remote-controlled toy cars, complete with flashing lights, proper gears and red enamelled bonnets to be delivered from Hamleys by a man in full livery? Who, for my thirteenth birthday, took charge of the party when Mum was ill with flu and escorted me, with ten of my friends, to the cinema, where we saw a '15' film (*A Fish Called Wanda*) then went to Pizza Express where he let us all have a glass of wine and tipped the waiter to go and buy me a proper birthday cake from the patisserie next door? Mike.

Actually, more often than not he's useless. He never turns

up, he has no idea how old you are or what you're doing, he's late, he's disorganized, and when he's there he often has no idea what's going on, but I suppose that's part of what makes him so fab – you never know what he's going to do next.

Mike is a high-powered lawyer, like Tom, and lives in New York where he works even harder than Tom does and has an infrequent succession of girlfriends. 'The law is my mistress, Suzy,' he'd say, in answer to Mum's hopeful enquiries about his love life.

'I don't care who your mistress is, you stupid man,' Mum would reply crossly. 'Have you got a girlfriend?'

Tom negotiated the crossroads through the village. A Christmas tree covered with twinkling lights shone through a cottage window, and in another I could see the glow of a television. The rain had stopped, and the temperature had dropped sharply.

'Mum told me yesterday that Chin's bringing her new man,' Jess said.

'I didn't know she was seeing someone.' Tom was obviously nettled by this information.

'Wait! It's not that Australian guy . . . Gibbo? She's bringing *him*?'

'Apparently,' said Jess. 'It must be more serious than we thought.'

'Must be, if she's willing to expose him to Christmas at home,' I said.

Chin was Dad's youngest sibling by a mile, and more like a cousin to us than an aunt. She was a designer: some of her scarves had been sold in Liberty and she also made necklaces and little bags. She lived in London too, but I hadn't seen her for a while, although she had a flat not too far from me, in Portobello Road. Even now she seemed the epitome of

13

chic Bohemian glamour, without even trying; the kind of woman who could walk into a junk shop and say, 'Wow, what a delightful eighteen-century French armoire for fifty p! I'll take it please,' while if I'd been in there three seconds earlier I'd only have spotted a rusty old baked bean tin for four hundred pounds.

She'd been seeing Gibbo for a few months now and all I knew about him was that he had long hair and wore flip-flops in November. Jess had bumped into them in Soho one evening, and Chin – who normally goes out with worldly Frenchmen or devastatingly handsome record executives who break her heart, rather than dishevelled young Australians who punch her jovially in the arm and say 'Let's get going, mate!' – couldn't get away fast enough.

'That's it, then,' Jess said. 'That's everyone.'

'You've forgotten your parents,' said Tom. 'Perhaps they don't count, though. I mean, it's their house. They're always there.'

TWO

It was my parents' house, but it felt like home to all of us. The home of the Walter family. It had been for over a hundred years, pretty amazing when you think about it. My great-great-grandfather, Sir Edwin Walter, had been a successful society artist who painted Victorian ladies who lunched. Elise was the dark-eyed eighteen-year-old daughter of a paper manufacturer. They had fallen in love when he painted her. He asked her father if he could marry her, and her father said no, that Edwin was a flaky London painter without roots, living in a shambolic studio in Hampstead, of all places.

So my great-great-grandfather, who until then had never thought about anyone but himself, went looking for somewhere to settle down, and found Keeper House. The owner had just died: his family had lived there since it was built in 1592, and he was the last of the line. Just one family, for three hundred years. It was small, dilapidated, unloved and scruffy, but my great-great-grandfather looked out over the valley, at the meadows, the fields and the stream, and up into the twinkling windows, and knew immediately he would live there with Elise. When he persuaded her father to bring her down to see it, family legend has it that all three stood in the hallway and toasted Elise and Edwin's future happiness. I've always loved that story.

Keeper House is built in a mellow golden stone that gleams in summer and glows in winter. It's L-shaped, with high, leaded windows whose casements jam in wet weather, long, rambling corridors with uneven floorboards, and evil hot-water pipes that rarely work and sound like the Edinburgh Tattoo when they do. It's a beautiful house, and we were lucky to have grown up there. It is encircled by a wall, and at the front there is a terrace of flagstones, worn smooth with age, where tiny white flowers spring up in the cracks each spring. At the back there is a long lawn and a walled garden, where rows of lavender stretch from the kitchen door, punctuated by tumbling, sweet-smelling roses, mustardy lettuce and the tastiest potatoes.

In summer it's the best place in the world to live. In winter, it can be a nightmare: freezing, draughty, prone to breakdowns and temperamental behaviour, but we never mention this out of politeness to the house – at least, I don't. I once found Mum hugging the ancient boiler and banging her head against its red-painted curves, moaning, 'Why do you do this to me?'

Tom took the last corner and we veered left down the driveway. Jess and I craned our necks like a couple of five-year-olds. 'There's Chin, and that must be Gibbo,' Jess said. I could see them all through the big leaded bay window as Tom brought the car to a halt – Mum, mug in hand, half standing, smiling, Dad beaming as he walked towards the front door, Chin and Gibbo following him, then Kate.

They filed out one by one. 'Hello!' we cried. 'Hello!' I hugged Dad, shook hands with Gibbo and kissed Chin.

'Darlings, you're here!' My mother was holding a stodgy-looking piece of cake, which she waved at us. 'Oh, I'm so glad to see you. You made good time, didn't you?' She kissed me and Jess, then Tom. 'Come inside, we're having a Bavarian *stollen* I've made.'

Jess and Tom rolled their eyes, just as Kate appeared. 'Hello, Tom,' she said, and gave him the kind of hug that the Rock would have been proud of.

As we entered, the smell of home flooded over me, a potent blend of damp old flagstones, burning logs and something baking in the Aga. Then I caught the scent of the Christmas tree in the hall and the boughs of pine that were laid along the windowsills throughout the house.

'I'll make a fresh pot of tea,' Mum said. 'Why don't you shove your bags upstairs so we don't fall over them?'

Jess and I lugged our suitcases up the carved staircase that curved over the hall, along the galleried corridor, from which you could drop things on the heads of new arrivals, past the alcove with the worn-out rocking chair and a bookcase crammed with green Penguins and cheap old cloth hard-backs, past our parents' room, to the corner of the L where my bedroom was, a long low room with windows on both sides.

I threw off my shoes, flung my bags of presents on to the bed, then went to open the corner casement. Out beyond me stretched the sloping valley, with the lights of Wareham in the distance, smoke curling from the occasional chimney. The clouds had cleared and the stars were out, shining in clusters above the fields. The mulberry tree on the terrace had been festooned with white lights that shone like magic in the dark. I could hear Mum talking to Kate in the kitchen. An owl hooted in the woods behind me.

'I'm home,' I said, and hugged myself.

There is a tradition in my family that on Christmas Eve we drink sloe gin. This is one of the many traditions that characterize the yuletide period of joy, which starts in October when we pick the sloes in the hedgerows above the house. Armed with plastic bags and hats, because it always rains, we all set forth from the house searching for the plump, blue-black berries that nestle between the thorns.

It's not easy, sloe-picking. A film executive from LA took me out to lunch in a glassy Soho restaurant this year and peered quizzically at my scratched hands, which looked rather dramatic against the white linen tablecloth. 'I do all my own stunts,' I said, then told him how I'd spent Sunday afternoon. He evidently thought I – and my family – was completely mad.

When Jess was little she looked like a monkey, not facially but in physique. She could climb anywhere, once Mum smacked her for climbing on to the roof at home and playing her recorder there (a bit like Brian May at Buckingham Palace, but smaller and with less hair). She used to put up the lights in the mulberry tree, scampering among the branches until she had nearly garrotted herself. When our late cat Seamus climbed up to the highest bookshelf in the study and refused to come down, Dad handed Jess a fiver and a ladder and left the room. She was brilliant at sloe-picking – small and lithe, she would have located lots of berries while the rest of us were crying, 'Ooh, where's the bag? I think I've found one!' This year she had excelled herself, so there was a lot more gin than usual to drink.

Later that evening we all gathered in the sitting room to taste the results of our hunter-gathering, and wish each other a happy Christmas. If I'd been at home in London, I'd have been settling down with a large glass of red wine and a plate of pasta mixed with butter and Marmite (don't knock it till you've tried it) in my bobbly old socks with my hair pushed back in a bobbly old hairband. But at home in Keeper House

18

the formalities of another age lingered: although no one dons white tie and tails or dusts off the tiara, I had still felt it necessary to run a brush through my hair, change my top and put on some more lip gloss. Mum and Kate, both creatures of habit, were modelling Marks & Spencer's festive collection – a riot of burgundy crushed velvet and elasticated palazzo pants.

Mum had put ivy along the sitting-room mantelpiece and around the lamps, and sprigs of holly on top of the paintings. She was pouring the sloe gin into little glasses and singing along to a Frank Sinatra CD, while Dad was handing round crisps. Gibbo, who had endeared himself to us by calling Chin 'mate' and giving her a fireman's lift up the stairs, was standing by the fire. He'd smoothed down his extraordinarily curly long hair with water and now wore a plaid shirt buttoned to the neck and a confused expression.

'No sign of Mike, then?' asked Kate, as she came into the room.

'He could still turn up, you know,' said Dad. 'He booked his flight and the car ages ago. Perhaps he'll call.' He looked hopefully at the phone, as if he expected it to suddenly say, 'He's on his way, sir, just passing Membury Services now in fact.'

'When was the last time you spoke to him?' Tom asked.

'Not sure – Kate, he rang you last week, didn't he?'

'Yes,' Kate said. 'When did he phone you?'

'Last week. But he left a message yesterday – it didn't make much sense. I think he was a bit the worse for drink, unfortunately. Still, I got the impression he hated work and wouldn't be able to make it.'

'How?'

'Well, he said he hated work, and that he wouldn't be able to make it.'

'Take a glass,' said Mum, distributing drinks. 'Ah, Chin,

19

don't you look lovely?' she continued, as Chin appeared in the doorway, wearing a beautiful black velvet skirt and a skinny wool top printed with roses and studded with little sequins – which Jess was staring at enviously.

'Thanks, Suzy,' said Chin, helping herself to a glass. 'So, young Lizzy, how's work?'

I cannot tell you how much I hate that question when I've just stopped thinking about work for the first time in weeks. I work as a scout for the film company Monumental, searching for books, magazine articles, TV programmes and, of course, scripts that would make good films. Then I develop these projects, and it's a sign of how totally stupid my job can be that I've been doing it for three years and only one film has come about as a result of my work. Two near misses one that got to casting stage but fell through for lack of money and a bastard American producer who pulled out, and the one I've just started working on, but that's it. 'Work's fine,' I said firmly. 'It's lovely to be on a break now, though. I'm exhausted.'

'I know what you mean.' Chin nodded. 'But I'm practically the only person I know left in the country. All my friends have buggered off to get some sun.'

I could well believe this since most of Chin's friends seem to be trust-fund millionaires who either run crusty cafés serving green tea in Notting Hill, design jewellery, write screenplays or check into Promises rehab centre in Malibu. 'Gibbo seems nice,' I said casually. 'Where did you meet him?'

Chin looked around. Gibbo was talking to Dad.

'Oh, here and there.' She said. Chin is always secretive about her love-life. 'He's a carpenter, so I thought he'd like to see the house. Especially the staircase,' she added unconvincingly.

I tried not to laugh. Very brave of you to bring him along.'

'Well, you know.' Chin took a swig of gin and briskly

changed the subject. 'So, we've done work. How's your love life?'

I didn't run away screaming 'Help!' at this question because Chin is very good with relationships – not because she wants to see everyone settled down and going to B&Q at weekends but because she is obsessed with the detail of people's lives.

'What happened with Jaden, the film writer?'

'He was called Jaden,' I replied.

'Nuff said. It's over, then?'

I wanted to get this bit of the conversation wrapped up as quickly as possible. 'It was never really under, if you know what I mean. We – well, I saw him a couple of times when he was in London. I might be seeing him when I go back. He's nice but he's bonkers.'

That, at least, true. I knew what she was going to ask me next. There was a brief pause. Then—

'So . . . have you heard from David lately?'

I shook my head vigorously and looked away.

'Your mum's been asking me. She's worried about you. But she doesn't want to ask *you*. You know how it is.'

'I don't want to talk about it,' I said.

'Don't you know where he's going to be for Christmas?' she persisted.

'No,' I said. 'And I don't want to.'

Chin squeezed my arm. 'I know, darling, I know.'

Embarrassingly I felt tears squeezing into the back of my eyes, and my throat constricted. I stared at the portrait of my great-great-grandmother and thought about how she would have celebrated Christmas in this house, nearly a hundred years ago. Had she loved her husband so much it almost hurt? Had she been afraid of her own happiness when she moved into this beautiful house? I looked at the non-committal dark eyes, at her hand on her silk lap with one finger marking the page of a book. She met my gaze, as she always did.

'Ooh, crisps!' Chin exclaimed, and passed me the bowl as Mum clinked two glasses together.

'I can hear the carol singers coming,' she said.

'Wha-hey!' Gibbo yelled.

We stared at him, and Jess peered out of the window. 'Yes, they're at the gate,' she said.

We processed outside and stood in the porch. The night was bitterly cold and a frost was creeping over the lawn. The carol singers, several of whom I recognised from the church in Wareham, stamped their feet and called greetings to Mum as she hurried forward to open the gate and let them in. We could see their breath rising in the air, wispy in the torchlight, as they formed a little knot, the children in front, muffled up with hats and scarves, eyes shining with the excitement of staying out so late.

They started with my favourite carol, the one that sums up Christmas for me, especially Christmas Eve and arriving home.

> *'It came upon the midnight clear,*
> *That glorious song of old,*
> *From angels bending near the earth*
> *To touch their harps of gold.*
> *"Peace on the earth, goodwill to men,*
> *From heaven's all gracious King."*
> *The world in solemn stillness lay,*
> *To hear the angels sing'*

'Nice carol,' I heard Gibbo inform Chin in a stage-whisper. 'Look at the bloke on the left with the big brown beard – it sticks out from his chin at like forty-five degrees! What a guy!'

Having been a little nostalgic and sad – in the way that happy family occasions can sometimes make you feel – I was suddenly overtaken with a fit of the giggles.

'And that old girl there. Look at her! She's mad as a bag of snakes.' Gibbo nudged me now, his eyes on Mrs Thipps, the organist's wife, who opened her mouth incredibly wide on every word and shut it with a snap as she sang.

When the choir struck up with 'Whence Is That Goodly Fragrance Flowing?' and Gibbo said rather loudly, 'What the hell are they singing about now?' Kate turned and said, 'Be quiet, you fool.' Amazingly, Gibbo smiled, said sorry, and was as quiet as a mouse for the rest of the recital. At the end, Mr Thipps came forward with a velvet cap and we all put in some money while Dad stepped forward with a tray of paper cups filled with sloe gin.

'A Nice Change From Mulled Wine,' enunciated Mrs Thipps, as she gulped hers down.

Gibbo turned back to the house, fighting hysteria, and as he did I saw Kate catch his eye. My aunt is a fierce creature, someone who doesn't smile a lot, but when she does she's beautiful. Her lovely dark green eyes sparkled and she patted Gibbo's hand. I was glad she liked him.

'Thank you, all, so much,' said Mum, as the group turned to leave.

'Yes, thank you,' we echoed. 'Happy Christmas! See you at church!'

We hastened, shivering, back into the warmth of the house. The wind was getting up now, and the french windows rattled. Tom threw another log on to the fire, and sparks hissed out on to the carpet.

'Supper'll be ready in a few minutes,' said Mum. 'Time for one more glass?'

If catchphrases were written on headstones, that one would do for both my parents.

'I'll do it,' said Tom, picked up the decanter and went round with it.

'Are you all right?' I asked.

'Yes, of course I am.' He looked surprised. 'Why wouldn't I be?'

'You're a bit quiet,' I said.

'Oh, God.' Tom laughed. 'I'm fine. I was just thinking about something I didn't do at work.'

'I'd like to make a toast,' announced Dad. Jess and I groaned. Dad loves to make toasts or little speeches – it's part of his ceaseless quest to reclaim the title 'World's Most Embarrassing Dad to Two Teenage Girls', which was his for several years during my adolescence.

'Shut up, girls,' said Mum, even though I know she agrees with us.

'Yes, shut up,' said Dad, placing his glass on the table. 'I would like to say a couple of things. It is wonderful to have you all here tonight. Lizzy, Jessica and Thomas, you've come away from all the important things you do in London, and we're all very proud of you and glad you're here. And my little sister, Chin, doing so well with her scarves and bags that not only have Liberty taken some more I hear a shop in . . .' he paused before he said the words, then pronounced them as if he were a judge asking who the Beatles were '. . . *Notting Hill* – yes? Is that it? – wants to do the same.'

'Oooh,' we all murmured.

'Leave it with the J.R. Hartley impressions, John,' Chin said, bashing his thigh.

The mulberry tree's branches rattled against the window and the logs crackled on the fire. Dad went on, undaunted, clearing his throat: 'I'd like especially to welcome Gibbo. It's great to have you with us for Christmas, and while this year you'll be substituting, ah, *raincoats* for *sunblock*, we all hope you don't feel too homesick' – honestly, that's the best Dad's humour gets – 'and we're very pleased to meet you. So, to us all, happy Christmas, and welcome home!' He raised his glass and drank, and we were about to follow suit when there was a loud crash in the hall. (Later, after the excitement was over, we found that a window had blown open half-way up the stairs and sent a little jug filled with holly flying on to the floor, where it smashed into tiny pieces, with one of the boughs of pine.)

We jumped, and Kate and Mum grabbed each other and screamed, like spinster sisters in a horror film.

Then the french windows swung inwards.

This time we all screamed. A shadowy, windswept figure stood outside. Dad brandished his minute gin glass at it, as if it were a gigantic blunderbuss. We all took a step back. The figure came into the room and flung off its trilby. 'Happy Christmas, everyone! I'm so sorry I'm late, but I'm here! God, it's good to be back! Is that a new armchair?'

'Mike!' Jess yelled, the first to recover. 'You're here! This is fantastic.'

'Damn you, Mike,' Kate said crossly, as we all breathed a sigh of relief.

'Suzy . . .' Mike threw his hat on to the sofa and gathered my mother into a hug. 'Look.' He fiddled with his coat. 'Oh. Damn . . . I wanted to be able to produce them with a flourish, you know. Ah, here they are. Ouch. Fuck. Sorry.' He pulled a limp, cellophane-covered bunch of motorway service-station roses out of his sleeve.

'It's lovely to see you, you annoying man. Thank you.' Mum beamed and moved to close the french windows. She started. 'Oh . . . my God. Is someone else out there?'

As the wind whistled and the chimney belched smoke into the room, Mike said, 'I'd like you all to meet Rosalie.'

He grinned rather shiftily, and a second figure appeared

from behind him, immaculately made up, not a hair out of place, despite the wind, an early-forties minx-a-like with – and this was obvious even through her cashmere coat – a spectacularly pneumatic chest.

'This is Rosalie,' Mike repeated. 'My wife.'

Rosalie stepped forward. 'It's a pleasure to meet y'all,' she said, and smiled, revealing a set of shockingly white teeth.

THREE

We're so British, my family. If we'd been Italian we'd have jumped up and down, waving our arms, demanding to know where Mike had met her and when. If we'd been Afghan, French or Brazilian we would have come out with at least some of the questions we were dying to ask. Instead we simply nodded and stood quite silently.

Then Kate broke the spell. 'Congratulations! Wonderful!' she said, then kissed Rosalie and Mike, who clutched her hand.

'Bless you, Kate,' he said.

Mum and Dad followed suit, murmuring politely, and Tom and Gibbo shook his hand bashfully. For all his Antipodean forthrightness Gibbo could clearly hear ancestral voices calling when an awkward situation loomed.

Mike hung their coats on the long wooden rack in the hall, and took Rosalie upstairs to show her their room, the long low one at the front of the house with the rose wallpaper, which Mum said was so appropriate for Rosalie, as if she'd known her brother-in-law was about to turn up with a complete stranger to whom he'd just hitched himself. We stood around like Easter Island statues, until they came back, five or so minutes later, looking rather ruffled.

'Get rid of that God-awful gin and let's have a proper drink.' Mike produced two bottles. 'We brought some champagne.' He whipped off the foil and wire, popped a cork and out it flowed, thick and creamy, into Dad's empty sloe-gin glass, which Mike now drained.

There was a silence. I shifted my weight from one leg to the other. Kate hummed and looked at the cornices.

'Let me get some more glasses,' said Mum suddenly, and hurried into the kitchen with Chin.

'We met at a law conference in November,' Mike said, out of the blue, as Rosalie smiled up at him.

'*This* November?' Dad enquired, like a man in the final throes of strangulation.

'Nuts, Rosalie?' Tom asked innocently.

'Shut up,' I hissed.

'Well, thank you – Tom, is it?' Rosalie breathed, and flashed him a brilliant smile.

Tom coughed.

'So . . . when did you decide to get married, then?' Dad stammered.

'Well . . .' Rosalie and Mike looked at each other and giggled.

'Well, John,' said Rosalie, 'you're not going to believe this, but we got married yesterday! City Hall, eleven thirty a.m.! Then we decided to get on a flight over here.'

'I'm going to check on the glasses,' said Tom, to no one in particular, and left.

'But how did you get a flight at such short notice, Rosalie? Aren't they all booked up?' Jess asked.

'*Weeeell*,' said Rosalie, 'you have a very wonderful uncle.' She clenched her hands into tiny fists and punched the air. 'Hey! Thank you for this man!'

I glanced covertly around me, not sure whom she was thanking. Us? The Lord? *Jim'll Fix It*?

28

She went on, 'He actually had me booked on to a flight the week after we met – he was always going to get me to come over with him because he wanted me to see your beautiful home. And, I must say, it's such an honour to be here. You truly have a really . . . beautiful home.'

'Oh dear, where are those glasses,' I said, and slid out of the room.

At the kitchen table, Mum, Chin and Tom were whispering like the three witches in *Macbeth*. They sprang apart guiltily as I walked in, then visibly relaxed.

'I was just telling them he met her at a law conference *last month*!' Chin hissed across the table at me.

'I know,' I said.

'And they only got married *yesterday*!' Tom said, slamming his hand on the table for emphasis.

'I heard that too,' I said.

They looked at me crossly, as if I was ruining their fun.

'I can tell you that she's just given thanks for such a wonderful man and she thinks our home is really beautiful,' I said, with a glance over my shoulder to make sure the coast was clear.

'Noooooooooo!' they choroused.

'Also that Mike booked her on the flight home *a week after they met* because he knew even then he wanted us to meet her.'

'Nooooooooooooooooo!'

'Yes,' I said, much gratified at their reaction.

'Is she a money-grabbing whore?' said Tom.

'Is she even a lawyer?' said Chin. 'She doesn't look like one.'

'I'm sure she's a very nice girl,' said Mum, suddenly becoming a grown-up again.

'But I bet she saw a picture of the house early on and convinced herself Mike's, like, a duke or something,' said Chin.

29

'I'm sure of it,' said Mum then she paused and collected herself. 'Well, anyway, it's lovely to have Mike home and I'm glad for him. She seems lovely and I'm sure they're very happy.'

We glared at her, disappointed. Mum picked up the glasses and another bottle of sloe gin – thank God for Jess's nimble fingers in October. We were positively racing through the hooch that night.

'Let's have one more quick drink and then supper.'

We glared at her again, and Tom sighed. 'Aunt Suzy, don't be a Goody Two Shoes.'

'Hello!' said a voice at the door. We whipped round, and there was Rosalie.

'Good grief, Rosalie, you made us jump! I was just getting you a glass. Everything OK?' said Mum, running her fingers through her hair.

'Yes, of course, Susan,' said Rosalie. She brushed invisible dust from her sleeve, smiling as if she was visualizing chapter two of a self-help book on forging relationships with strangers. 'Hi, Ginevra, hi, Tom, hi, Lizzy. I just wanted to know if there was anything you needed help with out here.'

'How kind of you, but don't worry. You must be exhausted. Go back into the sitting room – supper's nearly ready,' said Mum, with a glint in her eye. I could tell she was looking for something to like in her new sister-in-law. Tom, Chin and I shifted from foot to foot: we are not nice people and didn't want to like her.

'Come and help me set the table if you want,' I offered finally.

Rosalie looked delighted, and so did Mum. It was almost a touching domestic scene.

We went into the dining room next door and started with the cutlery. 'There are ten of us, and the plates are in that cupboard. I'll get them,' I said.

Rosalie painstakingly counted out ten knives and forks.

Was she a lawyer? She looked like a fully-clothed member of the *Baywatch* cast. Who moves their lips when they count to ten? I thought, then realized that I did.

'OK,' I said. 'The wine and water glasses are here. And the napkin rings – can you fetch that bowl from the dresser?'

Rosalie reached behind her and put the bowl on the table. 'Do you all have them? They're, like, silver!' she cried.

'Er . . . yes, we do. They *are* silver. We were all given one as a christening present, but my dad has my grandfather's – he died a few years ago. So there's a spare for Gibbo.'

'The Australian guy, right?' She paused. 'But, hey, since I'm a member of the family now, I suppose – shouldn't I have it? Gibbo's not, like, married to Ginevra, is he?'

She asked it so artlessly, but with such cunning, that I was taken aback. It was such a tiny thing, but I saw that it could easily be the Thin End of the Wedge, plus I'd recently watched a late night American made-for-TV movie starring Tori Spelling called *Mother, May I Sleep With Danger?* about a woman who keeps giving in to her thankless, dim cheerleader daughter which results in the daughter nearly getting killed by her boyfriend from the wrong side of the tracks who has a penchant for bumping off his inamoratas with a wooden chopping board. It is all super-ironic because the mother knows she could have prevented the near-death by being firm with her daughter from the get-go. Anyway.

'No, you can have this one,' I said firmly, and handed her a wooden ring. I looked at her. She bowed her head, as if admitting defeat, and I felt like Maximus Decimus Meridius in *Gladiator*, accepting the cheers of the crowd in the aftermath of a particularly bloody bout.

Mum came in. 'I'm going to ring the bell now,' she said, and looked at Rosalie. 'Or would you like to do it? First time in the house, and you're a member of the family now, aren't you?'

31

Damn you, Mum, I thought.

Rosalie seemed delighted, and swung the huge Swiss cowbell that my great-great-grandfather brought back from a painting trip in the Alps and which had stood on the shelf in the dining room ever since.

The others came in, and we all sat down. Jess poured the wine and Dad stood up. 'I'd just like to make a little speech.'

Saints preserve us! Two in one evening. By this stage I was wondering why I'd come home for Christmas at all, and feeling that my flat – even though the only food in it was those white beans you have to soak overnight so you never get round to cooking them – would be a lovely place to spend Christmas with a bottle of wine for company.

'Erm, well, here's to Mike and Rosalie,' Dad said, in a rush, drank and sat down. It was his shortest speech ever, but at what a bitter price: the sacrifice of my favourite uncle to a fake-bosomed troll who was, at that very moment, studying the cutlery to see if it was silver-plated.

'Thank you, John,' said Mike. He stood up, ruffling his hair with his hands – he always did that. 'Thanks very much.' He gave us such a big grin I thought his face might explode. 'God, it's fantastic to be at home again. Ahm – just want to say it means more to me than you can possibly know,' he said, swallowed and looked rather wildly up and down the table. 'Here we all are. It's Christmas Eve . . .' We waited, politely, for so long that I wondered if he was seeking confirmation of the date or had something else to say. Then his eyes came to rest on Rosalie and he gave her his sappiest smile. 'Happy Christmas, everyone,' he said.

Supper took on a dreamlike quality, as if we were all being filmed for a reality TV show.

The side of beef was delicious, as was the mash, but Mum's

Christmas Eve speciality, her mini Yorkshire puddings, had fallen by the wayside. I'd seen them earlier, all ready to go into the Aga in their little cups, but they never appeared on the table. Either they'd gone horribly wrong or we were two short and Mum had thrown them away rather than make Rosalie and Mike feel guilty. Hm. I watched Rosalie through slitted eyes as she munched happily away.

After supper, Mum and Kate had the usual stand-off about who was going to do the washing-up.

'Go and sit down, Suzy, you've done quite enough this evening.'

'Don't be ridiculous, Kate. You had to work today, *you* should be relaxing.'

'Not at all. I won't hear of it! Move out of the way!'

'No, *you* move out of the way.'

'Ow, you're hurting me!'

'Stop pushing!'

'God, this is ridiculous,' said Chin, from the doorway. 'Both of you, go and sit down in the other room. Why don't you get started on the sprouts for tomorrow? I'll bring you through some coffee and *we*'ll do the clearing up.'

Tom and I looked at each other. 'Jeez, thanks a lot, Auntie,' said Tom, but he went into the kitchen and started loading the dishwasher.

Kate dragged a sack of sprouts out of the larder, and she and Mum disappeared into the side-room, with the TV and comfy chairs. It was where we ate when we weren't having formal meals, lovely and sunny in daytime but surprisingly cosy at night too, with a big open fireplace, shelves of magazines, videos, gardening guides, reference books, photos of the family and postcards from around the world – lots from Mike especially. It was one of my favourite rooms in the house – we'd transformed it from what had been the servants' hall into what Americans would call a den.

33

The kettle whistled and I poured water into the cafetière as Tom plucked mugs off hooks. I could hear Rosalie gabbling in the hallway to Mike. Gibbo appeared and asked if we wanted any help.

'Don't worry, hon,' said Chin.

He whipped the tea-towel out of her hand and kissed her. 'Come on, gorgeous,' he said into her ear. 'Time for bed.'

Tom and I exchanged a glance of mock outrage.

'It's Christmas Eve. I'm not going to bed yet, even if it is with you, you . . .' Chin murmured something that made Gibbo stand up straight, blush and give a little cough. She patted his arm and went back to the drying-up.

'I'll be with the others, then. See you in there,' he mumbled.

'No fear. I want to watch a bit of TV – I've had enough family chats for one night,' said Chin.

'Oh.' Gibbo scratched his cheek. 'Rosalie's watching TV. Apparently her favourite film's on, so she asked Mum and Kate if they wouldn't mind watching it too.'

'Urgh,' said Tom. 'She's such a muscler-inner! I wonder what it is – *Weekend at Bernie's*? *Pretty in Pink*?'

'*Pretty Woman*,' I suggested. 'No, *Risky Business*. No! *Robin Hood, Prince of Thieves*!'

'I've got it,' Chin yelled. '*Showgirls*! In a tie with *Top Gun*!'

'Actually,' said a voice from the door, 'it's *Some Like It Hot*, and it's on now.'

We turned. There was Rosalie again. The world's quietest walker. Damn. There was total silence.

Then Rosalie spoke: 'Hey, where's that coffee? I bought some chocolates, and your dad says there are chips in the cupboard bit at the back of the kitchen . . .' She bustled through to the larder. 'Here, yeah,' she said, emerging with two big bags of crisps. 'I'll see you in there, but hurry up. Tony and Jack have just nearly been shot – they'll be getting to Florida any minute.' She walked out and we gazed after her in astonishment.

'Is she all bad?' Chin wondered aloud. 'Clearly not. And yet, my friends, it is easier to hate her than to like her, no?'

'I say you're all horrible people,' said Gibbo, picking up the milk jug and bending over to kiss Chin again. 'Come on, let's go and join them.'

Mike appeared in the hall as Tom and I were negotiating our way to the side-room with the mugs and the cafetière. 'Hold on,' he said. 'Let me get the door. Hey, Titch, isn't that the mug you painted for me in that stupid craft class you used to go to after school?'

'It wasn't stupid,' said Tom, defensively. 'It was really interesting. And you said it was the best present you'd ever had.'

Mike picked it up and considered it. 'I dare say. It's got a dent in the middle, though, hasn't it? Look.' He held up Tom's masterwork, fashioned in blue with 'Unkle Mike' in a childish, uneven script. As a drinking vessel it wasn't an unqualified success – goodness knows why we still used it. It sloped on one side and the handle bent in on itself, which made it difficult to hold. 'Looks as if it's had one or two too many, if you ask me. Can I take it back to New York?'

'Of course you can,' Tom said, rather chuffed. 'Sorry I forgot to wrap it.'

'So that's the way the land lies, is it?' Mike said. '*Très charmant*. No presents, after I come all this way.' His head drooped. 'Oh, well . . .' He brightened, taking the cafetière out of my hands. 'I haven't got you chaps anything either, so we're evens. But Rosalie and I are going to stop off in London before we fly back. We're staying at Claridges. How about we take you shopping, get you each a present, then treat you to dinner? Jess too.'

'Oh, do Jess and Lizzy have to come?' Tom asked. I kicked

35

him. 'Ouch! Blimey, Mike, that's really kind of you. Are you sure? Claridges, eh?'

'Well, in for a penny, in for a pound,' Mike said. 'Can't do these things by halves, can you? Let's give the coffee to the thirsty troops. And ssh – don't mention it to the others. It's a surprise for Rosalie and I don't want her to find out.'

If you'd told me eight hours previously that I'd spend the rest of Christmas Eve watching the World's Greatest Film with Mike's new wife, I'd have said you were mad. But that was what happened. Rosalie hadn't made a very good first impression – unless a brunette version of Anna Nicole Smith in a twin-set is your idea of a good first impression – but I had to admit she might turn out to be not too ghastly.

She helped with the sprouts and adopted the Walter tried and trusted technique – remove the outer leaves and cut a cross in the base, which helps them cook better. I love sprouts. Rather unsociably, Dad and Mike had disappeared into the study for a catch-up. I bet you any money you like that at no time did Dad say, 'So who on earth is she, bro?' No, they'd have been talking about some shares of Grandfather's that were currently worth zero, and whether the wall in the kitchen garden needed rebuttressing.

'So,' Rosalie said, toned thighs clamped round a bowl as we all sat in the side-room, intermittently roaring with laughter at the film, 'Suzy, you're a doctor, right? Where?'

'I'm a GP at the local surgery,' said Mum, deftly whisking off a rogue stalk.

'I'm sorry?' said Rosalie, looking blank.

'She's a family doctor at a clinic,' said Tom. He had performed a remarkable *volte-face* and become Rosalie's new best friend. He was even speaking with a semi-American accent.

'Wow,' said Rosalie. 'That's hard work, right?'

36

'Right,' said Mum. 'I'm lucky, though, I've got three days off for Christmas.'

'Gaahd!' screeched Rosalie. 'I don't know how you do it. I have such admiration for doctors and nurses and those who help.'

My mother and Kate shifted closer to each other on the sofa.

'Er, yes,' said Kate. She cleared her throat. 'So, Rosalie, what about you? What do you do?'

'Me? Oh, gosh, nothing real interesting. I'm an attorney with Wright Jordan Folland. That's how I met Mike. I head up their commercial property arm,' Rosalie said casually, tossing a pile of uncropped sprouts into her lap.

'Really?' we said in unison.

'Are you serious?' Chin said.

'Sure, why?' said Rosalie.

'I just . . .' mumbled Chin. 'No reason.'

'Well, that must be a much more stressful job than mine,' said Mum. 'Good grief, you've done so well to get so far, and you're so young! How old are you?'

'Oh, my God, my favourite bit!' yelled Rosalie, neatly deflecting the question as Tony Curtis cycled towards the hotel after a night spent kissing Marilyn Monroe.

'He's brilliant,' said Tom.

'Creep,' I muttered under my breath.

'Tony Curtis! What a man!' Tom continued, unabashed.

'I was his attorney a few years ago when I was living in California,' Rosalie said. 'Nice guy. Some asshole was trying to screw him around on the money and I guess I ironed things out. He gave me one of his paintings.'

'Oh, my God!' said Tom. 'You met him?'

'All part of the job, honey,' said Rosalie, tossing her hair off her face and putting the bowl on the floor. She smiled

37

at me as she looked up again and I smiled back, unable to resist her. 'So Lizzy,' she said suddenly, 'I want to know more about you. You got a boyfriend?'

The room fell silent – apart from the rise and fall of Gibbo's breathing as he dozed in the corner.

'No,' I said.

'But what about that David guy? Doesn't he live round here?'

'David?' I asked. How did she know about David?

'Mike and I met him for a drink in New York. I liked him.'

The atmosphere was as thick as stew.

'You met David?' breathed Jess. 'You saw him?

'David . . . Lizzy's—' Mum broke off. 'David Eliot?' She made it sound as if she barely knew him.

'I'm sure that was his name.' Rosalie looked confused. 'You guys dated, right? Journalist? Kinda cute, short brown hair, real tall?'

'Argh!' I said, in a kind of strangulated scream.

Chin sat up straight. 'Well, actually, Rosalie, we don't talk about him any more. Do we, Lizzy?' she said.

'No, we do not,' I said, as firmly as I could, though the mere mention of his name made me feel as if someone had scooped out my insides.

'I'm sorry,' said Rosalie. 'Hey, Lizzy, I hope I didn't—'

I raised my hand. 'Don't worry. David and I finished last year. He went to New York but his mother lives just over there,' I said, gesturing towards the window, 'in the village.'

His mother has a little orchard where David had kissed me in spring, surrounded by gnarled little apple trees, festooned with white blossom, and told me he was going to New York.

'Right. I'm sorry. Is that how you met? Down here?' said Rosalie.

'Yes,' I replied, plaiting my fingers in my lap.

Although I'd known his younger brother Miles for a while, I hadn't met David until he ran over my bike in his car after I'd left it outside the post office on a baking hot summer's day. When I'd heard the crumple of steel and loud swearing, I'd appeared at the doorway with an ice lolly to see it buckled round David's bumper. He took me for a drink to say sorry. We ended up spending the night in a room above the pub and the next four days together.

'Why did you split up?'

'Ask him,' I said flatly.

'I did,' said Rosalie. 'But he went kinda weird and said I had to ask you.'

I'd deleted the email Miles had sent me, only four months ago, confirming that in New York David had slept with Lisa, a friend of mine from university. I didn't want it in my computer: I knew the temptation would be to come back to it, like picking a scab. My best friend Georgy still has it, though, and has said she'll forward it to me if I need to read it again.

'Ha,' I said bitterly. 'Ha. No disrespect to newly-weds, Rosalie, but all men are bastards.'

'You'd better believe it,' said Rosalie. 'Apart from your uncle, honey – that man is good through and through. My first husband though. My gosh, that man was bad. Turned out he only married me so I couldn't testify at his trial. There. All done.'

'Blimey,' said Kate, recovering her poise before the rest of us. 'Er. thanks for doing those, Rosalie.'

'My pleasure,' said Rosalie, stretching herself on the sofa and patting my hand. 'I'm sorry it didn't work out, honey. But look at you – so pretty. You'll find someone much better. I did.' The irony was lost on Rosalie but not on us. 'Come on, let's watch this darned film,' she said.

Dad and Mike appeared, rather flushed, as Geraldine,

Daphne, Sugar and Osgood were sailing away. Mum stood up and went over to them. 'OK?' she asked.

'Absolutely,' said Mike. He dropped into the armchair next to me and yawned. 'I'm shattered, though. Er . . . Rosalie?' he said, as if he wasn't sure that was her name.

'Heigh-lo,' said Rosalie.

'You all right, old girl?'

'I'm just fine, Michael darling.'

'I'm pretty tired,' said Dad. He took my mother's hand and held it. 'Look at the sky,' Mike said. 'It's clear as you like, look at the stars.'

Mum turned off the overhead light. I always forget how many more stars you can see outside London, and there was a new moon, the thinnest sliver of a bright white crescent in the sky. 'It's Christmas Day,' she whispered. 'Happy Christmas, everyone.'

'Happy Christmas,' we murmured back.

'I'm off to bed,' she said, and padded out of the room. As I turned away from the window, I caught Rosalie gazing at Mike. I've never seen such naked, all-consuming love on anyone else's face. It lit hers, but there was something unsettling about it, which I couldn't put my finger on. When I told Tom on our way up to bed, he said, 'But they've just got married. Of course she's in love with him, you strange girl.'

But that didn't explain why it had been scary.

I stopped by the old bookshelf, picked out a Georgette Heyer I hadn't read for years, then went to my room, undressed and got into bed. How lovely it was to sit in bed, to feel my feet push down, along the clean, smooth sheets, to feel as snug and warm as anything in my new fleecy pyjamas, and not to have to worry about work, about crazy Jaden, about my boiler, which was on its last legs, about tidying the flat, about making sure Ash at work was

40

all right. It was Christmas Day. I was at home. All I had to do was enjoy being here, in my bedroom, which smelt of lavender, with the presents I'd half wrapped scattered across the floor and *Devil's Cub* on my knee.

I started to read: 'There was only one occupant of the coach, a gentleman who sprawled very much at his ease, with his legs stretched out before him, and his hands dug deep in the capacious pockets of his greatcoat . . .' But my eyes were growing heavier and heavier, and I must have fallen asleep, because in the middle of the night I woke up and had to turn the light off, and the book was still on my lap.

FOUR

When I woke again, bright sunlight was flooding into my room and I could smell cinnamon. I pulled back the faded curtains and my heart leaped. It was a bright blue day, and the view to the village was as fresh and clear as it was on a spring morning, but coated with the glittering frost of winter.

I showered and dressed in the clanking old bathroom, singing 'Hark the Herald Angels' very loudly, and rushed downstairs, eager for some pre-church bonding with my family. But everyone was already in the hall, putting on their coats.

Mum appeared with a plate and thrust it under my nose. 'Grab one of those muffins and let's move it,' she said, then pulled on her gloves like a member of the A-Team. I declined: I'm of the strong opinion that, when it comes to breakfast, if it doesn't have Marmite on it, it ain't worth it.

Jess came down the stairs, rubbing her eyes. 'Come on, Jess, we'll be late,' said Mum testily.

Every year my relatives get themselves into a frenzy about being late for church. I have no idea why. It's a twenty-minute walk, and we always leave with half an hour to spare. Now, short of a hurricane, driving snow, frogs dropping from the sky, we would be sitting in our pew with ten minutes to spare while every other member of the congregation rocks up fifteen minutes late, and stand in the aisles chatting and exchanging pleasantries.

Old habits die hard, and we set out straight away, crunching across the terrace flagstones. Dad opened the gate and Gibbo appeared barefoot in the doorway, trousers trailing on the ground, hair whipped up into a storm around his face. He wasn't coming to church, he said. It made him fall asleep. 'Bye, you guys,' he called, and waved, a piece of toast in his hand.

'What's he going to do?' asked Jess, a little enviously.

'He's a great cook,' said Chin. 'He's sorted it with your mum. He'll start the Christmas lunch so it's all ready to go when we get back.'

I doubted that Gibbo could start a fire with a can of petrol and a match, let alone a Christmas lunch for ten people, but I kept quiet.

It was a beautiful walk, along the well-worn path through the fields. We owned the first, and the rest of the land before the church was the village common, a long sloping expanse of meadow with a stream at the bottom. This morning it was frozen at the edges, though a little water trickled through the centre and a forlorn-looking robin hopped from branch to branch.

Mike was just ahead of me, humming, Rosalie's arm tucked through his. They made a comforting picture, his checked wool scarf wound tightly round his neck, Rosalie in her beautiful pale coat, little heels clicking on the hard ground alongside him. The crown of his head showed beneath his thinning hair and I felt a rush of affection for him, with a kind of protectiveness. He and Rosalie stopped and turned. I caught up with them and Mike put his arm round my shoulders. 'It's lovely to see you, Lizzy,' he said. 'God, it's nice to be home again, you know?'

'It's great to have you back,' I said. 'I wish you'd come over more often. Can't you go part-time and supplement your income with bar work over here?'

'Good idea,' said Mike. 'Bar work. Haven't been back for ages, you know.'

'A year,' I said.

'Pah! Not a year – I came back at Easter.'

'No, you didn't,' I said. 'You were going to, for Dad's birthday party, but you had to cancel.'

Mike appeared to be in the grip of some unpleasant memory. 'You're right, Titch. Matheson deal. Phones ringing off the hook. Screaming. I don't think I left the office for three days . . .'

'Ooh, Mike,' I said, 'you're *so* important and hardworking, aren't you?'

Mike had been supposed to make the speech at Dad's party, which had also celebrated my parents' silver wedding anniversary (I *know*! You do the maths . . .) but, typical Mike, at the last minute he had to cancel his trip and Chin made the speech. The party was good, but Chin was a bit of a flop, drunk and rambling. And, besides, she wasn't Mike, who would have told a story, played the kazoo, got the audience to sing along, then probably slipped over and lain, with aplomb, on the floor unconscious for the rest of the evening.

'Well, you're back now,' I continued, seeing that he was looking rather depressed.

His face twitched into a smile. 'And I can't imagine how I stayed away so long. I could give it all up and live in the shed in the garden just to be near the old place. Does that make sense or sound completely crazy?'

'No, it makes sense,' I said, because I'd been thinking that more and more often lately. 'But you can come back any time. You know it's always going to be here.'

'Not necessarily,' said Mike, darkly. 'Your dad might sell it and move to a bungalow on the coast.'

'Or form a nu-metal band,' I said.

'Or join the Rotary Club,' Mike replied, jamming his trilby on his head and smiling.

'Or the Steven Seagal fan club. Why did you meet David for a drink in New York?' I asked suddenly, hoping to catch him off-guard.

'Ah.' Mike stopped and looked down at me. 'Did Rosalie say something? I've met up with him a couple of times, actually. Since . . . er . . . you two . . . He's a nice bloke.'

'Bollocks,' I said.

Mike corrected himself: 'Sorry. He's Satan's master-worker, and I hope his eyeballs dry up, but that aside, he's a pretty nice bloke.'

We were approaching the village. Mike patted my arm.

'I'm sorry, Lizzy, my love, I should have told you but it isn't a big deal. Look at it this way. He doesn't have any friends, he's been ostracized from normal society, so that's why he doesn't mind meeting up with me.'

I released Mike's arm. 'Does he ever ask about me?'

Mike looked alarmed, as if this was some kind of test and he didn't know the answer. Then he said, slowly, 'He's mentioned you, but I've told him not to. He's a great bloke in many ways, but he's weak. The way he treated you . . . Bit crap, really. So we just don't . . . Well – you know. It's over, isn't it?'

I nodded.

'Dear girl, have I said the wrong thing?'

'No, no, not at all,' I replied. 'In fact you've said absolutely the right thing. Don't worry.'

Mike was saved by Jess running past. 'Come on, people,'

she called. 'We're nearly there – and it's Sandringham time.'

Every year we play Sandringham Church, a game Jess invented when she was a teenager and obsessed with *Hello!*. We all pretend to be a different member of the Royal Family walking to church on Christmas morning, waving to the crowd of well-wishers, though to those who choose to wait outside in the freezing cold on Christmas Day to see Prince Edward I say, Think about what you're doing and whether you need medical assistance.

Anyway, Mike is brilliant as Princess Anne, while I always get landed with someone totally duff. This year I'd got Sophie Rhys-Jones, Tom was Fergie, which is great (mad eyes, shunned by the others and sucking a finger as a toe-substitute), and Mum was an impressive Prince Philip, shouting at imaginary foreigners. We had to keep stopping to laugh and help Rosalie with her portrayal of Mrs Simpson (she offered).

The organ was playing and there was a buzz of excitement, and Mum, Dad and Kate paused to kiss people and chat. Tom, Jess and I grabbed two pews and watched our parents gesturing to Rosalie, smiling and explaining about Mike's new wife as something they were all over the moon about. Rosalie was loving it all, you could tell the words 'quaint' and 'cute' were hovering on her lips as she gazed at the stone carvings, the little gargoyles above the arched windows and the pretty stained-glass picture of the flight into Egypt.

'Is that Mary and Joseph?' she asked, sitting next to me and pointing as the other grown-ups chatted in the aisle.

'Who? Oh, yes, and that's Jesus. They're fleeing from Herod,' I said, niftily disguising that almost all my Bible knowledge comes from *The Usborne Illustrated Bible Stories*. 'Into Egypt.'

'Praise be,' said Rosalie, solemnly, bowing her head.

Kate had sat down and was tapping her watch crossly because the service was late starting and she *hates* that. It applies to all events in which she is participating but not the leader – church services, concerts and dinner parties.

A few seconds later the organ stopped, there was a shuffling sound, and it started up again, wheezing into 'O Come All Ye Faithful'. We stood up and sang as the choir shuffled down the aisle. As always, Silas Hitchin, the oldest member, brought up the rear, about fifteen feet behind the rest, singing a different carol – I think it was 'O Little Town of Bethlehem'.

Tom and I were convulsed with laughter and Mum turned to frown at us. I snatched my glove out of my pocket to shove it into my mouth, and the other sailed out to land in the pew behind.

Someone tapped my shoulder. 'Disgraceful behaviour,' a familiar voice said. 'Here's your glove.'

I look round and then blinked, to see if I was dreaming.

It was David. My David. David Eliot.

He was smiling at me, holding out my glove. I dropped my hymn book.

When I was eight I had nits and was sent home from school early to be deloused. It was horrible. I was one of only three culprits in my year so I was shunned. My parents had only just moved into Keeper House and I was new at the village school. My mother was accosted in the chemist, our doors were daubed with sheep's blood and we had to move to a new home. Well, not exactly, but I felt like a leper and, worst of all, even after I was 100 per cent nit-free, I had to sit in assembly with a row of girls behind me and the gnawing fear that overly acrobatic lice might leap across the gap. Ever since I've had a thing about people sitting behind me, and now was no exception.

As the carol finished, I took my glove and sat down. The

back of my neck felt cold, though the rest of me was hot and my heart felt as if it might burst out of my chest.

The vicar's Christmas sermon might have been the calendar for the Barron Knights' next UK tour: I have no memory of the rest of the service, except that I was seized with the desire to run screaming from the church and all the way home.

David Eliot was back. Why? When? How?

As we filed out, Chin hissed, 'Is that David?'

'Where?' I asked casually.

'Behind you! Leaving his pew! Kissing your mum and shaking hands with Mike! Looking gorgeous in a black coat! With—'

'Yes!' I said. 'Shut up!' I fingered the silky-thin tassels on my scarf, not wanting to look up. 'Say something to me, pretend we're having a great chat.'

'Hahahahaha!' said Chin, casting her eyes around the church, which was emptying rapidly. 'Good one, Lizzy!'

I stared at her in despair. 'God, you're awful, aren't you? Come on, he's nearly outside. We can go now.'

Gavin, the vicar, was relatively young and trendy. As I passed into the porch I shook his hand and stopped to say hello. Chin drifted off to join the others. 'It's Lizzy, isn't it? I've just seen your sister,' he said.

'Yes, it is. Happy Christmas, Gavin. That was a lovely service.'

Mrs Kenworthy from the choir brushed past. 'Sorry, Lizzy. Just getting your uncle Mike a history-of-the-church pamphlet.'

'Ah – for Rosalie, I suppose,' I said.

'Is that his new wife?' Mrs Kenworthy didn't sniff, but there was a degree of doubt in her voice.

'Happy Christmas, Lizzy,' said Gavin. 'Well, I hear the carol singers weren't the only visitors to Keeper House yesterday.'

Rosalie, in her pale pink cashmere coat, was standing nearby, talking politely to Mr Flood, who used to work the Earl of Laughton's whacking great estate nearby. He's retired now but must make an absolute fortune; he's in every single documentary about old agricultural practices, life in a great house before the war, after the war, during the war, and in those village reminiscences that people publish. He's even thought about getting an agent. The sight of this very old, hairy man grasping the cuffs of his too long shirt in his fists and waving them enthusiastically at the immaculate Rosalie was quite special, and I looked at Gavin, who is perceptive about these things.

'You've met Rosalie, then?' I said politely.

'Yes,' said Gavin, and I knew he understood it was a little strange for us all. 'But it is the season to be jolly, isn't it? And to welcome those without shelter into our homes,' he added, his face pink with pleasure at the relevance of the Christmas message.

'She's got an apartment two blocks from Central Park,' I told him. 'I don't call that being without shelter.'

'People find shelter in different places,' said Gavin. If he hadn't been a vicar I might have punched him, but it's the kind of thing vicars are supposed to say.

'You're right. Thanks, Gavin,' I said.

A voice at my side said, 'Hello, Lizzy.'

I searched desperately for Chin, and saw all of my family making their way to Uncle Tony's grave, so I turned and looked up at him. David sodding Eliot, the man who had ripped out my heart and used it as a doormat. He was so tall – I always forgot that.

'Hello, David,' I said.

FIVE

'Hello, Lizzy,' he repeated.

It had been such a long time since I'd seen him properly that I'd forgotten little things about him – the tiny scar next to his mouth, the hollow at the base of his neck. How dark his eyes were. I'd tried to remember all this so many times since he'd left, tried so hard to picture what it would be like to have him standing in front of me, and now that he was I almost wanted to laugh with the strange, strange shock of it all.

'Sparkling conversationalists, aren't we?' he said, gazing into my eyes. 'How are you?'

'Fine,' I said, pulling myself together. 'When did you get back?'

'The day before yesterday.'

'From where?' Of course I knew the answer to this but I wanted to sound as if his movements weren't of the slightest interest to me.

'Still New York.'

'Going well, is it?'

'Yes, thanks. I've seen your uncle Mike a couple of times.'

'Good,' I said briskly. 'Well, give my love to—'

'So, you've met your new aunt,' said David. 'That's a turn-up for the books, isn't it?'

'What did you think?'

'I think she's nice.'

'Yes, well,' I said, glad we were keeping the conversation afloat, 'I'm not sure about her, but she likes *Some Like It Hot*, so she can't be all bad.'

There was an awkward silence. *Some Like It Hot* was the film we had watched on the night before David left me. Sheesh, it's a long story, I'll get to it later.

Tumbleweeds rolled casually by and a church bell tolled mournfully (no, it really did, we were outside the church) David frowned and stared at the gravelled path. People were drifting away – I think. Suddenly I couldn't think of anything to say that didn't involve talking about us.

'How's Miles? And your mum?' I asked eventually.

'Mum's good, been working hard. Miles is fine, working hard too.'

All the rest of the Eliots were accountants, which I imagined must make for captivating exchanges around the family hearth.

'They're over there,' he said, pointing towards the lych-gate. Miles raised his hand in a gesture of greeting. I looked to where my family was standing, staring at us intently, making no attempt to pretend they were thinking solemn thoughts at my uncle's graveside. Rosalie even waved at David.

Suddenly the spell was broken and I remembered that he'd left me at Heathrow last year on a beautiful spring day, promising to phone every day, to write letters, emails, texts, telegrams, poems, essays and doctorate papers about how much he loved me. I never considered that we might break up. I remembered how his lips felt when he kissed me.

But as I looked at the man who had kissed me with those lips, I remembered he was also the man who, before the first month of our separation was over, had slept with someone else, then dumped me by email. Turns out it's not such a long story after all. Breezy, be breezier than a sea breeze, I told myself as a wave of enormous sadness washed over me. 'Well, glad to hear all's well.' I wrapped my scarf round my neck. 'Happy Christmas, David.' I allowed myself one last glance at him as I turned away. A fat wood-pigeon was cooing loudly in the yew trees skirting the churchyard.

Abruptly, David reached out and grabbed my arm. 'Tell Mike I'll be in touch. How is he?'

'Oh, you know, happy, successful, just closed a big deal, got married – so in quite a bad way, all in all,' I said, with a feeble attempt at sarcasm.

'I mean it. Tell him I'll give him a call. There's something I want to ask him.' I felt the warmth of his hand on my arm. He looked at me intently and I could feel his breath on my cheek. 'Don't hate me, Lizzy,' he said. 'It's not worth it any more.'

'I don't hate you,' I whispered. 'Let me go. I don't want to see you again.'

He released me at once, then caught hold of my hand. 'I'm sorry. I just – I want to tell you something. I want you to know—'

'No, David,' I said. My face flamed. 'I don't want to do this again.'

'I don't see why not,' he said. 'I talked to Miles about it yesterday and I've never understood why you wouldn't give me another chance.'

'What?' I said. My throat seemed to be closing up.

'I made a mistake, but . . . Come on, Lizzy, isn't it time you stopped being Miss High and Mighty about it?'

'How *dare* you?'

'You *always* do this!' David said, raising his voice. He swallowed hard, trying to bring himself under control. 'It's always *you* who's the one who's hurt, who has to be at the centre of attention. Did you ever think about how it affected me? I just hoped you weren't as selfish as I thought you were. But you were. And you still are.'

Tears welled in my eyes, just as Kate and Alice Eliot appeared beside us. They greeted each other, in unison, as we glared at each other. 'Well, *I* want to know something too,' I said. 'I want to know how you pulled Lisa in the first place. How soon was it after I'd gone? Or did you fix up a time to meet up for a quick fuck while I was still in the room?' David's mother looked totally shocked and she and Kate huddled together like the humble servants in *Dangerous Liaisons*, watching with trepidation from the sidelines.

'I managed to persuade you, didn't I?' David said, eyes glittering with rage.

'That's true.' I could have hit him. 'But you certainly punished me for it, didn't you?'

David was white with fury. I'd never seen him look like that at me or anyone else. He swallowed, took a step back, and said, in a much calmer voice, 'You're right. I'm sorry. I know I was wrong, but you were too. And since you'll probably never understand what you did, perhaps it's best we leave it at that. Bye, Lizzy.'

'You always have to have the last word, don't you?' I couldn't put my gloves on, my hands were shaking so badly. 'I know you better than you think. Goodbye, David.' (Please note this shows *I*, in fact, had the last word.)

As I walked towards Tony's grave I could feel David's eyes on my back, and had to cling to Kate's arm to stop myself running back and either stabbing him with a nearby icicle or throwing myself into his arms. I couldn't help it. I'd tried to stop feeling this way for nine months but suddenly the gates were open again and I felt totally miserable but incredibly happy because I'd seen him again.

I shook my head involuntarily and murmured, 'No' and Kate put her arm round me. 'You are bonkers, aren't you, darling? Never mind, we're going home soon and you don't have to see him ever again.'

'I know,' I said quietly. 'But I want to.' We were almost at Tony's grave. 'Was it ever like this with you two, Kate?'

Kate set her jaw in a firm line. 'Erm – no.' She bit her lip. 'We were never apart from the moment we met.' She smiled at the memory of the husband she had married when she was a slip of a girl and whom she had had every right to expect would be around for the rest of her life, not taken away from her when she wasn't even thirty and had a small child.

I was horrified by my selfishness. 'I'm so sorry, Kate,' I said. 'Forget about it – stupid David Eliot and his stupid bloody gorgeous eyes.'

She looked at me, perplexed, and kissed my cheek. 'You *are* bonkers, you know.'

'Conditions at base camp, the forty-eighth day after settling here by the graveside, are poor,' intoned Tom. 'Tom Walter had a simple wish, merely to visit his father's grave. But he was to be plunged into a horrifyingly tedious wait that no modern Briton should be expected to endure. In freezing temperatures, he was forced to watch as his cousin flew into a strop with a tall dark stranger from her past and screamed obscenities in a way that brings shame not only on herself but also on her family and friends. Are Britain's young women binge-drinking? Are they descending into a spiral of drink and drugs hell? Are they—'

'Yes, yes,' said Kate. 'Come on, let's get this over with.'

Since we were really only there to pay our respects and she was the one who'd brought the flowers, none of us was quite sure what to do next. There was a silence. Eventually Mike touched the headstone. 'We miss you, old man. Happy Christmas.'

'Happy Christmas,' we murmured softly. Each year on Christmas morning, Mum and Kate unpick the wreath of holly, ivy and mistletoe that hangs over the front door at Keeper House, and make it into a bunch of greenery to lay on Uncle Tony's grave. Now Kate picked it up from the grass where she'd left it and put it on the grave. 'Happy Christmas, Tony,' she whispered. Mike put his arm round her and kissed her hair. Tom's head was bowed and his lips were moving, as if he was praying. Neither of us remembered his father – when Tony died, Tom was a barely toddling two-year-old – but the loss had affected us badly. I slid my arm through his, and we walked away from the grave.

The wind was biting cold and cut into our skin, but the sight of the house across the field, its windows glittering in the winter sun, was calming. Mum, Dad and Rosalie walked together, chatting quietly, while Mike strode along behind them, his arm round Kate, who occasionally laughed at him. Chin, Tom, Jess and I brought up the rear.

'So, David Eliot, Lizzy,' said Chin, and I could tell she was trying to take Tom's mind off Uncle Tony's grave.

'Yes?' I answered.

'What were you talking about? It looked from where we were standing as if the two of you were about to fight.'

'We almost did,' I said. 'I'd forgotten how . . .' passionate he was, I wanted to say, but that sounded so corny '. . . worked up he got about things. Weirdo. Idiot. Jeez.'

'I don't understand him,' said Jess. 'Why's he so cross with you? He's the one who slept with your friend, for God's sake.'

'I know!'

'He broke your heart. You didn't go out of the flat for a week and you wore those pyjama bottoms through in the

55

bum,' Tom chimed in. 'He really has got a nerve, acting like you dumped him.'

I had trained myself to harden my heart against David after he'd sent me that email and since the terrible, short phone call when we'd decided to split up. I couldn't think about him without sadness, so I tried not to think about him at all. Early on I used to dream about him every night, tortuously realistic dreams where none of it had happened, then wake up and cry because it wasn't my real life. Then grit my teeth and get ready for work.

I'd just have to do that again now – forget how lovely he was, and how he had seemed generally perfect to me in the departments of height, looks, taste in things like films and TV and, finally, sex. I nodded at Tom, with tears in my eyes, cursing my selfishness and wishing I hadn't seen David today of all days.

Then I remembered something I'd learned on a slightly dubious self-motivational course at work which is that whether or not you have a good day is mainly up to you. So, I would enjoy the rest of Christmas and not let this ruin it. I tugged some ivy off a tree next to the path. The leaves were green, glossy and thick. I twisted them into a little crown and put it on Tom's head as we walked. 'I hate men – except you, of course, Thomas.'

'Thank you, Elizabeth.' He squeezed my hand. 'Good grief, what *is* he doing?'

We were still a little way from the house, and as we caught up with the others we could see a smallish figure emerging from the front gate, trousers and hair flapping in the wind. It was Gibbo, and as we got nearer it became apparent he was carrying a tray loaded with glasses of champagne. 'Happy Christmas, people!' we heard him cry, as he came towards us. 'Hurry up, it's good stuff here and I don't want to drop the tray.'

'You crazy man,' Chin shouted. 'Put some proper shoes on! I can't believe you're wearing those horrible old flip-flops!'

'Love me, love my thongs, woman,' Gibbo said, as we reached him.

'I think you might be a contender for the title of Greatest Living Australian, Gibbo,' said Mike, as he took a glass. 'Chin, I love your boyfriend, in an American, warm and fuzzy way.'

'Me too,' said Rosalie. 'You're a class act, Gibbo.'

'Thanks, Rozzer.' Gibbo handed her a flute. 'Here you go – take one, Suze.' I don't think anyone's called my mother 'Suze' since she was about fourteen. 'Get stuck in, everyone. Lunch is totally under control – you don't have to worry about a thing. I've been a bit experimental too, Suze, hope you don't mind.'

I love Gibbo.

SIX

As we entered the house there was a warm reassuring smell of something good happening in the kitchen, and Mum breathed a sigh of relief. Despite her passion for experimentation, she's still a megalomaniac when it comes to culinary matters. There was a brief but tense stand-off over ownership of the oven gloves (the kitchen equivalent of the remote control), but Gibbo emerged victorious and proceeded unchecked towards the Aga. Mum leaned against the doorframe, looking pale.

'Come on, Suzy, finish off your champagne,' said Kate, bustling in behind her. 'Gibbo, do you need a hand?'

'No, everything's under control,' said Gibbo. 'No worries, go and relax.'

'But I can't!' wailed my mother, grinding her teeth. 'You've disenfranchised me. What shall I do?'

'I can't believe you're a doctor and you're allowed to be so irrational, Suze.'

'You're quite right,' said my father, appearing behind me. 'Come on, darling, you can be *my* helper. We're going to hand out the presents in a minute.'

'Do I get to wear the hat?' asked Mum hopefully. 'I'll do it if I can wear the hat.'

'Yes, of course,' said Dad, patting her shoulder like he used to pat our ancient Labrador, Jockey, towards the end when he was old and confused.

We always open our presents after church on Christmas morning, and Dad is always Santa, with Tom as his helper. Long ago our grandmother knitted Dad and Tom bright red bobble hats to wear as they were giving out the presents. Dad's still has a white pompom, but Tom's fell off ages ago, and they're both rather lopsided and uneven because she was quite short-sighted when she made them.

I followed my parents into the sitting room, where Mike was on his knees lighting the fire, and watched my father trying to wedge Tom's hat on Mum's head. I wondered where its owner was. Tom was the only person I'd ever really talked to about David, and I wanted a debrief with him now.

'Are you OK, darling?' Mum asked.

'Yep, thanks, Mum,' I said. She snatched the better Santa hat away from Dad. 'We should have realised David would be there, I'm sorry.'

I was outraged that they'd known David was back and had said nothing about it, but I merely smiled. 'Mum, it's fine. He didn't kidnap and torture me, we split up. I can cope with seeing him for a few minutes each year, you know.'

'Did—' Mum began, but Dad tapped her shoulder and solemnly removed the Santa hat from her grasp.

I felt depressed. Both my parents had loved David, and neither of them understood why we split up, because I didn't tell them. I think Mum had thought we'd have an emotional reunion by the gravestones. Well, yet again I was going to have to disappoint her. I went back towards the kitchen, looking for Tom. As I passed the study I saw a movement out of the corner of my eye and peered through the gap between the door and the frame, where the wood had warped. Rosalie was sitting at my father's desk, still in her coat, with an open box file, scribbling notes furiously on a pad.

What was she doing? Why was she in there? I turned to go upstairs, and Mike was standing behind me. I jumped, and heard rustling in the study. 'What are you doing there?' he asked. 'You look like you're in a world of your own.'

'N-nothing,' I stammered. 'Is Tom in there?' I gestured towards the study.

His eyes flicked to the door. 'No, that's Rosalie. Hey, did you find the Sellotape? We were looking for some earlier and I've got one last present to wrap. Ah! Hello, gorgeous, any luck?'

'Yes, here it is!' said Rosalie, emerging from the study, holding a dispenser. 'Hey, Lizzy, how are you?' She slid an arm round Mike. 'Shall I run upstairs and do that last one?'

I couldn't tell if she'd worked out I'd seen her. Or if Mike knew I'd seen her, or if he even knew what she was doing, going through Dad's stuff.

'A wife and a present-wrapper, rolled into one. What more could a chap ask for?' Mike dropped a kiss on her shoulder.

'I'm going upstairs to get Tom,' I announced in a loud, peculiarly am-dram way. 'See you later.' I stomped upstairs thinking the world was going mad.

On the landing I paused to look out of the leaded window across the valley. What was David doing now? Was he with Alice and Miles, having a drink and opening presents? Was he pacing the floors, dashing tears from his eyes because of his stupid behaviour and thwarted love for me, like the Marquis of Vidal in *Devil's Cub*?

Ha. I gave a mirthless laugh, like a world-weary torch singer. I knocked on Tom's door. There was no answer, so I opened it slowly and looked in. Tom was lying on his bed, staring into space. 'Tom, darling,' I said, and sat down next to him. 'What's wrong?'

'Go away,' he said dully. The old iron bedstead creaked beneath us. 'I don't feel well.'

'Is it your dad?' I said, putting my arm round his bony shoulders.

'What do you mean?' he said, shrugging me off.

'Well, it's Christmas Day and all that. It must be sad.'

Tom turned back to look at me without expression. 'I don't want to talk about it.'

'But . . .' I didn't want to sound stupid. 'We visit his grave every year, why are you so upset this time?'

'I just am, that's all. It's different this year.'

'But why?'

'I've been thinking about something you said in the car yesterday. And about Mike and stuff.'

'Oh, God, what?' I said, alarmed that something I'd said and couldn't remember should send Tom into a decline.

'Nothing, just about us all in general. It's not a big deal, and it's none of your business. Go away and stop being so nosy.'

Downstairs I heard Mum shout, 'Change of plan! Lunch is ready! Presents afterwards!' followed by the dull clang of the bell. I didn't know what to say. Tom is more than a cousin to me: he's like my brother – but I often feel I don't know him very well. I went to his birthday party last year, in a wine bar in the City, and I knew lots of his friends but he seemed . . . different. More relaxed, happier. And I suppose sometimes the people who know you best are the ones you want to run away from most.

I stroked his arm again. 'Tom, whatever it is, I want to help. You know that, don't you?'

There was no answer so I got up and opened the door. Then Tom said, in a muffled voice, 'I'll see you downstairs, Lizzy. Thanks.'

'And the glory, the glory of the Lord . . .' boomed the CD player, as I went downstairs. I could hear Dad sharpening the carving knife in time to *The Messiah* and rushed into the dining room. The table was set, the fire burned in the grate, and the smell of Christmas lunch was drifting through the kitchen door. Mum and Kate were giggling: in a few short hours Gibbo had twisted them round his little finger, and I could see why. If I'd caught *him* rifling through Dad's desk I'd have told him to take what he wanted.

One by one we sat down and the dishes came forth from the kitchen. Slices of stuffing, sausage and chestnut, bread sauce, cranberry sauce, Brussels sprouts, and a huge platter of roast potatoes. And finally, with a flourish, in came Mum with the turkey. I sat on my hands to stop myself picking at anything.

Tom appeared at last, a grim expression on his face, and proceeded to down a glass of red wine.

As Dad finally sat down, we raised our glasses and said, 'Happy Christmas.'

I looked round at all of us and thought what a pickle we were in, even though we appeared to be a normal happy family enjoying Christmas. I wondered what Georgy, Ash and my other friends were doing. Were they as confused by their own family Christmas as I was? Whoever had said that each family was barking insane in its own way was right. Just look at the evidence:

FAMILY MEMBER	LEVEL OF WEIRD BEHAVIOUR BEFORE XMAS	NEW LEVEL
Gibbo	No prior knowledge. Prob high tho	Ditto
Chin	Esp when younger, not so much now	Same
Dad	Auditioning for role of Mayor of Town of Mad	Same

Mum	Mayoress. Both seem happy about it tho	Same
Mike	No previous weird/mad behaviour but now married to mad American who rifles through drawers!	Off the scale!
Rosalie	No prior knowledge. Suspect she could be a bona fide nutter however.	Go away!
Kate	Fairly high. Also repressed about many things. Scary. Made a postman cry last month	Wouldn't be able to tell either way, to be honest
Tom	Low, but potential for high	Suddenly high
Jess	Low, but signs of intelligent life in brain also low	Same

I'm sure our ancestors were all scavenging peasantry because I've never known anyone like my family when it comes to attacking a meal with gusto. Silence reigned as we ploughed through the mountains of food in front of us, with only Rosalie making an attempt at conversation.

'These are beautiful, Suzy,' she'd say, picking at a crumb of roast potato.

'Mmm,' my mother would answer, as her nearest and dearest guzzled, pausing only to open another bottle of wine. conversation broke out. I must say we were rather knocking back the wine but as they say, Christmas comes but once a year, and it is the season to be merry. It was probably nearing teatime but, just as at weddings, where one has nothing to eat for hours and then lunch at 6pm, we'd lost all sense of time.

After the pudding and mince pies, we had toasts where – yes! – we all propose toasts. When we were younger we found the adults desperately tedious by this stage: they were clearly drunk, found the oddest things hilarious, and would hug us, breathing fume-laden declarations of affection into our faces.

'Lizzy goes first,' said Chin, giving me a shove.

'I'd like to toast Mr and Mrs Franks, and Tommy the dog,' I said, getting up and downing the rest of my wine.

'Hurray!' said the others, except Gibbo and Rosalie.

'They live in the village in Norfolk where we go on holidays. They're gorgeous,' said Chin. 'You'll meet them there this summer. It's wonderful.'

Gibbo and Rosalie, bound together by fear of the unknown and the solidarity of the outsider, shot each other a look of trepidation.

'Jess, you next!' Tom yelled, prodding her in the thigh.

'I want to toast Mr and Mrs Franks too,' said Jess, determinedly.

'You can't,' I said. 'That was my idea. Think of someone else.'

'I miss them,' said Jess, her lower lip wobbling. Jess cries more easily than anyone I know, especially after wine.

'Me too,' said Chin, gazing into her glass. 'I hope Mr Franks's hip is OK.'

'My turn,' said Mike, standing up straight and holding his glass high in the air. 'To . . . to Mr and Mrs Franks and Tommy the dog.'

We all fell about laughing, except Jess. 'Mike! Be serious.' She glared at him.

'I stand by my toast,' said Mike. 'I send waves of love and vibes of massage to them, especially Mr Franks and his hip.'

'Oh, Mike,' said Jess, 'don't take the p-piss. You are mean.'

'Sorry, darling,' said Mike. 'I change my toast. To my lovely new wife.'

'To Mike's lovely new wife,' we all chorused. Rosalie beamed up at him.

Mum got up next. 'I would like to toast Kate,' she said quietly. 'It was thirty-three years ago this week that Tony met her and we always remember him today, but I want Kate to know we all . . . Anyway, we do. To Kate.'

'To Kate,' we echoed, and Kate looked embarrassed and buried her face in her glass.

Mike opened another bottle as Dad stood up. 'To the district council and their planning department,' he said darkly, and drained his glass.

Jess and I rolled our eyes. Dad is always embroiled in some dispute over the field next to our little orchard, which is owned by the local council. They're always threatening to chop down the trees opposite the house, or remove the lovely old hedgerow that flanks it and similarly stupid things.

'The district council,' came the weary reply.

It was Tom's turn. He stood up slowly and surveyed the room. I noticed then, with a sense of unease, that he had a red wine smile: the corners of his mouth were stained with Sainsbury's Cabernet Sauvignon. 'The time has come . . .' he began, and stopped. He swayed a little, and fell backwards into his seat. We all roared with laughter and raised our glasses to him. Somehow he got up again. 'The time has come,' he repeated, glazed eyes sweeping the room. 'I want to tell you all something. I want to be honest with you.'

Kate looked alarmed. 'What is it, darling?' she asked, balling her napkin in one hand.

Tom waved his arm in a grandiloquent gesture. 'You all think you know me, yes? You don'. None of you. Why don't we tell the truth here? I'm not Tom.'

'What's he talking about?' Rosalie whispered, horrified, to Mike. He shushed her.

'I'm not the Tom you think I am, that Tom,' said Tom, and licked his lips. 'None of us tells the truth. Listen to me. Please.'

And this time we did.

'I want to tell you all. You should know now. Listen, happy Christmas. But you should know, I can't lie any more to you.'

'Tom,' I said, as the cold light of realisation broke over me and I suddenly saw what he'd been going on about. 'Tom, tell us.'

'I don't think we're honest with each other,' he went on. 'None of us. I think we should all tell each other the truth more. So I'm going to start. I'm gay. I'm Tom. I'm gay.'

The old clock on the wall behind him ticked loudly, erratically, as it must have done for over a hundred years. I gazed into my lap, then looked up to find everyone else doing the same. Someone had to say something, but I didn't know what.

Then, from beside my father, Rosalie spoke: 'Honey, is that all?' she asked, reaching for a cracker. 'You doll. I knew that the moment I laid eyes on you.'

Another silence.

'Well, come on,' said Rosalie. 'Did any of you guys really not know?'

Kate cleared her throat and pouted. Tom was staring at her, with what seemed to be terror in his eyes. 'I have to say I've always thought you might be, darling,' she said. She reached across the table for his hand.

'Er . . . me too,' said Chin, and my mother nodded.

'And me,' Jess added, her lip wobbling again. 'I love you, Tom.'

'Oh, do be quiet, you fantastically wet girl,' said Tom. A tear plopped on to Jess's plate.

'Good on you, mate,' said Gibbo.

'Come on, Mike,' Rosalie appealed to her husband. 'Didn't you wonder?'

'I must say I did,' muttered Dad, which says it all, really. If Kate and Dad – people who think 'friend of Dorothy' refers to someone who is acquainted with Maisie Laughton's sister in the next village – can be aware of Tom's sexuality, then who had he thought he was kidding?

Tom looked discomfited. It must be awful to get seriously drunk and reveal your darkest secret to your family, only to discover that they knew it already.

'What about you, Lizzy?' said Tom. 'Didn't you wonder why I never talked about girls? Or boys?'

'Not really,' I said. 'I just thought you might be and you'd tell me if you wanted to.'

Mike agreed. 'I always wondered, Tom, you know. You asked for that velvet eye-mask for your twenty-first. I wondered then whether you were going through a *Maurice* phase. Jolly brave of you, must have been nerve-racking telling us today. I cancel my toast to Rosalie. Stand up, everyone.'

Our chairs scraped on the old floorboards. 'To Tom,' he said. 'You know . . . we're proud of you. Er. You know. For being your way. Here's to Tom.'

'You're proud of me for being my way?' said Tom, incredulously. 'Good grief! This is like being on *Oprah*.'

'Shut up, Tom,' I said. We raised our glasses and intoned, 'To Tom,' and sat down again.

'Well,' said my mother. 'Does anyone have room for another mince pie?'

SEVEN

By the time you've finished Christmas lunch, it's incredibly late, and even though you're stuffed you have to have tea with Christmas cake and Bavarian *stollen*, made by my mother, and by about nine p.m. you're starving – the huge amount you have ingested over the last four hours has stretched your stomach, which is now empty and needs to be filled again. So you have the traditional Christmas ham, accompanied by the equally traditional Vegetable Roger, which is what Tom called it once when he was little, and which is

Brusselsproutscarrotsroastpotatoescabbagestuffingandbreadsauce

but not necessarily in that order, all whizzed up in the food-processor, then served with melted cheese on top. I console myself with the thought that this was what kept Mrs Miniver going through times of stress.

Because it was a time of stress. I've been underwhelmed in my time (George Alcott, 1995, step forward), but never quite so much as by Tom's outing himself for the benefit of his family. The drama of the moment wasn't matched by the significance of the announcement. Ever since Tom showed me the picture of Morten Harket that he kept hidden in a secret compartment of his Velcro-fastening, blue and red eighties wallet, I've always suspected that he was as gay as a brightly painted fence.

Immediately after lunch, Kate ordered him to bed for a nap. He protested loudly (what a great way to start your new life, being sent to bed by your mother), but he was so drunk it was for the best.

We sat downstairs, opened our presents, then had tea. Tom's presents sat in a forlorn heap in the corner of the sitting room as we leaped up to thank each other, exclaimed with horror, amusement or pleasure at our gifts (all three, in Jess's case, when she unwrapped a parcel from her flat-mate without knowing it was a vibrator. I thought Dad was going to pass out).

I can't say with my hand on my heart that my immediate family were overjoyed by their presents from me but, then, Jess gave me a 'Forever Friends' key-ring and *Get Your Motor Runnin: 25 Drivin' Classix for the Road* on cassette, and I know the only place you can get those tapes is at a service station.

Mum and Kate both loved Tom's presents: bottles of wine, gift-wrapped in a couple of rather creased Oddbins bags.

'Ah, he knows just what to get his old aunt,' chuckled my mother, affectionately.

'Now, that's what I call a present,' said Kate, indulgently. 'Bless him.'

'Yes,' Chin said sharply. 'The masterstroke of asking for two separate plastic bags must have taken him ages.' She had given her sisters-in-law individually crafted, velvet-beaded bags and was quite rightly annoyed at the reception lavished on Tom's wine. As was I, but with less justification.

Later, as Mum and I were clearing up after the ham and Vegetable Roger I decided to wake Tom, so that he could enjoy a bit more of his Christmas Day, rather than coming to at three a.m. with a raging thirst. 'I'm going to go and get Tom in a minute,' I said to Mum, as we stood by the sink, washing the Things that are Too Big to Go in the Dishwasher.

Mum was in a philosophical mood. 'Ah, Tom,' she said, staring out of the window into the dark, windy garden. 'Lizzy, did you really never ask him?'

'No,' I said firmly.

'I don't understand,' she said, placing an earthenware pot on the draining-board. 'Didn't it ever come up?'

I felt a bit impatient, as if I was being accused of being a bad cousin/friend. 'No, it didn't.'

'But why not?' said Mum, lowering another dish into the soapy water.

'Because you don't ask big questions over a glass of wine or on the way into the cinema,' I explained. 'How do you say, "Hi, Tom, the tickets for Party in the Park have arrived and, by the way, do you prefer the manlove?" It was up to him to tell me if he wanted to. I'd do anything for him, he knows that.'

'I know, darling,' said Mum. 'I do understand. I'm just glad he felt he could tell us now. It was all so different in My Day.'

'Right,' I said, hiding a smile in a tea-towel and not particularly wanting to hear about the famous 'My Day', although I'd very much like a specific calendar date for it at some point. In My Day blokes were called chaps, rad fem med students like my mother wore Pucci tunics, had big hair with black bows on top, applied their eyeliner wearing oven gloves while sitting on a bumpy bus, and marched during the day against the Midland Bank or Cape fruits while in the evening they grooved and bed-hopped at someone's shabby stucco South Ken flat. In My Day you knew one chap who was 'a queer', usually a photographer or a film director, and you told people about it in a subtle way that implied you were a free-thinking liberal.

'Well, it's been quite a Christmas so far, hasn't it?' said Mum, wiping her hands. She advanced towards me. 'And I've hardly talked to you since you got back, darling. How are you?'

'I'm fine,' I said, alarmed by the sudden maternal probing.

'Was it very awful seeing David today?' she said in a casual way, filling the kettle.

From the other side of the house I could hear Mike and Gibbo doing something to Chin that was making her scream. I put my elbows on the counter. 'No, it was fine, thanks.'

'Do you miss him?' my mother persisted.

My elbows were soggy. I straightened hastily. 'Erm . . . in what way?'

'Oh, come on, Lizzy,' my mother said, crossly, I thought. 'Either you miss someone or you don't.'

'Not necessarily,' I said, patting my damp arms. 'What if there's more than one factor involved? What if, say, you were madly in love with that person and would still be with them if it was up to you? Then you miss them. But what if that person slept with your friend in New York a month after he moved there and after he'd told you he wanted to spend the rest of his life with you? Well, yes, you still miss them, but you kind of don't any more so much.'

My mother stared at me, involuntarily wrapping her arms round herself. 'What?' she said, with a catch in her throat. 'I knew it was serious, but . . . oh, my darling . . .'

'Yes, blah blah,' I said. 'But it turns out he's a lying so-and-so and I was wrong about him, so let's forget about it, shall we?'

'Yes, let's,' said Mum, and gave me a hug. 'I don't know,

you children. I know I'm always saying this, but in My Day . . .'

Thankfully, Kate came into the kitchen. 'I was going to go and wake Tom. He's been asleep for nearly six hours, you know. He told me he hadn't slept at all the previous three nights because . . . he wanted to tell us.' She smiled wanly.

'I'll go and get him,' I said.

'Be nice to him,' said Kate. I stared at her. Kate, the scariest woman south of the M4? Kate, who made the postman cry? I expected her to support her son but in a bluff, Kate-ish way, but there were tears in her eyes.

'Oh, *Kate*,' I snapped. 'Is it that much of a surprise to any of us? It's hardly like finding out about John Major and Edwina Currie, is it? I mean . . .' I tailed off. She was looking at me in a really scary way. 'I'll be off then,' I said hurriedly, and ran out of the door. I bounded upstairs, shoes clacking on the wooden staircase, and knocked on Tom's door. No answer. I banged again.

'Hello . . . ?'

'Tom, it's Lizzy. Can I come in?'

'Lizzy . . .' The voice was muffled and distant. 'Hello . . . ouch.'

I pushed open the door. 'Hello again,' I said, and sat on the bed.

'Hi,' said Tom, from beneath his duvet. 'Oh, God . . .'

'Your mum sent me to get you.'

'I can't go down there and face them.'

'Why not?' I enquired.

'I just can't. I made such a fool of myself earlier.'

'It doesn't matter, silly,' I said, stroking his feet. 'They don't care – none of us cares.'

Tom sat bolt upright and stared at me. His hair was incredibly amusing. It was springing out stiffly from his head at a 45-degree angle. I giggled.

'That's just it,' Tom said angrily. 'None of you cares. You knew all along. Here I am, carrying this awful secret around, living this double life where everyone at work and most of my other friends all know, and I haven't told you, the people who mean most to me in the whole world. And when I pluck up courage to tell you this terrifying thing, all you do is laugh. Well, I wish I'd never bothered.' He ran his fingers through his hair.

'I'm so sorry,' I whispered, horrified. 'Honestly, none of us is laughing at you. We're proud of you for having the guts to do it. Even if we did know. And I wasn't laughing about that just now – your hair looks mad.'

'I made a fool of myself,' Tom moaned.

'No, you didn't,' I said.

'Yes, I did. Don't lie to me, Lizzy.' He stared up at me briefly, then buried his head under the duvet again. 'Just go away,' he mumbled.

I decided honesty was the best option. 'Well, yes you did,' I said quickly, 'make a bit of a fool of yourself. But – oh, Tom, can't you see why? You had red wine round your mouth, you were swaying and you fell over! That was why it was funny at first, and that's what you're probably remembering – if you can remember it,' I added. 'And the only way to show it doesn't matter is if you come down-stairs with me now, have a coffee, and make the others laugh so that they think you're OK and they don't have to be embarrassed about it.'

'Perhaps you're right. But . . . I just don't want to go back down there.'

'Oh, come off it, Tom,' I said. 'Get a grip. Look at the sorry collection of humans downstairs. Jess? What does she care if you're gay, straight or a homicidal maniac? Gibbo? He's only known you a day – I hardly think this is a body blow to him. Chin? Her friends are always coming out of the closet – look at Marcus.'

'Marcus is *gay*?' said Tom, pursing his lips and making snake eyes at me. 'Fanbloodytastic.'

'And, Tom,' I continued, hoping I was on the home straight, 'what do you think our family's going to remember this Christmas for? You telling us what we already knew? I don't think so.'

'Mike . . .'

'Exactly,' I said, slapping his thigh. 'When you look at it objectively, your news hardly compares with the ageing lawyer uncle bursting in on Christmas Eve with his busty bride of two days and acquaintance of four weeks. Think about it.'

'Holy guacamole,' said Tom, 'you're right.'

'Of course I'm right. Come on, get up, you idiot.'

'Lizzy,' said Tom, hugging me, 'you're great.'

'Yes, I am,' I answered, and I allowed myself a moment of internal glow for my good deed.

'I'm not playing Shoot Shag Marry with you again, though,' said Tom, swinging his legs off the bed. He picked up a glass of water from beside his bed and glugged it down. 'You're terrible at choosing – you always pick completely the wrong people. And I don't just mean David. Remember when you said you'd rather marry Duncan from Blue over Ryan Philippe?'

'I stand by that,' I said, as Tom pushed me through the door. 'Duncan's gorgeous and he'll cut the mustard when he's fifty, but Ryan's pretty-boy looks will be gone in a flash.'

'You're hopeless,' said Tom, as we trotted downstairs together. 'Really you are. You're the one who needs the sympathy, not me. You couldn't spot a good thing coming if he was completely gorgeous and wearing a T-shirt that said "Good Thing Coming" on it.'

'I know,' I said, linking my arm through his.

'I hope so,' Tom said. 'What about Miles? You could always shag him – he'd be up for it.'

'You make me sound like a complete slapper,' I said, not without a note of pride in my voice.

'Oh, Lizzy,' said Tom. 'You wish. But listen to me. Anyone but David or that madman Jaden, and you'll be fine.'

I couldn't say, 'But I don't really want anyone but David,' so I said nothing except 'Come on, we're here.'

As we stood in the hall, I looked through to the sitting room. There, framed in the doorway, my father was enthusiastically poking the fire with the end of the bellows and Mike was leaning against the mantelpiece, holding Dad's whisky glass. 'Bollocks, John,' he said, as Dad jabbed ineffectually at another log. 'No, that one there! Get that one over it, fella'll burn for hours. No, no! Give it to me!'

'Get off!' said Dad, brandishing a poker, as if he and Mike were little boys again. Mike scowled and flopped into the armchair next to him, then picked up an old *Eagle* annual and popped a chocolate into his mouth.

Rosalie sat in one of the battered old chintz armchairs to their left, with Chin perched on the arm. They were both laughing – I could hear Gibbo reaching the end of a convoluted story.

Suddenly Mike caught sight of us. 'Hello, you two,' he said, leaping up and striding towards us. He slapped Tom on the back. Come and get a drink – get one for Lizzy too. Here, have one of my chocolates!'

I sat down on the one empty sofa and felt the old springs sag. Mike handed me a glass of whisky, and Rosalie winked at him.

'All right, darling?' hissed Kate across the room, under cover of Gibbo's story.

'Yes, thanks.' Tom grinned.

'And then,' Gibbo continued, 'they said, "Get out of Bangkok, and if you show your face in here again, we're going to put you in prison." And I said, "Well, that's not fair," and the bloke cuffed me and I woke up on a boat with all my stuff gone.'

'Right,' Jess said. 'Have you ever been to the street where they film *Neighbours*, Gibbo?'

Several more stories from Gibbo, a lot more alcohol and three Frank Sinatra albums later, our Christmas Day party broke up and, one by one, we trickled off to bed. Mum went first, followed by Kate, then Chin and Gibbo, till only the hard-core were left. Tendrils of ivy clattered against the panes as we talked. Each of us was eager to reassure Tom. Mike, with the grace of the seasoned conversationalist, picked up the baton and referred affectionately to Tom's 'break-out'. Tom, the lawyer, laughed in bashful but genuine amusement and threw it back, with a comment on Mike's new comb-over. My father, the erstwhile captain of his university debating team, rolled the thinning-hair and outed-nephew gags into one with an anecdote about Oscar Wilde that gracefully touched on each but undermined neither. Jess, whose grey matter I sometimes worry might be composed of dead skin cells, sat up suddenly and said she didn't get it, so we took the piss out of her until she dozed off on the sofa.

By the time I got into bed the wind was howling. I pulled the duvet tightly round me as rain lashed against the windows. A gate was slamming and creaking in the gale, and as I wondered when it would stop I heard Mike pad downstairs and venture out into the storm.

I peered outside and saw him, in a battered old woollen dressing-gown and stripy pyjamas, twisting a piece of wire round the catch. As Confucius so rightly said, 'There is nothing more pleasurable than to watch an old friend fall from a rooftop.' The wind wailed louder. Wait! It was a human wail. I got up, unfastened the window and looked out. Rosalie was hanging out of hers. '. . . eee . . .

76

areful . . . ike . . .' she yelled. 'Ohmigod . . . don't sli . . . Wet path!'

'Aaargh!' Mike shouted, and slipped. He got up, looking furious, knees and hands covered with mud. '. . . ucking . . . couldn't . . . simple thing . . . a gate?' he growled, his normally unruffled nature clearly very ruffled.

'Are you OK, honey?' I heard Rosalie say as the wind dipped momentarily.

Mike brushed himself off, spread his arms wide and beamed up at her, rain streaming down his face. 'I am coming back up to you, my sweet,' he bellowed. 'Wet, dirty, covered with mud and rust, I shall bring you this token from my garden.'

He picked up a handful of streaming wet gravel. 'I'm putting this down your nightie. Now lie still, I'll be up in a minute, to give you a—'

I shut the window hurriedly.

And that was Christmas. As I lay down, the events of the day rushed through my mind in reverse order, a bizarre kaleidoscope of images: Mike yelling up to his wife in the pouring rain; Mum washing up in the kitchen; Tom's red-wine smile; the clinking of glasses as we sat down to lunch; Rosalie flicking through the papers in the study; the hollows beneath Kate's cheekbones as she laid the wreath on Tony's grave; David at the church, looking at me with those dark eyes . . . and all the way back to this morning, when I ran downstairs, excited as a little girl by the prospect of what the day would bring. And then I must have fallen asleep. Perhaps it was inevitable that I'd dream about David. I hadn't for a while, those dreams where he still loved me and I could see him, hear him, so clearly that I was sure I wasn't dreaming and that we were back together again until I woke up. Six months ago I had them every night. And it was still the same feeling then, as now – it was still the most bittersweet torture of all.

EIGHT

In the year and a bit that David and I were together, I was sure of three things: one, that I loved him; two, that he loved me; three, that this was the way it was always going to be. I didn't worry about whether we'd get married or look at cots and sigh longingly. I never thought about the future because all that mattered was that I'd found him and he loved me.

I'll never make that mistake again. I learned a lot from David, but the most important thing is that loving someone so much your heart turns over with happiness every time you draw breath isn't enough. It can't save you; the only thing you can do is to try and get over it.

When we'd been going out for nearly a year, he was offered a job in New York. It was a good one – with a highly respected newspaper – and it meant more money as well as a step up the career ladder. In every way, it was the most simple decision to make – except one. I didn't want him to go, and he didn't want to leave me.

Of course, we were terribly adult about it. I never said, 'Oh, God, please don't go. I'll miss you so much. I'm glad you've got this job and I'm so proud of you but don't go.'

78

Sometimes now I wish I had, just so he knew how much I loved him. How much I *really* loved him.

It was strange helping him pack up his flat, having endless farewell parties and dinners, where the same conversations were rehashed over and over again. 'You'll miss him, won't you?'

'Yes.'

'Are you going out to see him?'

'In a fortnight's time.'

'Well, you've got email and the flight's really not that long, is it?'

'No.'

Sometimes, when I was having these conversations, I'd look up and see David watching me, as if he wasn't sure about something. As if he couldn't decide whether he wanted me to be weeping and devastated, or calm and businesslike about his going.

I loved him so much it hurt. When I closed my eyes and thought about him, my heart would clench – even if he was standing next to me. And I was almost as happy when he wasn't there, because having him in my life, loving him, knowing he lived in the same place as me, that I had held him and made love to him, made me feel gorgeously lucky, young, happy and in love. Until I knew I had to say goodbye to him.

On one of the first days of late spring, a beautiful English day when the trees, the grass and hedges are at their most green, we went together to the airport. We checked in his bags, then sat at a café in near silence. I couldn't cry: I didn't want him to leave a weeping, drooping fool (and I didn't want his last memory of me to be as a honking, pink-nosed pig with rivulets of mascara around my eyes and on my cheeks). As the time drew near for him to go through, the silence between us pooled, lengthened. I felt dizzy, hot, muffled with cotton wool. Suddenly I wanted to say, 'I love you. Don't go. I don't want to spend another night apart from you. I want to spend the rest of my life with you. I love you.' I opened my mouth: my throat felt dry.

The flight was called. David drained his coffee and said easily, 'Right, I'd better go.'

I should have made my speech then but he was swinging his backpack over his shoulder. Instead I said croakily, 'Did you pack the *Rough Guide* in your suitcase or have you got it with you for the flight?'

'In here, thanks,' he said, indicating his rucksack.

'Good.'

As I stood at the gate and kissed him, he drew back. I smiled brightly and swallowed.

'This is for you,' David said. He handed me a crumpled brown-paper bag. 'I should have given it to you earlier. Listen, I – oh, God, they're calling the flight again. I'm late. Open it when you get home. I love you, Lizzy. Tell me you love me.' His eyes were on me, almost pleading, alert, looking for something.

'Of course I do,' I said, clutching the package to my chest. He kissed me suddenly, turned and walked through. He didn't look back.

When I got to my flat, I threw myself on the sofa and cried as if my heart would break because it *physically* hurt, him having gone. Then I made myself a strong gin and tonic. I reread the letters David had sent me, looked at some photos of our holiday in France the previous year, and cried some more. I moped, drank more gin, put a scarf round my neck, which made me feel like a tragic film heroine or Edith Piaf, and sang 'I Know Him So Well' drunkenly into my remote control. Then I remembered the package. I tore it open, and found his copy of the *Rough Guide to New York*. Stupid man, I thought. He's given me the wrong present. He'd been annotating it for weeks, putting sticky markers on pages of restaurants, bars, shops, museums – anything people had recommended to him. Now he was half-way across the Atlantic and without this book, which had maps, and information on where to buy milk, headache pills and sheets – I started to cry again, huge racking sobs for him on his own and me on my own and him without his *Rough Guide*. He'd wrapped an elastic band round the spine as a marker and the book fell open at the title page, where David had written, '*Lizzy, I need you and I need this book. Bring it over soon. D. PS I tried to give you this ring last night. Wear it, I love you.*' It was threaded on to the elastic band, thin yellow gold, battered and beaten, with a cluster of tiny diamonds that formed a flower.

But it turned out that the old chestnut 'Absence makes the heart grow fonder' isn't true. Perhaps our relationship wasn't strong enough to survive our separation; still that doesn't explain why we split up, and every time I force myself to think about it, none of it makes sense.

When David had been away for a fortnight, I flew out to see him. I'd been to New York a couple of times before, for work, but I love it so much that flying there *and* seeing David again meant I was almost sick with excitement. While the dreary suburbs and endless grey roads into London must be a shock for your average tourist coming from Heathrow who's expecting castles and thatched cottages, New York doesn't disappoint. There, you arrive and the following things happen, as if you were in an episode of a super-merged programme called *Cagney and Lacey and Sex and the City*:

1. Woman with enormous hair and nails shouts at you to move on in queue for Passport Control. 'Hey, you! Yeah . . . you, lady! Move it!'

2. Get into yellow cab. Hurrah!
3. During drive past graveyards and factories, you look up and there in front of you is the river, with Manhattan, including real-life Chrysler Building and the Empire State, gleaming in the sunshine!
4. Three doors down from your scabby hotel there will always be a bar like an old hairdressing salon that stays open till two a.m., where Cosmopolitans are three dollars each, and an old guy plays brilliant jazz piano!

I love it. But now the thing I loved most was David's being there. The city would be ours, the wide streets, the park, the tiny bar I'd told him about opposite his apartment. We'd live in black and white and Gershwin would play in the background, like in *Manhattan*. We'd ride through Central Park in a horse-drawn carriage. We'd laugh in slow-motion and wear Gap scarves and David would push tendrils of hair off my face.

But it wasn't like that, quite. And that was where it all started to go wrong.

The night I arrived one of David's colleagues was having a party in a downtown bar. I wasn't tired. I wanted to go out and see the city, and I wanted David to cement his friendships with his new work pals. David wanted to stay in, watch a movie and have sex, basically. I pointed out we'd just spent three hours doing that. He said we could happily spend another three hours doing it, and came up with some suggestions that I've been wishing ever since that I'd taken up. We had a bit of a row and went to the party in a slight atmosphere, neither of us understanding why when we were so pleased to see each other.

And how life laughs at you when you don't realise it's about to. For as we walked into the bar, a trendy, dim-lit place off Spring Street where the seats were cubes in primary colours and everyone wore black, I saw Lisa Garratt. The frienemy to end all frienemies. Lisa, an old acquaintance of mine from university, Lisa, who by coincidence worked on David's paper too. Tall, tanned, muscular. She had thighs like tree-trunks, I remembered – she was captain of the ladies' rugby team. She was always louder, more confident, more energetic than everyone else around her at university – an irritating mix of sporty and horsy with a bad slutty-party-girl edge. She was the one who'd say, 'Hey, I know! Let's stay up late and play Scrabble all night doing tequila shots and strip poker at the same time!'

'Oh, God,' I murmured to David as we walked in. 'It's Lisa.'

He was checking in our coats. I smoothed his hair and kissed him, relishing the luxury of being able to touch him. 'Lizzy,' he said, pulling something out of my coat, 'Why did you bring gloves with you to New York? It's June.'

'I'm aware of that, thank you,' I said. I'm never quite sure what temperatures to expect around the world and I believe in being prepared. Gloves don't take up much room.

'Is this like the time you took that bobble hat to Prague because you thought it always snowed there?'

'No,' I said, affronted. 'I'm using the gloves to store things in.'

'It was thirty degrees in the shade and you packed a woolly hat because you thought Prague was snowy all year round, didn't you?'

'You patronizing ratbag,' I said, hitting him. 'Don't forget that you thought Adrian Mole was a real person writing real diaries until you were sixteen.'

'I wish I'd never told you that.' He kissed me. 'Hmm . . .' he said, a moment later. 'What were you saying before the glove debate, bobble-hat girl? Who's here?'

I remembered. 'Urgh, yes, Lisa Garratt. Does she work with you?'

'You know her?' David said. 'Don't you like her?'

'She's the original frienemy,' I said.

'The what?' David said, kissing my neck. 'Let's go in. Lisa's OK. I'll fetch you your gloves if you get cold. How's that for a deal?'

'I'm sure she is. It's just I'll have to pretend we're really friendly and I don't like her much. Hey,' I pressed closer to him, feeling his hard chest and strong arms round me, 'I've changed my mind, let's go home and have sex all night. I want to try the thing with the ice cube and the needle now.'

But David broke away from me and took my hand. As we pushed through the crowd he said, slightly brusquely, 'Come on, Lizzy, we're here now. She's nice, honestly. A real laugh. Hi, Garratt. How are you?'

Lisa was still the original boys' girl. She was a massive flirt, the biggest drinker, likely to start a fight, and to wear slaggy clothes. Because she was a real lad the blokes loved her company, and because she was a real sex bomb they all wanted to shag her, but thought it was OK because they could explain her away as 'one of the lads'. I'd never liked her at university and I didn't now. I saw her appraising me as she smiled a sharky smile and slapped David on the back. I saw her deliberately exclude me in the subtlest of ways as she drew David and the other men into her group. Jokes about the office, about the subway ride into work that day, about what was on TV last week. I couldn't make a fuss about it because I wanted David to be happy and have friends.

The rest of the weekend was fine, but it wasn't as wonderful as I'd assumed it would be. We didn't mention the future, although I was wearing the ring. I didn't know what it stood for, and I couldn't bring it up without sounding either ungrateful or hysterical. The thin end of the wedge was already there. It wasn't Lisa. I don't blame her. Well, I do, the evil whore: she was a woman on a mission. But it was other things too. We were separated, leading different lives. And neither of us noticed until it was too late.

A month after I got back from New York I had a bad row with David. It started when he told me he wasn't coming over for a friend's wedding, and escalated into all sorts of things. I missed him; I was miserable. He told me he missed me too. But while I was still living the same life, if without him, I'd heard enough to know that he was having a great time, try as he might to deny it. And, of course, I wanted him to – I wanted him to be happy. So I felt guilty about being jealous of him, and he – well, I don't think he missed me that much. I think he got along just fine without me.

He had this thing about how us being together was a big step – 'It's a big step', 'We're taking a big step', 'Our relationship is a big step' – which made the word step lose all meaning for me. I found it vaguely amusing, but now, in the cold, Davidless light of day, I realized he was trying to tell me that he wasn't in serious-long-term-relationship mode. So while I think he bought the ring meaning to propose, he must have bottled out at the last minute. And that says all there is to say, really, so the row ended with us both half-heartedly saying sorry and ringing off. What I should have done was call him back; I should have been the bigger person. But I didn't. I was afraid, and so I bottled it.

Then, three days of silence later, Miles rang up and took me out to dinner. Miles and I had been friends when we were teenagers; he'd lived in Spain with his and David's father till he was fourteen, then come back to Wareham, which was when Tom and I became his pals. David was at university then, in Edinburgh.

In addition to having a variety of jobs to pay his way up there, he volunteered to visit an old couple twice a week, did their shopping, and was on the committee for rag week, stuff like that. He rarely came back for the holidays, and when he had we'd never met him. I remember saying to Miles that he sounded like a Goody Two Shoes, and Miles offering me a Mayfair cigarette and saying, in a bored tone, that he was, and it was annoying to have such a *girl* for a brother.

Miles, Tom and I thought we were a right cool teenage gang. On my eighteenth birthday I went to the Neptune in Wareham with them and some friends from school, and got royally drunk. Miles and I even snogged. In fact, in the summer of our first year at university we nearly slept together, but Miles got stage fright and his enthusiasm, as it were, wilted. He was mortified, but I told him I took it as a sign that we were meant to be friends and that was what we became. Of course, it was a bit different after I'd met David and fallen in love with him, but old friends stay old friends whatever happens. They're there for you when things go wrong. They'll tell you what no one else will because they love you.

So, over dinner, with anguish on his face and in his voice, Miles told me that David was sleeping with Lisa, that she was virtually living in the apartment, that – and even now I think he could have spared me this bit – they had been caught in the photocopying room together. My David cautioned for fucking a colleague at the office, with his trousers round his ankles.

I called David, and he was out. I left him a message. I couldn't bring myself to mention her name. I just said that because of what had happened it was over and I never wanted to see him again. So, theoretically, I dumped him by leaving a message on his answering-machine, which is something you do to someone you barely know, not someone you'd wanted to spend the rest of your life with.

I had an email from him in reply, just as I was leaving work.

Lizzy

If you say it's over, then it's over. I think it's for the best and you obviously do too. I'm sorry for what's happened. Anything else sounds trite.

For what it's worth, I never thought this would happen. I've missed you.

D

And then another, thirty-two seconds later:

PS Keep the ring. I don't want it.

Lisa emailed Emma, a mutual friend from university, and told her (really – what a total cow): Emma rang and asked Georgy was it true about Lizzy and her boyfriend? Georgy happened to be at my flat trying to cheer me up. I could hear Emma's braying, strident tones from my end of the sofa, the first of what would be too many calls and questions about what had happened. Georgy looked at me – what should she say?

I leaned forward. 'Tell her it's not true. Tell her it was Lizzy's ex-boyfriend. Because he's not my boyfriend any more.' The *Rough Guide* was lying on the floor. I picked it up and put it on my bookshelf, the spine facing away from me and since then I've tried not to think about David and anything to do with him at all. I try not to. But, occasionally, I dream about him again and it all comes flooding back.

This time I dreamed we'd just split up because we'd both received anonymous letters saying we hated each other, and then David's father had died and he had to scatter the ashes in my flat, and I kept saying I needed to Hoover them up and he kept yelling that I was insensitive and horrible for not understanding those were his father's ashes.

I woke up as David was coming towards me in my flat, smiling at me with his dark eyes and kind, stern face and banging the anonymous letters together incredibly loudly. (It turned out Jaden had sent them out of jealousy. I know, I know.) I could feel myself swimming back into consciousness, as you do when you wake from a deep sleep, and I rolled over and looked at my watch. It was ten thirty a.m. already and after a few seconds I realized that Tom had woken me by banging my hairbrush on my dressing-table.

'Tea! Wake up, young laydee, wake up,' he screeched, as I rubbed my eyes and tried to focus on him. 'Mum's bouncing off the walls. She wants to go for a walk. So's your mum. Rosalie's wearing a fantastically humorous outfit – kind of Burberry meets the baroness in *The Sound of Music*, and I've already found her counting the pewter bowls in the dining room. Mike's about to make scrambled eggs for late risers, so get a move on.'

I stared at him in frank astonishment. 'Who are you?' I asked.

'Whadyou mean?'

'I mean,' I said, pulling my knees up under my chin, 'last night you were so drunk you passed out for three hours. How can you be so chirpy this morning?'

Tom handed me a mug of tea and strode to the window. He pulled back the curtains to reveal a grey, overcast day. 'I'm right as rain. Must have slept it off. And I feel fantastic. Everyone knows. No more secrets. No more lies. Layers stripped away. Family reunited. Ho, yes.'

I took a gulp of tea and, amazingly, felt better too. 'I'm so glad, Tommytom.'

Tom gazed out of the window, musing and stroking his chin. Then he stopped and picked up Flossie, my first doll, who had a tremendously exciting tulle skirt and light blue top and used to be the centre of my world but now led a nice quiet life, sitting on my windowsill next to Manfred, a boy doll with a willy it could wee through (it was French). Tom looked challengingly at Flossie, as if he expected her to give him some backchat. Her flecked-blue marble eyes rocked open as he picked her up and she gazed blankly at him. 'I want everyone to know what it feels like to be totally honest.' He put Flossie back on the windowsill. 'To free yourself from the tyranny of repression.'

'What?' I said.

Tom sighed. 'Never mind. No more secrets and lies in this family, is all I'm saying. Come on.' He threw me an ancient baggy jumper that my grandmother had knitted for me. I pulled it on and rolled out of bed, yawning. I felt incredibly tired.

'You look knackered,' he said.

'Tom,' I said, as I freed my hair. 'Can I ask you something?'

'Yes, of course.'

'Have you . . .' I stopped. 'Have you . . . Sorry, this is embarrassing. But you're right, let's be honest. Are you seeing anyone at the moment, then? Like . . . a . . . a boy?'

Tom shut the door again. 'Er . . . no, I'm not. Thanks for asking, though.'

'But,' I persisted, 'when did you last . . . So how did you . . .' I trailed off. 'Sorry, I'll be honest again. Right. When was your last relationship? And how did you meet?'

Tom avoided my gaze. 'Mind your own business.'

'But you just said—'

'I know, but I don't ask about your sex life so don't you ask about mine, OK? I'm not seeing anyone, I don't particularly want to. But if you must know, I'm not going without.' He turned in a mini-flounce and opened the door again. 'Come on, let's go downstairs.'

I opened and shut my mouth. 'Righty-ho,' I said. 'Great. I'm pleased for you.'

'Thanks. I'm pleased for me too.'

'So now we don't have any more secrets, do we?'

We headed downstairs and I smelt something nice coming from the kitchen. Oh, it was lovely to be home. Even when it was more of a lunatic asylum than usual. In the light of a new day, I remembered how much I missed it when I was in London.

Tom stopped so suddenly that I nearly bumped into him. 'You're so blind sometimes, Lizzy.'

'What do you mean?'

'Nothing. Don't worry about it. The truth is out there,' he added. 'It's important to catch it while you can.'

I scratched my head. 'I don't suppose you could give me an example?'

'I'm going to, just you wait and see.' He stared at me. 'You know, you do look exhausted. Didn't you sleep?'

'No . . . I did,' I said, brushing my hair out of my eyes. 'I just had a bad dream, that's all.'

'God, that bastard David,' said Tom. 'I still can't believe what he did to you.'

I was impressed by this display of emotional intelligence, but as always when a member of my family brought up *le sujet de Davide*, I found myself fighting the urge to climb into the wardrobe and hide. They all loved him, damn them, and I suspected that in some obscure way they held me responsible for the end of our relationship. I gritted my teeth. 'Thanks,' I said, and changed the subject. 'So you're really feeling all right this morning, then?'

'Tom's eyes lit up for the first time in ages. He looked about fifteen again. 'Ah sure am, Lizzy,' he said, in a southern drawl. 'Ah suuure am.'

I sat down at the table in the side-room, yawning. Jess appeared from the kitchen and sat down next to me. I poured us both some coffee.

From the corridor came a sound like the hoofs of a dainty pony, and there was Rosalie, with a tray of toast and butter. Tom was right; cashmere twin-set, Burberry scarf tied jauntily around the neck, tweed skirt and stilettos. Amazing.

'Hello!' she said merrily.

'Lo,' Jess and I grunted.

'Mike'll be along in a minute – he's just finishing the eggs. They look good, I'm telling you. It's a lovely day out there. Your parents and Chin have gone for a walk.' It was like having our own personal CNN news roundup.

'Where's Kate?' asked Jess. 'Has she gone too, or is she back at the cottage?'

Rosalie frowned. 'Oh, of course, and Kate too. Sorry.'

Kate and Rosalie were not destined to be best friends, I could see that. Apart from the fact that Kate was scary, and Rosalie was mad, Kate and Mike were close: they always had been, ever since Mike moved in with Kate and little Tom for about a year after Tony died. They still do things together, like go for long walks. Before all this Mike had sometimes stayed with her rather than at Keeper House. I think he sometimes found it a bit strange to stay in the house that might have been his cluttered with roller skates, wet gym gear and an endless succession of pink girls' toys manufactured in Taiwan, it must have felt as if it was yet wasn't his home.

At that moment he came in, carrying a pan of scrambled eggs and wearing a paper hat. He was still in his tatty old dressing-gown, which looked much the worse for his exertions of the previous night. He was singing 'La Donna E Mobile' in a fruity operatic tone. It struck me that he looked more at home here this Christmas than I'd ever seen him. Although if Mike's in a good mood and you're one of twenty people in the same room, within ten minutes you'll be doing the conga down the street, strangers from around the corner will be begging to join in, shops will hang out bunting and sell fireworks, and the council will declare a public holiday. I perked up at the sight of him.

'Elizabetta! *Mi amore*. Have some eggs. Give me your plate.'

Mike had inherited from our grandfather a gift for making perfect scrambled eggs. 'Hold on a second,' I said.

'Come on, stop dousing that nice bit of toast in sheep-dip and hand it over. How disgusting you are! Rosalie, my peach, my nectar called Renée, have you ever had Marmite?'

'Yes, and it was totally gross,' said Rosalie. 'My first husband had a kinda fetish for it. He had it flown over from Fortnum and Mason. God, some of the memories I have stored up here. Yeuch.'

There was a pause. Jess and Tom made choking sounds. Mike said, in outraged tones, 'Woman! Please! Remember you're talking to your second husband now, and his beloved nieces and nephew! They do not know whence your previous spouse and his extraordinary nocturnal proclivities hailed, nor do I wish them to. I do apologize, children. Don't tell your parents about her.'

Rosalie giggled.

'Aaargh,' Mike shrieked. 'You've distracted me with your bizarre Marmite routine and the eggs are overcooked now.'

'Oh, God, please don't worry,' I begged. 'Honestly! I'm starving – just dish it up.'

Mike slid the eggs on to my plate.

'What about me?' Jess demanded.

He held out the empty pan. Jess looked as if she might cry, but that was nothing new. 'Have some of mine,' I offered. 'I've got loads.'

'No, I'll make some more,' said Mike. 'It'll take two secs. Hold tight, Jessica. Don't cry.'

'I'm not going to cry! Jeez!'

Tom helped himself to another piece of toast.

'You OK there, Sparky?' said Rosalie, smiling at him.

'Sure am,' said Tom.

The phone rang. Tom, Jess and I glanced at each other guiltily, knowing that none of us had any intention of getting up to answer it.

Mike shouted, 'Someone get that, will you? I'm breaking eggs in here.'

I relented, and ran through into the hall, hugging myself in the sudden cold as I picked up the handset.

'Hello?' I said.

'Lizzy? It's me.'

'Georgy!' I yelled. 'I'll take this into my room, hold on.'

'Good – but hurry up. I can't talk for long. Uncle Clive's just arrived and we're all going to do handbell ringing in a few minutes. Oh, God, get me out of here.'

The purpose of any best friend worth their salt is to listen with apparent fascination while you rant about on a number of subjects, in this case 1. our families and how mad they were (Georgy's Uncle Clive and Aunt Matilda – who makes corn dollies – were contenders, but I won, hands down); 2. men, and the hieroglyphic language they speak (won that one, too, with my tales of David's reappearance by the grave); 3. random Christmas presents (Georgy is a glamorous girl who runs a top hotel in central London: her aunt gave her a single hyacinth bulb in a plastic bag – nice); and 4. what we were wearing to our friend Swedish Victoria's Pikey New Year's Eve Party.

But since Georgy isn't really a part of this story, and since our conversation would have been of no interest to anyone but ourselves, I felt a bit strange when I put down the phone twenty minutes later. For the first time since I'd come back to Keeper House, I felt myself peeling away from home life, and wanting to be in my flat, chatting and watching TV with Georgy over a glass of wine. It's good to feel like that, though – I always arrive at Keeper House dreading having to leave, and the desire to embrace my normal life can come as something of a relief, an affirmation that I am a rational twenty-eight-year-old, not a crazed dumped person, marooned at her parents' home, still in her pyjamas at eleven a.m. on Boxing Day.

I went back downstairs, where Mike was lighting a fire with the ecstasy of a ten-year-old. Tom and Jess were eating their eggs in companionable silence, while Rosalie gazed into the garden, hands folded in her lap, perhaps imagining herself as Queen Elizabeth I or the gracious hostess of some elegant soirée, gliding through the halls in a silk dress, Mike adoringly at her side.

The fire crackled and Mike rocked back on his heels to take a gulp of coffee. I ran my hands through my hair and bit one of my nails. I glanced at Tom, who looked relaxed and happy, and felt content again.

Rosalie turned to him. 'You must come and stay with us in New York. Mike's moving into my apartment, and it's pretty big. You're so welcome. I want to see you all over there before the year's out – hey, we're family now, aren't we?'

It's funny when I look back at that scene now. In a few days everything would change, and at that moment I had no clue of it, no clue at all.

NINE

By the end of Boxing Day, I wished Tom had taken up Rosalie's offer immediately. His new-found desire to help others and reveal the truth had accomplished the following:

1. Chin had threatened to kill him.
2. His mother had offered bodily violence against him.
3. He had made my mother cry.
4. And – this was a stroke of genius – he had probably managed to split up Chin and Gibbo.

I'm not sure where it all went wrong. I can see that after unburdening yourself as Tom had done, you might want to help others help themselves, and I can also see that he had imagined touching tableaux of grateful relatives kissing his hands and thanking the Lord he was gay for it had shown them the path to their own happiness. What I'd forgotten was that Tom is, and always has been, disastrously tactless. He has all the strategic acumen of – well, I'm not too hot on military history and it's been a while since I last read *Asterix the Legionary* – let's say, a really bad general. He means well, but he can't bring all the cohorts and squadrons together in a satisfactory way.

Tom's first course of action was to try to embrace Rosalie – both literally and figuratively – into our family. Because she'd been the first to speak up after his 'shock' announcement, he clearly now looked upon her as a worthy recipient of the most intimate family confidences. By the time the walkers came back we'd rustled up some lunch and, as we tucked into our turkey leftovers, Rosalie asked Chin why she'd cheated on her fiancé Bill with his best friend, then asked Kate whether she'd had any side effects from her hysterectomy.

Chin gaped, and Kate said, no – but the up-side was that she'd never have any more children like Tom.

After lunch Tom sloped off with his NBF Rosalie to watch *Chitty Chitty Bang Bang*.

'God,' breathed Chin, as she prowled around the sitting room, pursued by an emollient Gibbo, 'doesn't she have any tact?'

Kate stopped pacing in front of the fireplace. 'I blame Tom,' she said. 'Well, I blame her too, but I especially blame Tom.'

'Poor Tom,' said my mother, absently, on the verge of going to sleep.

'It's just so . . . *rude*,' said Chin.

'Well, yes,' said Mike, helplessly. 'Rosalie seems to absorb information like a sponge . . .'

'Well, tell her to mind her own business in future, OK?' Chin fumed. 'And, Kate, you can tell your son not to be such a blabbermouth.'

'And you, Chin,' said Gibbo, from the corner of the room, 'can stop sleeping with your fiancé's best friends.'

I shrank back into the sofa. Brave Gibbo. Brave, stupid Gibbo, we hardly knew ye.

'How *dare* you?' Chin hissed, advancing on him. 'For your information, even though it's none of your business, I wasn't engaged to Henry when I slept with Bill.'

Dad raised his eyebrows and retreated behind *England's Thousand Best Churches*.

'Oh, right, right . . .' Gibbo nodded. 'Well, that's OK, then.'

'*You*—' Chin spluttered.

Gibbo raised a long, looping eyebrow. 'What, Ginevra?' he said coolly. Suddenly I saw where the balance of power lay in the latest Chin relationship, and I liked it.

'Oh, forget it,' Chin said, and grinned. 'You're right. Nobody's perfect.'

'With the possible exception of the bloke who invented the Norton Commando,' said Gibbo, and went back to his motorbike magazine. Chin sat down next to him, beaten but happy. She tends to be the stroppiest girlfriend in the world, which is why the cruel record executives and suave men-about-town always dumped her, but now she just sat there quietly and tucked her hair behind her ear. Gibbo put his hand on her thigh and squeezed it. Chin smiled.

'Suzy, when does the surgery reopen?'

'Tomorrow.' Mum sat up. 'And John's got to go into town for a meeting with the solicitor about the planning permission for the roof, so he'll be gone quite early too. Mike, are you going with him?'

'Me? No,' said Mike, sounding surprised. 'I was going to take Rosalie for a drive, maybe stop off at a pub and have some lunch, show her a bit of the countryside. And possibly kit her out with a really good Groucho Marx disguise in case she says something to make you want to lynch her again.'

'Oh,' said Mum, 'I must have got it wrong . . . I thought you were the one who suggested the meeting.'

I sighed. Apart from Mum, no one else seemed to share

Dad's all-consuming interest in the roof. I knew it needed doing, but really . . .

'No,' Mike said, 'it's sorted out now, don't worry. In fact, I—'

The phone rang. Jess, on her way upstairs to fetch something, shouted, 'I'll get it.'

'Don't worry,' said Mike, leaping up. 'I will. I think I know who it is. I'll have a word with Rosalie, too.' He winked and disappeared.

Silence fell as everyone picked up their books or dozed off. I looked down at my lap and realized I'd picked up a birdwatching guide from the dresser in the drawing room, not my Georgette Heyer. 'Damn,' I said, and got up, but no one took any notice. Kate and Mum were having a nap, Dad was reading, and Gibbo and Chin were whispering in the corner by the french windows. The fire was crackling and spitting but apart from that it was quiet enough to hear the ticking of the grandfather clock by the door. I crept out quietly into the deserted hall and heard Mike's voice coming faintly from the study. I wondered idly why he'd gone in there to take the phone call as I went into the dining room and picked up *Devil's Cub*. Suddenly I heard him say, 'Yes, Lizzy's here – they're all in the sitting room. I thought you wanted me, old man.'

I know you shouldn't eavesdrop but, really, come on. My ears didn't exactly swivel and rotate like Inspector Gadget's, but they came quite close.

'David – I say, no, David – I don't think that's a very good idea.'

David? I flattened myself beside the dining-room dresser in case someone should walk past. My heart was pounding.

There was a pause, then Mike said, 'You want to do what? Why?' I could hear him drumming on the desk – a sure sign of irritation.

98

A floorboard creaked beneath me. The silence in the rest of the house was overwhelming.

'Think of how it'd upset things – think of Lizzy's feelings, David. You loved her, didn't you? What would telling her all this do to her?'

I breathed in and looked out over the courtyard to the fairy lights on the tree, shining brightly in the gloom.

'No, don't come round. It's really not a good idea. I mean it.'

The drumming continued, faster and faster. 'Come on, old chap,' he said finally. 'You can still be the good guy here . . . What? . . . OK, then. Good . . . All right, I'll speak to you soon . . . No, she'll be fine. You've done the right thing. Just leave her alone.'

I heard him put the phone back on to its cradle. 'Little shit,' he said, quite distinctly, then slammed his hand on the desk. Mild, sleek Mike, so affable and relaxed? I caught sight of his face as I walked out into the hall and my blood froze. I'd never seen him so angry, ugly almost, eyes smouldering.

I waved *Devil's Cub* at him as he emerged from the study.

'Lizzy-lou,' he said, as he saw me. His face instantly ironed itself, the creases of rage replaced with his usual affability. 'You look like a man who's just swallowed a fifty-pound note and doesn't have any cash left in the bank. Do I mean that?' He looked up in the air as if expecting someone to answer from above. 'What's up, Titch?'

'Ooh . . . nothing,' I said lamely. 'Who was that on the phone?'

'Christian Bell – you remember him? Nice chap. I was at university with him. Told him I was coming back for Christmas and he was ringing to fix up drinks. Now, come on, why don't we play a game or something?' He put his

99

arm round me and squeezed me tight. 'If it's Trivial Pursuit, bags me not with Jess.'

'Not fair,' I said. 'Bags me not with Jess either.'

I was thrilled that he was lying so I wouldn't know David had called, but I was dying to know what David had said. Did he want to apologize for what had happened? Or what he'd said yesterday? Was he starting a local branch of the Young Ornithologists Society? Had he fallen on hard times and decided he needed the ring back? Well, he couldn't have it. When people asked, in sepulchral tones, 'So, what did you do with the ring?' I replied sadly, 'I've hidden it away. I think it's for the best,' but in fact I'd accidentally dropped it down a crack in the floorboards in my bedroom and never got round to retrieving it.

David would find this amusing. I was always losing things and he was always finding them. I thought of the fury in Mike's voice as he hissed, 'Little shit,' and loved my uncle even more for taking care of it all.

'Hmmn,' Mike said. 'Why don't we go and find my tactless wife? I want to behave like a king. I want to lie on a sofa and eat chocolates and watch TV. Like a pharaoh. A pharaoh with a television.'

We stayed in all afternoon as the weather got worse. When *Chitty Chitty Bang Bang* ended, we moved on to *Murder on the Orient Express*. *The Wizard of Oz* and *The Wrong Trousers*. The wind raged outside and we lounged around until tea-time.

As we sat down to supper, Chin and Kate wedged themselves next to each other and glared at Tom. Chin had sworn to cut off his privates if he spoke to her again, and his own mother had told him that if he breathed another word about her gynaecological *histories*, she'd stick a fish knife in his leg. But Tom was undeterred. He turned to Mike and asked him what he thought of the Davis Cup – could Philipoussis stage a comeback against Capriati? I'm not sure I've got that right, but I'm fairly confident they were talking tennis.

Anyway, supper progressed in this vein. Dad was agitated about his meeting with the solicitor; he said nothing throughout the meal, but grated pepper over his soup for about three minutes, then ate it without turning a hair. Mum was quite looking forward to opening the surgery the next day. Getting back to work doesn't seem to fill her with the dull, vomit-inducing dread it does most of us, even if, like me, you don't mind your job. She was bright and sparky, joining in Tom's and Mike's arguments about Nasser Hussein's batting average (perhaps it was cricket they were talking about. Who knows?).

'You used to be so good, Tom,' she said. 'D'you still play?'

'I'm in a team at work, but it's not much cop,' said Tom. 'Wareham did pretty well last summer, though, didn't they?'

'They're still pretty useful – but they'll miss David this year,' said Dad, spreading butter on his roll. 'He was the star bowler, I seem to remember. Always saved the day.'

'Er,' said Tom hurriedly. 'Uncle John . . .'

I got on with my soup, wishing he'd shut up.

'How – um – how did they do in the end, then? Wareham,' Mum asked, in the silence that followed.

'They did jolly well, actually,' said Mike. 'Top of the local league.'

I stared at him. 'How on earth do you know that? Is the Wareham team newsletter distributed on the Lower West Side?'

'Internet, dummy,' said Tom. 'It's how I know Jimmy Gooch maintains his batting average. Unfortunately, it's also how I know he hasn't died and turned into slime, as I fervently hoped he would.'

'Ah, Jimmy Gooch,' said Mum wistfully. Tom coughed

and looked outraged. 'Nice boy. I know he was a bit mean to you at school, Tom, but it was his parents. Horrible people. The father was a drunk. He used to beat Jimmy up.'

'No, he didn't!' Tom exploded. 'That is a complete myth! It was the other way round! Jimmy Gooch used to beat his father up! He's an evil thug! He made a policeman cry!'

'I know you didn't like him, but he wasn't a bad boy. I was rather fond of him,' said Mum. 'He had terrible stress headaches, even when he was little. Poor mite.'

Tom put his elbows on the table, made a pyramid with his fingers and cleared his throat. 'Oh, honestly, Aunt Suzy, you're *so* naïve.' He then told my mother that all of the prescriptions she'd written for Jimmy Gooch at primary school had been sold in the playground for hard cash by the same Jimmy Gooch: he had claimed, to a circle of goggle-eyed ten-year-olds, that they were 'hard drugs what made your bits feel funny'.

My normally cheery mother, who had made a pet of Jimmy Gooch, was devastated. She sat in silence for the rest of the evening, which alarmed all of us, even Tom, then went to bed early, muttering that she needed to get up early and check her records.

I should never have left Tom and Gibbo alone together. After supper, I went to Jess's room. We sat on her bed, on the patchwork quilt she's had since she was tiny, and I took off my nail varnish. We were studying the ingredients of the remover – it smelt of almonds, but in a toxic way that wasn't pleasant – and chatting about what Jess would do next year after her course when we heard shouting.

We didn't pause. Like crack commandos, we leaped off the bed and jogged down the corridor. Screams were coming from the other end of the house.

A door slammed. *'I never want to see you again! I hate you!'*

'What's he done now?' I said, a wave of unease washing over me.

During their men-and-motors chat, Tom had asked Gibbo when he was going to propose to Chin. In touching and forthright language he had conveyed to Gibbo Chin's advancing years, her desire for children, her satisfying financial position and the sincere wish of her loving family to see her comfortably established. He left Gibbo with the distinct impression that he, Gibbo, was in danger of being regarded by our family as a cruel seducer, toying with Chin's emotions and playing her for a fool. He conjured up a vivid image of Dad and Mike as men who would break a man's neck like a cocktail stick for so much as glancing at their sister.

Gibbo, who was sincerely in love with Chin – and the only person I'd ever met who didn't take any notice of her when she was in a mood – was horrified. While he didn't particularly want to get hitched, he did want to be with Chin, and saw the wisdom, nay, the urgency of his position. (All of this I found out the next day at the pub, when the recriminations were flowing freely. At the time, of course, I was as confused as Ricky Martin.)

'What's happened?' I gasped, as Jess and I arrived at the scene of the crime. Gibbo was standing outside the bathroom, looking hopeless. There was a toothbrush and a slipper on the floor and an old print of *Marriage à la Mode* listing on the wall, clinging to a frayed wire. Chin was inside the bathroom, whence sobbing could be heard, along with muffled phrases like 'How could you?' and 'Go away, you piece of shit!'

'Oh, my God, what have I done?' Gibbo muttered, alternately wringing his hands and slapping his cheeks.

'Yes, Gibbo, what have you done?' echoed Jess.

At that moment Tom appeared, unruffled and wearing a

nightshirt. He looked like Wee Willie Winkie. Jess and I clung to each other and guffawed.

Tom glared at us. 'What's happened here?' he asked.

'I did what you said,' Gibbo said weakly. 'I told her I thought we should tie the knot, that she wasn't getting any younger, and I was about to get stuck into the speech about how much I loved her when she threw the toothbrush at me, then the slipper, then the yelling started and now she's locked herself in the bathroom.'

Jess slapped her forehead. 'You said *what*?' she whispered.

'HE SAID I WAS GETTING ON AND I SHOULDN'T WASTE ANY MORE TIME,' came Chin's agonized voice from the bathroom. 'THEN HE SAID, "HOW ABOUT IT, EH?" ' More indistinct noises.

The door to Mike's room opened and its incumbent poked out his head. 'I say, what's happening?' he called in a passable impression of Terry-Thomas. 'Everybody all right? Are you having a party?'

The bathroom door flew open and there stood Chin, wiping her nose with her finger in a distinctly ominous fashion. 'You low-down piece of crap,' she said softly, her face inches from Gibbo's. 'How *dare* you say I'm past it? How *dare* you ask me to marry you while I'm spitting out my toothpaste? I – I'm going to have you shot. No, I'm going to do it myself unless you get the hell away from me. You can sleep with Tom tonight and then go. I never want to see you again. You two,' she turned to us menacingly, 'go to bed and mind your own bloody business. And you – *you . . .*' We all stepped back when it was clear she was aiming for Tom. She grabbed him by the scruff of the night-shirt so that it rode up almost to his bottom. 'You!' She curled her lip and bared her teeth. 'You're starting to get on my nerves! I don't give a fuck if you're gay. You can be a one-armed bisexual Zoroastrian cannibal for all I care. Just stay the fuck out of my business. You think about what

104

you've done today. You've *ruined Christmas*. You've *ruined it!*' Her voice broke. 'This is the *worst Christmas* since the *awful one* and that's all because of *you!*' And with that she turned on her heel, walked into her room and slammed the door.

'Well, well.' Mike's tone was unexpectedly cheerful in the circumstances. 'There's a sleeping-bag in my room, Gibbo. You'd better grab it and bunk down with Tom for the night.'

'Don't get any ideas,' said Tom, pursing his lips, and trying unsuccessfully to make a joke of it. I glared at him. 'Oh, well, we can discuss all this in the morning. I do think Chin's overreacted somewh—'

'Tom,' said Gibbo, in a voice that seemed to come from beyond the grave, 'don't try to get out of this. You've got to cop responsibility for what you've done here today. You've made your aunt cry. And she's going to have me killed.'

'Jeez,' Tom said. 'I gave you a piece of helpful advice and you went off and told a woman in her late thirties that her eggs were drying up and time was running out and, frankly, she was lucky you were being seen in public with her, let alone shagging her. I'm surprised she didn't kill you there and then. Phew,' he said, shivering at the memory of Chin's basilisk stare. 'I'm going to have nightmares tonight. Night, you two. Night, Mike.'

'Night,' said Mike, handing Gibbo the sleeping-bag and closing the door. 'You'd better discuss this further tomorrow.'

'Good idea,' said Tom. He leaned against his doorframe. 'Lizzy, Jess – hey. How about we go to the Neptune for lunch? I'm meeting Miles there for a drink. We'll take Gibbo with us. Miles is a wise chap. He'll know what to do. Wow. I'm exhausted. Some people are so ungrateful.'

On Friday morning I'll be in Queensway, shopping and

having lunch with Georgy, I thought. I'll be out of this madhouse. I'll be in London, behaving like a sane person, not holding a bottle of almond-oil nail-varnish remover in a corridor at one in the morning watching my cousin in a nightshirt, my sister and my aunt's spurned lover trying unsuccessfully to undo the zip on a sleeping-bag.

TEN

We moved into Keeper House when I was seven. My grand-mother had fallen and broken her hip, and she and Grandfather had decided to move to a little cottage a hundred yards away. Dad had been offered a better job in an auction house nearby so our move to the country made sense.

I remember our first proper Christmas there mainly as a series of domestic accidents and arguments. My parents had a blazing row about where we should put our furniture, what to leave and what to keep. Dad felt everything should be left as it was, and only the furniture my grandparents had taken should be replaced. Mum felt Keeper House should be *our* home, not a kind of mausoleum to Dad's relatives. Then Grandmother had another fall after she'd drunk one glass of sloe gin too many on Christmas Eve. Tom had measles and had to stay at home with Kate. Chin had just left school and hated her parents for moving out of her home, hated Dad for moving in, and Mum for moving things around. And Mike had suddenly left his job with a tiny, rather bizarre charity (the objective of which escapes me now – something to do with real ale for carthorses, or being nice to second-hand bookshops) and gone back to

London, where he'd spent his dissolute early twenties, to take up a flash new job in a City law firm.

So, in later years my family referred to that Christmas as 'the awful one'. As we were walking along Wareham high street the next day, I wondered if this might be the one to eclipse it in the collective memory.

We'd left early to have a drink before Miles joined us. Mum had disappeared straight after breakfast to check her surgery records and find out what and how much Jimmy Gooch had taken her for. Dad had left for the solicitor's, very serious and smart in his suit. Kate had returned to her cottage after supper the previous night; Rosalie and Mike were going for a drive; and Chin was AWOL, but I knew she was there because she kept slamming doors.

After a brisk walk across the fields, Tom, Jess and I found ourselves in the Neptune, nursing hangovers with a sense of gloom and anticlimax. The Christmas decorations hung limply, the tinsel curling and dusty. Put us away, they moaned. We want to go back in the box in the cellar next to the crème-de-menthe that no one drinks. Christmas was two days ago: move on and get over it.

The Neptune was where I'd got so drunk on my eighteenth birthday. Bill, the landlord, had bought me a double rum and Coke as a present, and I'd found myself still there three hours and lots more drinks later, with my head down the loo reacquainting myself with the original double rum and Coke. Ah, memories.

We slotted ourselves into the alcove by the fire, the best spot in the green, cosy interior. It has a view of the main street through leaded windows, and the snug gloom means you can look out but not be seen by those looking in. There are two high-backed wooden settles, worn smooth by the bottoms of local habitués over the last three centuries.

They're joined at the end by an old oak-panelled wall, with a door in the middle, painted on the outside with the crest of the Radcliffes, the family who built Keeper House. It was for their personal use and favour, so that they weren't bothered by the lumpen proletariat. David and I had spent many a happy hour there, covertly doing things we couldn't have got away with in the open.

Gibbo appeared with a tray of drinks. 'Gin and tonic?' he asked.

We surveyed him gloomily. 'Me,' I said.

'Guinness?'

'Me, thanks,' said Jess.

'Pint of girly Carling?'

'Charmed, I'm sure,' said Tom.

Gibbo sat down and took a gulp of his Guinness. He smacked his lips and put down the glass. 'Well, Thomas, what the bloody hell am I going to do now?' he said.

'I honestly wouldn't have told Suzy all that about Jimmy Gooch if I'd known she'd get so upset,' Tom said passionately. 'I just thought she'd want to know the truth.'

'Oh, be quiet, you fool,' said Jess, rather crossly for her.

'No, *you* be quiet,' said Tom. 'You don't know what it was like, knowing I was going to tell you all on Christmas Day. I kept thinking, while we were all oohing about Rosalie and Mike, What are they going to say when they hear about me?'

'You're not wrong there,' said Gibbo. 'But (a) it wasn't exactly a bolt from the bleeding blue, and (b) . . .' he cleared his throat and glared at his new room mate '. . . it doesn't give you the right to play God. Seems to me . . .' He ground to a halt. 'I'm going to the toilet.'

'Poor Gibbo,' said Jess, after he'd gone. 'Chin's still furious with him. I talked to her this morning.'

'What did she say?' I asked.

Jess took a gulp of her pint. 'Not much. She used her eyes, mostly. And hand gestures.'

As if by magic, the door opened. 'Oh, my God,' I whispered. The three of us shuffled further away from the door of our safe haven and prayed Gibbo wouldn't emerge from the loo just then.

It was Chin. And she couldn't have been looking shiftier. Her lovely black bob was all but covered by a black beret and her coat collar was raised. Her brown eyes looked enormous in her pale face, which was partially covered by a large scarf. She looked like Inspector Clouseau's daughter. She paused, eyes darting about, then crept stealthily to the bar.

'Afternoon, Ginevra, how are you, then?' Bill bellowed. He's not overly keen on social chit-chat, but has always been fond of Chin, in his lugubrious way.

We stayed as quiet as church mice, praying he wouldn't mention our presence.

'Fine, thanks,' said Chin briskly. 'Gin and tonic, please. How about you? Good Christmas?' I could see her taking off her scarf and putting it on the bar.

Bill slapped a measure of gin on to the bar with a little bottle of tonic. 'Ice?' he boomed. 'Not so bad,' he continued, as Chin reached for her purse. 'Lemon?'

'Yes, yes,' she said impatiently. 'How much?'

'Straw?' Bill said, Eeyore-like.

'No!' Chin snapped. 'Why on earth would I want a straw with my gin and tonic? Just tell me how much.'

'On me, Ginevra. Season's greetings and all that,' said Bill, with the air of one announcing long delays on the motorway.

Gibbo appeared from the gents. 'Sit!' we hissed. Tom grabbed his shoulder and pulled him down.

Transaction over, Chin took her drink and disappeared to the other side of the curved bar, where I could just about make out the top of her head and one of her hands. Bill looked over in our direction, but we shook our heads and put our fingers to our lips.

'What's she doing here?' said Gibbo. 'I'm going to go and talk to her.'

'No,' said Tom, all previous thoughts of goodwill momentarily shelved. 'She's obviously not here to meet us. Don't interrupt her.'

'But I want to apologize to her! I want to let her know I didn't mean it and I don't want to marry her!'

'Not sure that's going to do the trick, Gibbo,' Jess said. 'Leave it for a moment or two, OK?'

'She has to talk to him some time, though,' I pointed out, 'and let him back into their room. He's wearing Tom's pants.'

The door banged open again. It was Miles Eliot, and as his gaze ranged round the bar I shot my head out of the Radcliffe and hissed, 'Miles! We're over here!'

'Hello, you lot,' he said, pulling his scarf out of his coat. 'Hello, Lizzy.' I was nearest to him, and he squeezed my shoulder.

'Get in.' I pushed him on to the settle next to Tom, and kissed him hello.

Miles managed to stay friends with Tom and me, all the while the thing with David was crumbling around us, and for that I thanked him. Heck, he was the one who told me about what David had done. But it couldn't be denied that it was a little awkward now that he was David's brother, and the one who'd had the courage to tell me the truth. I hadn't really seen him (apart from Christmas Day), since a dreadful night, about four months ago, just after the break-up. We'd gone out to supper and I'd just been so sad, it had been a pretty dire evening. It culminated in me bursting into tears all over my nice steak, because David liked steak. I know, pathetic. It's not exactly a controversial thing to like – who doesn't like steak, for cripes' sake? Miles had to take

111

me home in a cab and I snotted on his shoulder. I hoped he'd forgiven me. We'd emailed and texted, but never got round to fixing up another date. The one good thing about it was that it meant that what had happened before, between me and him, had been pretty much forgotten.

I like Miles. He's laidback and urbane, a bit bitchy, easy to get on with, and obsessed with QPR (why?). In direct contrast to his brother, to whom he is close but not in temperament, David being unlaidback, unurbane, crap at gossip and an Aston Villa supporter (again, why?).

'Er, what the hell are you all doing?' said Miles. 'Why aren't you with Chin? She's over there.'

'Yes, yes,' Tom snapped. 'We know that. We don't want her to see us. We've got a problem and we need your help. What I rang you about on Christmas Day is all fine now. We—'

'I don't need a drink, by the way,' Miles said, taking off his jacket.

'Good,' said Tom.

'Have this, mate, there's two here,' said Gibbo, sliding over a spare Guinness we'd bought earlier.

'Thanks, er – mate,' said Miles. 'We haven't met. I'm Miles Eliot.'

'Hi. Norman Gibson. Good to meet you,' said Gibbo, and shook his hand.

'Anyway—' Tom stopped. He stared at Gibbo. 'Norman? *Norman* Gibson? What's that?'

'Take a wild stab in the dark,' said Gibbo, closely examining one of the frayed cuffs on his shirt.

'Gibbo! Is that your name!' Jess cried.

Miles produced a folded-up copy of *The Times* and buried himself in it.

'You're called Norman!' I said. 'That's really weird – like calling your parents by their first names or looking at yourself in the mirror for too long—'

'Oh God, I know what you mean!' said Tom, turning to me in excitement.

'Norman Gibson,' Jess mused. 'No, I'm sorry. It just doesn't seem right.'

'Shut up, you blokes,' said Gibbo, whose ears were turning pink. 'I don't go a bundle on it either, but occasionally it slips out. Wait till you hear my middle name. Awful.'

'Tell us!'

'No way,' said Gibbo. 'Listen, if I ever marry Chin, they'll say it in church, so there's an incentive for you.'

'Ah, yes,' said Tom. 'Like in *Neighbours*, when Charlene married Scott and that was when we found out her middle name was Edna. Poor Kylie.'

Miles whistled under his breath. 'Listen, sorry to interrupt. This is really fascinating, I'm sure, but, Tom, what did you want to ask me?'

'Norman Gibson!' Tom cackled. 'Anyway—'

'Get a move on. What was it you rang me about on Christmas Day?'

Tom paused, took a sip of his drink. I craned my neck to see if Chin was in evidence, but she'd disappeared behind two old men at the bar. Bill was leaning against the till, polishing a glass and whistling sadly.

'Yes,' Tom said. 'The plan to get David round to talk to Lizzy, we don't need that any more. There are other problems afoot. Sorry, Lizzy, I should have told you this earlier.'

'*What?*' I said, leaping out of my seat.

Tom had the grace to look ashamed. 'I'm sorry, I was going to mention it, then everything else ran away with me.'

'Mention *what?*' I leaned forward. 'Tom?'

'It's not a big deal, honestly. Just that, well, I thought, after you saw him in church on Christmas Day, you probably really needed to talk to each other – you know, clear the air. So I rang up Miles and told him to tell David that

113

Mike and John wanted to ask his advice about applying for some crap thing like lottery money to restore Keeper House, including the roof. Then I thought he'd arrive and I'd get rid of the others for a bit and you two could talk properly.'

Jess was nodding, enthralled, as if this was the plot of a daytime soap. 'Right, right. Then what happened?' she asked, eyes wide as saucers.

'How dare you, Tom?' I said, furiously. 'It's none of your business. I don't want to talk to David and I don't want to see him.'

'Lizzy,' Miles said calmly, as I balled my hand into a fist. 'Slow down, it's OK. I thought you'd probably feel like that, so I told him to leave well alone and get out of it.'

I was about to say something when I remembered Mike on the phone the night before. Why had David rung, then?

'But what I don't understand,' Miles continued, 'is why David said he was going to meet Chin for a drink today. Ah, here he is now.' He leaned over serenely, as if the last piece in the puzzle was falling into place. 'Great pint of Guinness, mate, thanks a lot.'

Oh, no. I felt as if we were in the closing stages of a Gilbert and Sullivan operetta with people moving in and out, sighing hopefully and leaping around corners. Of course this was the nearest pub for miles around, and it was natural Chin should meet David here if she was going to meet him anywhere, but it was a bit much. I put my hands over my eyes and groaned, then peered through my fingers.

Sure enough, there on the stairs, his lean fingers unbuttoning his coat, stood David. He glanced in our direction and I held my breath, thinking he'd seen us. But then he headed towards the other end of the bar. I was just about to feel relieved when I saw Chin stand up and fling her arms round him. David responded, smiling at her with real warmth. They stood together for a moment, David holding her elbows and saying something. Chin bowed her head and looked downcast, then glanced up and grinned. She picked up her bag, talking all the time, and they moved towards the door. David held it open, then followed her out. I saw him dig his hands deep into his pockets as the door banged shut. It was such a characteristic gesture that my heart turned over.

Why was Chin having a clandestine drink with my ex, whom she'd had to help me get over a few months ago? Why was David meeting my young, attractive aunt, who was maybe single, maybe not? Were my family lying to me? Was I like Tom Cruise in *Vanilla Sky*, programmed by futuristic cyborgs to have the life I wanted but with a dodgy computer program that would suddenly reprogram with disastrous results?

Miles roared with laughter as we told him about our Christmas. We got quite annoyed with him when he was still chuckling five minutes later. 'God, you Walters,' he said eventually. 'You're all the same – you do realize that, don't you? That's why David thinks he misses you all so much – it's a kind of love-me-love-my-dog thing.'

'What?' I said. 'That's bollocks. We're not like that. What do you mean?' *Where were Chin and David going?*

'Well, we are *similar*,' said Jess, cutting across me. 'Of course we are, we're all related. But I'm nothing like . . . er . . . Gibbo,' she concluded triumphantly.

Miles sighed. 'Oh, Jess, you great mallet. You don't get the point, do you?'

Jess's wide blue eyes filled with tears.

'Don't be mean, Miles,' I said. 'God, you're evil. Say you're sorry.'

'I'm sorry, Jess,' Miles said, putting a placatory hand on

her sleeve. 'But you are all the same. You're as bad as each other. Look at yourselves.'

'What do you mean we're all the same?' Tom asked.

'No,' Miles said, after a moment. 'Forget it. Let's talk about Norman Gibson.'

'No, come on,' Tom said, shifting in his seat, 'what do you mean?'

'I mean,' said Miles, balancing his lighter on top of his cigarette packet, 'you rush around, doing Walter things, having Walter family love-ins, whooping it up and having a fabulous Walter time, and you never notice what's going on right under your noses. You're a dying breed.'

'That's rubbish,' I said, nettled. 'We're nothing like that.'

'Yes, you are,' said Miles patiently. 'Look at you. I've known you all for – what, more than ten years? And you never learn, any of you. You're like a heritage exhibition. Here's Tom, behaving like a three-year-old who's overdosed on Sunny Delight. And, Lizzy, look at you and my brother. You meet him, you tumble head first in love with him, like a little girl, and you can't cope with the first sign of trouble. Then there's Mike. For some reason he decides it's time he got married, picks up some pair of cashmere boobs with an ex-husband and a lucrative pay-packet and gets hitched three nanoseconds later. And Chin, so beautiful and talented, she could do anything she wants, hooks up with a bloke who might possibly be Mr Right, then treats him like shit because she doesn't know what to do with him if he is.'

He brushed an invisible speck off his coat. 'Sorry, Jess, you're right. You're not a berk compared to them, actually. You're the sanest of the lot. And you, Gibbo, get out while the going's good, mate. Run like the wind.'

'Hey,' said Tom, half standing, 'shut up, that's not fair. You apologize, OK? Don't talk about my family like that.'

Miles grinned ruefully. 'I know I'm being harsh, but I'm

playing devil's advocate. Can't any of you see it? Does any of you know what I'm talking about?'

'No,' I said.

'No,' said Jess, rubbing her nose.

'Me neither,' said Tom.

'Yes, absolutely,' said Gibbo.

Miles laughed. 'Look, I'm not trying to stir, I'm just saying it's great you're all so close still. Look at the three of us, and Dad, living out in Spain. It's not exactly Happy Families at our house, like it is for you. But sometimes you can't see the wood for the trees because you're all too busy being Walterish together.'

'But we like being together! We're a close family!' Jess cried. 'There's nothing wrong with that.'

'Nothing at all,' Miles said. 'But think about this. If you see a book lying around at Keeper House, I bet all of you'd know who was reading it and whether they liked it. But can any of you tell me what's up with the roof that's so bad your father has to go and see a solicitor in town about it as soon as possible after Christmas?'

'It's a leak,' said Tom promptly.

'Yes, a leak,' Jess and I agreed.

'That's it?' said Miles. 'Is it dangerous? Does the roof need replacing? Whose fault is it? Whereabouts is it?'

We were silent. Tom frowned. I didn't know what to say. A cold, slinking worm of fear slithered through me, starting in my stomach. I thought of Dad last night at supper, grating pepper and fiddling with his fork. He'd be back soon, surely, and then I could ask him. Suddenly I wanted to see him very much.

Gibbo piped up, from the end of the table, 'Well, whatever. I think they're great. And . . . well,' he coughed, self-consciously, 'I'd be happy to be uncle to any of you three.'

'Gibbo!' I said, flushed with warmth. 'That's so nice. We'd

117

love you to be our uncle. Frankly, you'd be a lot better than our new aunt.'

'I like Rosalie,' said Tom, uncomfortably.

Miles chuckled and stood up. 'I'll get some more drinks. Same again?'

'I know you do,' I said, when Miles had gone, 'but come on, Tom, there's something going on with her, isn't there? I don't trust her.'

'Me either,' said Jess. 'I saw her looking at the back of the grandfather clock yesterday after supper. She was looking at the date, really closely, trying to work out how much it was worth.'

'Jeez,' I said. I thought of telling them that I'd seen her in the study on Christmas Day but something stopped me.

'I heard her asking your mum if she'd thought of taking in paying guests, like a B and B,' said Gibbo.

'*No*,' I said.

'Well, not like a B and B,' he said. 'It was more like making it a luxury hotel. But your mum laughed and told her they'd never do that.'

'So I should bloody think,' said Jess. 'The nerve of the woman! She's funny, isn't she?'

'You're telling me,' Tom said. 'Still, she's mad about Mike. And it'd be fun to go and stay with them in New York, wouldn't it? The apartment sounds amazing.'

Miles appeared with the drinks, and sat down next to me.

'How are you, Miles?' I said. 'Apart from annoying. I haven't seen you for ages.'

Miles took a sip of his beer. 'I know. I was thinking the same thing. It's been frantic, especially at work – sure it has for you too.'

'Well – yep,' I said, knowing this was a competition I'd lose as Miles works all the hours God sends. 'I hope you're having a good break, anyway.'

'Absolutely,' Miles said. He looked at me quizzically. 'It's great to be home.'

'Yes,' I said. 'It must be lovely for your mum to have both of you with her.'

'She sends her love, by the way.'

'Oh,' I said. 'Give her a kiss from me. I love your mum.'

'Well, she loves you,' Miles said. 'I'm just sorry things are so weird between the House of Eliot and Keeper House at the moment. You know, she'd love to see you. You should pop in and say hello. Maybe next time you're down.'

I thought about this as Tom and Gibbo started up another whispered conference, Tom seeming distracted, Gibbo menacing, or as close to menacing as he can get without the effort of frowning. 'Ye-es,' I said eventually. Alice was the ideal mother of a boyfriend. As far as I could tell, she had no agenda whatsoever, other than that a glass of wine is a nice thing to greet your guests with when they walk through the door. She was blonde, little and pretty, obsessed with reality TV shows and ready-made meals from Marks and Sparks, and when David and Miles's cheating father finally slung his hook, she had thrown a party in the village. The memory of it still makes people wince as if remembering the accompanying White Russian-induced hangover. She was a part of my life that I had lost when David and I split up. I knew I wouldn't go to see her. It was just too weird, and I couldn't stand the idea that she might think I was being polite. I liked her much more than most other people, but that was the way it had to be.

'You never know,' Miles said, chewing a nail, 'if you went to see Mum, or dropped her an email, it might diffuse some of the tension you feel about it all. Does that make sense?'

'Sure,' I said.

'Anyway, it's just a suggestion. So, yeah. When are we

going to meet up, then? New Year? Let's go out and get hammered like the old days.'

'The old days when all it took to get us drunk was sharing a rum and Coke?'

'Yes.' Miles took another sip. 'I'm joining a club in the New Year so I'll take you there. But in the meantime there's a real old men's pub in a mews off Great Portland Street – went there the other day. It's tiny. Does amazing beer. That's quite near where you work, isn't it?'

'It is,' I said. 'You've got a good memory.'

'It's not that. I've got a kind of magnetic needle that can identify the nearest good pub to anyone's place of work,' said Miles, with some pride.

'No way!' Gibbo said.

I looked at Miles and raised my eyebrows – a code that tried to say, 'Please sort this situation out.'

Miles, raised his at me, then put his elbows on the table. 'Oi, listen, Gibbo,' he said. 'I've been thinking about this. I think I know what you've got to say to Chin.'

I smiled at Jess and tapped the side of my nose. 'Watch and learn,' I whispered.

'What?' said Gibbo eagerly.

'Tell her you're going back to Australia and she'll never see you again and that she can just get lost. That'll make her see sense.'

Tom sat forward. 'Hey, that's a good idea.'

'Yeah,' Gibbo agreed. '*Great* idea, mate. Good one.'

'Give her a flight number and stuff, make it look authentic.'

'Yeah, and ask her if she can come round to help with your packing. You can unpack it afterwards if she comes. She'll be in pieces. It'll work like a charm.'

They clinked glasses.

'Great one, Miles!'

'Thanks a lot!'

Jess and I exchanged a glance. This was Miles's great plan. The one that was so full of cunning and daring that Chin would fall right back into Gibbo's arms. Men. How crap.

ELEVEN

'Shall we get out the battle-wagon?' asked Tom, as we reached the house, now shrouded in darkness. 'For old times' sake?'

The best thing that had happened on the Awful Christmas was when Grandfather tapped Jess and me on the shoulder as we huddled together on the sofa in our scratchy Mothercare dresses, feeling miserable, and holding us each by the hand he led us out into the bitter cold. Our grandfather was exactly as a grandfather should be; twinkly-eyed, interested and interesting. He could fix anything, from a bicycle bell to a fuse and, of course, he made fantastic scrambled eggs. As we walked through the kitchen garden, clinging to his hands, we begged him to tell us what he was going to show us. He took us through the rows of cabbages and potatoes towards the old shed, tucked against the kitchen-garden wall.

'Here we go,' Grandfather said, fishing out his enormous key-ring. He flattened his thumb against each key in turn, flicking them aside as he looked for the right one. When he finally unlocked the door Jess and I peered in and gasped.

There, in the shed, was the most amazing contraption, a

122

metal tin on four wheels with a long handle to pull it along or steer it. Its red paint gleamed at us through the gloom. The wheel hubs were a bright, snappy yellow. Jess jumped straight into it.

'Your father, Mike and Tony used to play in this when they were young,' said Grandfather, as I climbed in after her and he took the handle to roll us out. 'It's called the battle-wagon.' He squatted on the grass next to us. 'You're here now and I thought it would be nice for you two to play in it.'

We spent the rest of the Christmas holidays in the iron-hard, frost-covered meadow, with Tom when he was better, steering wildly and screaming with excitement. The following summer we made a train line that stretched round the garden, and took it in turns to pull the others round, calling at each stop in turn and picking up the teddies and dolls we'd put there as passengers. I shook my head wistfully. 'Too many gin and tonics,' I said wistfully.

'I know what you mean,' said Jess, then opened the old wooden gate and stood aside as we trooped in. I could see no sign of life: everyone was still out. 'What time are you going back to London tomorrow, Tom?' she asked, as I unlocked the door and we stepped into the house, flicking on the lights in the hall.

'Morning,' said Tom, picking up a newspaper. 'And I won't stay long now. I want to get back to Mum's to pack and spend the evening with her. Ooh, Prince William.' He flung himself on to the sofa in the sitting room.

I turned to find Gibbo behind me, not knowing what to do. 'Why don't you go and make some tea?' I suggested.

'Good idea,' he said, and disappeared towards the kitchen.

I picked up a letter on the hall table and wandered after him, unsure what I was going to do. The woolliness of the gin was wearing off. Why had David and Chin met up when

123

was he flying back to New York soon? In the cool of the darkened passage I leaned against the wall and inhaled deeply, trying not to get upset now that I was on my own. I'd seen him again. I stood quietly, listening to Gibbo humming under his breath as he put the kettle on, and Jess and Tom chatting in the sitting room. Jess was lighting a fire – I could hear the dull thud of logs falling into the grate.

I couldn't imagine that Chin was doing the dirty behind my back. It was unthinkable. And seeing Miles always brought back memories of David.

'Er . . . Lizzy?' Gibbo's voice came tentatively from the kitchen. 'Shall I get out the rest of the Christmas cake? Lizzy?'

I heard a car in the near distance and looked out of the window, pretty sure that it was Mum and Dad's. It was, and I could see them talking with the interior light on. Then Dad opened the door and got out. My lovely parents, I thought, my heart swelling. The roof. Must ask them about the roof. Suddenly I realized this was my last night at home too. I'd persuade Tom to stay and get Kate to come up here instead. We'd have a proper family supper, lots of wine, perhaps a game afterwards. Maybe I could even persuade Mike to show Gibbo how he could walk up walls, like Donald O'Connor in *Singin' In The Rain* – he hadn't done it for ages. Not since the broken ankle, anyway.

Hurrah. I was still here, we were all still here. Were our problems so bad we couldn't sort them out and get on with it? No, of course not.

I heard Mum and Dad walking through the courtyard, Dad throwing the car keys up in the air. They jangled as he caught them, and I remembered Christmas Eve, just before Mike had arrived with Rosalie. How long ago that seemed now. I went to open the door and Gibbo glided behind me,

124

carrying the tea tray.

'It's Mum and Dad,' I heard Jess cry from the sitting room.

Our front door is heavy and old. As I heaved it open, I said 'Hello, how's the roof? Is it in the . . .' But the words died on my lips when I saw their faces.

'Not now, Lizzy darling,' said Mum, as Dad shuffled past me without saying anything. 'We just need to discuss something. Give us five minutes. Ooh, you've made the tea, Gibbo. Bless you. Where's Chin?'

'Out,' I said, fear rising. 'What's happened?'

'Nothing, we just need to . . . Where's Mike? And Rosalie?'

'I don't know, Mum. They've been out all day.'

Mum took off her hat and fluffed up her hair. 'I'll be along in a minute. Don't worry, darling, Dad's fine. It's . . .' her voice faded away. 'We're fine.'

I was left in the hall, gazing after them as they disappeared into the study and shut the door. A floorboard creaked and all was silent again. I couldn't wait out here so I went into the sitting room, chewing a painful hangnail.

Tom was in the doorway, obviously having seen everything. His face was set, eyes hooded. 'They'll be out in a minute? What's it about?'

I shook my head.

Gibbo was on the sofa reading the local paper. I sat down in a battered armchair and Tom put a cup of tea for me on the low bookshelf that ran along the wall beside me. I smiled at him, and he grimaced, then smiled back. We were in this together.

Next to the teacup was a photo of Dad, Tony and Mike as teenagers, all huge ears, buck teeth and long spindly legs, with a chubby, long-haired, gorgeous little Chin. The boys were leaning over with their hands on their knees, smiling, and Chin was holding up a teddy bear at the camera. The house was in the background, and in the top left corner an open window flashed as it caught the sun. My grandmother was leaning out, a tiny figure, waving. It's one of my favourite photographs. I picked it up and looked at it, drinking in every detail. Mum and Dad were talking loudly in the study.

Suddenly there were footsteps across the courtyard again. The door swung open and Chin appeared. She looked defiantly at Gibbo, who tossed his (slightly matted) hair and went back to reading the *Wareham and Crozier Gazette*, with the apparent concentration of one for whom every page holds the location of buried treasure.

I looked at Chin through narrowed eyes. 'Hello,' I said. 'Where have you been?'

'Where's Mike?' she said grimly.

'He's gone into town,' said Jess, getting up. 'Hello, Aunty dearest, have you had a nice day? Have some tea.' She poured a cup and handed it to Chin, who still stood in the centre of the room.

'Are John and Suzy back? I've got to find Mike. This is terrible,' she said.

'What is, Chin?' said Tom, alert.

'I've just had a drink with David Eliot,' Chin said, turning to me.

'I *knew* it!' said Gibbo, throwing down the paper. 'I *knew* you would!'

'Shut *up*, Gibbo!' said Tom. 'Of course you knew she did! We saw her, you complete idiot!'

'You saw me?' said Chin. 'When?'

'In the Neptune. We were in the Radcliffe. We saw you both arrive,' said Jess wearily. 'Gibbo and Lizzy both think you're having a secret affair. Me and Tom don't. Chin, did you know his real name was Norman Gibson?'

Chin spluttered. Drops of tea flew out of her cup and into the fire, where they hissed on the logs. She glared at

Gibbo. 'Of course I'm not having an affair with him! Please! Sometimes I wonder if growing all that hair takes up space in your brain.'

'You snobbish, stuck-up, thinks-a-scarf-is-a-really-important-work-of-art spoilt little princess!' yelled Gibbo, leaping to his feet.

'Yes,' said Chin, holding up her hand. 'Look, Gibbo, I don't have time for this now. We'll sort it out later.' Suddenly she looked tired. 'We will. We both know that, frankly, you're lucky to get me. Do sit down. Honestly.'

Gibbo did as he was told, rather more relaxed. 'Maybe. But you know why you're with me too, you randy little whore.'

Chin blushed and almost giggled.

'Oh, God,' said Tom, covering his ears. 'Please don't talk about your sex life. I'm begging you.'

'I'll go with that,' said Jess.

The door opened again, and in came Dad. My heart contracted. I seemed to see him properly for the first time in years. His hair wasn't the light brown I'd always known it to be: it was grey. He stooped. Suddenly he looked about twenty years older. He rested his hand on the old dresser where we kept the family photographs, and looked as if he was trying to work out what to say. 'I'm afraid there's been some rather bad news,' he began.

Mum came in behind him, and caught hold of his sleeve. She had been crying.

I looked round at everyone: Chin, now sitting next to Gibbo on the sofa, underneath the watercolour sketch of my great-great-grandmother who looked so like her; Tom, sliding his tiny mobile phone over and under his fingers; and Jess, her curly hair bobbing up and down as she nodded at Dad.

'It's rather complicated, and I still can't quite believe it, but . . . to cut a long story short, I've done something incredibly stupid. Well, several incredibly stupid things.'

Mum seemed about to say something, but my father gently eased away her hand in a protective, rather than dismissive gesture. He stopped and stared at the floor.

'I'm afraid we've got to sell Keeper House. As soon as possible,' he said.

Spring

TWELVE

Memo

To: Elizabeth Deborah Walter (a.k.a. Me)
From: Elizabeth Deborah Walter (a.k.a. Me)
Subject: Money-raising Plan to Avert SOKH (Sale of Keeper House)

1. Do a sponsored trek to the jungle and raise cash.
2. Have a bring-and-buy sale where someone brings a piece of Dresden china or a small old Norse chessman and it turns out to be worth millions of pounds – this was always happening in Blue Peter during their bring-and-buy sale appeal of 1985; sick children, old ladies who had no money or hordes of Brownies would leap around and say, 'I can finally buy a new Brownie Hut.'
3. Sell flat and release valuable equity something or other.
4. Become a prostitute.
5. Marry a millionaire.

Monumental Films, the company I work for, has glamorous but impractical offices just north of Oxford Street, in that secret, pretty area to the west of Charlotte Street. Glamorous, because they're in a lovely old Georgian town-house, with high, stuccoed ceilings and original fireplaces; impractical, because it was built as a home for Georgians, not as offices for people to run a multinational film company in the twenty-first century. The Americans can't understand how we operate out of a building where you can't knock two rooms together to make a screening room because it's listed – and they're right, I think, much as I love it. There's a primary school next door, in a beautiful old Victorian building, complete with neo-Gothic bricked arches and tiny steeples on its roof, which I look out on to from my desk. I can see the children playing in their break and I often wonder who lives round there. It seems such an unlikely place to go home to, right in the heart of London, a stone's throw from Soho on one side and the formality of Regent's Park on the other. Who are those children's parents? The people who run all those crazy little Spanish bars on Hanway Street? Lap-dancers from Spearmint Rhino? Shopkeepers who live above their own newsagent's or drycleaner's?

One morning in late January, I was gazing out of the window in a desultory fashion, mulling over my Save Keeper House memo instead of preparing notes for that afternoon's meeting. The idea that home and my parents were only a short journey up the motorway was as remote as those comforting, warm things always are in the alcohol-free, dark and bitter days of January, when you are back to being a London girl who has a job, bills to pay, wears high heels that are uncomfortable but gorgeous, likes champagne cocktails, runs for the bus (and rarely gets there in time, mainly because of the high heels). The memory of

Christmas seemed from a different age, although it was only a few weeks ago. Almost as if vignettes from those few days were playing somewhere in an altered universe, suspended in a snowglobe, as if characters like Rosalie and Gibbo didn't exist in real life, we had conjured them up in our imagination. And, anyway, as I had to keep reminding myself, Keeper House might not be home for much longer.

It was breaktime at the school and the children were huddled together like a group of penguins. It was a freezing day, dull and cold, and I pitied them, having to spend their break out in the playground rather than lying on a sofa in front of the TV. That is one of the blessings of being a grown-up: no organized sports, and no having to play outside. Otherwise it might be nice to be eight again without anything major to worry about.

The house had been on the market for two weeks. I still couldn't understand why the roof problem and our insurance shortfall were so incompatible that we had to clear out. But, of course, us being us, I didn't ask and no one told me. Instead I lived in hourly terror that someone would put in an offer. Conversely, when I heard from my parents that people had been to look round and hadn't offered, I was cross. Who could see that house and not want to live in it? What idiot could walk through the wood-panelled hall into the sitting room, see the huge fireplace, the battered old chairs, the snowdrops at the edge of the kitchen garden and the lawn and say, 'No, this isn't quite right, I'm after something nicer'?

So I'd decided to Take Action. Even if it came to nothing it would stop me sitting at work chewing biros till the ink exploded in my mouth. Instead I would sit at work and stare out of the window, formulating master plans of Wellington-like cunning and strategy. It was a legitimate

133

excuse, I decided, for not doing any work. Only the list wasn't going very well. To recap:

1. Do a sponsored trek to the jungle and raise cash. Or pay someone else to. I would rather eat my desk than trek through a jungle.
2. Bring-and-buy sale. Unfortunately I don't remember the Wareham one producing anything more than several chipped floral plates, lots of jam (80 per cent of which was my grandmother's), and bizarre cream plastic kitchen accessories from the 1950s.
3. Sell flat. Well, my maths is not great, but even I know a one-bedroom flat behind an off-licence on the Edgware Road (dodgy end) does not equate in value to a six-bedroom house in the English countryside.
4. Prostitution. My least favourite option, but if I charged fifty pounds a time I could buy Keeper House after ten thousand punters. Or maybe if I got a few regular clients and charged them £200 for the whole night, that would be (pause to work it out on the calculator) £200 x 7 times a week – I could give it up after 357.142857 weeks, which is 6.86813 years. Blimey. I'd always thought being a proz was a not-ideal but quite easy way to make money. *Au contraire.*
5. Marry a millionaire. Unlikely – but millionaires have to marry someone, don't they?

The script for *Big Yellow Taxi*, the project I was working on and the cause of roughly 40 per cent of my chewed pens, slid off my lap and on to the floor as I bit my lip, scribbled a couple of things down and went back to staring at the children. Suddenly the bell rang and they all jumped into a line.

'Hey, Lizzy,' said my friend Ash, as I scrabbled on the scratchy blue carpet tiles for the pages. 'What on earth are you doing?'

'Being useless,' I said, arms full of paper.

'I wondered what you were doing this lunchtime,' said Ash. 'Sally and me are going to the pub.'

'I can't,' I said, shuffling the sheafs into some semblance of order and clacking them smartly on the desk. 'I'm too busy, I'm afraid. I've got to make notes for our big meeting about *Big Yellow Taxi* this afternoon.'

Ash peered over my shoulder to look at my nicely printed memo. ' "Become a prostitute . . . Marry a millionaire," ' he read out slowly. 'What are you on about?

'Nothing,' I said. 'Tell me something. Who's coming to the meeting with Jaden? It's not terrifying Fran, is it?'

'You set it up, Lizzy, not me,' said Ash, lolling against the door of the office I shared with Lily, our boss. 'You're the golden meeting organizer, who organises meetings, who Lily loves so much, and who is so obliging she starts sleeping with the scriptwriter to get really creatively close to the project—'

I sprang up, pushed Ash away from the door, and slammed it. 'Shut *up*, Ash,' I hissed. 'No one knows about me and Jaden. It is *not* a big deal, I've slept with him twice. So be *quiet*. If I hear anyone else knows I'm pulling your fingernails out one by one.'

Ash laughed, maddeningly. 'Oh, this is well good. I've got you exactly where I want you, haven't I, golden girl Lizzy? Show me your bra and I won't say a word.'

'No.'

'Yes! Or I'll tell Lily.'

'No,' I said briskly. I tucked my pen behind my ear. 'I'd rather lose my job, thanks. Go away now, please.'

Ash didn't move. Instead he swung his lanky frame into Lily's chair and wheeled himself over towards me. 'So, how *is* it going with Jaden? Go on, tell me. I'm being nice, not annoying.'

'Urgh,' I said wearily.

'Urgh?' Ash repeated. 'That's good. Wow, you must be really pleased. I'll mention you said that this afternoon.'

'No, I don't mean urgh Jaden, I mean urgh in general. It's just . . . It's nothing. That's why I'm not talking about it. I mean . . . I might see him again, I'm not ruling it out. But it's not going to last. It's just a bit of fun.'

Ash was the wrong person to have this conversation with – he's the one bloke I know who thinks commitment and long-term relationships are lovely and good, not things to run screaming from into the hills. He looked at me reproachfully, in the way men do if you admit you're not 100 per cent keen on one of their own sex. As if to say, 'You're lucky someone picked you at all. We do the dumping, not you.'

'Oh, Ash. He's nice, but . . .' I didn't want to sound like someone who uses men then casts them off at whim. 'We're just friends who've slept together a couple of times. No big deal. He doesn't want more. Neither do I.'

'Why?'

I tried to look brave and sad, like Audrey Hepburn. 'Because . . . because of *last time*. David.'

'But that was six months ago.' Ash was nonplussed. 'And he treated you like shit.'

'It wasn't six months . . .' It was more, and I should have been over it by now. But I couldn't say what I really thought, which was that the idea of being with someone who wasn't David was just *so wrong* it was best not to think about it. And use Jaden as a distraction from having to think about anyone else.

'Anyway,' Ash continued, leaning back in his chair and changing the subject with the insouciance of man. 'I wanted to catch up with you about Lola. Remember, that girl from Victoria's Pikey party? Do you think you could get me her number?'

He ran his hands through his hair, in a slightly self-conscious gesture. I considered best how to answer. Should I refrain from pointing out, for the third time, that he should just give up and stop trying to get her to go out with him? Ash is gorgeous, but I worry about him. He needs a nice, well-intentioned quiet girl who thinks he is Mr Charisma, but he keeps falling for credit-card-wielding harpies who expect him to fly them to St Kitts regularly.

'Oh, decisions, decisions,' I said vaguely. I waved my notes at the window. 'Look at the little children. See how they play.'

'Seriously, Lizzy, I really like her. What about it. Will you call Victoria for me?'

'Twiglets! In my desk! Fantastic!' I said, changing the subject cunningly. I opened the bag. 'Want one? I was thinking, you know,' I continued, 'Lily wants to see the rewrites Jaden's been working on, but I still don't think he's nailed it yet.'

'Oh, yes, he has,' Ash said, leaping joyfully upon my unwitting *faux pas* and making a fnaar-ish face. 'He certainly has nailed it. All over his flat, so I hear. Especially in the hall. Cor! Oh, he most certainly—'

'Do be quiet,' I said, with asperity, congratulating myself on having successfully led him away from Lola. 'Shut up now, please.'

'But you still haven't said. How much do you like him? Are you going to start going out, d'you think?'

People are so nosy, I thought. I'm not *engaged* to Jaden, I'm not even seeing him, and just because Ash happens to know what's gone on he thinks he can ask me all about it. 'No, it's something different. You know? That's why it's nice.'

'I'm not saying you're about to marry him,' Ash said. 'But . . . well . . .'

*　　*　　*

137

It was true that since Christmas I'd started seeing more of Jaden, rather than just sleeping with him by accident, which was what I'd done before Christmas. It was also true that I was project-managing the script he was working on. It was true too that no one at work, apart from me, Jaden and Ash 'Mouth of the South' Ghosh knew about it, but it wasn't that big a deal. I liked Jaden, but talking about it with anyone made it sound like it was going somewhere, and it wasn't. I'd never had a non-relationship before. It was great.

However, Jaden was coming in for a meeting that afternoon with Lily, Ash, the script consultant, Fran from the New York office – producer/kick-ass scary, once slept with one of Lily's boyfriends – and me. I had to tell him and Fran that the concept still wasn't working, and we needed to decide how to approach the next stage of development. Added to that there were several weird things about seeing more of Jaden, which meant I was constantly on the verge of laughing every time I saw him, and unable to decide whether he was wise or bonkers but a good shag.

It is weird – but not unpleasant – seeing someone when no one else knows about it. You don't have to have endless conversations, like the one above, with your friends about whether you like him or not. It was weirdest of all getting busy with someone who wasn't David. It never was before him. Why was Jaden's stomach tanned even in January? Did he use a sunbed? Or was he so Californian he remained naturally golden throughout the year?

Why do people drink wheatgrass juice? It's the most disgusting thing ever. Last Saturday Jaden and I went ten-pin bowling, which was brilliant. Then he led me into a juice bar. If Kate had happened past and seen me sipping wheatgrass juice mixed with ginger and seaweed, she would have run screaming into the road. He called me Q E Three – and I couldn't decide if that was a cute new nickname or a subversive piss-take of my nationality and accent. Or a dig at my hips, which I often felt myself were the size of an ocean liner.

Heigh-ho. I needed to do a memo like the one for Keeper House about Jaden, but every time I thought about it a wave of impatience with myself engulfed me. Get a grip! I'd think. Make the most of having a no-strings fling and stop harking back to some ill-intentioned shagger of last year and get over it – woo-hoo, up with Jaden. Then I'd see him and he'd say something like 'Toxins are clogging your pores, which is why your nose is becoming engorged' and I'd want to smack him, then run screaming into the road . . .

This was partly why I was dreading that afternoon's meeting. I had a nasty feeling Jaden would try to give Lily some ginseng or ask Ash how long he'd been gay. I'm fond of him, but while he's a great writer, he doesn't perform well in public because he's a bit mad.

While this was all going on in the daily foreground of my life, the backdrop was the sale of Keeper House. It popped into my head at the most inappropriate times. I'd started doing degrees of separation in my idle moments, waiting for the bus, on hold on the phone, sitting in a bar holding a drink in my hand. Champagne cocktail, lovely glasses, champagne glasses at home – how would we divide everything up when we had to move out? Watching *Friends* on Channel 4, trailer for *Property Ladder* in the break – where would Mum and Dad move to? Could they afford a house after the money was divided up between Dad, Mike and Chin or would they have to move into sheltered housing? Playing Cluedo the previous weekend with Swedish Victoria and her friends, staring at my card of Miss Scarlett, I realized she reminded me of Rosalie. Why were we selling just because the roof needed repairing? It didn't make sense. Why had Rosalie been leafing through Dad's papers?

The awful thing was that as most of my family had no idea what was going on, it felt remarkably as though we were in semi-freefall. Mike and Rosalie were back in New York, having had some row with Dad and Mum about selling the house before they left that neither side would talk about. I'd tried to get Mum to tell me to no avail, and Mike was impossible to get hold of. Tom was working hard and wouldn't return my calls. Jess had sliced off the top of her little finger on New Year's Day. She'd kept it in a bag for a while – it was like a tiny fleshy hat. She said it was Art. Mum said it was a bit of finger in a bag.

The only good thing was that I thought less about David. Before Christmas I'd tried so hard to push him to the back of my mind and all of this made it easier.

Actually, there was one other good thing, much more important than that. Chin and Gibbo were engaged. I kept forgetting about it, then suddenly remembering that my aunt was marrying a lanky carpenter with matted hair. The wedding was in a few months' time, and they were both delirious about it. So it was dead nice at the moment being friends with a crazy Californian who made me do gentle cleansing yoga, brought me bamboo shoots and took me to see soporific Japanese films or jive dancing at a fifties club near the Brockwell Lido. Especially when he was coming in for a meeting today where we had to act like nothing was going on.

They were due at five o'clock. My assistant Marie had gone out and bought some lovely biscuits from the cake shop down the road. I always forget it is deeply naff to be seen eating biscuits in a high-level meeting.

'They're here,' Marie said, as she appeared in the doorway of the meeting room where Ash, Lily and I had gathered in the late afternoon. Ash was contemplating himself in the huge antique gilded mirror, licking his fingers and smoothing down his trendy sideburns. I tried not to be irritated by this. Ash is annoying in many ways but he's flacking good at what he does. Lily, who oversees the UK films in development, is a mad small Rottweiler with crazy curly hair. She was pacing up and down, brown eyes snapping, gearing herself up for a fight with Fran.

'Can you go and get them from Reception, Marie?' I asked. 'Thanks.'

'Late, I suppose,' said Lily, glancing at her watch. 'Yup. Three minutes. Tih. Pick. Al.' She resumed pacing until Ash got her to sit down.

A lot of this stage of the development of a film, I've discovered, is about placating egos and compromise. It's a huge waste of time. That is why so many terrible films get made – because no one's in charge of the original reason why someone loved a script, an idea or a book. It is diluted by an actor who won't fly, so the Second World War RAF film becomes about a navy SEAL, in Iraq filmed in the Nevada desert; or a producer who likes big boobs, so a comedy-drama about a small town in Vermont turns into a flesh flick about a stripper who liberates a repressed community through lap-dancing; or, in the case of *Big Yellow Taxi*, the head of the UK office hates the US producer because Miss UK was shagging her boyfriend one night and he yelled out Miss US's name. Aha.

As the voices along the corridor grew louder and nearer, I gripped the edge of the carved wooden chair, and realized my hands were slimy with sweat. This meeting had to go well – it just *had* to. Otherwise . . . I might as well give up.

'Here they are,' Marie said brightly. Fran and Jaden walked in, Fran dressed from head to toe in black, and Jaden in black with a frivolous touch of dark khaki about

141

the trousers. Fran slammed her sunglasses on to the desk and sat down, not making eye-contact. Jaden sat beside her and touched his tongue to his top lip as he looked at me. Oh honestly, I thought, feeling momentarily turned on, but more like a Girl Guide leader and wanted to say, 'Don't be ridiculous,' which gave me strength.

'Fran, you know Lily?' I said, playing dumb.

'Yuh.'

'And this is Ash Ghosh. You met last year.'

'Yuh.' The claw-like fingers tightened round the sunglasses.

'And, Lily, Ash, you know Fran and Jaden, of course.'

'Yep,' said Lily, sitting opposite Fran and bitch-staring her.

'Er . . . yes,' said Ash, smiling at Jaden, then settling back in his chair.

'Tea, coffee?' I said brightly to the Americans, like an air-hostess at the beginning of a long-haul flight.

'Black coffee,' said Fran.

Lily glared at her again.

Ash said, 'I'd love a tea, please. And, Jaden, what is it that you want?' And he smiled at me evilly again.

I made a mental note to devote my life after this meeting to ensuring that Ash went to the sixth circle of hell.

Someone cleared their throat.

'Lizzy, do you have any ginseng?' Jaden asked.

'No, just tea or coffee, Jaden.'

'No hot water with a slice of lemon?'

'No.'

'Just hot water?'

'No!' I said, much louder than I'd intended. 'I can get you a glass of tap water, but other than that, decide if you want tea or a bloody coffee and let's get on with it, shall we?'

Four heads snapped up in shock.

'OK, then,' Jaden said, nodding sagely. Fran gazed at me as if to say, Hey, lady, you're not the pathetic sap I thought you were. And thus I will now take real pleasure in pulling you to pieces.

'Right,' I said, gulping and gritting my teeth, which is hard to do at the same time. 'Let's press on.'

THIRTEEN

There is a me who sits in meetings and makes conference calls and sends on average thirty-seven emails a day (so our IT department tells me, though I'd bet roughly 97 per cent of them are to Georgy and Tom), and there is also a me who lives at Keeper House and lies on the sofa in the side-room reading and eating biscuits, going for a walk if it's summer, throwing another log on to the fire if it's winter.

Sometimes, when I'm struggling on to a bus on my way home or waiting despondently in an endless queue at Prêt à Manger with my pathetic tomato and Brie baguette in my hand, I realize I could be at home in three hours if I jumped off the bus, or ran out of Prêt. I torture myself with imagine-if: just one more night at Keeper House without the executioner's axe hanging over us; just one more day of freedom before the Christmas that changed everything.

But real life isn't like that. And when these feelings of yearning washed over me I'd remind myself that I was twenty-eight and should get a grip. Also, that if I went home to live with Mum and Dad I'd be a twenty-eight-year-old who lived at home with her mother and father doing . . .

well, not very much. I'd be a societal drop-out. Georgy and Victoria would sigh into their gin and tonic and say, 'Of course I miss her, but she'd become so weird it's probably best she went into retreat never to be seen again by the general public.'

And David would murmur to Miles next time he was over, 'I always knew she'd been left out in the sun too long as a child.'

It was this train of thought that got me through the day. I am, like most of my family, much given to amateur dramatics, but we are pragmatists, and after a while that takes over. It was ever so, and it was so at the meeting, where I eventually assumed some kind of control and began the tricky business of untangling the mess that the project had become.

To do them justice Lily and Ash make a great team and when Marie had dispensed tea, coffee and water, I outlined some of our concerns to Fran and Jaden. Lily and Ash backed me up, he playing good cop, she bad, a role she relishes with Fran. Alas, after ten minutes, the tension in the air was not so much palpable as taking human shape. And Jaden had contributed absolutely nothing. Lily was looking at him with disdain, and Ash was casting me pitying glances: Lizzy's new shag is made of balsa-wood, Oh dear. Jaden sat there and smiled, sipping his water, oblivious to the hostility. I could have killed him. Problems with the central character? He said nothing. No one liking the final setpiece? He was silent. Dialogue slow and stilted? He raised an eyebrow but remained mute.

'But I don't understand,' Fran said finally. 'It's called *Big Yellow Taxi*. How the hell is it going to work if there ain't a yellow taxi in it?'

'The taxi's a symbol,' said Ash, smiling at her. 'We don't need it to keep the magic of the story – this wonderful story.'

'Yeah, but lose the taxi,' muttered Lily, swinging her feet so they hit the table legs.

'Hey.' Fran pointed at Lily. 'You're not working with us. Listen to me. How can you have a film called *Big Frigging Yellow Taxi* when there's no taxis in it and you want to make the central character a waiter, not a taxi driver? Lily, you gotta use your head, OK?'

'Paul hates the title too,' said Lily, quietly, producing her trump card.

'How do you know?' Fran snapped.

'I spoke to him earlier about the V and A party and I asked him then,' Lily hissed.

'What's the Vee 'n' Eh party?' Fran snarled.

'It's the première for *Always and Forever* in March at the Victoria and Albert Museum,' Ash interjected. 'It's a bit of a Monumental shindig, state-of-the-nation kind of party. You've been sent an invitation, Fran.'

'I'd better have, honey.' Her tone was glacial. 'Well, I'm seeing Paul in New York next week and I'll be discussing this with him then, you can bet your bottom dollar.'

There was a pause. Paul was our managing director. Lily pointed at Fran, in a splendidly symbolic but otherwise useless gesture, and slid back in her seat, as if to say, 'I've won.' I looked at the ceiling. The title had been Fran's idea. Of course Lily's always hated it. Oh, Jeez. I chewed my pen and cast around for an idea. Suddenly, for no reason, a picture of Mike trying to walk up the wall of the side-room last Christmas and falling over popped into my mind. I smiled to myself and willed the image away. I looked up, tears welling, and caught Jaden's eye.

'Well,' I croaked. Lily and Ash looked at me in horror as the pause bloomed into an awkward silence. Shit! Shit! Say something – anything.

And then a voice in the corner spoke: 'Why don't we just change the title?'

'Whaddya mean, Jaden?' said Fran suspiciously. 'Don't you like it?'

Lily stared at Jaden, mistrust writ large across her face. 'It's about more than just the title, Jaden. I think we're all looking at this film in totally different ways. Perhaps . . .'

Jaden smiled at her, and loosened his tie. 'I love the title, Fran, but I accept that the rewrites I've done mean this isn't the script we started with. What a great title. And what a great idea. Perhaps they're not coming together properly yet. I take responsibility for that. But, my gosh, this is an exciting project and I'm so pleased to get feedback from you guys. Ash – thanks a lot. You're right about the scene in Piccadilly Circus with the thousand white doves. Perhaps it would be hard to film. And, Lily, I'm really interested in your ideas about the interplay between the Iranian bookseller and the gay policeman. Can I run a couple of things past you when I've thought about it some more?'

Lily was dazzled by the guileless face before her, smiling with such charm. 'Yes . . . yes, of course you can.'

Jaden clenched his lips and his fist briefly at her, in a show of mutual bonding and support. He turned to Fran. 'And, Fran, I think these guys are so right. I can tell you do too. This film isn't about a yellow taxi in London, is it? It's about people. People who need . . . people. Outsiders, lonely people, a big city, you know, the idea that there really is . . . well, someone out there for everyone. We need each other. Heck, even the five of us round this table! God, I love this idea so much, Fran. Remind us how you came up with it again?'

Fran looked up into Jaden's blue eyes. 'Oh, gad, I'm so embarrassed. It's a long story.'

'I didn't realize this was your idea, Fran?' said Lily, with something akin to interest.

'Oh, it's no big deal. Just a passion I've always had.'

'No big deal? Fran, you're being modest again,' said Jaden.

Fran smiled.

Lily smiled at her.

Ash smiled at Jaden.

And Jaden . . . Jaden smiled at me.

And I grinned back, captivated once again by this strange, but really rather great man. 'Right, then,' I said, clearing my throat. 'Back to business. Jaden, why don't you talk us through some of the new ideas you've had for the reunion scene in the railway station at the end?'

It was almost seven when the meeting ended. Lily and Ash accompanied Fran out. She pointed at me as they stood on either side of her. 'Hey,' she growled.

'Yes?' I said, leaping in alarm.

'I like you. You should go to LA.' And with that gnomic utterance, she walked through the door.

'OK, crazy lady,' I said to myself, and finished stacking the cups. I went back to my office to flick through the notes I'd made. The sound of laughter echoed down the corridor. I was scribbling something when the light from the internal window darkened suddenly. I looked up. There was Jaden. 'Hi,' I said.

'Hi,' he said cheerily. He came over and took my hand. The pen dropped to the floor. He pulled me up so we were facing each other.

'You were great,' I said bashfully.

Jaden kissed the back of my hand, turned it over and kissed the palm. 'Fran loves you, you know. Well, she's right. You're quite something, Lizzy Walter,' he said, slid his hand round my neck, pulled me to him and kissed me.

I was glad to hear it, but I couldn't agree. My contribution to the meeting had been zip, and I couldn't help thinking, fleetingly, that if I wasn't sleeping with Jaden, he wouldn't have helped me out. God. Was I being rewarded for being great in the sack? But Jaden was a great kisser, so I surrendered to it and stopped worrying about it and even whether anyone could see us.

The phone rang, right by my thigh, and I jumped. Jaden moved his arm round my waist and kissed me again. 'I'd better get that,' I murmured.

'Forget it,' said Jaden. 'Let go. What are you doing later, QE Three?' He kissed me again.

'No, I must get it,' I said suddenly, and pushed him away. He sat in my chair and watched me. I leaned against the desk and picked up the receiver. 'Hello,' I said, smoothing down my skirt. There was a pause. I could hear the *Archers'* theme tune playing in the background.

'Oh, hello, darling, it's Mum.'

'Hi, Mum,' I said, collecting papers on my desk and shuffling them into a nice organized rectangle. Jaden tapped his watch. 'How are you?'

There was a low grumbling sound in the background at the other end of the line.

'Amontillado, thanks, darling,' said Mum. 'Sorry, that was your father. Look, I can't speak for long. Shula's about to tell Jack Woolley the truth about Pru Forrester.'

'What?' I said. There was a chiming sound, which I knew was Dad handing Mum her sherry and clinking her glass against his. I could picture them now, in the sitting room, Mum in her chair by the fire, next to the radio, the sharp smell of woodsmoke mixing with the faint scent from the bowl of lavender on the bookcase, next to the photo of little Jess, tanned and scratched, sitting in the treehouse she'd made on holiday in Norfolk when she was seven. I could see it all, like the words on the page of a well-worn book, and my heart clenched.

'Some good news. Or bad news. Both, really.' There was a pause as Mum took a sip of her drink. 'Darling, the Caldwells came to look at the house again today. They've offered – five grand over the asking price. So we've accepted. Keeper House is sold.'

It was bitterly cold when I left work that evening. I'd packed Jaden off in a cab, persuading him I was fine. It was to his credit that he didn't believe me but he knew I wanted to be alone. I walked out on to the street. The pavement had been gritted that evening and my shoes crunched as I passed the smoky, brown-tiled pub where some of my friends from work were gathered. As I peered through the window I caught sight of Ash waving his arms around, as Sally and Jon laughed at him. Jon half turned to look in my direction, and I shrank back so they wouldn't see me and yell for me to come in. I scurried past the tiny French café, where I often got my lunchtime sandwich. The wooden chairs were folded up and chained to the painted green railings outside.

When I got to Luigi's, the Italian deli, I stopped and stared aimlessly in the window. I couldn't be bothered to walk to the bus stop: I just wanted to curl up and fall asleep under the chocolates and the coloured twists of paper, then go back to the office early tomorrow, rather than think about everything else. I gazed in at the sides of marbled, burgundy meat, the cheeses piled beneath the counter, the jars of artichoke hearts and oily, sun-dried tomatoes for what seemed like ages before I noticed that the shop was still open. I wandered in.

'Good evening, signorina,' said Luigi, behind the counter.

'Hello,' I said, picked up a focaccia and some pasta and handed them to him. I stared at the painted green, white and red Italian flag above the chalk board over his head as he sliced some ham for me.

'*Uno momento, signorina*,' he said suddenly, left the guillotine, and disappeared into the back of the shop. I heard loud shouting between him and another man. I gazed about me listlessly. Something in the corner of the shop caught my eye and I turned towards it: thick, creamy daffodils, their centres a pale, sunny yellow, their petals bursting open in an old blue and white enamelled bucket. I gathered up three bunches and put them on the counter as Luigi emerged.

'*Mi dispiace, Signorina*,' he said, wiping his forehead on his apron. 'My son. He is so rude, so rude. All day he lie and play guitar. He hate the cold, he no like winter, he will not get a job. What is the world coming to? Do you know?'

'Absolutely no idea,' I answered truthfully. 'These daffodils are beautiful, I haven't seen any yet this year.'

'They are the first we have,' Luigi said, wrapping the prosciutto in thick, waxy paper. 'Look outside you. Is dark, is oh-so-cold. But spring is coming, and then it will be summer – ah, the sun on my head, after these months!'

'Ye-es,' I said slowly. 'Spring is coming.' My heart lifted.

'And then all this is over, no more winter. There you go, my darling, *grazie, grazie mille, ciao*.'

I swung out of the shop with my flowers and the parcels of food in a little brown paper bag, and carried on walking, turning the same thoughts over in my head.

Spring would be here soon, then summer, then it was all over. Finished.

The boiler, which had been threatening to go on strike since before Christmas, packed up when I got home. It greeted me with a thuggish clunk, whirred plaintively, then lapsed into silence. Yes, I thought, as I stood in the freezing cold kitchen, holding my hands over the kettle as I waited for it to boil, I would be glad when winter was over, and now we knew the house was sold and that everything was changing, everything would be much simpler.

I made a vow, as I crawled into bed wrapped in four jumpers, clutching a hot-water bottle. I'd go back in May for the wedding, but that was it. Not before then and not after. My dreams of running away back home had to be over, *kaput*.

So I didn't go back to Keeper House that weekend for Dad's birthday, as I was supposed to. Or the next weekend, when Chin went up to start planning the wedding with Mum. The house was gone, David was gone, Uncle Mike was effectively gone. These were all facts. I didn't understand them but that was what they were, and imagining dreams you may have on the bus or lying in bed on Saturdays are all rubbish.

I carried on with my life, putting David and last year behind me as best I could, reminding myself frequently that in the grand scheme of things nothing really terrible had happened, and hoping I could be left alone to get on without the bother and mess of other people. Well, I tried.

FOURTEEN

The Caldwells – Stuart and Simone – had lived in Wareham for a few years. Simone had grown up in the village, then gone to London to become a model. She had met and married Stuart Caldwell, millionaire founder of Caldwell Tarts (Tom sniggered). I should point out now that Simone (who was approaching forty, but could have been thirty or sixty-five) had been called Sarah when I first knew her, had no boobs and buck teeth. Now she had a perfect white smile, a year-round tan, and definite augmentation had taken place in the area between her neck and ribs. Stuart was a bear of a man in Ben Sherman checked shirts that strained across his chest.

Before SOKH I had neither liked nor disliked the Caldwells. I had issues with them for naming their children Sharleen and Dior (A boy! Called Dior! You are *asking* for that child to have his head bashed in), for Simone addressing her husband as 'Babes' and for the rumours in the village about Stuart's allegedly dodgy business practices. Post-SOKH I hated them with the white-hot intensity of a thousand suns, and especially augmented Simone, whom I saw as the catalyst of SOKH, an evil genius who was driving my parents out of their home because of a crazy lust to right years of her family's wrongs. She planned to start by taking out the kitchen and dining-room to build a heated indoor swimming-pool, or so she had told Bill at the Neptune.

I was at work, eating a very late lunch, when Mike finally returned my call, a few days later. It was so nice to hear from him, especially after the silence from every other member of my family since the sale had been agreed – the if-we-don't-mention-it-perhaps-it'll-go-away policy. How very us. I slid down in my chair and eased out the lever so the back rocked down. 'Maybe,' I conceded, piling Jaden's drafts of the script on top of each other, then resting my feet on them. 'Mike, can I ask you a question?'

'Sure,' said Mike. He cleared his throat and whispered something.

'Sorry, have you got a meeting or something?' I said, alarmed. I'd been to Mike's office last year when I was visiting David. It was incredibly impressive. All the fittings were ochre marble and his desk was the size of a bus. He had a view looking up Park Avenue, over Grand Central Station, with Central Park off to the side. It was ultra-swank. Mike, being Mike, kept drinks there, a huge pile of magazines, a TV and video, and showed me how to bet online and trade in stocks and shares. He also had a CD player with dreadful, dreadful CDs, like Michael Bolton, Curtis Steigers, and Leather and Lace 3. He took me to lunch at the restaurant in Grand Central Station: we drank kirs and watched the celestial scene overhead and the bustling commuters beneath us.

Anyway, I could picture him in his office, his feet on the table too, loosening his tie and making like the great New York lawyer that he was. It's always easy to picture Mike. The very act of conversing with him was a comfort. I didn't need to worry that he'd come over all serious and emotional and I knew I'd feel better afterwards.

'Fire away, young woman,' Mike said. 'It's just my chef asking if I want my oysters with lemon juice or Tabasco, you know the kind of thing.'

'Mike,' I said. 'Will you tell me the truth if I ask you something? It's important.'

After a pause he said, quite seriously, 'Of course, ducks. What's the problem?'

'Why are they selling the house?'

'What do you mean?' I said to Mike slowly.

'I mean . . . I don't understand why things have come to this. Does that make any sense?'

'Kind of. How so?'

'Well . . . It's just that . . . OK, I know the roof needs work, and that's expensive and everything. It's just . . .' I knew it would sound wrong however I said it. 'I know roofs are awful and pricy and it's a big job. But this is our home, all of ours. Well . . . I just think perhaps Mum and Dad haven't thought this all through properly. Selling Keeper House, getting rid of all that just because they need some money for a roof. I wonder if there's something we don't know. Like . . . I don't know.' I trailed off.

Mike was silent for a moment. 'Have you spoken to your parents?' he eventually said. 'Asked them about this? It's important stuff, y'know. Perhaps you should confront them about it. Not aggressively – just ask if there's something they're not telling you.'

The idea of asking my parents if they were defrauding us of our home because they were secret boozers or because they'd murdered someone and hidden the body under the floorboards wasn't appealing. But perhaps he was right.

'On the other hand,' he said, clearing his throat awkwardly, 'you could leave it. I should think, even if there is a reason you don't know about, they're not dancing for joy at having to sell the place. Perhaps they haven't looked after it. Perhaps my old ma and pa weren't up to it either and that's the problem. I know what you mean, old girl, and I'm pretty upset about it too. There's no place like home and all that.'

'No!' I said. 'There isn't, and I—'

But Mike continued, unheeding, 'I look out here, you know, lovely view, the park and all that. The station. Best city in the world. But I still can't help wishing. Well. Y'know . . .'

'Wishing what?'

'Well . . .' he sighed. 'Lizzy, don't you sometimes wish you were little, and back at Keeper House, that you didn't have anything to worry about? Running around in shorts on the lawn. Playing with the dog. All that sort of thing.'

'Er . . .' I wondered if he was losing his marbles. 'Oh, you're talking about you.'

'Yes,' he said eagerly. 'God, I wish I could go back.' He sounded glum. 'But I can't.'

'And you wouldn't want to, anyway,' I said. 'Didn't Dad set a rocket off in your face when you were ten? Weren't you in hospital for a week? And didn't he have a gang who bullied you, even though you were the oldest?'

'Ha. No, it was Tony who set the rocket off,' Mike said. 'But, yeah, nasty bullies. They wore those Red Indian feather things. Used to ambush me in the lane on the way back from school. Broke my finger.' He fell silent.

I tried to buck him up, feeling the conversation had taken a somewhat maudlin turn. 'Well, then, you wouldn't want to go back, really, would you?' I said. And although it was super-tempting, *I* didn't want that either. I just wanted everything to be *right* again. 'You're the one who got away, Mike,' I said dramatically. 'Be free. Make that change. Leave this cursed house behind ye, while ye be still young.'

'The old days were the best, you know,' he said darkly, then added, 'still, thanks. You're quite right, Lizzy.'

'Good,' I said, pleased I'd cheered him up a bit. 'Anyway, I just . . .'

He interrupted: 'But listen, Lizzy. About your ma and pa, the house and all of that side of the coin. Take my advice, eh? Sometimes you have to let things slide, even when they're important to you. Don't upset the apple cart unnecessarily. You know?' I did, and he was right.

A harsh voice was suddenly on the line. 'Mike? I need to make a call – can you get off now, please?'

'Sure,' he said, his tone altering. 'Give me a few seconds, my love. I'm on the phone to Lizzy.'

'Whatever. But I've got work to do, unlike you.'

It was Rosalie, of course. Clearly not in the best of tempers. 'Hi, Rosalie,' I said tentatively. 'How are you?'

'Fine, honey,' she said brusquely. 'I'd love to chat, but I can't. Come see us soon. 'Bye.'

There was silence again.

'The old ball and chain not particularly pleased with your uncle this morning,' said Mike.

'I thought you were at work?'

'Ah, no. I'm working from home today, got some rather complicated reading to do and wanted a bit of peace and quiet. I'm – erm – getting under her feet, poking my nose in where it ain't wanted and all that. Anyway, Titch, I'd better go, as you can tell.'

'Is Rosalie OK?' I asked, worried.

'What? Oh, yes, absolutely fine. Don't worry, old girl, can't blame her, sure I'm an absolute pest to live with. I'll take her out to supper tonight, lay on the charm, she'll be right as rain tomorrow. Better go now. 'Bye, darling, 'bye.'

Since Chin was the youngest of her siblings, the only girl, and had lost her mother while she was still relatively young, Mum and Dad, Mike, Kate and Tony, when he was still

157

alive, had taken a parental attitude towards her, as if she was an adorable, if wayward little girl who needed coddling and cherishing. She and Tony were closest in age, since he was the youngest brother, and his death – when she was only fourteen – had hit her hard. She started bunking off school, and got terribly thin. The family still talked about Tony, but she hardly ever mentioned him.

Gibbo had proposed to her on New Year's Eve at Keeper House. Mum, Dad and Kate were there too (not during the proposal, of course) and Mum reported back that it was very romantic. We were all over the moon about it because we adored Gibbo and he and Chin were so obviously perfect for each other. He loved the way she cackled at his terrible jokes and smoked Sobranies – the bright blue, green and pink cigarettes with the gold filters; he loved her messiness too. She loved the way he was funny, inventive, interesting, and that he was a good, solid person, who found fashion and frippery unimportant. They both liked art and design and spent ages together in museums trailing round in perfect harmony. Gibbo loved to cook and Chin had a mammoth appetite. Most importantly, Gibbo was unimpressed by Chin's tantrums, unlike my family.

Mum wanted to help Chin assemble her trousseau in a married-womanly way, like someone in a Victorian novel. She wanted to release Chin's inner Bridezilla, infect her with Wedding Lust, but Chin found the whole thing hilarious – or so she said. 'Bless Suzy,' she said, when I spoke to her a few days into her engagement. 'I love your mother but she's got it all wrong. She keeps dropping hints or offering to show me her wedding dress, or saying should we have a meeting about this or that. I think she's doing it to take her mind off everything, but it's not going to work. I just want a simple wedding. I don't care about things like the font on the invitation or where our wedding list is going to be.

Although Liberty has some lovely things. It's all such rubbish.'

Mum was bitterly disappointed, but Chin, supposedly, despised the cult of the modern wedding and, indeed, marriage itself. She had yawned her way through the endless elegant weddings of her chic friends, had deliberately worn either bridal white or funereal black, snorted when a groom made a soppy speech, and generally eyed with disdain anyone who apparently saw their wedding as more important than the marriage they were embarking upon. I'm sorry to say she lost more than a couple of friends this way (although in the case of one, a dippy girl who set free a hundred white doves after her wedding in Oxfordshire, right next to fifteen electricity pylons, I applaud Chin's decision to shout, 'You total berk,' at her).

However, in the month since the engagement, Chin's attitude had changed, and it was a good thing: most weddings take years to plan and she was doing this from scratch in less than five months so that it could take place at the house before we had to go. Kate could have planned a royal wedding, but snorted every time Chin suggested spending more than three pence on anything. Dad was in charge of drinks and outside structures and fittings (the marquee and wine glasses). Mike was doing nothing, but that was fair enough: he was geographically challenged. Tom was working like a dervish so couldn't be any help either. Gibbo hadn't been entrusted with anything important. Jess and I had offered to help, but been turned down by HQ. I was secretly relieved, as this chimed with my desire to stay away from my family, but I still felt guilty. And I wanted to talk to Chin. I was sure she had some idea about what was really going on. She'd been so weird when she'd come back from that drink with David, the night Dad had told us the house was being sold. She knew something, but I had no idea what.

* * *

159

As February was blustering into March, and the wedding and the move were only a couple of months away, Mum took the day off from the surgery and came up to town on the train. I took a longer lunch hour than usual and met her at Paddington. She and Chin were going to Liberty for the trying-on of wedding dresses, and I'd promised to escort her into town. I couldn't wait to see her, even if only for forty minutes. I missed her.

However, on the rare occasions Mum comes up to town I do have to remind myself that she spent her crazy student years in London and later brought up two small children here. And that she marched to Ban the Bomb, burned her bra, and made hash brownies for her friends (my godmother Stella told me this once, not Mum). Now she behaves as if she were being dropped into Viet-Cong era Vietnam, eyes darting about, alert and ready for lurking thieves who might attack, handbag worn diagonally over her body like a school prefect, and sensible shoes in case of the need to run.

'Hello, darling,' she trilled when she spotted me on the main concourse. 'Lovely to see you. Keep moving,' she hissed, under her breath. 'Aah!' A young man in a suit bumped into her, turned, and said, with a smile of apology, 'I'm so sorry,' put his hand on her arm and moved on in the shifting sea of people.

'Well, really,' said Mum, trying to be annoyed and clutching the handles of her Royal Academy oilcloth bag closely to her chest.

'That was your fault, Mum,' I told her, sticking my finger at the base of her spine and propelling her towards the Bakerloo line. 'Come on, let's get moving.'

I also have to remind myself that my mother is in charge of the diagnosis and treatment of illnesses of over one hundred people who call her their doctor. How a woman who can spot the early signs of a most virulent strain of meningitis can be incapable of working a ticket machine is beyond me. It's not exactly brain science – and she's *studied* brain science, for heaven's sake.

We stood in silence at the ticket machine as a resentful queue built up behind us. Mum jabbed a few buttons blankly.

'It looks like Greek to me. What on earth does it all mean?'

'Oh, God, Mother,' I said, cracking. 'Here, let me do it. First of all, do this up, though –' and I zipped up the purse that, despite her strictures about muggers and thieves, Mum was waving around with cash aplenty poking out of it, much to the interest of a gaggle of lounging schoolboys at the next pillar. I punched the buttons and slotted in the money. When the ticket slid out and I handed it to Mum, she looked at it as if it was growing legs and trying to samba. 'Well, whatever next?' she actually said.

'Oh MUM!' I said in exasperation. 'Stop acting like a caveman and get a move on. They had ticket machines when you were living here twenty years ago, don't be so annoying.' Chastened, my mother scurried after me, her Marks and Spencer Footgloves humming slightly on the rubber floor. The schoolboys straightened up with interest as we approached. 'Alright then, *muvver*?' asked one of them, elongated and slightly repellent, as only fifteen-year-olds can be.

Mum whipped round. 'I'm not your mother, thank God. Go back to school, you ridiculous child,' she said, and sailed on towards the barrier, where she presented her ticket to the guard and said, 'I'm terribly sorry, I've no idea how to work these things, could you possibly zoom me through? Oh thank you so much.'

I slapped my hands to my cheeks. The teenage boy shot me a look of sympathy.

*   *   *

I knew we wouldn't talk about anything serious on the Tube; my family delights in the art of repression and the idea of being emotional on public transport was beyond the pale. Kate once famously said to a screaming six-year-old Tom, when he banged his knee on the metal pole in the carriage, 'Darling! *Not* on the Tube, please!' As we stood on the platform, waiting for a train, I asked, 'Have you started looking for somewhere else to live, then?'

'No, darling. Not yet. But it shouldn't be too hard, I hope. I bumped into Alice Eliot yesterday in Wareham. She thinks she might know somewhere that would be perfect.'

Alice, Kate and Mum were still friendly, even though Alice was responsible for bringing the Cradle of Evil (David) into the world.

'Right,' I said.

We were silent for a few moments as the crowd around us swelled.

'Aren't you going to ask about it, then?' Mum said.

'Sorry,' I said. 'Sorry. That's great, where is it?'

'It's a kind of bunga. In Danby.'

'What?' I said.

Mum shifted on her feet. 'Oh, darling, a bungalow! Bunga. Anyway, Alice Eliot knows a dear old couple who are selling their house – they're going into a retirement home. The son's going to rent it out. Alice thinks it'd be perfect for your father and me. We're going to see it tomorrow, actually.'

'Renting? A *bungalow*?' I said. It might have been a septic tank. 'In *Danby*? Oh, Mum, are you sure?'

'No, of course not,' she said, surprised. 'We haven't seen it yet, but it sounds great. And we don't . . . well, we don't want to buy just yet. It's thirties, art deco, pretty big. Lovely leaded windows, nice big garden. You and Jess would both have a room, and there's lots of storage space. And . . . we'd get a sofa-bed and some camp beds for everyone else. I'm sure we could fit in whoever wants to stay. You know, for Christmas, and things like that.'

I swallowed. 'Can't you . . . can't you rent somewhere in Wareham? A nice little cottage? Or buy somewhere?'

'Nice little cottages in Wareham cost about as much as five-storey houses in Kensington, these days,' Mum said.

'But, Mum—'

'Lizzy, darling,' she said impatiently, 'I know selling the house is horrible. It's *really* horrible. But it's going to happen. We have to leave. And we have to live somewhere else – unless your father and I take up residence in the hedge opposite Keeper House.'

'I can't . . .' I said, my voice high and wavering.

'I know, it's awful,' Mum said, putting her arm round me. 'But it's happening. Look.' She paused. 'I've lived in . . . ooh, about eight different houses in my life. More, probably. And I've been happy in most of them, apart from the flatshare in Bloomsbury with that Spanish girl who tried to get into bed with me. Ines. What a strange girl she was.' I coughed. 'Yes,' Mum said, chasing her own train of thought, 'But, darling, my point is that I've had three homes with Dad, and everywhere I've lived with him, I've been happy. We've made a home wherever we've been. So we'll make another one wherever we end up. We'll still be together, and that's what matters.'

'It's not the same,' I said sullenly, knowing I was behaving badly.

'Thank goodness, here comes a train at last,' Mum said. She squeezed my shoulder. 'I know it's not the same. But, darling, the reason you love the house is because we've all been so happy there. We'll be happy somewhere else, you know. A home – oh, it sounds so trite but a home isn't just bricks and mortar. OK?' The train bellowed into the station.

'I just don't think it'll ever be the same.' I said. 'We'll always miss it.'

'I know,' said my mother, positioning herself in front of a door as it opened. 'Sometimes I wonder, though . . . It – well, never mind.'

'What?' I said, checking my coat pocket for my Oyster card.

'It's not important. Perhaps you'll see in time. Come on, darling, here we go.'

The Tube doors opened exactly in front of Mum. How did she know where to stand on the platform? I'd never been able to work it out. I shot a quick glance at her, but she was back in Lady from the Sticks mode again, staring up at the Tube map and calling 'Lizzy! How many stops, then? Quick, let's get these seats, oh excuse me, thank you so much!' to various fellow passengers, and I knew the moment had passed.

'How far have you got with the wedding plans?' I asked, once we were sitting down and the train was on its way into town.

'It's going to be lovely,' Mum said. 'Chin and I have decided on a theme of pink. But not ghastly old-fashioned pink . . .' here she hesitated, and I realized she was repeating parrot-fashion what Chin had told her '. . . more a sort of *pale*, *vintage* pink, pink and cream, really, so we're having lots of pink and cream flowers. Chin's got a lovely friend who's a florist – Mando. He's been just *lovely*. Strange, though.'

I'd met Mando the previous year. He wore sunglasses in March and put his hand on David's thigh, and kept moving it up, so far up that David had to actually shift in his seat, then get up and go off and pretend to make a phone call.

'That sounds gorgeous,' I said. 'And the roses along the kitchen wall will be out then – you can use them, can't you? Perfect timing.'

'Oh, no, Lizzy. Wrong pink,' said Mum.

'Wrong pink?' I said. 'You're joking.'

'Well, it all has to co-ordinate, doesn't it?'

'Hm,' I said.

Mum yielded a little. 'Those roses are lovely, yes, but we must have what we must have.'

'Oh, yes, we must,' I said. A thought struck me. 'But I thought Chin didn't care what flowers she had? She said pink at a wedding was bourgeois.'

'She's changed her mind.'

'Oh, Mum,' I said. 'You've given her Wedding Lust, haven't you?'

'No!'

'Well, you've made your bed,' I said prophetically, 'and now you'll have to lie in it.'

She looked worried, so I changed the subject. 'I spoke to Mike last week, did I tell you?'

Mum perked up considerably. 'How was he?'

'At home.'

'Yes?' Mum said, rifling through her bag to check its contents again. 'What did he have to say for himself?'

Her tone was rather cool. I remembered Mike's words: 'Don't upset the apple cart.' 'He was really sweet,' I said. 'You know Mike, he can sort things out in your head for you – he knows just what to say.'

'Yes, he does,' said Mum. 'That's quite true. How's Rosalie?'

'Finding Mike a bit annoying. She was quite snappy.'

'Hm,' said Mum. 'Well, *she*'s made *her* bed, hasn't she?'

'What do you mean?' I said.

'Well, in My Day one didn't marry people after one had known them less than a month.'

'Luckily for Dad, eh?' I shot back, quick as a flash, then chuckled, with pleasure at my quick wit.

'Watch out for that woman,' Mum said, obviously nettled. 'That's all I'm saying.' I hoped she might be close to telling me something juicy, but she merely shook her head. 'Oxford Circus, here we are!' she said, and stood up.

Outside, by the stall selling tourist tat on Little Argyll Street, we said goodbye. 'I'm sorry I can't come with you,' I said.

'I am too, darling, but we'll see you soon, yes? You'll be down before long, won't you?'

She was already looking down the street, trying to make out the black and white mock-Tudor Liberty building. 'Yes, yes of course I will,' I said. 'Look, I've really got to go now. Good luck with the bunga tomorrow, and give my love to Chin. Dad too.'

I watched her sail down the street, then turned and walked back into my London life.

FIFTEEN

And then, suddenly winter was over. A week later – one month after the sale had been agreed – I felt spring coming, one clear evening in early March. As I came out of South Kensington Tube station, I saw the florist on the traffic island opposite put away the pink and blue hyacinths, the irises and tulips, and look up at the sky, which was still just light. I took a gulp of fresh air, inhaled through my nostrils and knew that spring was on its way. It was hard to believe, after the long, long winter, yet impossible to ignore.

As I walked to the traffic lights, I shivered, wrapping my shawl around me against the chill: it was still cold. I knew when spring was coming at Keeper House because the cherry tree outside my window came into bud. In a month's time, it would be at its best – a frothy fuschia riot of velvety flowers arching against the wall and over the edge of the lawn. Now, at this moment, it would simply look like a mass of tangled black branches. It was only from my window that you could see the tiny green buds that held the promise of summer. I wouldn't be there to see it this year. Because of the solemn vow. And next year one of the Caldwells would be looking out of that window.

I stopped on the corner of Cromwell Road and searched for my invitation to the party. The V&A loomed ahead of me, dark and forbidding except for the floodlit entrance where a steady trickle of guests was streaming in. The wind blew my hair and I smoothed it back as I gazed up at the building ahead of me. I've always loved the V&A, ever since Grandmother read *Ballet Shoes* to Jess and me one wet summer at Keeper House. When it was raining, the Fossil sisters and their nanny would walk up Cromwell Road and go to the V&A because it was free and they were so poor. After Chin moved to London to do her fashion degree Jess and I (still quite young) were put on a train once a year to meet her for the day, and she would take us to the V&A. It was always a magical occasion, and followed a strict formula. We always got the Tube there and the bus back. We went to see the costumes and the Great Bed of Ware. As Chin sketched, her pencil rasping across the thick paper, Jess and I would gaze open-mouthed at brocade skirts as wide as four people, velvet bustles, silk bias-cut thirties dresses and chiffon prints, jabbing our greasy fingers against the glass and hissing, 'That one! I like that one best!' We always bought postcards of our favourite dresses. I have them still, a collection gathered over the years, and each dress looks strangely ghostly: an expressionless white dummy wearing a beautiful taffeta and silk ballgown that, two hundred years ago, a wealthy girl wore to dance at a party.

Afterwards Chin always took us to lunch, or tea, at Pâtisserie Valerie on Brompton Road, where Jess once famously insisted she could manage a Florentine *and* an éclair and was sick. Then, if there was time, we'd wander up to Harrods, and would walk through the Food Hall, licking our lips and grimacing alternately at sugared almonds in dear little glass pots or oozing, smelly cheeses.

When we got home, incredibly late (or so it seemed –

probably it was only about nine o'clock) and dropping with exhaustion, we were allowed as an added treat a late supper at the kitchen table, in our pyjamas, something like soup or welsh rarebit.

The memory of all these things came back to me as I stood outside the museum. I hadn't thought about our dream days with Chin for such a long time but lately, since Christmas, I'd started to remember lots of things from long ago. Our house in London, before we moved. How cold Grandfather's hands were when we hugged him. Kate in brightly patterned headscarves. The wall by the tiny kitchen garden where a brick was missing and Tom hid his chocolate when he was small. And the last time we came to the V&A, when Jess and I were old enough to know it was the last time just because it was. Chin didn't sketch that day: she was nursing a hangover and couldn't hold a pencil without shaking, so she claimed. Instead, we went and looked at eighteenth-century silverware, which is one of the most boring ways to spend an afternoon, and as we trailed past yet another amazing filigree candlestick, I thought resentfully of the gleaming white mannequins in their dresses on the floor below unseen by me on this most looked-forward to of days.

The Monumental film for which this was ostensibly the post-première party, *Always and Forever*, was a film I'd had nothing to do with. It was also an excuse for us to throw a party – and we'd just had our best ever year. I had to go, and if I had been in a better mood I would have enjoyed it. There would be lots to drink, goody-bags, work pals and the chance of a cab ride home, but I just wasn't in the mood.

Still, a party's a party, and some people would be there from LA and New York whom I needed to talk to and might not see at the office. I was still flavour of the month, bizarrely, after my meeting with Fran in January, and all was going remarkably smoothly with *Dreams Can Come True* – Jaden's suggestion for what had been *Big Yellow Taxi*. I knew it'd only last until something dire happened, like the child star we'd hired checked into teenage rehab for coke addiction, so I wanted to capitalize on it. Lily and Fran were going to be there together – incredibly, they'd been best gal-pals since the meeting. And Ash had been at the pub with our various work pals and Jaden, and I'd said I'd meet them there.

I'd been at home that afternoon, waiting five hours for a boiler repairman, who had claimed not to have received any of the fifteen messages I'd left at work, home and on his mobile asking where he was. My flat was still freezing. Last year, when this happened, David had known a great plumber, called Brian, I thought, who happened to be round the corner when we rang, came straight over and replaced a rivet valve something something, got rid of an air socket bubble, and coated the lagging with pipes or something again. I absolutely *loathe* that air of helplessness that afflicts perfectly intelligent girls just because they don't have a boyfriend and I was determined I could sort this out by myself. I was going to. I do not know the intricacies of the boiler world, I told myself. It is not my profession. I will calmly and simply hire someone to facilitate this. Thus will my flat be heated. Only, nearly five weeks later I was on my third plumber and the flat was still freezing cold. That very morning a pigeon jumped up and down on my window sill as I was shivering and making myself a cup of tea. It seemed to be laughing at me, saying, It is warmer out here than it is in your flat.

What I ought to do, I knew, was email David, calmly and simply, and ask for Brian's number. But perhaps subconsciously I'd broken the boiler as a means of contacting David so that was the last thing I should do, no matter how much I wanted to – no matter how much I longed to tell him what was going on with Keeper House, and that I was freezing cold, that Chin was being a nightmare about her dress being ready in time and that I was worried Ash might have started stalking Lola. And I wished I could ask him about the fact there might be a job for me in the LA office, acting as liaison development executive for a year. Part of me wanted to go, and part of me was terrified by the idea. And I wanted to tell him that, although everything was good with Jaden, I still missed him so much that I couldn't breathe properly sometimes when I thought about him, about what it was like with him.

So I didn't email him, and the plumbing industry continued to ignore me, not that the two were linked of course.

As I went into the huge marble hall, dodging the disgruntled, smoking journalists outside, I could hear the party, a distant burble of noise. It's fine arriving at parties late when you know everyone, less fine when you have to network and be professional. I squared my shoulders and walked past a battered old wooden angel, brightly painted, with a rather smirky smile. His right hand was raised in benediction.

'Lizzy,' said a voice at the end of the corridor. 'Hey, I've been looking out for you.'

'Hello, Jaden,' I called, walking towards the light and the noise.

'How about some pineapple juice? I'm having some. I don't want to drink this evening and orange juice converts to sugar, then fat if you drink it late at night.'

The wooden angel's smirk seemed to stretch a little wider.

'Thanks, mate,' I muttered, and hurried past him.

SIXTEEN

When he caught up with me Jaden kissed me. 'Any good in there?' I asked.

'No,' he said, taking my arm and steering me gently past tombs and monuments. 'The tie on the back of your shoe is undone and you're going to trip over it. Let me do it.' He bent down and retied the thin suede ribbon.

That's what I like about Jaden – he's surprisingly capable.

'I was going out to get some air – it's kinda hot in there. This way,' he said, and propelled me into the crowded room. As I scanned the masses for Lily, Jaden looked at me calmly. 'Why are you so late? Is it what we talked about last time? Are you feeling like you're in Avoidance Strategy Mode?'

That's what I *don't* like about Jaden – he talks like a book written in a language I don't understand.

'I'm fine,' I said. 'I want a dri— Ah, thanks, Lily.'

'Where have you been?' Lily demanded, as she thrust a glass of lukewarm champagne into my hand. With other bosses this might sound like a reprimand, but with Lily it was a sign that she had something to tell me. 'Nicole Hegerty's over there,' she said. 'Look, Lizzy! I can't believe it! What shall I do?'

'Calm down,' I said. 'You don't have to talk to her. Just ignore her. She's going back to LA tomorrow, isn't she?'

'Yes, but she wants to talk about the development-executive position. She wants it filled by June. Oh, Lizzy, are you sure you don't want to go? You could move to LA and I'd never have to deal with her again, I could speak to you instead. Come on, you'd love it.'

'I'm sure I would,' I said, laughing. 'You're always saying that. But I'm not moving to LA to do some random new job just so you don't have to speak to Nicole Hegerty and that's that.'

Nicole Hegerty was another kickass producer from Monumental in LA who had once gripped Lily by the neck after we'd lost the option on a book she'd wanted. She is Fran's boss, whippet-thin and looks like she's lived off her own muscles for the last decade. That, and vodka. She has a voice like a rattling dustbin lorry. And a vocabulary to match.

'Your loss,' Lily said. 'You'll stay in London and ossify. You'll never move on. You'll still be here in ten years' time and then you'll come to me and say, "Oh, Lily, why didn't I go? I'm so stupid!"'

Appraisals with Lily are very much in this vein.

'Very true,' said Jaden, showing his white teeth. 'Lizzy, is this true? About LA?'

I frowned at him, to discourage him from asking too much while Lily was around. 'The job's true – it's a liaison thing between the London and LA offices. But I'm not leaving. Why would I want to?'

'Why wouldn't you?' Jaden said. 'It's seventy degrees there at the moment.'

A picture of myself rollerblading along a boardwalk wearing a strappy top and cut-off denim shorts floated into my mind's eye. I batted it away. 'I hate hot weather,' I lied.

Jaden nodded in an annoying way. 'Well, maybe you should think about it, you know? Make a change.'

Someone pushed against me, laughing raucously. Suddenly a flush of panic surged through me. I wanted to go home.

'Argh, there she is,' said Lily, suddenly, as Nicole Hegerty moved closer.

'I can distract her if you want,' offered Jaden.

Lily threw him a grateful smile. 'God, you're gorgeous, but don't worry. If you go to her from me she might smell my scent and that could lead her back to me and—' She caressed her neck ruminatively. 'No, I'm going to disappear. Lizzy, have another drink. You're awfully pale.' She reached up and pinched my cheeks, hard.

'Ouch!' I yelped.

'Sorry,' she said unapologetically. 'You need a bit of colour. Ooh, press packs. I must read one.' She hared off.

As I turned back to Jaden I heard the unmistakable tones of Nicole Hegerty behind me. 'Lily! Hey there, Lily, how are you?'

I stood firmly behind a large man in a tweed suit, hoping she wouldn't spot me, and Jaden moved closer. 'How was your day?' he asked.

I looked round to see if any of my colleagues was nearby before I answered. 'Fine, fine, fine. Ordered some new shoes off the internet, talked to Fran about *Dreams Can Come True*. She's really pleased with the way things are going and she loves the new title. And the bloody plumber didn't turn up *again*. Jaden, do you know a good plumber? No, of course you don't.'

Jaden held my wrist. 'No, Lizzy. *How was your day?*'

I was still considering my response when, to my right, a woman in a silk poncho suddenly said, 'No, Pasha and Jemima refused to squat so we had to cancel the shoot.' I giggled and thought of how much Tom would love this. I hadn't seen him for ages. What wouldn't I give to be at home on my sofa with him, watching *The OC* and having a glass of wine? 'Sorry,' I said, recovering myself. 'No, my day was fine, honestly.'

'Have you spoken to your parents about going home?'

'Noooo,' I said warily.

'So you're not going home this weekend, then?'

'Nooo,' I said, edging towards the canapés and scanning the crowd for Ash.

'Why don't you want to go back?'

'I do want to. It's just I'm busy this weekend.'

'But isn't this, like, the fourth weekend in a row you've been busy? Aren't you avoiding the issue? You're gonna have to go back some time, you know.' Jaden's face loomed over me, moonlike and nosy, like a huge tanned conscience.

I suddenly got cross. 'Look, Jaden,' I said, jabbing his chest with my finger and trying to sound like Penelope Keith, 'just mind your own business, will you? I don't know why you think it's got anything to do with you.'

Jaden was unperturbed. 'What about your aunt's wedding? The one with the funny name. Aren't you going to have to go back to the hall then?'

'It's not a hall, it's a house. Ginevra.'

'But what do you call her?'

'Chin.'

'Why?' Jaden was rocking on the balls of his feet, staring at me intently.

'Uncle Tony couldn't say Ginevra when she was born. He could only say Chin, so I suppose that's how—'

'Is he the one who died?'

'Yes.'

'What did he die of?'

'He had a heart-attack. He was twenty-eight. He had a little son – Tom.'

'Do you remember him?' Jaden persisted.

'Not really,' I said, downing the rest of my champagne and hoicking another glass from a passing tray in one fluid movement. 'He was blond. He was very handsome, funny. Nice. I'm probably wrong. I was nearly three, so I don't actually remember. Ah, look, there's Ash. What a shame we can't continue this little chat where you're incredibly rude and ask me lots of personal questions, which are absolutely not your business at all. I do so wish we could.'

I should have known better than to try to get a rise out of Jaden. He doesn't work like that. 'I'm sad about it too,' he said, smiling, as Ash appeared at his side.

'Are you?'

'Yes, especially that you don't think it's any of my business. You're sleeping with me, and you still don't want me to know anything about what's happening with you. And, man, this is crazy, none of you talking about it. Don't you think it's crazy?'

'Er . . .' I bit back the urge to tell him to take the stuff he'd left at my flat and never darken my door or my bra strap again. 'No?'

'But they're selling the house, Lizzy! They're selling your home! I know how emotional you are about it. Don't you even want to know why?'

'I know why,' I said. 'The house needs a new roof and loads of work doing and we can't afford it. If we sell, they all still get some money. That's the way it is, and if you don't mind . . . let's change the subject. OK?'

'Well . . . OK,' said Jaden, reluctantly.

'And another thing. I'm not sleeping with you. That makes it sound almost like we're going out. We're enjoying occasional sex together. Which is great. And sometimes we go ten-pin bowling. But that's it. OK?'

Ash was gaping at us. He closed his mouth, then said, 'Hi, Liz. You made it, then? Nice of you to come.'

'I know,' I said. 'Leave me alone. It was the plumber. He didn't turn up. Again. So shut up.'

Ash elbowed me. 'You shut up.'

'No, you shut up.'

'No, you.'

'No—'

Jaden watched this indulgently. 'I guess that's the nice thing about working in an office. You get to bond, be intimate with people.'

'Yes, we do,' said Ash. 'In fact, only last night in bed, I was saying to Lizzy, as we were being intimate and bonding, "Hey, Liz—"'

'No, really shut up, Ash,' I said hurriedly, having observed Jaden's bewilderment. 'We're just being silly, Jaden. Ash is a sad single loner who has to construct fantasy romances in his head, and since he doesn't have any friends, the only people he knows are his colleagues.'

'Talking about yourself again, eh?' said Ash, smirking into his glass.

'No, you are.' I elbowed him.

'No, you are.'

'No, you.'

'No, *you*,' Ash said, and pushed me. I stumbled backwards into someone. Ash muttered, 'Oops, sorry,' and I found myself face to face with Sophia Gunning.

She gave me a death stare as she righted her champagne glass, whose contents she had deftly managed not to throw over herself, then turned the glittering full beam of her smile on me. 'Lizzy! How *lovely* to see you!'

Speechless with horror, I gazed moronically at her beautiful chiffon and lace top, which I had coveted for weeks from Whistles. Typical that the world's biggest bitch Sophia Gunning would have my top.

Ash and Jaden had, magically, straightened themselves, as

if they were soldiers on parade and were also gazing moronic-ally at the glacial beauty of Sophia, an ex-schoolfriend of Chin, who happened to be one of Monumental's most promising executives. She had relocated to LA a couple of years ago.

'Hi, I'm Sophia Gunning,' she said, holding out her hand and giving Jaden a dazzling smile.

'Huh,' said Jaden. 'I'm . . .' He paused and I could see he was trying to remember his name. 'I'm—'

'Sophia,' I interrupted. 'This is Jaden Adler, a screenwriter. He's working on *Dreams Can Come True* for us.' Sophia looked blank. 'It used to be *Big Yellow Taxi*, remember? And this is Ash Ghosh,' I continued. 'He's a development executive. We work together.'

Sophia scanned them for a nanosecond. 'Jaden Adler! I've heard so many good things about you,' she said, shaking his hand so warmly that if you didn't know her as well as I do you'd swear it was sincere. She gushed on: 'And *Dreams Can Come True* sounds *wonderful*,' she continued. 'I know it's going to be *great*.'

Ooh, you lying ho, I thought.

Jaden gulped, staring at Sophia's thin, tanned hand as she released his. A diamond-studded watch, its elegant silver links too big for her stick-like wrist, slid down her caramel-coloured arm as she took a step back. Before he or Ash could say anything else, Sophia turned to me. 'So, Lizzy darling, I hear Chin's getting married. In May? Well, that's news! Who to? Everyone's getting married but me. I'm such an old maid!' She shook her white-blonde hair, her beady blue eyes on me.

'Oh, no one you know, a weird Australian called Gibbo. He's a real character and they've had their ups and downs, but she's mad about him.'

Sophia smiled patronizingly, and I hated myself for putting

Gibbo down like that. Likewise, I knew how much Chin hated Sophia and would loathe this conversation if she could hear it. I added, 'At least, he's unusual, but very good-looking and incredibly intelligent . . . He worships her. It's so great.'

Sophia's smile hardened. 'Gosh, when I knew Chin she only went out with losers who were vile to her. Well, that's wonderful. I'm so happy for her. Do tell her. I'd love to see her again . . . So, what does . . . what does her fiancé do?'

'He's a carpenter.'

Sophia snorted. 'How fascinating!'

'Like an old-fashioned woodworker. He does carvings, makes beautiful cabinets. I've seen photos of his work.'

Three blokes in identikit black suits, white shirts with thick collars and huge, pouffy silk ties, all good-looking, greasy and jowly, were jostling next to us, clearly wanting to attract Sophia's attention. One leaned over and said, in Eton-meets-mockney tones, 'Arhm, Sophia, mate?'

'Well,' Sophia said, making as if to move, 'that all sounds wonderful. You're having the wedding at Keeper House, I expect? Of course. Chin is lucky, getting married from there. We used to play wedding in the holidays. We'd line up the dolls and teddies as guests and walk down that beautiful staircase with sheets on our heads pretending we were on our way to church. Don't you remember, Lizzy?'

'Er . . . sort of,' I said, not wanting to remind her that I was at least ten years younger than her.

'Oh, it was such fun,' Sophia continued, smiling in an almost humane way. 'What a gorgeous place, Lizzy. We were always so jealous of Chin growing up there, and you, of course. Well, it'll be perfect for a wedding, won't it?'

'Yes, it will,' I said quietly.

'You can have the marquee right at the back of the garden, where the lawn becomes that wild meadowy bit.'

179

'We are,' I said.

Sophia was getting quite excited. 'God, I'd forgotten how beautiful it is. Chin and I always said we'd decorate that stone porch gate with flowers so the guests can walk through it on their way to the marquee. And she always said she'd have people waiting out in the courtyard at the front serving champagne as everyone arrives.'

'We are,' I said again, deflated. I was longing to tell Chin of this exchange, but the reason we hate Sophia Gunning down my way is that, having been best childhood pals with my aunt, she waltzed off to LA with one of Chin's record executives. (We think she did Chin a favour, but understandably Chin went off her.)

Just then my mobile rang. I pulled it out of my bag, feigning annoyance, but glad of the diversion. 'I'm so sorry, I'll get rid of it. I thought I'd turned my phone off,' I said, and glanced at the screen. 'Actually I'll have to take it – I do apologize. Nice to see you, Sophia.'

Jaden, Ash and Sophia gazed after me as I hurried importantly out of the room. Out in the corridor two or three suits stood around talking earnestly into their mobiles. I pressed mine to my ear. 'Hello, Mum,' I said.

'Darling,' came my mother's voice, speaking incredibly loudly as she always does when communicating via The Mobile. 'So sorry to disturb. I was just wondering – do you want those Thames prints in your room?'

'Eh?'

'Those prints of the Thames, do you want them? I'm not packing them yet but Mike did say he'd always liked them and I thought . . . If you were particularly attached to them then of course you must have them. But I wasn't sure.'

'I don't know what you're talking about.'

'Those three framed prints in your room of the Thames. Edwin Walter's. I was just starting to sort out what we want and what other people want. Also, footstools, darling, have you got any? Because we seem to have about ten. You must take one next time. I like the—'

I interrupted: 'Mum, I'm at a work party. I'm standing in a corridor at the Victoria and Albert museum. Please, can we have this discussion tomorrow?'

'The V and A? How lovely! Kate, Lizzy's at the V and A!'

I could hear Kate muttering in the background and sounds of stomping and clanking. 'How's Dad?' I said.

Mum's voice remained bright. 'Oh, he's fine, darling. Very busy sorting everything out. Meetings with solicitors, and so on. And he's had a lot on at the auction house, which is a good thing, I suppose.'

'Yes,' I said.

'I did wonder, though,' said Mum, 'have you heard from Mike again?'

'No,' I said. 'Not for a couple of weeks. Why?'

'No reason,' my mother said hurriedly. 'We haven't heard from him for a while, that's all, and I want to talk to him.'

'About what?'

'Oh, nothing for you to worry about.'

'Anything wrong?' I said.

'Good grief, no! All fine here, yes, absolutely fine,' Mum said, sounding like Captain Mainwaring in *Dad's Army*. 'But if Mike calls, tell him to ring us too, will you?'

I gave up. 'Yes, of course.'

'Listen, darling,' my mother continued, infuriatingly pulling the plug first, 'I'd better go, I've got things to do.'

'*You*'ve got things to do! You called me out of a party! Honestly, Mum,' I said, huffily.

'Chin's coming down this weekend to sort out the decorations and the marquee, and we're going to work out the seating plan. Are you free? Do you want to come down, darling?'

'Er, no, sorry,' I said, 'I don't – I can't. I've got a party. And I promised someone I'd help. With something.'

'Oh, right,' said Mum. 'Well, maybe next weekend. It would be lovely to see you.'

'I don't know, Mum,' I said. 'I'm busy at the moment. I'll see if I can come for Easter.'

'OK, darling. Well, lovely to speak to you. Enjoy the party. Kate sends her love.'

Bums and damn and fuck. I pressed the button and leaned against a wall next to some ancient Korean death masks. Why was it all so hard? And why didn't I want to go home and why was everything so strange? I looked down at the phone screen again and noticed I had a text message: 'Hello lizzy. Free for supper and catch-up next thurs? Hope all gd miles x'.

I hadn't seen Miles since Christmas even though we'd sworn to meet up after New Year. He'd been in touch before this but I hadn't got round to fixing something up. I texted back to invite him to mine next Friday instead, the same night as Jess and Tom would be there.

'Let's get you out of here. I'm hungry, I want some proper food.' It was Jaden. He pushed my hair away from my neck and kissed my skin.

'I can't just go—'

'Yes, you can. Who's going to notice? Ash told me to take you home and Lily's drunk.' He gestured at my diminutive boss, who was glassy-eyed and gesticulating at an un-responsive Nicole Hegerty, who was stone-cold sober and staring at her bemusedly. He turned back to me, kissed me, and said, 'You're lovely, Lizzy, you know that, don't you?'

'Er . . .'

'I know we don't see lots of things in the same way, but can I just say one thing to you tonight?'

182

'Of course,' I said, inwardly cringing.

'Don't look so horrified.' He took my hand. 'Just think about the LA job. Take it seriously.'

'Don't be stupid,' I said.

'Hey, no big deal,' Jaden said, holding his hands up. 'I know you think I'm some strange beancurd-eating Californian who talks a lot of crap, but doesn't one small part of you think it could be kind of cool? But if I'm saying it to you, you'll never take it seriously as a suggestion. I know you won't. It's all about boundaries with you.' He sighed. 'And now you'll laugh at me.'

'I'm not!' I said, appalled that I was coming across as some sarcastic laughing cow. 'I don't laugh at you.'

'No, I know you don't, and I don't mean it like that . . . I mean . . . I know you've had a rough time, and I know about that guy David—'

'Jaden,' I said, putting my finger to his lips, 'stop it, it's fine.'

'Let me finish, Lizzy. Perhaps a change would be good for you.'

'It wouldn't,' I said. 'That's not what I need.'

'I don't think you know what you need. I'm not saying I do either – I'm not saying anyone does. But that's fine. I'm not trying to say – anything. But it might be cool, you know. You could come live with me for a while.'

'And what would I do there?' I said, knowing where this was going.

'Well, you'd be away from a lot of stuff. And we could do as much or as little of this as we wanted.'

'Of what?' I said.

'Going home together, QE Three. Your place tonight, I think.'

'I think not,' I said. 'The boiler, remember. It's your turn, partner. Come on, let's go.'

Jaden kissed me again, and that lovely momentary feeling he gave me, of being carefree, came over me. And a tiny part of me wondered if he might be right. He took my hand and we ran out, down the steps into the fresh spring night.

SEVENTEEN

The next day, deciding I had to take positive action, I emailed Mike. My purpose was several-fold: to do some digging about him and Rosalie, to get him to reveal some actual information about SOKH and, finally, to ask him to ring David on some other pretext and get Brian the plumber's number. I had remembered one more thing about him: he had referred to himself as Spanish Brian throughout our previous encounter. That wasn't much help, but surely it was better than nothing.

Mike didn't reply. Three days went past, during which I forgot about it, caught up with Ash and his love for Georgy. Ever the romantic, Ash had forgotten about Lola, the love of his life, and moved on to Georgy, whom he'd met a couple of times but who had blanked him up until the previous week when, at the pub with me and assorted others from work, they'd got drunk and snogged. Last week they'd been out on a date, slept together, and Georgy – who is never around and when she is even I, her best friend, find it virtually impossible to get hold of her – hadn't been in touch since. In desperation, Ash had written her a letter with bullet-points explaining why their love would be true if she'd only

185

go out with him. He hadn't sent it, thank God – I'd managed to stop him in time. Every time I think that I am becoming a crazy stalker or that I obsess too much about an ex-boyfriend, I look over at my friends or relatives and see them being even madder than me, which gives me succour.

Take Mike. I wondered how he and Rosalie were getting on, now the initial thrill of wedded bliss was over. Until he'd met her, Mike was what you would call a confirmed bachelor – in the non-gay sense. He suits himself – in an entirely charming way, of course, and I couldn't help thinking he must be finding it odd to live in a strange apartment, having to fit his stuff in with someone else's, adjust to their way of living. The benefits, of course, were that the apartment was a prime piece of Manhattan real estate overlooking Central Park and he had a wife who was supposedly crazy in love with him. I found myself thinking about him a lot. The sale of the house was hard for him, especially coupled with this new stage in his life.

Worryingly, my email was bounced back, and although I tried a different address he never replied. In the back of my mind it bothered me: I had a creeping feeling about Rosalie, almost as if she was trying to isolate Mike from his family. He would do anything for an easy life; I couldn't see him resisting her for long. Would he let her keep him away from us? I didn't want to believe it, but as the weeks went by I started to accept that he might.

The next week I had Tom, Jess and Miles round for supper. I'd invited Georgy too, but she was flying to Sorrento that night to oversee the opening of some new luxury hotel, the lucky cow. She was going to be away for five weeks in the sun in a flash hotel in Italy. Her life is considerably nicer than mine, which should make me want to hit her. I hadn't seen Tom properly since about 450 BC – he could have become an astronaut or a bra designer for all I knew. Or Miles. Or Jess, come to that. There were things we needed to discuss: Chin's wedding and whether we would kill her before the happy day because she was driving us all up the wall; the Caldwells, for whom we all nursed an enjoyable loathing; and, finally, Gibbo's stag night and Chin's hen party, which Tom and I respectively were organizing and which were going to be great, except Tom's idea of a bonzer night out and Gibbo's were quite different. What none of us would discuss was the sale of the house.

On the way home that Friday I went to Luigi's and got lots of antipasti, tomatoes, scraps of bresaola and prosciutto, garlicky olives, some lovely oily focaccia, olive oil and lemons. I was so pleased at this vision of my simple, elegant delicatessen-style Friday kitchen-table supper, with low key but exquisite food served in an atmosphere of relaxed chats and wine, that I forgot how cold the flat was. As I stood glaring at the boiler, I ate most of the ham and all of the artichoke hearts by mistake. As my gaze drifted away from the boiler and roamed idly to the counter and the empty clear containers I realised my faux pas. First rule of elegant dining: do not eat the guests' supper because you are an oinky piggy pig. I slapped my hand to my mouth, still chewing, screamed swear words at the boiler whose fault it clearly was, slapped it viciously, then stomped into the sitting room just as the phone rang.

'Hello,' I snarled.

'Lizzy, it's Miles. I'm just checking about tonight. Is it eight o'clock?'

'Yes. Have you eaten?'

There was a silence. 'No,' said Miles, after a moment. 'No, I was . . . well, I was assuming you were providing food since your text message said, "Come round for supper." Silly me. Was I wrong?'

'No,' I said, refusing to rise to the bait and not wanting to have a long chat with someone whom I was about to spend the evening with (why do people do this, I ask myself? I do not know, it is annoying, I answer myself.) 'See you at eight then. Bring a jumper by the way.'

'Have you lost all your clothes?'

'The boiler's still not working and it can get quite chilly. Well, very chilly. And the plumber who was supposed to come isn't till . . .' I stopped, overwhelmed by anger at modern plumbing standards. Then I made my first mistake of the evening. 'Miles, I wouldn't ask you this normally, but can you do me a massive favour? You usually speak to David on Saturday afternoons, don't you?' – for they did, David would ring during Final Score on Grandstand and Miles would read out the football results, up to Division Two – 'Can you ask him something for me?'

'What, Lizzy?' Miles said, with a *faux*-horrified gasp. 'The enemy? Sure, what is it? You've changed your mind about him?'

'God, Miles, get a grip.' I was horrified to find myself blushing. 'No, it's really stupid. So don't bother. In fact,' I said, changing my mind again, because I was sick of (a) behaving like a four-year-old and (b) living in the Arctic, 'do bother. Could you ask him for Spanish Brian's phone number?'

'David, what's Spanish Brian's phone number?' Miles repeated.

'Yes,' I said. 'Thank you so much, Miles, that would be super-helpful.'

There was a pause. '07387 843312,' Miles said.

'Or whatever, yes,' I said. 'Who knows?'

'Do you want me to repeat it?'

'No,' I said, confused. 'I'll make sure I have a pen and paper handy when you ring me tomorrow afternoon so you don't have to. Just speaking slowly will be OK, I'm sure.'

188

'No, Lizzy. That was Brian's number,' Miles said.

'How do you know? Have you used him too?'

'No,' said Miles, casually. 'David's standing right here, he's reading it off his phone. He's staying with me this weekend.'

Someone who wasn't me said, 'How marvellous. Do bring him along to the relaxed-kitchen-table supper tonight.' I had no idea why I said this. It was my second mistake of the night – third, if you count accidentally wolfing the food before the guests had even arrived.

There was a pause at the other end and I could tell that conferring was taking place.

'He'd love to come,' Miles said. 'We'll see you at eight. In jumpers. Great. Looking forward to it.'

I hadn't chosen my first meeting with David since our split – standing in church with him had been an accident. But the second was entirely my fault and now I had just an hour to prepare for it. He was coming here, to the flat, where we had spent so much time together. Should I divest my home of David-related things? I wanted to, I didn't want him to think I was sentimental about anything. I couldn't bear the idea of his pity. So I ran round with a plastic bag and collected up the following: a silver photo frame with a picture of me and David under the Eiffel Tower; a letter he'd written me, which was tucked inside a book on the mantelpiece (unlikely he'd go book-browsing, but still too much of a risk), a tie he'd left here when he went to New York (hideously expensive and a bit kipperish but trendy), a video of *Some Like It Hot*, which he had given me for Christmas the previous year and, most importantly, my first-year hall photo at university, an hilarious group of self-consciously groovy students standing in three long rows that I usually kept rolled up and had forgotten about. But the previous week Georgy had come round and we'd found Lisa Garratt (admittedly after painstakingly searching for her with a slow-moving finger going along each line). She was in among a group of boys – oh, what a surprise. Georgy had got out a pen and written, 'Look for me down the docks,' in a speech bubble next to her and I had scratched out her face with a pin. Reading that, it makes it sound as if we are psychos, but show me a girl who isn't slightly imbalanced at some point in her life when it comes to men and I will show you one of George Bush's brain cells.

Everything went into a plastic bag and into a corner of my bedroom out of harm's way. Then I changed into a low-cut top and zooshed my hair up. Then I changed out of the low-cut top into one with long sleeves and a high neck, then de-zooshed my hair. I put on S Club 7's *Greatest Hits*, changed it to Chet Baker, took off Chet Baker and put S Club 7 back on. *Tough!* I thought. You always hated S Club 7! Well, screw you! You're a guest in my home, you cheating bastard, and you can bloody well listen to S Club 7 and appreciate the melodic structure and beauty of 'Never Had A Dream Come True' for once, and I hope it grates on your very soul all night.

'Ha-ha!' I yelled calmly at Jess and Tom, when they arrived just after eight. 'Nothing special. David's coming with Miles tonight, thought I should forewarn you.'

Jess and Tom gaped, as well they might.

'Coming here? To your *home*?' Jess asked, in hushed tones.

'Yes,' I said more calmly, handing them each a glass of wine.

'In your *flat*? My God, how *can* you?' hissed Tom.

'He's my ex-boyfriend, you know, not a serial killer.'

'He might as well be,' muttered Tom, gulping his wine. 'Well, I shall have something to say to David Eliot.'

'Oh, yes, me too,' said Jess, a martial gleam in her eye.

'Please, Tom, Jess, don't say *anything* to him,' I begged.

'That's the worst thing you could do. If you want to help me, make out I'm completely fantastic and over him. Don't be cross with him and *don't* make out he's broken my heart.'

'But he did break your heart, he should know how much he hurt you,' said my doltish sister. 'It's freezing in here, by the way. Have you still not got the boiler fixed?'

I couldn't stand the idea that David might feel I hadn't moved on and was scratching out people's faces while he was gadding about in New York, indulging in a spot of light shagging with Lisa Garratt on the photocopier. 'I mean it,' I said firmly. 'If you love me at all, do this for me.' I allowed my bottom lip to tremble just a little.

They were both won over. Jess patted my arm and Tom said, 'Fine.' He looked around, taking stock of his surroundings, including me. 'God, this is *such* a fantastic album, isn't it? What a strange top you've got on, though, Lizzy. You look like a vestal virgin.'

I laughed a hollow laugh and went into the kitchen, hoping against hope that the food would have multiplied itself since I'd last looked at it.

About ten minutes later the doorbell rang and with a shaking hand I answered the intercom and let them in. My policy was to be calm and cheery, as if to say, 'Well, this is rather strange, isn't it? But we are All Adults, aren't we? So welcome to my home. Would you care for some dry white wine?'

The anticipation is the worst, I think, the knowledge that you will definitely see him, and being unable to predict what will happen and whether you will acquit yourself properly. As I heard the steady thump of their feet on the last staircase I pinched my left arm to ward off a rising tide of hysteria. Calm down, you stupid girl, I told myself. This man moved away, slept with someone else and dumped you. How dare you get into such a state about it?

191

I gritted my teeth, flared my nostrils and held my head high. God, I hated him for invading my home and ruining what might have been a lovely evening.

There was a knock on the door. The outsiders were outside. An evening with David loomed ahead and there was no way out. I looked at myself in the hall mirror, checked my teeth for lipstick, smiled at myself in a pathetic way. Then I opened the door.

EIGHTEEN

'Hi,' I said, in a normal voice, though my heart was thumping. 'Come in. I'm sorry it's so cold. Hi, Miles.' I kissed his cheek. 'Hi, David, lovely to see you.' I kissed his cheek too, but I didn't look at him. Then I stood back and smiled brightly. Miles grinned so kindly that I wanted to hug him. Behind him, David stood awkwardly.

'Right,' I said. 'I would say, can I take your coats but you might be better to keep them on.'

'Don't worry, we're jumpered up,' said Miles. 'Here's some wine, and some flowers.' He took off his coat.

'Great,' I said. 'Well – David, it's not like you don't know where the bedroom is! Would you mind popping the coats in there and, Miles, can you come with me and open the wine?'

Miles flashed me a look of surprise and inwardly I congratulated myself. David, startled, disappeared with the coats down the corridor. I licked my lips, my mouth was dry, and smiled at Miles. 'Come with me, darling. Can you be wine person this evening if I put you in charge of the corkscrew?'

'Course,' said Miles, and winked for which I loved him. We went into the kitchen.

While we were in there, I heard David saying hello to my sister and Tom. After a few seconds of stony silence he came in. 'You got rid of the Puddlesmasher.'

'He's being dry-cleaned.'

The Puddlesmasher was a long, floppy, penguin-like toy I'd had since I was very small. He used to be my mother's, and there is an adorable picture of her when she's tiny, with curly hair, in a little spotted dress, clutching him and smiling toothily at the camera. He's black and white with peachy pink webbed feet, and usually hung on a hook above my bed. That sounds like I'm the kind of girl who has a large pink armchair bursting with cuddly toys and uses Forever Friends stationery. I am not. It's just that the Puddlesmasher's great. David always thought he was hilarious.

'Right,' said Miles, as David and I stared at each other, unsure what to say next. 'Who wants some wine?'

'Me, please,' we said simultaneously.

I regrouped mentally as I took my glass. Be firm. You're doing really well. Don't let him feel sorry for you. 'Thanks so much for coming,' I said to him. 'Can you give me Spanish Brian's number now, before we forget about it? Imagine if you left and we'd forgotten the whole point of you coming over.'

'Yes, absolutely,' David said, clearly trying not to goggle at my marvellous insouciance. 'Do you – can I have a pen and paper? Better still, why don't I just call him now for you?'

'Oh, would you mind?' I said airily. 'That's really sweet of you. Here's the phone. Do you mind going into the hall to talk to him? Thanks.'

David disappeared again. I shut the door on him and turned to the others. 'Pour me some more wine, will you, Jess? And, Tom, S Club 7's finished. Press play again and let's have it from the beginning, shall we?'

*   *   *

We made a strange group that night, and it was sad, when I thought about how it would otherwise have been. It was sad to see David, Tom and Jess standing in my sitting room chatting awkwardly about David's flight over.

'So, David, where do you live now?' Jess said politely, as I handed round crisps and olives.

'Greenwich Village,' David said. 'In an apartment building.'

'Is that where you've always been?' Tom asked, equally politely.

'Yes,' David said. 'It's a great neighbourhood. I can walk to work – that's the beauty of Manhattan.'

'Right,' said Tom. 'How interesting.'

I could have said lots of things, as I offered the olives to David and stole a glance at him. Like, do you remember that gorgeous day we walked all the way from your apartment in Jane Street up to Central Park, from the south to the north of the island, and how we stopped and had a burger half-way in a crusty old diner by the Empire State Building, between two Persian-carpet shops? And if you do remember that, what do you think about it now? He smiled briefly at me, as he took an olive, then asked Jess about her course. I went into the kitchen and started to lay the table.

Miles was in there, humming softly and pouring wine. There was something reassuringly familiar about his bulk. 'OK there? Shall I take more glasses out?' I asked.

'Sure,' said Miles. 'They're lovely. I found them in the back of the cupboard. Are they antique? Crystal? Where did you get them?'

'Er,' I said.

Miles looked back at them too. 'Oh, God, David gave them to you on your anniversary, didn't he?' he said. 'Shit, Lizzy, I'm so sorry.'

'It doesn't matter,' I said. 'They're nice, and I never use them. Leave it.'

'No way,' said Miles, opening and shutting cupboard doors. 'God, I'm an idiot.'

'You're not!' I said. 'Don't – oh, OK. Yes, that's it, there.'

Miles emerged, red-faced, clutching a box. 'Here we go. What vintage are these?'

'Ikea, 2001,' I said. 'Bought twelve, only six left now, three pounds for six.'

'Bargain,' said Miles. He flipped open the box, plucked out the glasses, flung the wine from the old glasses into the new ones, and slipped the cut-glass lead crystal goblets David had bought when we'd been in Paris into the wrong box. I knew they would stay there, traces of wine still in them, for a long time. He crouched, pushed the box into the back of the cupboard and stood up. 'Right, Captain,' he said. 'Ready?'

'Thanks,' I said, and picked up the tray.

And that was sad, too.

'This looks lovely,' Tom said, as I brought out the platter of forlorn-looking food that unfortunately constituted the elegant Friday-night kitchen supper. We all looked at the meagre plate in silence.

'I ate some of it by mistake,' I said. 'Really, I'm sorry. I didn't mean to. So I'm not that hungry. I'll just watch you eat.' I couldn't have eaten a thing anyway.

'Come on, Lizzy, that's ridiculous. I'll feel terrible,' said Jess.

'Honestly,' I said, panicking. 'Please.'

'If David wasn't here, there'd be enough,' Tom said pointedly. 'Very true,' David said. There was a silence. He looked at Tom, then poured himself a glass of wine, sat back and reached into his coat, which he had kept on. He pulled out two bags of Mini Cheddars. 'I brought along my own supper,' he said. 'I remember this happening before.'

Miles frowned at him, but I knew what he was talking about. 'The evening of the pie,' I said.

'Ye-es,' said David, opening the bags of Mini Cheddars and pouring them into a mound at the side of the platter.

'Oh, God, I remember!' Tom said.

'What happened?' Miles asked.

'Lizzy spent all afternoon making a pie – why didn't it work, Liz?' Tom asked.

'When I put it into the oven all the pastry slid off and crumbled into the meat,' I said, trying to make out like that was how cool people cooked pies.

'So she threw it away, and – where did we go?' Tom turned to David.

'To that pub in Maida Vale with the Thai restaurant upstairs.'

'God, yes,' Tom said, punching David's arm. 'Anyway,' he went on. 'We got back to Lizzy's after the pub, and some friend of hers from university – you were trying to set me up with her, weren't you, Lizzy?'

'No,' I said, lying.

David laughed at me. 'You were, Lizzy,' he said. 'Marina. You said they'd be perfect for each other because they both loved US sitcoms.'

'God, yes,' Tom said, and shuddered. David chuckled, and patted him sympathetically on the back.

I wondered whether he had been aware that Tom was gay all along, then knew, with a quiet, depressing certainty, that he had.

'She draped herself all over David – she thought you were going out with me – and Georgy sat on the sofa and got pissed, and then Ash arrived with that girl he was seeing – Gemma? And then you threw the pie in the bin and screamed, and all we had to eat was the green salad she'd made to go with it,' he finished, looking around the table.

'Yes,' said David. He nodded gravely at me, but his smile was amused. 'And then you made me go out to the corner shop and buy some Twiglets and – ironically – some Mini Cheddars. So it was serendipitous that I brought some this evening, I think.'

'It's not serendipitous,' Tom scoffed. 'You've got a good memory, that's all. You don't go out with Lizzy if you want to stuff your face all day. Either she's got there before you or she's thrown it away.'

'That's not why I went out with her, certainly,' David said, and laughed. It was a nice laugh, somehow acknowledging the awkwardness of the situation. As if he had said, 'it was ages ago. Look how mature we can all be about it now.'

And that was sad, too.

After that it wasn't awkward. I laughed and joked – we all did. Miles flirted outrageously with me, which was great, and Tom was friendly and nice to David. Only in the brief pauses, as someone passed the food or asked for another glass of wine, did the masks start to slip.

As alcohol relaxed me I found my part easier to play. And Miles can rise to any social challenge. He has small talk in abundance, and can chat lightly on any subject under the sun.

'So, Tom,' he said, leaning forward, eyes glittering above his red wine, 'had any dates lately?'

We'd just finished the main course (a handful of Mini Cheddars each, some bread, one artichoke, and a minuscule slice of bresaola, alas), and had spent the last ten minutes arguing over Tom's choice of stag night for Gibbo. He wanted to take him on a group outing to *Singalonga Sound of Music*, and we were trying to persuade him that this was a terrible idea, which he strongly disputed.

Tom pushed his plate away, and dabbed at his mouth

with a napkin (a square of kitchen roll). 'Mind your own business,' he said.

'Come on,' Miles pressed him. 'I want to know you're laying waste the gay scene in London, that you spend every leisure hour applying false eyelashes and glitter and rushing out into Soho.'

'No,' said Tom, shortly. 'I was at work yesterday till one o'clock in the morning, and the night before that till three. Tell me how I'm supposed to pull when I'm working hours like that.'

'You could always try trawling the men's loos in the office – you never know what you might come across.' Miles pursed his lips in a *faux*-camp way and smiled.

'Shut up, Miles,' David said.

Tom didn't seem to mind. 'Is that how you get your dates, Miles? Good for you, my friend. Needs must, eh?'

Miles laughed. 'Fuck off, Walter.'

Tom turned to David and said something about a bar in Soho that Jess had found recently and Miles swivelled to face me. 'OK?' he said, in a jokey tone.

I glanced round to see if the others were listening. 'I'm fine. It's weird, though.'

Under the table, he patted my hand surreptitiously. 'It must be. Look, I'm so sorry about bringing him tonight. I forced you into a corner, I shouldn't have done that whole thing with the plumber – it was really inconsiderate.'

'Don't worry about it,' I said, putting my hand on his. 'It's nice to see him again, under normal circs, too. Well, kind of normal circs.'

The conversation from the other side of the table suddenly became animated and Tom said something funny to David, pointing his finger and laughing.

'How are you feeling about it now?' Miles asked. 'Like it's all for the best? Or like it was a big mistake?'

'Er . . . Bit of both, really,' I said noncommittally. 'What's done is done, and there's no going back.'

'And do you *really* think that?' said Miles, quietly.

The others erupted again. 'You fell out of the cab!' David yelled at Tom.

Jess threw back her head and laughed. 'He did! You're right, he did!' she said. 'Lizzy,' she appealed to me, 'didn't Tom fall out of the cab the night we all went to that cheesy Sloanes' club in South Ken?'

'I bloody never did,' said Tom, crossly.

'You did, I'm afraid,' said David, patting him comfortingly on the back and smiling broadly. 'Let me refresh your memory. You hailed the cab and we all queued to get in, and you climbed in first and opened the other door and fell straight out on the other side.' He turned to me. I sat up straight and Miles's hand slid off my leg. 'Didn't he, Liz?'

'You did, Tom,' I agreed. 'You rolled into some iron railings and you said, "Where am I?"'

'I completely dispute that,' said Tom.

'Tough,' said David. His eyes met mine. 'We were witnesses. Lizzy had to take you back to our flat, remember? Her flat, I mean.'

I nodded, smiling at them both. 'That is also true.' I slumped back in my chair, feeling slightly sick as I remembered how things had been and how they were now.

Miles turned to me again as the others carried on chatting. 'Anyway, my love, I'm going to take you out to supper next week to apologize for bringing my horrible brother.'

'You don't have to,' I said.

'No, I don't,' Miles said, 'but I want to.'

'It wasn't your fault. It's – well, it's David's fault, I suppose, then mine, and so on, but not yours, well—'

Miles interrupted. 'I insist. What are friends for?'

'OK, then,' I said. 'Nice. Where?'

'You *are* ticklish!' Tom screeched. 'Jess, you bloody liar, you so are ticklish! Everywhere!'

'I'm so absolutely not,' replied Jess.

'This great new members' club in Covent Garden I've just joined,' Miles said, running his fingers up and down the stem of his wine glass, trying to ignore the others. 'Ha. David tried to get in last year and they wouldn't have him. Membership full. But I got in. He's gutted.'

'Revenge is sweet,' I said, as David grabbed Jess in a neck-lock and tickled her till she screamed.

'Does anyone want any coffee?' I said after pudding (a few fondant fancies), as I pushed back my chair with a plate in each hand.

'Peppermint tea for me, please,' said Jess.

'Coffee,' said Tom, lighting another cigarette. I wedged the salad bowl under my arm. 'Coming right up,' I said. 'David, how about you?' I knew what he'd say, just as I knew he loved Colmans and hated grainy mustard. Just as I knew he loved ham and his favourite meal was steak with béarnaise sauce.

He looked tired and a little drunk. Bearing in mind the lack of food and the abundance of alcohol this was no surprise. 'Coffee, please. No milk,' he said. He pulled the bowl from under my arm. 'Don't carry that, Lizzy.'

I went into the kitchen, smarting at his patronizing ways. He followed me. 'Thanks. I can cope you know,' I said, taking the bowl out of his hands and switching on the coffee machine, which was one of the noisy ones that rattles and steams the moment you go near it.

'I didn't mean that. I meant . . .' he pointed, '. . . you've got olive oil on your top now – there, look.' He moved towards me and touched the inside of my arm lightly, then paused and looked at me. I froze, cheeks burning, heart

201

thumping. I grabbed his finger and held his arm in front of me. The kettle whistled behind us. I looked up at him. My breath was coming in shallow gulps. Slowly, he bent his head and kissed me. And I remembered how our lips always met perfectly, as if by instinct. I remembered the taste of him, the feel of his skin on mine, the sensation that was like nothing else as he pulled me to him desperately.

And then the doorbell rang. We sprang apart. David put his hand on my arm. 'I'm sorry. I didn't mean to—' He cupped my chin in his hand. 'Lizzy. Oh, God, Lizzy. Don't you ever wonder . . . why this happened?' His dark eyes were staring at me, with a mixture of fear and eagerness. The doorbell rang again.

'Lisa,' I said, coming to my senses. I stroked his hand one last time, to remind myself of how he felt. 'Lisa Garratt, you remember?'

'Is that really it?' David said. And at that moment, Miles appeared in the doorway.

'It's a bloke called Jade on the intercom,' he said. 'I think he's American. He sounds like a nutter. Shall I tell him to fuck off?'

At the age of sixteen, when one is most vulnerable and prone to think one is the most hideous creature in all of creation, I was unlucky to be cursed with buck teeth and terrible skin. I also had a weird mullet, which meant that my hair, which is sort of wavy and past my shoulders, was cropped at the top of my head, and ballooned out, as if I was wearing hairy dumb-bells, to my shoulders. I played chess and the oboe and bared my top teeth, flaring my nostrils, when I concentrated.

How I wish, therefore, I could have revisited that sixteen-year-old and told her the glad tidings of great joy that lay ahead of her: that a mere twelve years later she would be in the situation I was in when I heard Jaden's tread on the stairs. Yes, there I was, about to kiss my ex-boyfriend in the kitchen when my current boyfriend rang the doorbell.

'Lizzy,' David began.

'Sorry,' I mumbled, and pushed him away.

'Lizzy!' David said again, his voice urgent. 'Will you listen to me?' he said, speaking fast, as if he knew time was running out. 'Lisa and me – it meant nothing, OK? You're over-reacting. You don't have to be so bloody brave all the time, you know. It's—' His shoulders slumped. 'Oh, forget it.'

I could hear the front door opening.

Right, I thought. Let's skim over the part where David calls sleeping with someone else (a) nothing and (b) me over-reacting. I didn't know how he could have done that with someone else after all the promises we'd made to each other. Was that stupid of me?

And I realized I could fall for him again at the click of two fingers, flick of a button. That having him in front of me was still what had made me happiest in my life. And that was why, if I stood any chance of getting over him, I had to walk away.

Jaden picked that moment to come into the kitchen. He'd been with Ash all day, working on rewrites. His hair lacked its customary gelled care and there were faint dark circles under his eyes. At that moment he seemed more human to me than he ever had before. He stood in the doorway and looked at the pair of us. 'Lizzy, I'm sorry if I'm intruding,' he began. 'You said it might be OK for me to come over after Ash and I were done and . . .'

He knew, of course. He wasn't judging me but he was jumping to conclusions about what was going on here and I couldn't bear him to think that. I walked towards him, and imprinted myself on him, pressing myself to him, suddenly glad of his comforting presence in a strange evening. I kissed his lips and ran my hands through his hair, then stood back and smiled into his eyes. 'I'm glad you're here,' I said. 'I thought you might have gone straight home.'

'I found a plumbing guy for you,' he said, stepping back a little.

'You what?' I said, aware of David glowering at me. I reran the words in my head. 'A plumber?'

Jaden nodded. 'Well, it's been bugging you, so I just asked around. He's great. I got him to come over tomorrow. Simon – the director, you know? – recommended him. So, that's my contribution to human happiness for the week. And now – oh, I'm so sorry.' He turned, obviously realising he must acknowledge David because I wouldn't. 'Hi there,' he said, holding out his right hand, while the left rested gently on the waistband of my jeans. 'I'm Jaden Adler. We met last year, but I don't expect you remember. It was at a party for Lizzy's work—'

David started, as if he'd been miles away. 'Yes, of course I do,' he said, came forward and shook Jaden's hand. 'Nice to see you again.' He stood back and regarded him with a strange expression. 'You were writing a screenplay about a co-dependency workshop in Silicon Valley, I seem to remember. How's it going?'

'Oh, yes. That's not really a current project,' Jaden said, as I squirmed inwardly. 'I'm over here for a little while, working. With this girl here.' He squeezed me to him.

'Yes, he is,' I added half-heartedly, and squeezed back.

David looked at us. 'That's great. Lizzy, I was about to say—'

'Oh I'm sorry,' Jaden interjected. 'Did I interrupt?'

'No – God, no,' David said lightly. 'Don't worry. Miles and I were just leaving. What I wanted to say, Lizzy, was . . .' he turned to put his glass on the counter, then back to me, '. . . have you heard from Mike lately?'

'Mike?' I said blankly. 'Oh, *Mike*. No, not for a while. Why? I have been wondering where he is actually.'

'Me too,' said David. 'Never mind, just asking. I'll call him when I get back to New York. Anyway, thanks for a lovely evening.'

Don't go, I wanted to say. Or, Do you remember the last time you were here? The night before you left for New York. When we stayed up till dawn. And at the last minute you gave me that ring, and told me you loved me. And do you know how many times since then I've cried about you, in this flat?

Perhaps I might have said something if we had been alone, but we weren't, and I felt incredibly tired. I blinked and smiled at him, and he looked at me, then Jaden. Silence fell upon us.

Thank God for Miles: as if by magic he appeared in the doorway from the sitting room, where he, Jess and Tom had been lying about chatting, or pretending to while they were earwigging on the scenes in the kitchen.

'Hello,' he said, shaking Jaden's hand and dispelling the awkwardness that lurked among us. 'Nice to see you again, Jaden. Right, then.' He looked at his brother and, all of a sudden, David seemed distant to me again, a stranger.

'Are you ready to go now?' he asked Miles, almost rudely.

'Sure am, bro.'

'Well,' said David, advancing towards me, 'I'm sorry for being a bit heavy earlier. It was lovely to see you, as ever.' He kissed my cheek and shook Jaden's hand again. 'Great to see you, Jaden. Take care of this one, eh?'

Jaden and I followed him and Miles into the hall. I stood in the doorway and waved them off. They waved back, as if Jaden and I were their parents sending them off to school.

Well, that's that, I thought, as I shut the door. Great. At

205

least I know where I stand. 'Sorry for being a bit heavy earlier.' Yes, we shouldn't have kissed drunkenly in the kitchen, but somehow I felt as if a weight had been lifted off me. Yes, that was it.

NINETEEN

Chin and Gibbo's wedding was at the end of May – perhaps the best time of year for it. If the sun shines it's warm, but not too boiling so you're sweating in complicated underwear and seeking shelter under a tree where you sink into the ground on your high heels, get stuck and have to be pulled out by someone who is laughing at you. As spring arrived, even in London, my feeling of dread about the house was harder to ignore. The signs that summer was on its way were evident, the wedding was close, and things were coming to a head in my relationship with Jaden. Decisions had to be made, things had to be said, and yet I buried my head in the sand, hoping it would all sort itself out without my intervention.

I began to find myself thinking more and more about my grandmother, the most efficient woman known to womankind, who tried – mostly in vain – to instill this discipline in me. When I was little and my grandparents still lived at Keeper House, Grandmother always went into town on Thursdays. If I asked to go with her, she would take me by the wrist and lead me into the kitchen. She had a little notebook in a National Trust slipcase that she used as a kind of to-do and shopping list, and throughout the week she would jot notes in it. Last year I'd found one in an old Tupperware box of keys and string. She had curiously childish handwriting, clear and open. 'Upholsterers – price for stuffing dining room chr. Linseed oil. Seeds: pots, lettuce, radish, check last yrs. Tacks. Lightbulbs – Robert's study lamp, side room x 3. Culpepper's. Sheets in spare rm. Candles, lots. Nuts. Check w R when Wine Soc to deliver sherry. More Campari.' And so on.

I would sit at the kitchen table, swinging my legs, thighs sticking to the *faux*-leather seat, and watch Grandmother translate her notes into a concise shopping list on the next page, and we would sail into town in her 'little runaround'. Grandmother's motto was, 'Never put off till tomorrow what you can do today', and that was why Keeper House was always polished, waxed, scented, tidy and well cared-for, even if it tried its best to foil my grandparents' and later, my parents' efforts to keep it so.

My motto is almost exactly the opposite: I'll worry about that tomorrow, because tomorrow is thankfully another day – to paraphrase Scarlett O'Hara. But as March went on I realized the status quo would have to change fairly soon, whether I did something about it or something happened to change it.

I love Saturday morning. It's my favourite time of the week, without a doubt. If I'm out a lot in the evenings during the week, Saturday morning is often the only time I have to potter about in my flat, water the plants, drink coffee and read the papers in an aspirational lifestyle way.

Actually, most of that's a lie. I do drink coffee and potter about, but then I lie on the sofa and watch TV, and it's an absolute luxury, because lazing around is my favourite thing to do. Some people get their jollies from opera, football or bonsai trees. I like lazing around, and Saturday mornings is when I indulge myself. The closest I get to doing housework on Saturdays is pushing some old magazines into a pile on the floor with my toe or transfering an empty wine bottle from the kitchen counter to the place on the floor where empty wine bottles go. Then I stand up, brush my pajamas off as if I've been doing heavy manual work, and say, 'Phew!'

About two weeks after the dinner party, I was lying on the sofa reading a magazine, when the phone rang. It was a lovely spring day, cold and clear, and the sun was shining through the skylight, helpfully illuminating the dust on the floorboards. CD:UK was on, and I was eating a huge chocolate croissant I'd bought the night before on my way back from the pub (I love Sainsbury's Local, I really do). The flat was warm: Spanish Brian had heeded the call of his erstwhile client and done a sterling job on a blocked pipe. Jaden had been gracious in defeat.

Who is it? I thought indignantly. I wriggled my toes in their pink bedsocks to test how much they wanted to swing off the sofa so I could answer the phone. Not very much. I took another swig of coffee. The phone continued to ring. Jaden had said he'd call me over the weekend, but I was feeling cheerful and relaxed and didn't fancy being told otherwise. Screw it, I thought, and carried on reading. They'll leave a message or try my mobile. What if it was Jaden? I reached over and turned off my mobile.

I ran through my mental checklist for the weekend. One, finish croissant. Two, tidy flat. Three, have rest. Four, meet Chin in Harvey Nicks. Five, Ash's birthday party in gastropub in North London. Six, do not call Jaden when drunk.

Jaden was going back to LA in a couple of months, and while I should have thought it was a good thing, I was surprised to find I didn't. I was trying to wean myself off him, but it was harder than I'd thought. Strangely, the more time I spent with him, the less bonkers I found him.

The phone rang again. I sighed, rammed the rest of the croissant into my mouth and heaved myself off the sofa to answer it.

'Lizzy?' It was Tom.

I swallowed fast. 'Hi. Did you just call?'

'What? No. Listen.' Tom was out of breath and I could tell by the odd sounds he was making that he was jumping up and down, as he often does when he's excited.

I sat down again. 'What?' I asked, and settled back to hear some long involved story about what had happened to him the previous night. The change in my cousin over the last couple of months was subtle but noticeable. He wasn't camp, he didn't go around trying to make up for time wasted in the closet, but he was clearly keeping himself busy.

'You're never going to believe it – well, actually, I don't think it's going to come as *that* much of a surprise, come to think of it—'

'*What?*' I said, annoyed.

'Rosalie's left Mike. No one knows where she is.'

I stood up and stubbed my toe. It was agony. '*What?*' I repeated.

'Rosalie and Mike!' Tom was still jumping up and down: his speech came in gasps. 'Mum rang me this morning – she'd just spoken to Mike. Rosalie left, she didn't tell him where she was going but she says she wants him out of the flat in a week. And he hasn't got anywhere to go.'

'But – what do you mean, she's left him?' I asked, turning off the TV. 'She wants to end it?'

'Yup. Mum didn't say much, except Mike's totally cut up about it. Apparently he got home from work and she'd packed her bags and was standing in the hall, waiting for

210

him. She said she was going to stay with a friend and she was giving him a week to get out.'

I thought back to my conversation with Mike a few weeks ago and Rosalie's snappish intervention. Well, what a surprise. She had thought she was marrying her very own romantic hero, and he had turned out to be an overgrown schoolboy. I felt no sympathy for her. But then I remembered Christmas Eve, the look of adoration on her face. I'd thought it was the real thing. But obviously she'd been wrong – and what did I know about judging the real thing? 'I don't understand it,' I said. 'Did she tell him why?'

'You know what Mum's like. That's why I was ringing. You've got to call your mum or Chin. They'll know. All Mum said was Rosalie told Mike it had been a mistake. The marriage, I mean.'

'I'm meeting Chin for lunch. I'm going to help her do some shopping for the wedding,' I said.

'What kind of shopping?' Tom sounded suspicious, with good reason.

'Er . . . bride apparel,' I said vaguely, because these days I had no idea what Chin was talking about most of the time. 'She needs bits of material. And stuff. Meet me there. Harvey Nicks café, one thirty.'

'OK. Can you believe it, though, Lizzy?'

I thought about it for a minute. 'Actually, even though it sounds silly, I can't. I know he was mad about her, but I really thought she loved him too. Just goes to show, doesn't it?'

'Ye-es.' Tom sighed. 'It's . . . it's strange.'

A couple of hours later, I hurried into the Harvey Nichols café to find Tom and Chin already there. I'd forgotten to tell Chin Tom was coming, and now I hoped she wouldn't mind. She nurses a grudge for ever, and I didn't suppose

211

that Tom was out of the doghouse yet for his 'advice' to Gibbo over Christmas. Given all that had happened since, you might think she would have decided to let it lie by now, but through the whole of January she had not been on speakers with Tom. Then Gibbo had worked his magic: he'd asked Tom to be an usher at the wedding, as well as giving him responsibility for the stag night. (*Singalonga Sound of Music* had been jettisoned in favour of Tom's latest plan: Morrissey in concert followed by a meal at a Polish restaurant in Soho. Talk about gloomy.) I'm sure the fact that Gibbo has virtually no close friends in the UK had nothing to do with his being asked. Since Chin was exhibiting early signs of being a total Bridezilla, she called Tom to get his measurements for the waistcoat the ushers were to wear because she didn't trust Gibbo to take them down correctly. Talk of fabrics had led to reconciliation, and now all was sort of OK between them.

They looked up as I approached and Tom raised his eyebrows. 'Have you talked to Suzy?' he asked.

'Yes, and she says—'

'Hello, darling,' said Chin, jumping up to kiss me. 'Thanks so much for doing this with me. Sit down.'

I sat down. Tom kissed me. 'Hello,' he said, and made a face in the direction of Chin, rolling his eyes, turning down the corners of his mouth and dropping his jaw. 'That bad?' I mouthed at him, as Chin fished around in her bag.

'Now,' said Chin, getting out a huge A4 lined book and a large fat fountain pen. 'Let's talk tulle.'

'What?' I said simultaneously with Tom, as I took off my jacket. We giggled. I picked up the menu.

Chin bit her lip and started to write. 'Order a drink, darling,' she said. 'I thought Peter Jones first. That new haberdashery department's fucking awful, but it's still Peter Jones.

212

Also, I saw some beautiful pink ribbon with pretty little polka dots in John Lewis last week, so if they don't have it there, we'll have to pop to John Lewis. Or maybe you could and I could go on to Selfridges to see about those shoes.' She drew a vigorous line through something and frowned. 'Tom, we may need to divide and conquer even more. How are you at bartering?'

Tom was bewildered. 'Where? What?'

'Perhaps you should go to Berwick Street market and get the material.'

'What material?'

'Come on, people!' Chin slammed her book on to the table. 'Let's focus, OK?'

Tom and I stared at her. 'What are you talking about?' my cousin demanded.

'Tulle for the underskirt of my dress,' Chin said. She closed the book and stared at Tom. 'I thought you said you were here to help?'

'Why would I say that?' Tom asked aggressively. 'I'm gay, I'm not bloody Danny La Rue. I'm here to drink wine and find out what happened with Mike and Rosalie, and I haven't done either yet.'

'Oh, well, that's just charming, isn't it?' said Chin, snappishly. 'Typical of you, Tom, you're just so selfish.'

I thought it wise to intervene. 'Hey, Chin, shush. You can't ask Tom to barter for tulle in Berwick Street market. They'd eat him alive. Remember the church fête last year?'

We always go home for the Wareham church fête in June. Last year it was on Midsummer's Day, which was beautiful and hot. Kate sent Tom off to buy fir-apple and parsley jelly, or something like that, to have with our barbecue that evening. She told him to barter, because the Prufoots always over-charged. The chutney and jam stall was always run by hairy Lila Prufoot, who ran the village shop, and this year her daugh-

213

ter Mavis, aged ten, was helping her. To cut a long story short, Tom tried to barter with Mavis and ended up with a fat lip and a broken toe, as little Mavis threw him a punch and dropped a pot of damson and apricot jam on his foot.

Chin smiled self-consciously at Tom, and put her hand on his. 'Sorry, Tom.'

''S okay, Chin. Thanks for letting me be an usher.'

'Don't thank me, thank Gibbo. He really likes you. All of you. Which is weird, considering how mad you were at Christmas.'

'Yeah,' Tom and I answered ruminatively. We sat in silence for a few moments. The spell was broken only as a waiter walked past, and all three of us snapped to attention and tried to catch his eye.

'Oh, Chin, I keep meaning to tell you,' I said, as Tom twisted in his seat and flashed his pearlies at the waiter, who had ignored us. 'Guess who I bumped into at that Monumental party at the V and A a couple of weeks ago?'

'Who?' said Chin.

'You'll never guess,' I said, enjoying myself.

'No, I won't. I don't do the "guess" thing. Tell me.'

God, Chin was a pain sometimes. 'Sophia Gunning. And,' I added maliciously, 'she looked fantastic.'

Chin ground her teeth. 'That bitch,' she said. 'What a whore! What did she say?'

'Actually, she was OK,' I said. 'She told me she missed you.'

'Like a hole in the head, which is what I'll give her if I ever see her again,' Chin muttered. 'God, I really need a drink now. Hello,' she said, as the waiter approached. 'Wine, please. Red?'

'Yes, please,' said Tom and I together.

Ah, the simple gift of wine that brings families together.

* * *

214

'So ever since they got home after Christmas, Rosalie'd been totally different,' Chin said. 'It's hard for Mike – he doesn't want to slag her off, but he's terribly upset about the way she's behaved. And, of course, he's worried about her. Where the hell can she have gone?'

We were standing at the counter of one of the great wonders of the Western world: the haberdashery department in Peter Jones. Which, on a Saturday in March, was full of people buying things for summer weddings and thus emitted a high-pitched frequency of stress that only dogs, brides and their mothers could hear. Apart from a short, violent row when Chin lost Tom and me and found us five minutes later, laughing hysterically at the novelty buttons, we had shopped together in remarkable harmony for hooks and eyes, ribbons, lace trimmings, Wundaweb magical hemming gauze and normal buttons, and were now waiting to hear about the mystery of tulle from one of the nice ladies who worked there.

Tom was stroking the cream ribbon and blue lace garter he'd bought Chin as her 'blue and new'. 'I just don't understand,' he said finally. 'I really liked Rosalie. I thought she was lovely.'

My phone buzzed with a text message. I opened it. 'Hi, Lizzy, I would like to hook up tonight. Give me a call and I will come round. I will call you later. Jaden.' Not for the first time, I wondered why we were employing as a writer a man whose text messages read as if they were written by a Vulcan.

'I know you did,' Chin was saying impatiently, but not unkindly. 'I did too. At least, I was starting to warm to her before . . . this.'

'Actually, she was great after Dad said the thing about the house,' I said.

We were silent. None of us had mentioned SOKH yet, and

no one had discussed the scenes that ensued that night after Dad's announcement. Mainly because there hadn't been any.

Anyway, Rosalie had been great that night. She made everyone tea – yes, really. She drew Dad apart from the group, sensing that he was the one from whom everyone wanted answers, which they weren't going to get. She got him chatting earnestly about church architecture and the finer points of Norman fonts, and never once looked glazed and bored. We, however, all sat around stunned and Mike, devastated, slunk off early to bed.

Chin shivered and straightened. 'She's nice, I'm not saying she isn't. It's just . . .' She tailed off as a sales assistant walked past, carrying a roll of sequins destined for someone else.

'What?' Tom said.

'Well, don't get me wrong. I want Rosalie and Mike to be happy. I just wonder, perhaps, about . . .' Chin paused, as if she was choosing her words carefully. 'I don't know. Why she married Mike, maybe. It was very quick, wasn't it?'

'What do you mean?' I said.

'Yeah, what?' Tom demanded. 'Are you saying she only married Mike for a reason?'

'Don't be naïve, Tom. Everyone marries someone for a reason. It's the reason in question that worries me.'

'Well, Mike married her for a reason, didn't he?' I said.

'Yes, of course he did,' Chin said, opening her fist to count the pearl buttons she was holding. 'Mike's Mike. He's my brother and a hopeless romantic who loves the big gesture. And what's bigger than deciding you've fallen head over heels in love with someone you've only just met and that you're going to marry them right away? It's typical Mike.' Her expression softened. 'OK. I reckon Rosalie married Mike thinking she was getting the English-lord-in-the-stately-home thing, and then she comes over to England, sees that the house isn't really Mike's, then hears three days later that it's being sold to some thug who owns a dodgy biscuit company and that in future the Walter family home isn't some Elizabethan manor house, it's – well, take your pick,' she said, sliding the buttons on to the counter and ticking off each possibility angrily on her fingers. 'Kate's box-like cottage, which has two hundred back issues of *Horse and Hound* but no shower. Lizzy's box-like flat, which is dusty and full of empty bottles. Tom's minimalist yet box-like loft, which is full of broken gadgets. My house, which is a house but still the size of a box. Or your mum and dad's box-sized new bungalow.'

(For, yes, Mum and Dad had loved the horrible bungalow in Danby and they had signed a rental lease for a year. As a result of this I was liking Alice Eliot less and less.)

At the mention of the new house my stomach clenched. 'How depressing,' I said, holding up a paper tape-measure.

'I know,' said Chin. 'I know, pet. But that's the way it is, unless one of us can come up with a fail-safe get-rich-quick plan. I've racked my brains but I can't think of anything. So the house goes. There you are.'

'How can you be so blasé about it?' I said.

''Cause I'm not Mike,' said Chin. 'I'm my mother's daughter, you know. Your grandmother was a pragmatist. No point crying over spilt milk, and all that. If any of us could think of a way to stop it we would, but it's not going to happen. And you know – well.' She stopped.

'What?' Tom said.

'It might not be so bad for us, you know. Letting the house go. I sometimes think . . .' Chin sighed, and shifted her weight from one leg to the other. 'I sometimes think it's not as great for us as we think. Our family. We're more than just the house – we're still a family without it. And I wonder sometimes whether we need to get a grip on reality. A bit,' she amended, on seeing how aghast Tom and I were. 'I don't mean – but look at Rosalie. And look at us. She knows exactly what she's doing. We have no idea. Mike especially.'

'That's not fair,' Tom said, upset. 'Chin, that's not true. You're basically saying Rosalie married Mike because she thought she'd be Lady Muck. She's not like that.'

'Oh, isn't she?' Chin said. 'She's in her forties, she's success-ful but she's alone, and along comes lovely Mike, a bit useless but fantastic, falls in love with her and proposes. All of a sudden she isn't alone any more and she's living in a castle – when your mum and dad can be moved out, that is.'

'Oh, my God,' I said, suddenly remembering something.

The others turned to me.

'What is it?' Tom said. 'Lizzy, you look like you've seen a ghost. What?'

'On Christmas Day,' I faltered, wishing it wasn't true, 'I saw . . . We'd just come back from church and I saw Rosalie in Dad's study, going through some old box files, the ones Dad keeps the papers for the house in – the agreement signing it over to Mum and Dad, the lease when Edwin Walter bought it, even the original land sale. Everything. She was reading and making notes.'

'I *knew* she was up to something!' Chin said.

'Are you sure?' asked Tom in disbelief.

'Totally,' I said. 'I've just remembered something else. Mike appeared as I was standing there, wondering what she was doing. He was kind of embarrassed. He tried to pretend Rosalie was looking for some Sellotape or something. I'm sure he knew what she was up to. He covered up for her, and then she comes out sweet as you like and we have some joke about wrapping presents.'

'No way,' said Tom, and Chin swore under her breath.

'Do you remember I had that drink with David?' she said.

'When?' Tom asked.

'The same day we found out about the house,' I said, trying to sound casual. 'Yes, what happened?'

'Well, we were just catching up, really.' Chin looked shifty. 'I didn't do anything about it, because of everything that happened afterwards. And he saw you all hiding from him as he walked in – that's why we left.'

'Oh, God,' I said.

'Yes,' Chin said sternly. 'Stupid of you. Anyway, it's just that he said something weird. But I think he was wrong. He was a bit pissed off because Lizzy and the rest of you were pretending not to have seen him. Like the playground. She should have just gone up to him and said hi.'

'Hello, I'm still here,' I said, tapping Chin's shoulder, although I agreed with her and inside I was dying at the thought of how childish it must have seemed to David, how strange it must have been for him to see his brother with his ex and her family. 'What did he say?'

'About you?'

'No,' I said firmly, although I desperately wanted to know. 'About Mike.'

'Oh,' Chin said. 'Well, he asked me if Mike was OK for money at the moment. And I said, "Yes, of course, why wouldn't he be?" And David said he'd heard that he'd lost his job.'

'What?' Tom and I exclaimed.

'Mike hasn't lost his job,' Tom said. 'We had a long chat about it. What the fuck was David talking about?'

'He was just trying to stir,' I said, although I knew that that wasn't David at all. 'In any case,' I said. 'Rosalie wasn't with Mike for money, that's for sure. She doesn't need it – she's got loads. She wanted the life. She's a property lawyer, for Christ's sake, she knows whether she's on to a good thing or not. I bet she thought she was with Keeper House. Lady of the manor and all that.'

'I don't know,' said Chin. 'There's something odd about it, that's all.'

'Still,' Tom said, 'Rosalie hasn't actually done anything *illegal*, has she? The worst you can say of her is that . . . well, she's a bit of a fantasist.'

'A fantasist who marries a man she only met a couple of weeks before, then rifles through his family possessions and walks out on him a couple of months later,' said Chin. 'And where is she now? Found someone richer than Mike? I wouldn't be surprised, you know.'

'God, do you think that's it?' I said.

'Mike's well out of it,' Chin said, fingering some broderie-anglaise ribbon. 'You mark my words, she'd have had us out of Keeper House faster than you can say "knife" if she'd been able to.'

'I liked her,' Tom said stubbornly.

'I thought I liked dresses and things, and then I started planning this wedding, and let me tell you, if I see a square inch of lace ever again I'm going to throw up. Good grief, where is that woman?' She passed a hand across her forehead. 'Anyway, it's a bloody strange thing for David to say, don't you think?'

TWENTY

On the bus going home I kept thinking about Rosalie and Mike. The old truth that you never understand anyone else's relationships, even if you're their closest friend, was so true. I would never have expected Mike to show up on Christmas Eve with a total stranger as his bride – or that I would end up liking her and believing she was in love with Mike and that they'd probably be very happy together.

As the bus trundled up Park Lane, I stared out of the window into Hyde Park. The late-afternoon sun shone across the grass, and clumps of daffodils waved in the wind under the trees. This time last year David had been getting ready to go to New York.

After we had broken up I had had brief flashes of blinding optimism, thinking sometimes that Miles might have exaggerated, that I'd overreacted and we could get back together. Sometimes I thought about David and Lisa together. And when I thought about how much I missed him and remembered what it was like when we were together, I felt silly afterwards, because even though I didn't want to admit it, I knew it was over, and that he simply hadn't loved me enough. I couldn't think without blushing about the evening

I'd kissed him again. The way I'd flirted with Miles, enjoyed hurting David. That and then been all lovey-dovey with Jaden. It was all so horrible, and I wasn't that kind of person.

Perhaps, though, I *was* that kind of person, and that was why David had slept with someone else. As I jumped off the bus at the Saturday market on Church Street my phone rang again, reminding me I had to call Jaden, then factor in some lazing-around time before I went to Ash's. I'd got him a birthday present, a book about film directors, but I was looking for something else: the market has an excellent selection of reasonably priced clothing, which Georgy, who only buys from Bond Street, turns up her nose at but which I love. In my flat there were at least five bags containing some nylon top or cheap-looking cardigan that I had bought at the market in a moment of weakness.

My friend Pete from university runs a stall in Alfie's covered antiques market. He sells nice trinkets and interestingly designed things that take his fancy, so I wandered over to see him and ended up buying Ash a cool plastic ashtray, bright orange and globe-shaped. I trailed around, eyeing silver, old clocks, costumes and books. Outside again, I resisted the charms of a grey pencil-skirt for only ten pounds, which even I, with my shopping blindness, could see was cheap and nasty and would ruche up in all the wrong places. Instead I bought a potted plant and a cheap bottle of Gordon's gin and went home, glad that I'd purchased something, having been shopping all day and unable to spend any money – unless you count paying for five yards of pale blue silk taffeta in John Lewis because the bride has suddenly discovered she's left her purse in Peter Jones and has a total melt-down on the shop floor. I don't.

At home, I wearily dropped my bags to the floor and sank down on to the sofa. My phone rang again, and since I knew

Jaden would carry on calling till I spoke to him (he didn't believe in games or playing hard-to-get) I answered it. He was calling from an unregistered number.

'Hello there,' I said, rather coldly, and went into the kitchen to put the kettle on.

'Where on earth have you been?' said Jaden. 'Thank God, Lizzy, I've been trying you on your mobile and at home all bloody day.'

He sounded absolutely miles away. And a bit funny. 'Are you OK?' I asked.

'Yes, I'm fine, I'm just relieved to have got hold of you. It's – it's nice to hear your voice.'

I froze. It wasn't Jaden. It was David. Calling me.

When I sometimes fantasized about David ringing out of the blue, I was always in a chic bar laughing at sophisticated *bons mots* from several gorgeous men, wearing my fantastic new boots and flinging one leg over the other. He would be desperate to chat, and I would say, regretfully but gaily, 'David, I'm so sorry about this, but I'm really going to have to go. I can barely hear what you're saying and I must rejoin my companions. Thank you so much for calling, all good wishes, goodbye.'

'Oh, my God, it's you,' I said. 'Ouch,' I added, as I stamped on my foot. Behind me, the kettle started squealing and rattling on the hob.

'What on earth are you doing?' said David. 'What's that wailing sound?'

'Arhm . . .' I turned off the kettle and thought frantically. 'It's a protest. I'm in Trafalgar Square with some protestors. Friends. Protesting friends, you know.'

Why had I said that?

'What?' said David. 'You're at a protest? You? For whom? Or against whom?'

It always irritated me that David said *whom*, really

emphasizing the *m*. I drew strength from this. I looked out of the window. A bull mastiff was mauling a rubbish bin. 'Well, Battersea Dogs' Home,' I said. 'They – it needs to be heard. And that's all there is to it. So . . . how are you?'

'I'm fine. I didn't realise I'd be tearing you away from, er, your protest. I got your mobile number off Miles. You've changed it since . . . Anyway, you've changed it.' He paused. 'Look,' he went on, 'I'm really sorry to bother you but I . . .'

'Yes?' I said.

'I wouldn't have rung but I thought I should. I didn't want to . . . you know, talk to you.'

I did wish David wouldn't make it quite so plain, whenever he spoke to me now, that he'd rather be sharing quality time in a cell with Jeffrey Archer than talking to me. It made me feel even sadder about the inequality of our old relationship. And it made me want to shout things at him, like Did you know I had to take a week off work after we split up? Did you know I started crying on the bus two weeks later and an old lady called Martha put her arm round me and that made me cry even more, so much so that the conductor thought I was having a fit? Did you know any of that? No, of course you didn't, and I would never tell you.

'Thanks,' I said coldly.

'Sorry, bad choice of words.' The line crackled. 'Lizzy, I don't have much time, I'm afraid, I'm working today and I'm late. I'll have to go soon.'

'To shag someone in the photocopying room?' I said in my head. 'Right, well, what is it?' is what I actually said.

'Well,' David began. 'Sorry, I'm not putting this very well.'

'What?' I said.

'It's about – God, this sounded OK when I was thinking it through but now it just sounds fucking ridiculous.'

'Don't swear,' I said automatically, which is what I used to say as a reflex whenever he did. One Lent, his mum tried to make him pay her a pound each time he swore. He was thirty at the time. She'd worked out she could retire to Jamaica after two weeks, but he never paid up.

'I'd forgotten that,' David said. He sounded remote.

'OK,' I said. I could feel it in my chest – the tightness, the shortness of breath like a panic attack . . . the delirious rush of being someone else, someone I used to be. I pulled myself up. 'I saw Chin today and she told me about you seeing us at Christmas. At the pub. I'm sorry, I hope you don't think we were – well, we *were* avoiding you. But not in a rude way.'

David coughed. 'Oh, Lizzy, for God's sake, that doesn't matter. I'd forgotten about it. Good grief, I'm a big boy, you know, I can cope with – I was meeting Chin for a drink to talk about stuff. Look, we're getting off the subject.'

'I'm so sorry,' I said, irritated. I try to apologize and it turns out he was grateful to us for hiding from him. Cor, this conversation was going well.

'Be quiet for two seconds, will you?' David cleared his throat. 'I was just ringing to see if you were OK about last time.'

'Last time?'

'Well, what happened in the kitchen. I – I was just ringing to say . . . were you OK about it? Because if not, I'm sorry, I shouldn't have done it.'

'You shouldn't have done . . .'

'I shouldn't have kissed you. I was drunk.' He cleared his throat again. 'Lizzy?'

'Yes, hello,' I said. 'You were drunk.'

'Yeah, wasted. I drank far too much, there you were, all the old memories, haze of red wine – then bam!'

'You were so mashed you jumped on me,' I said.

'Er . . . yes. No. Well, I wasn't *that* drunk. I'm not saying I was so pissed I didn't know what I was doing but, well, you know how it is.'

Jesus, he sounded almost *jaunty*. 'No,' I said pointedly.

'So . . . er . . . were you OK about it?' he said.

'Me?' I said, trying to buy myself a few seconds. 'Me? Ha.'

'Right,' David said. I could hear him breathing as he walked up and down the corridor in his apartment.

'What are you doing?' I said, playing for time.

'Putting my coat on. I'm going to be late.'

'Right,' I said. 'No, of course I was fine.'

'Were you?' David said.

'Me?' I laughed, and tried to toss my hair in a devil-may-care fashion. 'God, of course. Yeah. It wasn't all you, you know. I was drunk too. Really, I was knee-walking drunk. Yeah. I was sick everywhere afterwards. *Everywhere*. I was much drunker than you.'

'Right, then,' David said.

I carried on: 'It was great to see you, though. Tom and Jess were really pleased. So thanks for coming. Sorry about the food. That's why I was so drunk I expect, no food and all that. Jaden had to put me to bed, yeah. After I'd been sick everywhere. Because I was so drunk.'

David cleared his throat. 'Well, good. That's partly why I wanted to make sure everything was OK. I didn't want to cause any problems with you and – Jaden. Make you think anything weird was up. That's great about Jaden and—'

Someone else's voice floated over in the background. 'David?'

'In a minute,' David shot back, under his breath.

'Who's that?' I asked sharply. Lisa. Oh, my God, she was there. He called me while she was in his apartment. I leaned against the wall.

David said, in a low voice, 'I can't explain now.'

'Yes, you fucking can.'

'Don't swear,' he said softly.

'Don't make old jokes with me when your new girlfriend's listening in to our conversation,' I hissed. 'I'm going now, goodbye.'

'Lizzy!' David said sharply. 'Don't go. Liz?'

'I'm here.'

'It's not my new girlfriend, as you put it. God. Women. It's . . . Well, it's a bit awkward. That's also why I was ringing.'

'Mm?'

'It's . . . Rosalie. She's . . . She's staying with me.'

'*What?*' I said, not believing my ears.

'Yes. And I'm not sure . . . Do you know what's happened?' He sounded hesitant. 'With her and Mike?'

'Oh, yes,' I said. My mind was racing. What was going on? Men. They were as straightforward as a room full of rubbish.

'Have you spoken to Mike?'

'No,' I said impatiently. '*Rosalie*'s staying with you? David, why?'

There was a pause. Then David lowered his voice so I could barely hear him. 'She's really upset. She needs someone to look out for her. We're . . . close.'

We're close. What the fuck does that mean? I thought, as a horrid suspicion took root. I swallowed. It absolutely couldn't be that.

'Look, has anyone said anything to you about why she left?' David said.

'No,' I said, my mind full of half-answered questions. 'Stop a minute, David. Does Mike know where she is? Mum says he's been really worried about her. We all are. Can't she just ring him and tell him she's staying with you?'

'I'm going to do that later,' David said. 'I need to have a chat with him, anyway.'

'David, is that why you were ringing?' I said.

'I wanted to apologize,' David said. 'I didn't want you to find out Rosalie was here, not yet, anyway. She needs some time to – well, think about stuff. God, this is awkward. So you haven't spoken to your parents?'

I put my hand on my chest to calm myself, and tried to keep my voice steady. 'No, I haven't.'

'Miles says you won't go home and see them, that you're avoiding them. Is that true?'

'No,' I lied, my mind whirling. 'It's not really your business, David. I haven't been home yet because . . . well, I've been really busy. I've got lots to do. My boss wants me to go to LA for a year and I don't want to. And other things. I—'

I wished more than anything that I could ask his advice. About LA; did he think it might be a good idea? About Rosalie and Mike. About why we were having to sell the house. About Jaden. But I forced myself to concentrate on the matter at hand.

'What? You're so busy you can't hop on a train and go and see your parents?' David said. 'For one night?'

'It's not that,' I said. 'It's—'

'Or are you too busy with your new boyfriend?'

'What?'

'Sorry,' David said immediately. 'It's none of my business what you do in your spare time. I just – I think perhaps—'

'Hold on a second.' I was so furious I choked and coughed. 'Hold on a second,' I said again. 'How dare you? For a start, you're right, it's absolutely none of your business what I do now, not after what you did. For a – well, for seconds, I'm not the one providing a shoulder to cry on for someone when she's at the root of all this trouble anyway! And I can go home whenever I want, thanks very much. So. Just mind your own business, David. Or, since you can't do that, at the very least stay out of mine. I mean it.'

'With pleasure,' David said acidly. 'As ever, you've jumped to every one of the wrong conclusions, Lizzy. You're always banging on about that bloody house, how much you all love it, and at the first sign of trouble you bury your head in the sand and bleat about how awful it all is.'

'What?' I said, tears springing into my eyes.

'You're all like that, all of you. Take Mike, living in a fantasy-land, not caring how much he hurts other people. But you're as bad, Lizzy. I used to love that about you, your elaborate daydreams and ridiculous fantasies, but it's not funny any more. Go home and see your parents. Ask them why the house is really being sold. Get them to tell you the truth. Then go to LA if you want. Forget about it all, start a new life. Just take charge of something for once. Stop living in a dream.'

In the background, I heard Rosalie's voice: 'She'll find out, David. Just leave it alone.'

I hadn't realized until then just how much David disliked me. But I heard the disdain in his voice, the weariness, the lack of anything approaching respect, and in many ways that was the worst thing of all.

'Anyway, listen,' he said. But I'd had enough.

I said softly, 'No, David, you listen to me. Don't ever, *ever* call me again and don't *ever* talk like that about my uncle or anyone in my family. I'm glad Rosalie's moved in with you. She didn't waste much time, did she?' I took another deep breath. 'It shows the kind of person she is. I never really liked her – none of us did. So you're welcome to her. In fact I could almost say you deserve each other. I'm putting the phone down now.'

I turned it off. I was shaking so much I had to sit down again.

The next day I went home.

TWENTY-ONE

Kate had said she'd meet me off the train on her way home from the butcher's. I stood waiting for her outside the red-brick station, shivering and rueing my decision to wear my new pale blue, rather thin spring coat (not appropriate here but Lovely! Tweedy, a frayed trim with large pockets but very slimming). As Kate's battered Mini Metro came into view round the corner and pulled up in front of me I clapped my hands together in relief.

'Freezing, isn't it?' I said, once we were on our way to the house.

Kate didn't answer. She chewed her lip as she negotiated a tricky T-junction. She hates needless yabber, as she would say.

I tried my luck once more. 'Any news from Mike?' I asked hopefully.

'Nope, nothing,' she said briefly.

We drove along various lanes in silence. The banks and hedgerows were coming to life again: the daffodils were out in force and pale yellow primroses were dotted beside the road. I felt strangely calm to be going home, despite the big deal I'd made about it. Don't think about it now, think about

231

it later. Think about it before Chin's wedding, worry about it then, I'd told myself, as winter slid into spring and time ran out. Now, driving along the roads I knew so well, with the sun shining in through the windscreen, I wondered how I could have stayed away so long when soon I wouldn't be going to Keeper House ever again. It seemed stupid beyond belief.

We turned the last corner, and I could see the side of the house opening up before me. Kate slowed to let another car go past, a flashy black jeep with bull bars and blacked-out windows. It screeched to a halt just past us as we turned right, and someone yelled, 'Mrs Walter! Hey, Mrs Walter!'

Kate stopped, and we both turned. Two long, rather bony white legs appeared from the jeep. 'Oi! Mrs Walter! God, these bloody shoes . . .' Suddenly the legs slipped out on to the muddy road, followed by the unmistakable surgically enhanced torso and face of SOKH's evil nemesis, Simone (née Sarah) Caldwell. She was wearing a red Lycra mini-skirt, black platform wedges, and a huge black padded jacket, like bouncers wear outside nightclubs. Even at school, Simone had been a stranger to leisurewear. She had her car keys and a mobile phone in one hand, and a little boy in the other.

'Oh, Mrs Walter,' she said, hurrying towards us. She peered in through my window at Kate. 'I'm so sorry to bother you.'

I could see the front door of Keeper House opening, and I didn't want Simone to notice. What was she doing here?

The boy under her arm whimpered.

'Shut it, Dior,' she said. 'Now, which one are you? I'm so sorry about this, my memory's terrible. Stu's always saying to me, "Simone, your memory's terrible." '

Kate was looking at her with something akin to horror, mixed with alarm. 'I'm Kate,' she said.

232

'Are you the one whose husband died?' Simone asked tenderly, leaning over me. Kate nodded. 'So . . . you were married to – what was his name?'

'Tony.'

'That must have been awful. Was it awful?'

Kate nodded again. 'Well, er, yes,' she said.

'Look, I'm sorry to bother you,' Simone said, shifting Dior on her hip. 'Shut up, all right? I just wanted to see if I could pop round again some time to have a look at the upstairs so I can start thinking up ideas, get a feel for what needs doing.'

'What you think needs doing, you mean,' Kate said pointedly.

'Yeah, that's it. But I don't want to intrude, OK? So I was just driving past to see if anyone was in, you know. Is now a good time?'

'No!' I said suddenly, making Kate jump. I wanted to punch Simone's stupid face in. How dare she be hanging around outside, like a vulture? I smiled at her briefly. 'Now's not a good time, Simone.'

'Well, when will be a good time?' Simone said.

'I'll get Mum to give you a call,' I said. ''Bye.'

'OK, that'd be great,' Simone said, unperturbed.

I pressed the button and closed the window. 'That was a bit rude,' Kate said. She drove on, leaving Simone waving and smiling in the middle of the road.

Stupid Simone, the horrible, silly witch.

Kate pulled into the drive and stopped the car. I gazed up at the front of the house, trying to recall what it had felt like to come back before all this, at Christmas. Why couldn't I remember? It looked the same as ever, welcoming, mellow, beautifully proportioned, generous, tidy and sprawling at the same time, but somehow completely different, as if already it didn't belong to us, as if it wasn't our home any more.

233

Mum and Dad had heard the car and were waiting by the door, Dad with his arm round Mum. As I got out they came rushing over. I gave them each a big hug. The gravel crunched beneath my feet, the old familiar sound.

'Who was that?' said Dad.

Kate might be scary but she's not a snitch. 'Simone Caldwell. She wonders if maybe you could call her. She wants to pop round later this week to have a look upstairs.'

'Again?' Dad said. 'Good grief. Why doesn't she just move in now?'

'She'd like that, John,' Kate said. 'She's got a crush on you, I've always thought so.'

'No, she hasn't,' Dad said stoutly.

'Of course she has,' Mum said. 'How many times did she come to look round the house? Three. And each time she followed John from room to room, looking like – oh, I don't know. Me at a Kinks concert. Waah! Oh, John!'

She and Kate dissolved into hysterical laughter at the idea that anyone could have a crush on poor Dad. Suddenly I remembered that he'd found Simone once, when she was a teenager, drunk and unconscious in the hedge by the bus-stop down the road from Keeper House. He had brought her back, stuck her head under the tap and given her some strong black coffee. For this reason he had earned himself her undying devotion, and this was why Mum was convinced she had a wee crush on him. Perhaps it was also for this reason that she'd decided her greatest wish was to live in the house where her greatest humiliation had taken place.

'Well, enough of that,' said Mum. 'It's nearly time for lunch so let's have a drink. Oh, it's lovely to see you.'

Dad followed her and they disappeared into the kitchen. Kate went to park the car round the side, and I was left alone in the hall. After the jangle of the Tube, the rattle of the train and the bangs and thumps of Kate's car, the sudden silence was deafening. I could hear my heart thumping. I looked up to the window by the stairs, where the sun poured in, casting an amber shadow on the wooden boards where I stood. Dust motes danced in each shaft of light. Through the window I could see the other arm of the house to the right, and the rows of green shrubby lavender. In the near distance I could just make out the lichen-covered cherub statue that stood at the centre of the walled garden.

Well, I was back where I'd wanted to be all along. Why wasn't it enough? What had I been expecting, when Kate's car turned into the drive and I saw my home again after three months away? That everything would feel better again? Next to me, the grandfather clock ticked quietly, but I felt as if time was standing still, that this moment would stay with me for ever.

I was glad I'd come back, but I had no idea how I was going to tell Mum and Dad about Rosalie. The back of my jaw tensed and I gritted my teeth. Well, I thought, as I swallowed hard and wiped my nose, let's get on with it, girl. I picked up my overnight bag and felt like Julie Andrews arriving at Captain von Trapp's enormous Schloss.

Kate appeared behind me. 'What are you doing, standing in the hall like you've seen a ghost?' she said, placing her car keys on the hall table with a clatter. She pulled open the poppers on her battered green Husky jacket and hung it on the coat rack, as I watched. It was cold in the hall, though the sun was bright. It was too early in the year for the house to have properly warmed up yet, and Dad would still light a fire in the evening. But the cold didn't bother Kate. She slapped her hands against her thighs.

'I'll go and sit down,' I said, suddenly feeling like a spare part. I wandered into the sitting room, where the afternoon sun had not yet penetrated. It was dark and chilly, and I pulled the curtains a little further back. As I did so, I remembered Mike's face appearing at the window on Christmas Eve, and the shadowy figure behind him who would cause so much trouble. Poor Mike. Grey ash from a previous fire, probably the night before, lay in the grate. A forgotten coffee cup stood by the fender. I picked it up and placed it on the table as the door opened and Mum came in with some wine. 'I made a quiche,' she said hopefully.

'Lovely,' I said, although the thought of food made me feel ill.

Mum handed me a glass. 'Dad's just coming,' she said.

Kate appeared at the door. 'Come in, Kate, sit down,' Mum said.

'Oh, Suzy . . .' Kate hesitated. 'Shall I just go and start the greens?'

'Don't be silly,' Mum said firmly. 'It's all under control. Lizzy, darling,' she continued, 'when are you going back?'

'In the morning, Mum. I've got to go to work.'

'Oh. I'd thought you might be able to take tomorrow off.'

'I didn't know I was coming,' I said. 'I told you on the phone. I can't just take tomorrow off without giving anyone any warning.'

'Couldn't you pretend to be ill? We haven't seen you for such a long time, darling.'

'Mum!' I said. 'You're a doctor! You can't go around suggesting people skive off work!'

Mum looked crestfallen. 'Chin's coming down next weekend to measure the garden again,' she said.

'I'll be down then too,' I said, 'if that's OK. And the weekend after that – I've got a couple of days' holiday spare so perhaps I could make it a long weekend. Help you with the preparations, and everything.'

Mum smiled radiantly at me. 'Oh, Lizzy, that would be wonderful. I just think you'll regret it if you don't spend as much time here as you can before we have to go. Jess is coming next week for ten days. She's doing a project up here and she gets two weeks off to do it.'

'God. Students!' Kate muttered.

'Great,' I said. 'Perhaps Tom'll come too.'

'He is,' Mum said.

Of course he was. I'd been so selfish cutting myself off from the house and my parents since the sale had happened.

'How's Miles?' Mum said. 'Have you seen him recently?'

'Yes,' I said. 'I had him round to supper the other night, actually. With Tom and Jess. David, too. It was nice.'

'Oh!' said Mum, looking amazed. 'Uh-huh. David – that's nice. How is he?'

'He was fine,' I said nonchalantly. 'He only came because he was over for the weekend, staying with Miles.'

'Righty-ho,' Mum said. 'Well, that's lovely. God, this bloody radiator.' She leaped up unexpectedly. 'It bangs and bangs and absolutely no heat comes out of it. What's wrong with it?'

'It's the boiler,' Dad said, appearing in the doorway. 'I give up. It's the Caldwells' problem now, not ours.'

'Lucky them,' Mum said. 'Two months' time, and I'll have a boiler that works. Imagine that!'

'Mum!' I said, shocked at such sacrilege.

'That was Mike,' Dad said, sitting down.

'Oh, really?' said Mum.

'I didn't hear the phone ring,' Kate said, looking startled.

'You were still outside,' Dad told her.

'What did he say?' Mum said.

'How did he sound?' Kate said.

'OK,' Dad said. 'Actually, not great. Still no news, I told him.'

This was the moment I should speak up, I thought, and say what I'd come to say. But my heart quailed. It was just too awful – and I'd probably got it all wrong. I couldn't

237

just tap my glass with a pen and say, 'I have an announcement. I think we should get Mike on speaker phone for this. I have a strong suspicion that his wife of two months has shacked up with my ex-boyfriend.'

'Poor Mike,' was all I said.

'And poor Rosalie,' Mum said.

'Not poor Rosalie,' I said.

'Well,' Mum said hurriedly, 'I think we can eat. Come on through, darling. How's work?'

Dad struggled out of his chair again, grumbling, and we walked through to the dining room. It was so strange being back there in the dark cold house, these three adults and me feeling like someone they'd just invited in off the street. Already it wasn't the home I'd grown up in. Something was missing.

'Work's good, thanks,' I said, and stopped. You can always tell if people are asking out of interest or just want a marker that the question's been asked.

'When Tom was here last week he was saying something about you having a trip to LA,' said Mum, as she brought in a tray from the kitchen. 'John, napkins.'

'Shall I get the mustard, Suzy?' Kate said.

'Oh, yes, please,' Mum said, placing the quiche on the table. 'Salt and pepper, too, thanks.'

'Yes,' I said, putting some bread on Dad's plate.

'Knife?' Kate said, popping her head round the door.

'Long trip?' Dad said, handing me a napkin.

'Maybe,' I said.

'How long's long?' Mum said, slicing the quiche up. 'Can you toss the salad?'

'Well, I don't know,' I said, grabbing the salad servers. 'It'd be exciting, though, wouldn't it?'

'Ooh, yes,' said Mum. 'I'd love to go to California. Beryl and Graham Edwards went last autumn on a tour of the

238

wine-growing region. They stayed in San Francisco for a few days afterwards. It's a beautiful part of the world, you know. Absolutely stunning, they said.' My mother is one of the few people I know who can take a job offer at a film studio in sleazy, smoggy, eight-lane-highway LA and turn it into Beryl and Graham's vineyard tour complete with souvenir tea-towels. I handed her the salad.

'Well, that's exciting,' Dad said. 'Would you be able to have some holiday afterwards?'

'I don't know,' I said. 'Really, it's up in the air at the moment. This quiche looks delicious, Mum. So, the bungalow – that's all going OK, is it?'

'Yep,' said Dad, briefly. 'Survey's fine, couple of problems with the electrics, but we got them sorted out. We should be in there by June, all being well.'

His words echoed around the large, empty room where at Christmas we'd been scrunched up together along the table, nudging each other for lack of space. I shivered.

'Are you cold, darling?' Mum said.

'No, not particularly,' I said, lying.

'The heating's terrible at the moment, I'm afraid. The whole thing is.' She sighed, and I followed her gaze to where the daffodils sprang out of the edge of the lawn, beside the kitchen garden. 'Still . . .'

An afternoon gloom settled in the room, and outside the bare soil of the garden beds was black, empty, crowding in on the view. We sat in near silence for the rest of the meal.

After lunch, Kate went back to her cottage, Dad lit a fire, and Mum put on some music. Then we went into the kitchen to clear up.

'So, next weekend,' Mum said, 'Tom and Jess are coming, and Chin, of course. No Gibbo, unfortunately – he's away teaching a course.'

'Teaching?' I said, almost dropping a plate in amazement.

'Absolutely,' Mum said, with pride. 'It's a woodwork workshop. The basics of carpentry, that sort of thing.'

'Well I never,' I said. 'I think he'd be a great teacher, though, don't you?'

'That's the funny thing,' said Dad, coming in with some logs. 'I wouldn't trust him to walk upstairs without falling over, but I'd trust him any day with a jigsaw and a power drill.'

'Deffo,' I said.

'Your mother wants him to build some cupboards in the new place,' Dad said. 'I think it's a good idea, don't you? He's made some beautiful things.'

'Oh,' I said, hating yet another mention of the bungalow. 'I don't know. You should wait till you're in there and think about it then.'

'Maybe,' Dad said.

'But we know what we want,' said Mum, wiping down the surfaces with a cloth. 'Budge over, Lizzy.'

'You won't properly till you're in there. Perhaps you should leave it a while.'

'We know what we want,' Mum repeated, running the tap. 'Something simple, clean, no hassle. A back door that doesn't swell every winter for starters.'

'A roof that doesn't leak,' said Dad, putting coffee into the cafetière.

'A bath that isn't a hundred years old and takes over an hour to fill,' Mum said.

'Well, you won't have any of that stuff in the bungalow, will you?' I said.

'No,' said Mum. 'We won't.'

You are my parents, I thought, and you are perfectly willing, happy even, to give up this house, sell it for reasons I don't understand, and move on without a backward glance.

'It's just,' Mum said, 'that sometimes I think it might be a good idea for all of us not to have this house any more.'

'You're wrong,' I said, with a lump in my throat. 'Don't say that.'

Dad poured water over the coffee. Mum folded up the tea-towels and slid them neatly into the rail of the Aga. 'We didn't choose to leave, Lizzy,' she said eventually. 'We're making the best of it. We don't have much choice.' She moved towards me. 'It'll all be OK, you know, because we've still got each other, and our girls, haven't we?' She hugged me. 'That's what's important, isn't it?'

'Yes,' I said, tears springing to my eyes. 'That's what's important.' I squeezed her hard.

'The house isn't part of us, and we'll be fine without it. But when I think about leaving the place, where you grew up, and your dad and Tony, Mike and Chin – and their dad and Uncle Charles before them, and before them . . . Oh dear.' she wiped her nose on one of the tea-towels. 'Brrraaah,' she said. 'Sometimes it makes me a bit sad.'

'Oh, Suzy,' Dad said, putting his arm round her and kissing the top of her head. 'Come on, old girl. Where are those chocs Miles brought the other day?'

Mum looked about her. 'Damn, I just saw them – I'm sure.'

'Miles?' I said.

'Yes,' Mum said. 'He was down seeing Alice. She gave your father some chocolates as a thank you – he helped her start her car a couple of weeks ago. Miles dropped them off.'

'Ah,' I said, pleased. 'I saw him last week. How was he?'

'Oh, ever so well,' Mum said, sloshing milk into her coffee. 'He's nice, isn't he? So easy to talk to. And so funny.'

'Yes, he is,' I said, eyeing the chocolates.

'He was telling us about that friend of yours from work,'

Mum said. 'He did a hilarious impression of him. What's his name?'

'Ash?' I said.

'No . . .' Mum rubbed her forehead. 'Weird name. Something to do with porous rocks.'

'No,' Dad said patiently. 'You're thinking of jade. It's not a porous rock, anyway. His name was Jaden.'

'Oh, God!' I said, laughing. '*Jaden*. Oh, Mum.'

'Where's he from?' Mum said. 'Such a strange name.'

'California, actually,' I said.

'And he's a friend from work?' Mum said curiously.

'Yes,' I said.

'Lizzy?' Mum said, ultra-cautiously. 'Ooh. Right.'

'No, Mum,' I said. 'Don't get all excited. He's – well, Jaden. How do I describe him?' Jaden is a gorgeous, funny, kind, intelligent man with whom I have a close, companionable friendship. Oh, and he's great in the sack too. But, before you get too excited, he is also a tanned, slightly camp, intense, beansprout-lovin' freak of whom I am fond but no more than that. However, I didn't think that was the best way to put it.

'He's . . . well . . .' I paused. 'He's someone to get you through the long winter months.' Perhaps that wasn't either.

'Ah,' said Dad, who looked as if he'd been forced to sit among a studio audience and watch a taping of *Trisha*.

'Right, then,' said Mum, wearing an expression that said more than I had thought it might. 'He sounds nice.'

'He is,' I said. 'He's great. Mad, though. He's going back to LA soon – I'm going to miss him.'

'Well, you'll see him if you go over there, won't you?' said Mum, who wasn't really listening now, having become distracted by the little plant on her side table.

'I will,' I said. 'What was Miles saying about him?'

'Oh, he was just quite funny about him. He sounded quite . . . Californian,' Mum said.

What's wrong with that? I wondered. Bloody sight better to be 'Californian' and get things done than mouldering around all day moaning about how awful everything is and letting things fester. I felt a sudden rush of loyalty to Jaden and the slices of lemon he kept in a labelled Tupperware box in his man-bag, so he could have one in some hot water whenever he felt his system needed cleansing. The thing is, I always used to think hot water with lemon was a complete waste of time – why drink it when you could have wine? – but actually it's rather refreshing. And that was symbolic of Jaden, in a way. Good grief, listen to me.

'Lovely coffee, darling,' Mum said, wiggling her toes in front of the fire.

'Have a choc,' Dad said, handing me the box. He picked up the bellows.

'Hey, they work!' I said, pleased. The bellows had been temperamental for about two years, since Mike had used them at Kate's birthday dinner to see if you could blow up a balloon with them then stepped on them by mistake.

'Actually,' Dad said, 'Miles mended them last week. Brilliant idea. He used a furniture tack to keep the flap section in place. I don't know where he got it from, but well done him. They work like a charm, now. He was funny about it. I'd thought we were having a pretty good chat, but he got all embarrassed that he'd helped, didn't want to outstay his welcome, and practically ran out to the car.'

'Ah, bless him,' I said. 'He's always been a bit like that. Don't worry.'

'But he couldn't have been more helpful,' Mum said. 'It was nice to see him. He's been a good friend, hasn't he?'

'Yes, he has,' I said.

I could see Mum's eyes were starting to close, so I said in a rush, 'Mike still doesn't know where Rosalie is, then?'

'No, no idea,' Mum murmured. Dad rocked back on his

heels and stood up. 'We might have seen the last of her. Terrible shame, because I was starting to like the idea of her. But no. I think in Mike's book it goes under the heading "The Ones Who Got Away". Silly man.'

'I don't know,' I said. 'Do we have the full story yet?'

Mum darted a look at me, and then at Dad, but he had sunk into his chair and was already asleep.

TWENTY-TWO

It was awful saying goodbye to the house, and to Mum and Dad, early on that Monday morning, climbing into Mum's battered old estate and being flung out unceremoniously at the station as she was late for work, to have to squeeze up next to a man who smelt of stale beer all the way back to London. But I'd be home again on Saturday – and now that I knew I could go back, and that it wasn't too awful, other things fell into place. For the first time since Christmas, I felt as if my life wasn't standing still any more.

I'd caught such a ferociously early train that I got to the office at an unheard-of hour. I stopped off at Luigi's to pick up two lattes, one for Ash, one for me, and as I stood in the queue I ran over the checklist in my head of the various things I had to do that day. Work was a bit of a nightmare at the moment, and the thought of running away to LA grew more appealing with every minute. The location for our biggest project of the year, *The Diary of Lady Mary Chartley*, had fallen through.

It was going to be an amazing film, the true story of a girl from an aristocratic family who had an idyllic, sheltered life before the First World War and then watches as an entire generation of the young men she has known is wiped out. Eventually, this girl, who's never known anything more distressing than a buckle falling off her shoe, goes to France to be a nurse. Not a dry eye in the house. Lily was bouncing off every wall in our office as this was a huge deal for us and it was supposed to start shooting in a few weeks' time. It was our big boss Paul's grand passion, and now it looked like it might come to nothing. The Americans were getting involved and even Lily's new best friend Fran was pissed off. So I was keeping my head down, trying to get on with things and avoiding Lily as much as I could.

But as I was pulling up the blinds on Monday morning and realizing I was so early that the children in the school opposite were still in the playground, Lily rushed in to our office, looking ashen.

'Lizzy! Oh, God, Lizzy, what a nightmare. I hate Americans, did you know that?'

'You *are* American,' I said, turning on my computer.

'No, I'm not,' Lily said in outrage. 'My father was. Pennsylvania Dutch. My mother's from Ireland. And Jamaica.'

'Wow,' I said.

'Wow nothing,' Lily said, flinging herself into her chair and typing something, fingers racing furiously across the keyboard. 'Anyway, I hate them. That Fran's a witch – did you know that?'

'I thought she was your new best friend,' I said, spreading Marmite on my toast from Luigi's.

Lily ignored me. 'And if bloody Paul rings me once again from his frigging breakdown centre and starts yelling about *Lady Mary* I'm going to scream. He can shove it. It's a stupid film! They don't know what they're doing. They don't understand this kind of film. It's not freaking *Miss Congeniality*, for God's sake.'

'Righty-ho,' I said. 'It kind of is *Miss Congeniality*, though, isn't it?'

'Don't be stupid, Lizzy,' Lily snapped. She said, as though reciting something, 'It's a beautifully paced, moving story about the tragedy of war.'

'But it's not, though,' I said, settling in for the long haul. 'It's got a bit of Sandra Bullock in it. Come on, Lily.'

'No, it hasn't!' Lily yelled. 'Have you actually read it? It's so moving! She's so great!'

'Yes, she is,' I said, 'but she's a young girl, having a good time until war breaks out. She kisses boys! She steals a brooch from her horrible aunt! She's a real person! And if you make it into some worthy do-gooding film with loads of sub-RSC faces in it it'll play for two weeks at the Curzon Soho, then disappear without trace.'

Lily glared at me, then smiled. 'You're wrong.'

'I'm right,' I said. 'You know I'm right. You need a Hollywood star in it, you really do. It's got to be relevant to people today otherwise they won't go and see it.'

'True.' Lily sighed. 'True. God! Fuck – what if you're right? Can you call Nicole Hegerty this afternoon and schedule a call about it all? She likes you. Horrible woman.'

'She's not horrible. She's just different from you, Lily. A bit.'

The famous Nicole Hegerty wasn't actually that bad. Granted, she was scary, but she got the job done and she treated you with respect, which is more than a lot of film people do.

Lily drank some coffee. 'Have you looked at the job spec for that LA job I sent you?'

'No,' I said, keeping my eyes on the screen and typing fast. 'I'm not interested. Sorry, Lily.'

'You're making a mistake,' Lily said. 'For me, mainly. How much better would my life be if you went? So much better.' She paused. 'Hey, do one thing for me, will you, sweetheart?'

'Yep,' I said. I didn't look round but I stopped typing.

'Just think about it, will you? It's a real job. I don't think you get that. Someone's going to take it. If it's not you they'll get someone else in to do it. Just have one last think about it, OK? It'd be perfect for you. That's all.'

'Why, though?' I said. 'Are you trying to get rid of me?'

Lily patted my knee. 'You're good, Lizzy, really good. I don't want to lose you. But you need some perspective at the moment. You need to look around you a bit more if you're going to make it to the next level.' She whirled round in her chair and started typing again.

'Right,' I said. I took a sip of my coffee. 'Er, what do you mean, perspective?'

Lily carried on typing. 'Look, Lizzy, you're a talented girl and I know you've had a hard time lately. This is your chance to wipe the slate clean. I know you can do this job. And the timing's perfect. You've had your eye off the ball a bit recently, haven't you?' She paused at her screen. 'You haven't done anything wrong. I'm just saying – go to LA, prove how great you are to me and everyone else. Get back in the game.'

Lily never has a go. She's not one of those bosses who likes pretending to be friends, then behaves like a total bitch. Or one of those bosses who doesn't care whom they trample on to get their way. She's a great nipper of problems in the bud. If she's not happy about something, she'll usually find some way to sort it out before it becomes a problem. I glanced at her gratefully. 'Thanks, Lily,' I said, and got up to take Ash his coffee.

'Sure, whatever,' she said, waggling her head. 'Off you go, then.'

* * *

I looked at the job spec, as she'd asked. And I liked the sound of it. I thought about it. And I knew who I wanted to talk it over with. I hadn't seen Jaden since before all this began, only once at the office since the dinner party, but we'd spoken on the phone several times, and he'd said he'd cook me supper on Wednesday. I'd eaten at his place once before, with some other friends from work, as I knew his food was almost inedible, I had a sandwich in the office at about tea-time. At the end of the day I paused only to take off my elasticated M&S support pants in the loo and put on my best black lacy ones. I left the office as it was starting to get dark, throwing a casual lie at Ash that I was going to meet some old friends in a pub.

He regarded me with an expression of bewilderment. 'Have a good evening, then. With your friends. Who are old. In a pub.'

'Thanks, Ash. See you tomorrow.'

Ash sighed, and went back to his computer.

Whether he felt pity for me in general, or because he thought I was way off with Jaden, I have no idea. I think the truth is closer to his belief that Jaden and I were wasting time with each other when we could have been out sourcing potential life-partners and planning joint mortgages.

He is also a fanatical film buff, so that lunchtime, while we were sitting in his office eating sandwiches, I'd tried a different tack. 'Have you seen *The Philadelphia Story*?' I said, opening my apple juice.

'Of course,' Ash said.

'He's James Stewart in that,' I said, taking a swig. 'Jaden is, I mean. He's the sexy reporter bloke who gets Tracy Lord all in a lather. But she knows it's just a bit of fun.'

'And who are you?' Ash said, interested.

'I'm Tracy Lord,' I said, affronted. 'Obviously.'

'Oh, right,' Ash said. 'Really?'

'Yes!' I said.

'Who's Cary Grant, then?'

'What?' I said. 'Where?'

'In your version of it,' Ash said. He drummed his pencil on his desk. 'Who's Cary Grant?'

'Good question,' I said. 'It's not Jaden, though.'

'I'm bloody glad you realize that, at any rate,' Ash said.

However, after supper, as I surveyed the orange sitting room of Jaden's nightmarish, rather than retro, seventies-throwback flat, I asked myself why I was always so rude about him when he wasn't there. I rolled back on his bean-bag and nursed a glass of wine, while he grabbed some fruit from the kitchen. Perhaps it was that the idea of Jaden is much more ridiculous than the actuality. In real life he's . . . nice. He's so calm and mad in his own way that I could be exactly who I wanted to be with him, so I was actually just myself, no games.

I'd been right about the food. There were beans, each the size of a small purse, as a starter, then beansprouts in some weird tomato and peanut dressing for the main course. It tasted like horse bedding. I shuddered at the memory and downed some more wine.

My host reappeared with some lychees and sat down next to me. 'Sorry about the bean-bags,' he said, for the second time that evening. (Apart from a TV/video and a stereo system, the bean-bags, three chairs and a table comprised the furniture in Jaden's sitting room.) 'My flatmates really love them. I'm not so sure.'

'Where are they tonight?' I said.

'At a party for some guy they know. On a boat. It's highly probable they won't be back tonight. Anyway,' he peeled a lychee and handed it to me, 'thanks for coming here. I know you don't like it.'

'It's not that,' I said. 'It's just a bit . . . studenty. Maybe. But it's nice.'

'Yeah. I know what you mean,' Jaden said reasonably. 'In the place I've got in LA, I can drive to the ocean in five minutes, and I can see three palm trees out of my bedroom window.'

'Nice,' I said enviously. I could see brick wall and Paddington Green Police Station from my flat. I had a sudden vision of waking up, opening my window and looking out over the Californian hills to the bright blue sea.

Jaden handed me some more lychees. 'So, you went home,' he said conversationally.

'Yup,' I said.

'And how was it?'

'It was fine. It was . . . great, actually.'

'I guess it must have been kind of depressing, though. Like if you make doing something into a big deal, whether it's good or bad, it's always a let-down when it finally happens.'

'Yes,' I said. 'You're right.'

'Good to be at home where you belong, though, right?'

'Oh, yes,' I said confidently. 'It's just—'

'What?' Jaden said, busying himself with another lychee.

I remembered how overwhelming it had been to step through the front door, to stand there and know I was home again. But . . . 'It's funny,' I said. 'I always feel safe there, I'm always hoping I can go back there. But . . . it's just something my mum said. In the kitchen. I've been thinking it's so important, Keeper House, being at home. And, actually, it's not. Is it?'

I was thinking of Mike, alone in Rosalie's flat, wondering where she was. Not knowing she was with David, in an anti-Walter pressurized environment, a bit like a can of anti-freeze, actually. I was thinking of Mum and Dad, making

251

the best of a bad deal and looking for the good points in their new home, of Tom, working himself far too hard. I wanted them to be happy – we didn't have to have the house for that. I didn't have to be there to feel at home. And I didn't have to have home to help me do things. Perhaps it was the opposite.

'It's not important, no,' said Jaden. 'My sister lives in Houston, Mom lives in Colorado, Dad lives in Michigan, I live in California, and we take it in turns to spend Thanksgiving at each other's houses.'

'Really?' I said, intrigued.

'Well, not Dad so much since he married Kelly,' Jaden said. ''Cause she's not something my mom's particularly thankful for.' He smiled. 'But when we're all together, we're . . . together. You know? And I'm happy about it. I go back to Colorado, where I grew up, mountains, snow all year round, and I love it. I feel at home at my mom's, I see my old friends, I go places I used to go on my trail bike. OK? And then I get home to LA. I'm by the ocean, I can do my yoga, I can walk on the beach, make miso soup and do all that other crap you think is kinda funny.'

'Yes, that's exactly it,' I said. 'Completely. That was what it was like this weekend, I suppose.'

'Anyway, about that,' said Jaden, sliding the smooth burgundy lychee stone out between his lips and putting it into the bowl at his feet. He wiped his fingers carefully on a piece of tissue, and turned round on the bean-bag to face me. This took more shuffling than one would have thought, so we were both giggling when he'd finished.

'OK, hear me out, QE Three,' Jaden said, picking up another lychee and running a nail over the spiky shell. 'You know I'm going back next month?'

'Three weeks' time, yes?' I said.

Jaden nodded. 'I booked my ticket yesterday, and it cost,

252

like, nothing. And that got me thinking, and then I just thought, Lily's offered her that job so why don't I ask Lizzy properly to come and stay with me there?'

I was nodding politely and thinking how nice it would be for this Lizzy person to go to LA with Jaden, when I suddenly realized he was talking about *me*. 'You mean *me* come and live in LA with you?'

'Why not?'

'But . . . what? To *live* there?'

'Yeah.'

'What? No,' I said. I struggled on my bean-bag, suddenly finding it constricting rather than relaxing and cheerful, and stood up.

Jaden got up too. He took my hands and turned me to face him. 'Hey, calm down,' he said.

'I am calm,' I said. 'I'm sorry, Jaden, it's a great idea, and I know I've been thinking about it, but it isn't going to happen.'

'Let me finish,' said Jaden, his eyes twinkling. 'I've started this all wrong. I don't want you to move to LA to be *with* me, that's not what I'm trying to say.'

'Oh,' I said, not without a little relief.

'And I don't mean, get over yourself, like I'd want to move in with you, either. OK?'

'Righty-ho, then,' I said, sounding insanely British and buying some time while I tried to work out what he was on about. 'That all sounds brillo.' *Brillo?*

'No, listen,' said Jaden. 'Let me say my piece. I've thought it all out, I think it's good. You're not exactly happy at the moment, are you? Your family's gone into meltdown, you're losing this great house, you're frustrated with your life here and you won't do anything about it. It takes you, like, a month to get your boiler sorted out, and that ex of yours, who you were making out with in the kitchen a couple

253

of weeks ago –' I opened my mouth to protest but Jaden raised his hand, unperturbed, and went on '– I'm not an idiot, Lizzy, it was kind of obvious what had been going on and, anyway, it's not a big deal, I understand. Anyway, he's still bringing you down. And that brother of his, what is he? Like, your stalker?'

'Miles?' I said, confused. 'No, we're just good friends.'

Jaden raised his eyebrows. 'I don't think that's what he thinks.'

'Bollocks,' I said. Me and Miles – urgh, even thinking about it was deeply deeply weird. He was David's *brother*, for God's sake.

'Whatever, don't worry about it, it's not a big deal. I don't think. But anyway, Lizzy,' he went on, 'if I were you I'd want a change. Why don't you do something about it?'

'Er,' I said.

'Well, it's up to you. But I really like you, Lizzy, you're great. I'd love to have you live with me. We've got a cool house-share and it's a five-minute drive from the beach. It's like a block away from Bette Davis's house. And the Monumental office there is great – it's small, it's just starting out. What's stopping you? You go there for a year, you wear sunglasses, get a tan, enjoy yourself, stop thinking all those crazy thoughts that are running around in that crazy English head of yours.'

Think about it. California. Sunshine all year round. Film stars. The ocean.

'And the brunch place next door to me does this great wheatgrass-juice shake. You'll love it,' he added.

My eyes bulged. Jaden smiled. 'I'm actually joking. Well, it does do wheatgrass juice, but it does waffles too. No-carb, no-fat waffles and maple syrup with no sugar. It's LA, after all.'

I am one who dithers over whether to have tea or coffee in the morning, and I find it's the really big decisions I can actually think through logically, without running around with my hands in the air. We were standing by the mantelpiece, which was adorned with a collection of Jaden's self-help books. *The Make A Change Manual* by Dr Ken Boomio was nearest to me, and as I gazed idly at it I saw that the line on the front cover said 'Change Your Way to a Whole New Betterness!'.

'I need to talk to Lily,' I said.

'The job's yours, Lizzy. She's said so already.'

I looked at Dr Ken Boomio's grinning face. And I thought of my grandmother saying, 'Never put off till tomorrow what you can do today.' Oh, to hell with that, I thought. I've spent the last year trying to understand things and getting more confused by the minute. I don't want to have to worry about it any more. How liberating it would be to surrender for once, and go with the flow, instead of sticking in the same old rut. And what if, when I did that, I sorted things out at the same time?

'Jaden,' I said, 'it's the maddest idea I've heard in a long time, but it makes almost perfect sense.'

I wasn't going to up sticks and move to California for ever, of course. I might not even go at all. But I thought about it all night, as I lay in Jaden's bed, counting the brown waves of the wallpaper through the silvery moonlight, with Jaden next to me on his back, arms resting neatly on his chest. And I thought about it the next morning after we'd had sex and Jaden was in the shower. I sat in bed with a cup of tea, looking at the rows of his neatly folded khaki, stone and brown clothes in their Habitat fawn-coloured clothes hanger, feeling content as a watery sun shone through the grimy window.

And I thought about it on the way to work, repelled by the rank smell of an unwashed old man next to me on the

Tube, and a trashy girl reeking of Calvin Klein on my other side, and during the horrid bun-fight queue for the lifts, one of which was broken, the other of which smelt of pee. And suddenly, instead of wanting to run back to Keeper House, I realized it wouldn't solve anything and I needed to get away from all of this. And Jaden, with his nice white teeth and yoga mat, his biscuit-coloured hands and trousers, his promise of the ocean and no strings attached, might have provided the answer.

It was a lot to think about before eight fifty-six on a Thursday morning. I wouldn't tell Mum and Dad and the others until there was something to tell them, but as I ran up the steps to the office and pushed open the black front door, it was exhilarating to think that I'd taken a step towards something different.

Lily was at her desk when I walked in.

'Lily,' I said. 'Yes.' Her eyes flicked over some text on the computer screen.

'If I were to take that job in LA, would I get an allowance for a pair of Gucci sunglasses and the hire on a Corvette?'

'Seriously?' Lily asked.

'Seriously,' I said.

'No,' she replied. 'But you'd get a pay rise and two free return flights a year. And that's your lot. Maybe a relocation package. Probably not.'

'OK,' I said, humming as I sat down at my desk. 'OK.'

And, with that, I set in motion a move to the other side of the world with a man I wasn't in love with.

TWENTY-THREE

I said nothing to anyone outside work about going to LA. I wanted to let the idea swirl around in my mind for a while without having to deal with the questions, the details. The funny thing about a big decision is that the moment you make it is never accompanied by a bolt of lightning. I don't know when the moment came that I knew I was going. I only know that, the following Saturday, as I sat in the back of Tom's car with Miles (who was also going home for the weekend), on the way down to Keeper House, I felt free. Perhaps it was because I'd already been back. Perhaps it was because, finally, I'd found something to get excited about.

'Has Mike heard from Rosalie yet?' said Miles, as we came through the outskirts of the village.

'Not as far as we know,' Tom told him. 'Poor Mike. Jeez, was I wrong about her!'

'I thought you were,' Miles said. 'There was something dodgy about her. Sexy, though. Those tight cashmere sweaters. Blimey.'

Yes, I thought. Do make sure you tell your brother they have to be handwashed. With every day that had passed in the week since she'd left him that Rosalie hadn't contacted

257

Mike, I had felt even more the responsibility for telling him and the others where she was. But I didn't want him to find out from me. I wasn't going to do her dirty work for her. Poor Mike – the humiliation of his niece ringing up and announcing he was being cuckolded by someone twenty years his junior was not something I wanted to inflict on him.

We saw Stuart Caldwell disappearing into the Neptune as we drove through Wareham to drop Miles off.

'It's the future lord of the manor,' Tom said.

'Oh, yes,' I said, watching Stuart's bulky frame disappear into the gloom of the pub.

'Want me to hunt him down and kill him, Lizzy?' said Miles. 'Drown him in a vat of beer?'

'Shout, "SOKH is avenged!"' Tom added. 'Yep, go on. She'd get you to do it, you know. And I bet you would, just to impress her, you big girl.'

Miles winked at me and jerked his head at Tom. 'I'd do anything for her, you know that.'

'Indeed,' said Tom. '"Oh, Tom,"' he went on in a high-pitched voice, '"I'm going to have to go in the back with Lizzy. You'll have to put this case of wine in the front, it won't fit back here. Ooh, she's so lovely."'

'Good gay impression, my friend,' said Miles. 'You should do it for a living. Oh, sorry, you already are.'

'Well—' Tom began.

'OK, OK, you two,' I said. 'Shut up, Miles. Tom—' for I could see in the mirror that Tom's face was arranging itself into a mutinous expression. 'Here's David's – we'll see you tomorrow teatime, yes?'

'Miles's, you mean,' Tom pointed out. I winced.

Miles took my hand. 'God, you're freezing.' He took the other, and rubbed them with his own warm, gloved hands, then kissed my cheek. ''Bye, gorgeous. 'Bye, Tom. Thanks

258

a lot, mate. Really appreciate the lift. Let me get this wine out. Or perhaps I should leave it in the front seat, so Lizzy and I can sit together on the way back, you know. Because that's how I pull the ladies. I'm *that* smooth.'

''Bye,' I said. 'Come on, Tom, let's get going.' The curtains were twitching and I knew Alice would be out in a few seconds, and I didn't particularly want to see her.

Miles put up his hand in a valedictory gesture, and we drove off.

'You two,' I said.

'Well, he's annoying,' Tom said. 'Always on at me about the gay thing. It's so boring.'

'You were old muckers together. It's probably hard for him, takes a bit of getting used to,' I said.

'You all seemed to cope with it OK.'

'Oh, boys, boys,' I said.

'And I don't care what you say, he's got a thing for you.'

'Tom, don't stir,' I said, because Tom can be like this. 'So what? He's always had a bit of a crush on me, but that's only when he's not going out with someone else. I'm like his fill-in woman.'

'Well, you shouldn't be,' Tom said. 'You should be doing other things.'

How little you know, I thought, visualizing myself in a breakfast meeting with George Clooney at the Chateau Marmont. Suddenly I wanted to tell Tom, but then he said cattily, 'He's only doing it to make David jealous.'

'Tom,' I said tiredly, 'I can't imagine anything weirder than going out with Miles. It's never going to happen. So what if we flirt? So what if we get on really well? He's fun, I hardly ever see him, and after all he's done for me, I owe him.'

'Yeah, whatevs,' Tom said, and I knew the subject was closed.

Was it really only a week since I'd been home? The hedgerows and trees along the lanes seemed a little more alive, showing more green than before. Tom slowed down to go through a rather deep puddle.

'Nearly there,' he said. 'Right. Have you thought of your Chin bingo line?'

'My bingo line is . . . It'll be something to do with the path on the way to the marquee. Will they put tarpaulin down if it rains? So people's shoes don't get muddy.'

'I think you're being too practical,' Tom said. 'It's going to be much more pointless and idiotic than that. Can we guarantee the roses will be in full bloom on that exact day, or something? Mark my words. Oh, speak of the devil.'

He pulled over, stopped the car and we were home. It was strange but it didn't feel like last time, and it didn't feel quite like home.

Chin was in the courtyard as we got out of the car, striding along with her hands in the pockets of a beautiful belted cashmere cardigan. 'Hello, loves,' she said, kissing us. Mum was lurking behind her.

'Hello,' she yelped. 'Shall we—'

'Let's just finish up here, shall we, Suzy?' Chin said firmly. 'While we're here. I just . . . Crouch down, will you?'

Chin and Mum crouched on the ground and squinted up at the wall leading to the gate and the main garden beyond. 'Nope, it's no good,' Chin said, flinging her notebook back into her pocket.

'No,' echoed Mum, who clearly had no idea what she was talking about.

'Don't you have it somewhere in a book, Suzy? It's extraordinary that these roses have been here for well over a hundred years and you don't even know when they're going to be in bloom. Two hundred people will traipse through this gate after the wedding to be greeted in all probability by a lot of brown dead rose-heads. God, when exactly *will* the roses be out?'

'Bingo!' shouted Tom. I high-fived him.

'What?' Chin said.

'We – we're here! Hurrah!' I said. 'Bingo, Mum!'

'Bingo!' Mum yelled.

'Ah, they're here,' said Dad's voice. 'Hello, darling.' He kissed me and hugged Tom. 'Right.'

We stood in a little circle in the courtyard. Mum and Chin fell silent. I knew something was up.

'Let's go inside and have some tea,' Mum offered. 'Brrr, I'm cold.' She looked down towards the lane. 'Oh, look, Tom, there's your mother. She said she was going to pop over.'

'All OK, Dad?' I said. Mum seemed worried and Chin gazed into the distance.

'It will be,' Dad said. 'That was Mike again,' he said to Mum and Chin.

'Again?' said Chin.

'No news – have you told him?' Mum said.

'Yes, but he's getting desperate. Poor bloke.'

'Poor bloke, my eye,' said Chin, with unexpected spite. 'Kate, hello. Mike's rung again.'

'Again?' said Kate, as we went into the hall. 'He is . . . God, Mike.' She wiped her muddy wellies on the mat outside and kicked them off, as Mum disappeared to make tea.

'I'm going to phone Mando about the roses,' Chin announced. 'I'll be upstairs. Call me when you're done.'

Tom and I mooched into the sitting room and flopped on to the sofa. Dad lit the lamps.

'Poor Mike,' Tom said.

'Yes,' I said, with feeling. 'We don't know the half of it, I'm sure.'

Dad spun round. 'What do you mean by that?'

261

I was taken aback by the harshness in his voice. 'Nothing,' I said. 'Just – I feel so sorry for him. If we knew where Rosalie was, our worst suspicions might be confirmed or otherwise. You know?'

Mum came in with the tray as Dad stared at me. 'Darling, I don't think that'd make a blind bit of difference. It's to do with Mike, not Rosalie,' he said, after a while.

'It might make a difference if you knew who she was with,' I said heatedly, then changed tack. 'Why are you so down on Mike? She's the one in the wrong.'

Dad laughed shortly. Mum started pouring tea. She shot him a look under her lashes. Kate sat down on the sofa next to Tom. 'How are you, darling?' she said.

'Good, thanks, Mum.' Tom kissed her. 'You'll never guess who I saw this week, by the way. Do you remember—'

'Hold on,' I said, and stood up. Then I felt like a bit of a berk and sat down again. 'Can we get one thing straight? You don't know all the facts. About Mike and Rosalie, I mean,' I said, since my parents and Kate were staring at me as if I'd gone mad. 'Look, I wasn't going to tell you this—'

'Lizzy—' Dad said.

'John, shut up,' Mum said, with urgency.

I took a deep breath. 'I know where Rosalie is,' I said.

'Oh!' Mum said.

'Exactly,' I said firmly. 'She's – well, she's with David. I think . . . well, I don't know. But they're living together. She moved in last weekend.'

'I know,' Dad said. He looked from Mum to Kate.

'You *know*?' I said. 'I didn't want to tell you because – and you *know*?'

'I know,' Dad repeated.

'Does *Mike* know?' I said. 'Are you going to tell him? God, this is . . . Why on earth didn't you say anything?'

He cleared his throat. 'Well. There's something we need to tell you – I don't know why we didn't tell you from the start. You see, we've all been keeping a few secrets.'

'Eh?' Tom said.

'I'm going to the study to get some things,' Dad said, and stalked out.

I had a dreadful, lurking suspicion, something hovering just outside my realm of comprehension, various ideas and images all rushing together and then Mum said, 'Yes. It's about Mike. It's . . . Well, where Rosalie is isn't important compared to what he's done.'

'What's he *done*?' I whispered, hardly wanting to frame the words.

Kate spoke up: 'Your uncle,' she said, face pale, her hand in Tom's. He's – he's not quite the lovely man you – we – think he is.' She looked at my mother, who nodded, then said, in a cold voice, 'Mike's the reason we're having to sell the house.'

The sound of footsteps in the corridor made me turn my head, and Dad was in the doorway with several box files under his arms. 'Right,' he said, as he laid them on the sofa. 'We – we didn't want you to find out about this. We didn't want to worry you. But I understand why you feel you deserve an explanation. And you're not children any more. Kate, it's rather appropriate you're here, isn't it?'

Tom and I looked at her, completely at a loss. She smiled at us wanly.

Mum handed Dad a cup of tea. He lowered himself gingerly into his armchair. 'Give me a moment, and then I'll explain why we're selling the house.'

When I remember the happy, often hilarious hours spent in the drawing room at home, playing raucous family games, Grandfather sleeping in the big chair in the corner, Jess and

263

I lying on our stomachs scribbling in drawing-pads with felt-tip pens in front of the fire, I often think what a strange picture the five of us must have made that day in March, so bright outside but dark and full of shadows in the room. We sat there, I between Tom and Kate on the sofa, Mum nearby, as Dad, glasses perched on his nose, lifted documents out of files, smoothed them on his knee, and passed them to me. These papers were always locked away; they told the story of the house. It was these that Rosalie had been looking at on Christmas Day, a few short months ago.

I learned that Edward Radcliffe, who built the house in 1592, had had a wife called Cicely who died in my bedroom, giving birth to his son, Thomas, in 1599. I learned that in 1664 Mary Kirke, Thomas's granddaughter, ordered the planting of the lavender and roses in the garden. I learned that Edwin Walter's son Julian built the gate leading to the meadow at the back. And that Julian's younger brother, Francis, was killed at Ypres in 1914. He was twenty-nine. All these things, waiting for me to know them, in this house all the time, and I only heard them now as we were leaving, packing up, and my sadness about leaving our family home, which had lessened in the last week or so, started to creep back.

'The thing is,' said Dad, putting another sheaf of papers back into a box, 'I doubt you've ever really given it much thought, but you must know that the house isn't ours.'

'What?' Tom said.

'Not mine and Suzy's. Grandfather left it to Mike. He's the eldest.'

'So, why isn't it his, then?' I said.

Dad spoke slowly. 'It *is* his – or, at least, the casting vote is his. If he decides to sell we all get a share of the proceeds, but he's the only one who can force a sale and the house is in his name.'

'But why doesn't he live here?' I asked.

'He didn't want to. When you were little, he went to live in New York and it all happened quite fast.' He looked at Kate who was gazing down at her hands, resting in her lap.

'Anyway,' Dad went on, 'when Grandfather and Grandmother decided to move out so we could move in, Mike signed a deed of covenant putting the house in my name, not his. Tony had died several years ago, Chin was far too young, and when Grandfather died, Mike was settled in New York and didn't want to come back. We were the only ones who were in a position to take on the house. It was that or lose it. Mike had made his feelings quite clear.'

'How could you be so sure? Why did he hand it over to you?' I asked. Dad was silent.

'I think,' Kate said slowly, choosing her words with care, 'when he left, all those years ago, he wanted a fresh start. He needed to get away. From – well, he felt – he felt he had to go.' She looked down, and fell silent again.

Mum and Dad were watching her. I looked at all three in turn, then at Tom, who was looking at his mother strangely, his brow furrowed.

'Oh, Lizzy.' Mum sighed. 'You have to understand what Mike was like when I first met him – when I first met your father's family.'

'Well . . .' Dad said, shuffling and uncomfortable.

Mum ploughed on: 'It was easy to be seduced by it all. I was. The house, the family, they were all such *good fun* – and Mike especially. He was at the helm with Tony. The pair of them were golden boys, couldn't do anything wrong. But Tony – well, he was just special. I wasn't aware of it then, but he was.' Mum reached out and touched Tom's hand. 'Wasn't he?' she asked Kate, casually, as if she wanted confirmation of the price of a pint of milk.

Kate nodded. Mum gave her a private smile, sisters-in-law together, and I saw them as outsiders for the first time.

'Mike was different,' she went on. 'With Tony it wasn't an act – with Mike it is. He's never been happy, always restless, always wants what he can't have, the grass is always greener. And that's – well, that's thrilling, exhilarating, but it's not for life. It's not real. That's why I married your dad – that's why people get married, I think. It's real life. Mike doesn't understand that that's what makes you happy.'

Dad was still fiddling with the papers, but he leaned against Mum and said, 'She's right.'

'Of course I'm right,' Mum said, and took some papers from him.

I still didn't see where this was leading.

'I don't understand what this has to do with the house, though,' Tom said, echoing my thoughts.

Kate got up, grabbed the tea-tray and clattered out of the room.

'Darling,' Dad said, clutching a box file on his knees, 'Mike looked at the covenant – well, he got Rosalie to do it – and he realized that the house is worth quite a lot of money now.'

'So?' I said. 'Big deal. He's rolling in it.'

'No, he's not,' Mum said shortly. 'He's bankrupt. He lost his job about six months ago. And now we discover he owes about three-quarters of a million pounds.'

'What?' I said. 'Mike?'

'Mike?' said Tom. 'Are you *sure*?'

Dad nodded.

'But . . . how come?' I said hoarsely. 'How – how did it happen?'

Mum went on, in a toneless voice, 'I'm afraid that's your uncle, darling. He's always been one to fly by the seat of his pants. He was made redundant last year – some irregularities, nothing really bad – and he invested money he didn't have in an online stocks-and-shares company.

266

He borrowed more and then more and . . . I'm afraid he used Keeper House as collateral for the loan.'

'Uncle Mike? But . . .' I felt as if someone was trying to explain the plot of a soap opera I didn't watch with characters I'd never heard of. 'Are you sure you've got this right? It really doesn't sound like him. He must have been defrauded, or set up, or something.'

Some irregularities? What did that mean? We all knew Uncle Mike was a crazy spendthrift, but that was just his style. It was part of what made him such fun when we were younger – you never knew if he was in clover and buying a shiny red MG or selling his furniture to afford bread and milk. Then I remembered David's harsh, angry words of only a week ago: 'You're all like that, all of you. Look at Mike, living in a fantasy-land, not caring how much he hurts other people.'

'Darling, you shouldn't blame him too much,' Mum said. 'He's had some bad luck. Unfortunately, he and Rosalie have proved to us that control of the house is still his, and I'm afraid that means we have to sell, whether we like it or not.'

I found my voice at last. 'But he can't! He can't force you to sell!'

'I'm afraid he can, Lizzy,' said Dad. 'And he has. He couldn't have done it without Rosalie, though, I'm sure. He must have known he could do something like this. I just don't think he ever thought he'd be able to pull it off, though, until he met her. She crystallized it for him. I don't think she wanted to, but she did. Well, you know the old saying – "Fancy a house, marry a property lawyer." I blame myself.'

'Don't be silly, John,' Mum said sharply. 'I blame Mike. Well, I blame Rosalie, too, but Mike first and foremost. She rang us last week from David's. She was distraught. She was head over heels in love with Mike and I don't think she thought about what she was getting into. Well, she's left him now, which I suppose is for the best. He was using her.'

'But I thought he loved her?' Tom said, in a small voice.

'I'm sure he persuaded himself he *could* love her,' Mum said. 'The sad thing is she's probably the best thing that'll ever happen to him, but he's too immature. Too selfish. He won't realize till long after she's gone, and in the meantime he's broken her heart and there's this –' she waved her arms, 'to deal with. That's Mike. I knew he'd let us down one day but not how badly.'

'Let's not talk about it any more, shall we?' said a voice at the door. It was Kate, her hands in her pockets, leaning against the frame, her bright gold hair shining in the pale sun. 'It's my fault he went and it's my fault he still feels so hurt, all these years later . . . And that's why he doesn't care any more. He can sit there and be jolly and underneath be lying to us. That's the truth. So.' She collected herself, then went on: 'The apportionment of blame after the main event is satisfying but pointless. Let's just not talk about it.'

I wanted to ask what she meant. I wanted to say, 'But, Kate, you and Mike, what happened?' But, of course, I didn't. She left the room, and Tom reached for the tea, and I knew I wouldn't ask.

We drank our tea in near-silence. I looked across at the photo of Dad, Mike, Tony and Chin outside the house. It was in this room, three months ago, that Dad had told us all that the house had to be sold. We were packing up, moving out, and our family was becoming more fractured and distant as a result. Because of Mike, who had sat there with his head bowed and forehead lined after Dad had broken the news. Because of Mike, who'd married Rosalie who, it turned out, hadn't wanted to be queen of her own British castle, simply to help the man she loved get the

268

proceeds from it. The proceeds from the sale of a golden-stone house that people had lived, loved and died in for four hundred years were going to pay off electronic, paper-less debts, run up in a matter of days. Because of my uncle Mike, the eldest son, whom I loved and who had casually reached in and ripped out the heart of our family.

TWENTY-FOUR

It turned out that much of what Mike had said and done at Christmas had been a lie: that the sole purpose of his visit was the hour-long conversation he had had with my father on Christmas Eve while we all lay around like a family of lotus-eaters watching *Some Like It Hot* and yelling about how great it was to have him home, as Rosalie sat with us. How she must have laughed at us. What idiots she must have thought we were as, in the study, Mike was explaining, calmly, brutally, to Dad that he had to sell our home. My darling dad had kept this conversation to himself all through Christmas, waiting till the twenty-eighth when he could go and see our family solicitor. There, he reread the deed of covenant that he and Mike had signed when Mike moved to New York, the document that confirmed the house was in my father's trust but belonged to Mike, although all three siblings benefited from a sale, according to the terms of Grandfather's will, it was ultimately Mike's house to do with as he pleased. And it pleased him to sell it.

I pieced this and more together from Mum and Dad during the next few hours and over supper. Later, when Tom, Miles and I met at the Neptune we agreed how *Alice in Wonderland* it all felt, like when you are little and allowed to stay up way past your bedtime, and everything seems strange and dream-like. The Mike I knew wasn't a nasty man, a criminal or a bastard: he was our *uncle*, we loved him, he looked out for us and made life better. So what he'd done didn't make sense. It was a bit like finding out your teacher's first name, or seeing a friend's parents kissing – wrong, strange, odd.

It wasn't just the sale of the house. It was what Mike's behaviour had meant over the years. Did he really not care about any of us? Could he put us all aside so easily, so thoughtlessly? It was chilling to think about his real nature, if one disregarded the patina of charm. And then I remembered the missed birthdays, the late arrivals, the broken promises, nearly thirty years of half-forgotten disappointments. Our parents refused to condemn him outright – to us, anyway: Mum and Dad were too bogged down with the practicalities of the sale, preparations for the wedding and the move, as was Kate, and Kate was bound by some other code of secrecy. I was sure now that Mike had been in love with her, but it wasn't as simple as that. I had to understand that there are always parts of people's lives of which you know nothing, things that happened before you were born or that have nothing to do with you.

So that night at the Neptune, we drew our own conclusions. Mike was a dastardly, creeping, thin-moustachioed skunk, the black sheep of the family, a liar, a cheat, and we – Tom and I especially – cursed his name. We couldn't have known what would happen in the weeks to come. We didn't even know where he was – Rosalie had moved back into the apartment and all she would tell Tom, sharply, when he rang was that Mike was in a motel, she didn't know where, and was looking for an apartment. He didn't reply to our emails. He didn't even call to apologise, hadn't spoken to Mum and Dad since he'd left at Christmas, except to confirm the sale price of the house. The saddest thing of all was, if Mike had had to become the villain of the family it should have been for something colourful and terrible – as a highwayman or a pirate, not as the pathetic shell of the golden boy he had once been.

Yes, we passed a strange evening in the pub. Tom and I got steadily drunk as the evening wore on, and alternately ranted or were silent. Miles was good enough to sit with us while we occasionally burst out with things like, 'Why can't he just sell something in America?', 'What will we say to him at the wedding?' or 'Why did he do it?'

'I tell you something,' Tom burst out, after a prolonged silence. 'I'm sticking with the good ones from now on. Gibbo – now, there's a good bloke. No trouble, nice, polite, not a cheating, lying thief, like Rosalie, or – or Mike, or even David. Sorry, Lizzy.'

'That's OK,' I said.

'Sorry, Miles, too,' Tom said.

'No sweat,' Miles said. He paused. 'So – David must have known, mustn't he?'

'About what?' Tom said.

'About Mike. Must have. And he did nothing about it.'

'Fucking typical,' I said. 'Yes, I'd love another wine white, please, Tom.'

'White wine, you mean,' Miles said. 'Are you OK there?'

'Yes,' I said. 'I'm fine. How about you?'

'I'm great, thanks,' Miles said, disentangling his hand from my frenzied grip. 'It might be time for you to try a spritzer. How does that sound?'

'Lovely,' I said, as Miles got up.

'Stag night,' Tom said firmly, as he came back with the drinks. 'I'm going to give Gibbo a night to remember. Hurrah. No nonsense, bloody lying people getting in the way. Great! Gibbo's the best, isn't he?'

'Yeah!' I said.

Tom leaned forward conspiratorially. 'Let's ring him. Let's tell him we think he's really great.'

'OK,' said Miles. 'We should go home now. Come on, finish your drinks. Honestly, the pair of you.'

'Shut up, *Dad*,' I said, as we tripped out of the pub into the cool April evening a few minutes later. ''Bye, Bill! 'Bye! 'Bye, Bill!' I felt Miles's arm through mine, comforting and solid.

'Come on, Liz,' he said softly. 'Let's get you both home, OK? Get some sleep. It'll all look brighter in the morning.'

Things didn't look brighter in the morning. I slept badly, and woke up with a terrible hangover. It was overcast and misty, a damp, cold day. I helped Mum and Chin with the seating plan and the order of service, then felt so terrible I crawled back to my room and flicked through my old back issues of *Vogue* for an hour. Dad was busy in his study, and Mum and Chin were in wedding-catering heaven. I felt like a spare part, so when Tom phoned from Kate's and said he wanted to get back to London that afternoon and did I want to come with him, I said yes with some relief. I wanted to go back to my flat, and think about California and my new life. Which I still hadn't told anyone about.

At one thirty, Tom's car beeped outside. Mum, Dad and Chin came out with me to say goodbye.

'Hello, Miles!' Mum exclaimed, as she saw him getting out of the car.

'Hello, Mrs Walter,' Miles said. He took my bag.

'Gosh, you do look well,' Mum said. 'John is so grateful to you, you know. That bit of leather you fixed on the bellows – well, it's transformed them.'

'Really?' said Miles. 'I'm so glad.'

'Yup,' Dad said, in his usual loquacious way. 'Thanks, Miles.'

Chin kissed me.

'See you on Friday,' I said.

'What's Friday?' she replied.

I groaned. 'Chin, don't say you've forgotten! Your bloody hen night, that's what. OK?'

'God, of course,' Chin said, slapping her hand over her mouth. 'I've been so busy. Yes, can't wait.' After a pause she said, 'It's not actually a hen night, is it?'

'What do you mean?' I asked.

'I mean it's you, me and Jess. It's not forty pissed under-dressed girls parading round in those limos, is it?'

'No, of course not,' I said. 'It's *Les Misérables*. You love *Les Misérables*! And we're having cocktails at Claridges. I told you that ages ago.' She smiled apologetically, as if she'd been thinking of something different and much better. 'Well, there you go!' she said brightly. 'That's something to look forward to, isn't it?'

'Sure is,' I said.

She leaned forward. 'Don't worry about Mike,' she whispered. 'I know we all hate him at the moment, but it could be worse. We'll talk about it on Friday, OK?'

I was touched – Chin's softer side is as rarely spotted as the N6 night bus.

She stepped aside as Miles put my bag, plus some scones Mum had made for me, into the boot.

''Bye,' Mum called. 'See you soon, darlings.'

''Bye,' we called back.

'Well,' said Tom, as we drove off. 'It sure is mighty fine to go home once in a while. Visit the folks, find out how the old clan's doin', what people have been up to.'

I leaned back and ran my hands across my eyes. I was tired.

'Step on it, Tom,' Miles said, from next to me. 'I've got a dinner reservation this evening.'

'Ooh,' Tom said, with mock-interest. 'Who with?'

'Mind your own business,' Miles said. 'And I'll mind mine.'

'Oh, God, not this again,' I said. 'I'm going to sleep.'

'Put your head on my lap,' Miles offered. He produced a jumper from his bag and folded it. 'Go on, you'll be comfortable that way.'

So I did, and as I was falling asleep, Miles stroked my hair, and started arguing with Tom about Jonny Wilkinson, a conversation that lasted all the way back to London.

After that weekend, I felt I had to start telling people that I was taking the new job, and more than ever I felt ready for it. I just wished that there was someone close I could talk it all over with, but good advice-givers were thin on the ground. I tried ringing Georgy but she was still in Italy. Tom was busy and stressed with work (a.k.a. putting the final touches to the gayest stag night ever), and Jess, whom Mum had told about Mike when she went home the day after we left, would get upset if she was the only person entrusted with this knowledge. In the old days I would have rung Mike – he would have been the perfect person to chat to: he would have understood what I was about to do in leaving everything behind and going to America. I thought Chin might understand, even if she had turned into a mad person who shouted bewildering things like 'SUGARED ALMONDS!' and 'VOILE IS SHABBY!' at me and her other nearest and dearest. But she wasn't around much either. She was always busy with the wedding. I understood that, but she seemed different in another way too, somehow – suddenly unavailable, even when she was there. Before all this she'd been someone you'd naturally tell things to. She was nosy, and cutting, but never judgemental.

*   *   *

On Friday, I tripped into work, thrilled that it was Friday and that I had a really good evening to look forward to all day. Half-way through the morning it came to me that tonight was the stag night too, and although I'd left messages, I hadn't yet spoken to Tom in a last-ditch attempt to persuade him to inject a note of masculinity into the proceedings. Or, if not that, at least a note of something that Gibbo might want to do. So I phoned him at work. I might as well not have bothered. The conversation went something like this:

Me: But can't you see that while you might love the idea of drinks at the American Bar and then *Chicago*, it's not necessarily Gibbo's idea of a great stag night?

Tom: So what are you saying? I've planned a crap night out? Thanks a fucking bundle, Lizzy. I've really thought about this, I spent ages investigating what Gibbo might like to do.

Me: And what you came up with was that he'd like to see Michael Greco in *Chicago*? And it must be sheer coincidence that you have fifteen pictures of Michael Greco in your flat and four different recordings of *Chicago*, on vinyl *and* CD.

Tom: Yes, that coincidence took both of us by surprise.

Me: What a load of rubbish.

Tom: Shut up.

Me: How many people have you persuaded to come?

Tom: Well, Miles is coming, which is good, because a few people have cancelled this week and I've got to take the tickets back to the box office tonight. And we've got a nice surprise for Gibbo too.

Me: A striptease by a Brighton antiques dealer?

Tom: I'm a very busy lawyer. Go away now, please. Goodbye. (Puts phone down.)

Although he was annoying at times, I still trusted Tom's advice so at lunchtime I dashed out to the Holy of Holies

– TopShop – to take back some lemon stilettos that he had told me were cheap and nasty, like something a group of Munchkins from the Lollipop Guild in *The Wizard of Oz* might have worn. I wasn't sure he was right but I couldn't look at them without laughing now, and it is wrong to be looking down at your feet and snorting during a meeting, as I had found out yesterday during a high-level chat with Lily. So I consoled myself while I was there by buying a lovely spring/summer vintage Liberty print flared skirt with cute deep pockets on either side.

On my way out of TopShop, clutching the bag – which also contained a gorgeous suede belt and a black crocheted wrapover top – I veered behind Oxford Street and walked towards Great Titchfield Street to grab a sandwich before I went back to the office. I walked up to Luigi's, and was pleased to see the little tables and chairs that dotted the patio outside occupied by some hardy shoppers enjoying the first of the spring sunshine. I dashed in, joined the queue and called Ash at the office to see if he wanted anything. We had a shouted conversation above the braying of the two girls at the first table outside. I got off the phone, made my purchases and was turning to leave when I heard a familiar voice. The braying girls were Chin and Sophia Gunning, both in outsize black sunglasses and silk scarves, pretending to be best friends.

'Blimey, this is a coincidence when I'm seeing you in a couple of hours, isn't it?' I said, as I kissed my aunt and smiled ingratiatingly at Sophia Gunning. 'What are you doing here?' I said to Chin.

'Guy, in Liberty's,' Chin said briefly, sitting down again. 'He's making my shrug. I've got my final fitting this afternoon.'

'He's making you shrug?' I asked stupidly. I felt like a huge large giraffe, standing up while tiny Chin and Sophia sat daintily far below me, sipping their coffee. I picked up an Amaretti biscuit from the uneaten pile on the table and put it in my bag.

Sophia's eyes flicked up to me with a look of total disdain, which she immediately masked with laughter. 'Ha-ha-ha! Oh, Lizzy, you're so funny.'

'No, Lizzy,' Chin said patiently. 'He's making me *a shrug*. To wear over my dress. Cream cashmere, lace trim. It's going to be gorgeous.'

'I'm sure it will,' Sophia said, fluttering her eyelashes at Chin, who fluttered hers back. 'We're bunking off this afternoon, aren't we, darling? I'm going shopping with Chin and we're going to be *so girly*. Then we're going for cocktails to have a proper catch-up. Oh, Chin,' she said passionately – I wanted to delve into my bag and whip out an Oscar for her incredibly convincing portrayal of the Girl Who Isn't A Total Bitch – 'it's *so good* to see you again!'

Even Chin could not help but look flattered.

I coughed. 'Excuse me,' I said, leaning over, 'Chin, tonight's the night, remember?'

'What's tonight?' Sophia said, without interest, looking at her tiny silver phone.

'It's her hen night,' I said proudly. 'Isn't it, Chin?'

Sophia wasn't really listening. 'Oh, my good God, Jeremy's texted me. Jeremy! He's so naughty! Didn't I tell you about him, Chin?'

Chin slammed on her sunglasses and got up. 'You text him back. I'm just going to have a little word with Lizzy. See you in a min.' She grabbed my arm, and strode off round the corner. Luigi was watching us and waved at me.

'Hi,' Chin said, when we got round the corner.

'Hi there,' I said.

'Listen, Lizzy,' she sounded brisk, 'have you gone to much trouble over tonight? Be honest.'

'Er . . . no, of course not,' I said, worried that she'd got cold feet or fear of condom-veil presentation. 'Why?'

Chin looked airily about her. 'Well, I was just wondering if we could do it another night, that's all.'

'Oh,' I said. 'Why?'

Chin sighed, then said, in her disarmingly sweet, clear voice, 'Look, tell me if this isn't on. I know we're doing our pizza thing tonight—'

'After the cocktails at Claridges,' I pointed out weakly.

'Yes, of course,' Chin said impatiently. She tossed her hair, and shoved her hands deep into the pockets of her beautiful black coat. 'But I've been to Claridges about five times in the last few months. I'm a bit sick of it. And, well, it'd be nice to see you both but, let's face it, we're going to be seeing a lot of each other over the next month or so. The thing is, Sophia rang me yesterday. Do you remember you saw her at that work party thing?'

'Yes, I do,' I said.

Chin looked round her again, then practically hissed, 'Give me that Amaretti. I'm starving. She eats bloody nothing.'

I handed her a biscuit from my bag and she wolfed it. 'Lovely. God, that's good.'

I scrunched up my eyes to see if I was in a dream.

Chin sailed on, oblivious to my (a) confusion (b) rising anger. 'Anyway, it was great to talk to her. She really enjoyed seeing you, and she'd heard about Keeper House from her mum – she was sweet about it. She said she'd thought she should give me a call for old times' sake and that we should meet up. Anyway, to cut a long story short, we arranged to spend today together. So, yes, we're going shopping this afternoon and out for drinks tonight. To the Sanderson. So, unless you had something really special planned, I thought it'd be OK to call a raincheck for tonight.'

I looked at her in amazement as she crumpled the biscuit

279

paper and threw it neatly into a bin a few feet away. Several things about this speech irritated me intensely. One, Chin was the kind of person I'd always suspected might ditch someone at the last minute for a better offer, but I'd never dreamed she'd do it tonight. Two, she was supposed to hate Sophia Gunning, but obviously Sophia Gunning came higher in the social pecking order than Jess and I did, and if she was seeking Chin's forgiveness (or, more likely, was at a loose end on her last night in London, the friendless witch), Chin would be willing to dole it out. Three, why the name-checking of the bar at the Sanderson? Was this a covert message that she liked it much better there and we ought to have taken her there too? Finally, the whole if-you-haven't-planned-anything-special tack was a monstrously rude way of saying, 'If you'd planned a better evening, I wouldn't be dropping you for someone else.'

I was suddenly the kind of furious where you don't really want to get into a ding-dong or unforgivable things will be said. So I just said, in a voice that could have frozen vodka, 'That's a real shame, Chin. Jess and I were looking forward to tonight. And, no, we hadn't planned anything. Well, nothing we can't change anyway.' I wasn't going to tell her I'd bought those tickets now. If she didn't want to come out with us – fine.

Chin stamped her feet impatiently. 'So you don't mind, then. Sorry about this. We'll do it some other time, OK?'

I pushed my bag on to my shoulder and made to leave. 'I do mind, actually, but if you'd rather go out with Sophia I'm sure Jess and I would be horrified to think we were holding you back.' I sounded like a pert housemaid. 'Anyway, I'd better go. I'm going to be late getting back. I've got a few things to sort out *now*.'

Chin was totally oblivious to this, damn her eyes. 'Thanks, love. I'll tell her you said 'bye. You never know, she's probably quite a useful person to know at Monumental, isn't she? I'll put in a good word for you – maybe she can get you a job in New York or LA or something!'

How little you know or even care, I thought. 'Whatever,' I said, not wanting to talk to her any more. 'Have a good day.' I said mentally adding her to the ever-growing list of my relatives without whom I'd be better off.

Chin reapplied her lip gloss, then said, 'Thanks, Lizzy. Sorry about this – and thanks a lot! 'Bye.' She hugged me. 'I'll see you soon, OK? Sorry,' she said. 'It's the only day she can do before she goes back to LA.' Then she walked off. I watched her go, unable to believe quite how rude and ungrateful she was. And she had no idea! Bloody cow. I breathed deeply. Palm trees, the ocean, waffles. What a witch. Well, I'd see about that.

I stomped back to work, hurled myself into my office, slammed the door and sank into my chair, still in my coat. Then I had a brainwave. I rang up the *Les Misérables* box office and cancelled our tickets, rang Jess and told her to come to my office instead. Then I picked up the phone.

'Tom, it's me again. You said two people cancelled on the butch men's stag do earlier this week. Are those tickets still spare? And, if so, have you got room for two more people tonight?' I explained about Chin's awful behaviour.

'Of course,' said Tom's voice, reassuring and kind. 'What a cow Chin is. Hurrah, this is going to be great! Gibbo'll be so pleased!'

'Really?' I said. 'I can't imagine we're his top choice of stag-night companions.'

'Well, we've regrouped and I've changed the title of the evening. It's not Gibbo's stag night any more. It's Gibbo's Friends and soon-to-be-relatives Wish Him *Bon Voyage*. It's now just an excuse for us to have a nice evening out and then get mashed. Good, no?'

281

'Great,' I said.

'Right. Better go,' said Tom. 'See you at the Savoy at six thirty. Don't be late. Hey, I'm really glad you're coming. Bloody Chin! I'll have something to say to her next time I see her. She's getting worse and worse, don't you think?'

'She is,' I agreed. My heart swelled with love for Tom, then shrank again when he said, 'And don't wear those hideous Topshop lemon stilettos.'

A few hours later, Jess and I hurried through the chrome art-deco revolving doors at the Savoy and into the plushly retro lobby, trying to look as if such a place was run-of-the-mill to us. We ran up the stairs to the American Bar, where our eyes fell upon a knot of boys, sitting self-consciously in black tie and trying to make polite conversation. They looked like waiters on a busman's stag night. Miles saw us first, and his eyes lit with relief, then Tom and Gibbo stood up to greet us. Gibbo resembled an anorexic penguin in evening dress. It wasn't a look I'd have picked for him. His jacket appeared to be sliding off him and I made a mental note to warn Chin, if I ever got over my fury, never to let him wear it again.

'Well, this is the best man, Bozzer,' said Tom, gesturing to a short, rubbery man with a deep tan and small blue gimlet eyes. 'He flew in from Sydney yesterday. And this is Frank.'

'Hello, Lizzy,' said Frank. He had been Gibbo's boss at a fruit and veg stall where he'd worked briefly last summer. He was tall and thin with wispy white hair and the air of an absent-minded ghost. I couldn't imagine him yelling 'Five punnets for a pahnd!' but there you go.

We shook hands with the rest of the crew, an assortment of people Gibbo had worked with, or who had saved his life in various improbable situations, and even one bloke whom Gibbo had met on a train last year, who'd become a friend because he'd offered Gibbo a banana.

'Let me get you girls some drinks,' said Miles. I watched his retreating back, and thought that how much more he looked the part in black tie. It seemed to belong to him in the way it never quite does with many men.

'How do you know Gibbo?' I asked Ian, presuming that the usual rules of hen-night small-talk applied at the beginning of a stag night, too.

'I met him a couple of years ago, near Cairns,' said Ian.

'Nice,' I said. 'It's supposed to be beautiful there, but I've never been.'

'Oh, it is. Gorgeous part of the world.'

'So how did you actually meet?' I said.

Ian looked bashful. 'I saved his life, actually.'

'Blimey,' I said.

Gibbo overheard us, and slapped Ian on the back. 'He sure did!' he exclaimed. 'I was hanging out at a café by the beach, drinking a beer. Then suddenly I turn dark purple and go rigid. They think I'm dead, right? And Ian – he's a doctor, thank God – he just happened to be there. Otherwise I'd have been a goner. He bent down, reached into my throat and – ' he leaned forward, and said in sepulchre-like tones – 'and he pulled out a bit of rope that big – I was choking to death. Had a knot in it. This size.' He held his hands six inches apart.

Ian nodded modestly.

I was confused. 'But, Gibbo, why didn't you notice you'd swallowed it?'

'Who knows?' said Gibbo with interest. 'Who knows. Ah, mate, great to have you here!' he said, and slapped Ian on the back again.

Miles caught my eye as he shifted back on to the bench

283

and handed Jess and me a martini each. 'Classic,' he murmured. 'Vintage Walter situation.'

'Shut up,' I said, but I couldn't help smiling.

'How are you?' said Miles. 'Still on for tomorrow?'

'Sure am,' I said. 'Where were you thinking of going?'

'Well, it's going to be pretty nice weather, apparently, so I thought Richmond Park. I've got a big rug and I can pick up some food on the way. We can go for a bit of a stroll afterwards. How does that sound?'

I looked round the crowded bar, filling up with ever more bejewelled, skinny men and women, then at Gibbo, Bozzer and Tom, who were chatting together, and Jess, talking to Ian and his mate Phil. 'That sounds great,' I said. 'Here's to tomorrow.'

'Definitely,' said Miles.

So we all sat there, an odd collection of people if ever there was one, as the old Italian waiters circled and polite bubbles of early-evening conversation drifted around us.

'Well, what a week,' Tom said, stretching out his feet. 'How are we all, after last weekend's revelations?'

'I still can't believe it,' said Jess, and sipped her martini gloomily.

'Me either,' said Tom. 'I've been calling Mike all week, but I haven't heard a thing from him. Bastard.'

'What's it going to be like at the wedding?' Jess said. 'He'll still come, won't he?'

'I'm sure he will,' I said. 'You know our family. We'll all smile and pretend everything's fine. And—'

'What?' Tom said.

'Well, he should be there, shouldn't he?'

'I don't see why,' said Tom coldly.

'He should see what he's done,' I said.

'I suppose,' Tom agreed. 'But, still, it doesn't make you look forward to it, particularly.'

'Why?' said Jess.

'Well,' I said, 'we're moving out four days later. The bloody packing cases'll be everywhere, and Mike, and we'll be pretending everything's OK. And – and—'

'And David, too,' said Jess. 'He'll be there.'

'Perhaps he won't,' I said hopefully.

'He *is* coming,' said Miles. 'He's flying in the day before. He's going to see Dad in Spain afterwards. He and Chin are close, aren't they? Sorry.'

'Of course,' Tom said. 'I'd forgotten.'

'Oh, great,' I said, although I knew this was true. Like most of my family, Chin thought David was the bee's knees. They liked long walks, too. Ugh, some people.

'Well, you can have a reckoning with him,' Tom said consolingly. 'Get really drunk and tell him what a wanker he is.'

'Ye-es,' I said. 'But I'd rather do it with a devastatingly handsome new boyfriend on my arm. I tried to bribe Jaden to come but he's back in LA. And anyway,' I said, remembering the conversation I'd had with him earlier in the week, 'he was really annoying about it. He said I was being negative about the past and trapping myself in a holding booth.' I made a pshaw noise. 'God, he's so hilarious sometimes.'

'I think he's right,' Tom said.

'Shut up!' I said. 'What does it even *mean?*'

'It means you're stuck in a rut and you won't try new things. You just keep going back to some point in your past and blaming it for everything,' Tom said helpfully.

'Well, it's not bloody true,' I said crossly. 'You don't know the first thing about it.'

'Oh, yes? Give me an example of something new you're doing, then,' said Tom.

'Well, I'm moving to LA in two months' time,' I said conversationally.

285

Jess started.

'What did you say?' Miles said, at my elbow.

'I said,' I took a deep breath, 'I'm moving to LA. I've got a job out there. For a year. I just want to – to try something new. See what's out there.'

Tom floored me. 'That's a brilliant idea. Lucky you.' He kissed me. 'I'm going to miss you so much. Can I come and stay? God, I'm proud of you.'

Miles raised his glass to me.

'So am I,' Jess said. 'But, oh, Lizzy, I'm going to miss you. Can I come and stay too? Can you rent a house by the beach?'

'I'm going to live with Jaden for a bit,' I said. 'His apartment is by the beach. It'll be for a couple of months till I find somewhere. So I've got one friend there, which makes life easier.'

'Cool!' said Jess.

'It'll be great,' said Tom. 'God, this is weird. You're going to LA!'

'I know!' I said. 'I'm so glad you're pleased. I haven't told Mum and Dad yet – I don't know what they'll think.'

'They'll think it's a great idea,' Miles said, 'and they'll be so proud of you, too.'

I was shaking a bit: I hadn't realized it would be such a big deal to tell the others, and I was taken aback by how quickly they had embraced it. Perhaps they'd been longing to get shot of me, I thought gloomily.

Tom and Jess were discussing the best time for them to visit when Miles touched my shoulder. 'So, this is really happening?' he murmured into my ear.

'Yes,' I said.

'I'm going to miss you, Lizzy.'

'Well, me too,' I said. 'It'll be weird not seeing you for ages. Especially after this last year when we've been friends the way we used to be before – well, before David. And now this.'

'Well, it's good in that respect,' said Miles, gazing into his drink.

'How?' I asked, as Gibbo came over and squatted beside Tom and Jess.

'Well, it draws a line under you and David, doesn't it? And you need that. You'll come back after a year and it'll seem like ancient history. At the moment you're still raw.'

'I'm not, really,' I said frankly. 'I'm over him now. I just – I thought he was the one. And it takes time to realise that you were wrong about something like that. Jaden helped me do that, actually. It all seems like a million years ago now.'

'Really?' Miles said curiously.

'Really,' I said. 'For example, for a long time I saw you simply as David's brother. But for the last couple of months – well, I don't look at you like that now. I see *you*. Miles. My friend. You're a better friend to me than David ever was.'

'I hope so,' said Miles. 'Let's talk about it more tomorrow. I think Gibbo wants us to go now.'

'Righty-ho, then,' I said.

Tom stood up officiously. 'Right, people, let's get moving,' he said, and everyone got up to put on their coats. 'OK, get up, put your coats on. Now, where are the tickets? And where's my wallet? I must go to the loo. Can you hurry up, those of you who need to use the facilities before we go, please? We'll meet back here.'

'We're all ready,' said Jess, as Miles passed me my coat. 'It's just you.'

'Right,' said Tom, and dashed off.

Gibbo appeared between me and Jess. He tapped Miles's shoulder and gestured that he should step to one side. 'You don't mind, do you, mate?' he said, linking his arms through

Jess's and mine. 'Well, this is what I call a pretty bonzer night out,' he said, as we walked out of the bar. 'Off with my soon-to-be nieces for some real twenties musical action. Rock on, Tommy.'

'Yes,' Miles murmured behind us, as we went out into the early April evening. 'Vintage Walter situation.'

TWENTY-FIVE

It's fair to say that the Gibbo's Friends and soon-to-be relatives Wish Him *Bon Voyage* night was an unqualified
success. Bozzer taught Tom how to wolf-whistle in the
interval of *Chicago*, and he proved such a natural that he
was cautioned by the ushers in the applause after 'Give 'Em
The Old Razzle Dazzle'. Frank and Miles discovered a
mutual love of racing, and spent the rest of the evening
discussing form and swapping tips. Gibbo and Jess burnt a
hefty sum on sweets at the bar and ate them, enraptured
by the show – Gibbo because of the flesh on display, Jess
because it was short and the plot wasn't too complicated:
after eight she tends to fall asleep if she sits in one place
for too long. Tom and I whooped and cheered whenever
Michael Greco appeared. I'm ashamed to say that Tom 'I
wasn't officially gay this time last year' disgraced us by
standing up during the curtain call, shouting, 'Beppe! Here!'
and pointing at himself.

Afterwards we went to Miles's club in Soho where we
drank ourselves stupid: and a party was in full swing to celebrate the club's first anniversary. A Party with a Disco. Gibbo
did something so hilariously noteworthy we all separately

wrote it down so we'd be able to remind Bozzer to mention it in his speech (I found my piece of paper the next day, I had written, 'Gboo hands crypt ?? why!! For' Thank god for Miles, he remembered.) So we danced ourselves stupid after that, and one of the last things I remember is Gibbo trying to samba with Frank, and Bozzer staring with unnatural intensity at Jess as I slid off the leather banquette and folded myself up neatly under the table.

So it was with a rather delicate gait and a hazy memory of the previous night's events that I emerged from my flat the next day as Miles's car purred outside on the cobbles. I raised my hand in greeting, then gingerly placed the rug, some bottles of water, Twiglets (emergency rations) and some radishes (I always keep them at the back of the fridge: excellent hangover cure, trust me) in the back of his open-top Mercedes, which I coveted with a deadly covetousness.

It was a lovely day, and if my stretch of the Edgware Road had had frivolous luxuries like trees and birds, the former would have been rudely green and the latter chirping merrily. Miles watched as I pulled unsuccessfully at the door handle and slumped weakly against the car. 'I think I'm going to be ill,' I said. 'I can actually smell the wine going into my liver. How disgusting is that?'

Miles came round to my side of the car, opened the door and pushed me on to the seat. 'No, you can smell the chicken liver pâté in the picnic hamper, you alky,' he said.

'I *am* going to be ill,' I said, resting my head on the dashboard.

'Lift your legs into the car, Lizzy.' He shut my door. 'What you need is another drink. I've got some fizz in the back and we'll have a glass when we get there. Just sit back and enjoy the fresh air. It'll do you good.'

I didn't argue, even though the air where I live is 90 per cent lead and 10 per cent carbon monoxide and not fresh at all. Miles put on his shades and edged the car out on to the Edgware Road. 'I just hope it was worth it,' he said, as we hit the Westway.

'What? Feeling like this? I don't know,' I said. 'I can't really remember the last part much. But what I do remember I really enjoyed.'

'You looked like you were having fun.' Miles was trying not to laugh. 'You offered to give Frank a lapdance.'

'I didn't!' I froze. 'You're lying!'

'I wish I were. I don't think he heard you, though. He was too busy gazing at Jess's tits.'

'Don't be vulgar.'

'He *was*. You slow-danced with Bozzer, then sat on Gibbo's lap and told him you wished he was your blood relative, not Chin.'

Sadly, I remembered doing both of these things. 'Oh, God.'

'And you tried to kiss the barman when he gave you a free drink.'

'I did, didn't I?'

Disjointed memories of the evening flew at me, as if I was Tippi Hedren in *The Birds*. I shrank into my seat and closed my eyes to try to block them out, as Miles turned on Jonathan Ross and laughed callously at my shame.

We drove in silence for a while, listening to the radio. The sun shone as we headed west and I soon started to feel more human. As we turned off the Upper Richmond Road towards the park, I sat up again and took a sip of water. 'Argh,' I said.

'How are you feeling?' said Miles.

'Better,' I said ruefully. 'How about you? Aren't you at all hung-over? You were getting through the wine like – like a hot fish through butter.'

'Speak English, Lizzy,' said Miles, patiently. 'You're still making no sense. Talking of which, how much sense were you talking last night?'

'Er . . .' I said warily. 'I don't know. Depends. What did I say?'

'You said . . . well, you said some interesting things when you were drunk.' Miles paused, giving me ample time to reflect on what I might have disclosed on a number of potentially embarrassing topics.

'Don't. Tell me.'

Miles is the kind of man for whom parking spaces magically appear. We pulled into one he spotted in a tree-lined street exactly like the one we had lived in before Keeper House. He switched off the engine and turned to look at me. 'OK. You said you'd slept with that dorky American.'

'Oh.'

'Is it true?' Miles took off his shades and opened the door.

'Not sure,' I said, stumbling out.

'What's his name again?' Miles said, opening the boot and taking out the hamper. 'Jonquil? Jabba?'

'It's Jaden – and be nice.'

'You clearly are.' Miles leaned into the boot so his voice was muffled. 'Isn't he a bit of a wanker, Lizzy? What the hell were you doing with him?'

'Er . . .' I was thrown by this. 'Well, he's a bit *strange*, but he's not a wanker.'

'Yes, he is,' Miles said, standing up. 'Come on, let's go. I know the perfect spot.'

'Right,' I said, pissed off. I stood in the middle of the road. 'Er, Miles, shut up about Jaden, OK? I don't care what you think of him, but don't be rude about him to me.'

Miles had walked on ahead but he stopped, turned, and saw the look on my face. 'Sorry, Lizzy,' he said awkwardly.

'That's OK. Just . . . you know.'

'I was out of order. I shouldn't have said that.'

'Fine,' I said, relieved. I unbent a little more – he looked shaken. 'And I'm not going out with him. We're just good friends. Who have sex. Occasionally. He's nice.'

We were at the entrance to the park. A little boy on a fat-tyred bike zoomed between us and ahead the land fell away into a haze of grey and green, carved up with white paths.

'It's this way.'

We set off, cutting through the middle. Miles was silent for a while as we walked. Then he said, 'So, are the two of you not . . .' He tipped his head to one side and winked lasciviously, 'wna-wna any more?'

I laughed. 'No, we're not. It wasn't really about that, although it was pretty great . . . whatever, you know what I mean.'

Miles sighed. 'Again, no, I have no idea what you mean, but I get the gist. So will you . . . wna-wna in LA with Jaden?'

'No!' I said. 'Well, I might, but on a strictly now-and-again basis. Is that all?'

'Sorry,' said Miles. 'I'm just jealous.'

'Of course you are,' I said. 'That reminds me. I tried to snog you last night, didn't I? How embarrassing. I'm so sorry.'

'Here's the spot,' said Miles, obviously not listening. 'Let's get comfortable. I'll pour you a drink.'

Miles threw the rug amid the long grass and the sun beat down. I put on my floppy straw hat and lay on the ground. Miles had certainly come prepared: there was a cool box with bottled water, orange juice and the afore-mentioned champagne, and one of those old-fashioned wicker hampers, with a checked lining and dear little sets of plates and cutlery, stuffed with sandwiches, crisps, pork pies, the pâté and my favourite Scotch eggs. We munched happily for a while. I could hear children playing in the distance, and the rushing sound of the wind in the bracken all around us. The grass was long enough to hide in, and there was something curiously comforting about that.

After we'd demolished most of the picnic, I started packing away the things while Miles lay back and smoked a cigarette. 'Thanks so much, Miles. That was perfect,' I said, as I sat down beside him again.

'Have some more champagne,' Miles said, sitting up. 'Come on, it's the last bit.'

'I shouldn't really,' I said – it had gone straight to my head.

'You know you want to,' Miles said. 'Come on – how many times in one week does a girl decide she's moving to the other side of the world?'

'Oh, go on, then,' I said. We clinked glasses and sat in perfect harmony for a couple of minutes. I looked at Miles out of the corner of my eye. It was surprising, sometimes, how very much like David he looked, although his hair was longer and wavier and he was shorter. I thought about Jess, how people always said we were similar, and how we both thought that was rubbish. Perhaps it was true, though. I tried to picture what Jess would look like with my hair and vice versa. Then I wondered what we would look like with Mum's short, curly hair. Then I realized I was wasting time in drunken, pointless speculation, and turned to Miles to tell him, only to find he was fast asleep. I touched his shoulder, but he didn't move, so I pushed him harder.

He half opened one eye. 'Hello,' he said.

'Hello. Sorry, you were asleep, and I woke you.'

Miles reached behind me and pinched my ribs. 'Evil girl,' he said.

'Ouch!' I yelled, and pinched him back, then grabbed his arms and held him down. 'I've got you. Admit defeat,' I said, laughing down at him.

'You've got a caterpillar in your hair,' he observed.

I screamed, and my hands flew up to dislodge it. Miles caught my wrists and rolled me on to the ground. I screamed again and laughed as he loomed over me, his hands pinning mine to the ground. 'Ha!' he said.

'You bastard.' I was laughing so much now that I could hardly breathe. I could feel the soft wool of the blanket on my arms. 'God, I can't believe I fell for that. Ow.'

I kicked my legs in the air, pushing him from behind. He fell forward on top of me, so that our faces were millimetres apart. Then something changed. He stopped and looked at me. He let go of my hands and stroked my shoulders. And I reached up and kissed him, sliding my arms round his neck. He was breathing hard, his body was heavy on mine, and perhaps it was the hangover or the champagne, but something about him, about doing this, felt right. I reached for him as he kissed me, pulling him closer.

Then Miles stopped. He sat up again and took my hand. 'Well,' he said.

'Well,' I said.

'I didn't expect that to happen.' He rubbed his head.

I sat up and picked some grass out of his hair. 'Neither did I.'

There was a silence.

'I—' Miles began. He picked up the empty bottle and put it into the hamper.

'What?' I said, suddenly feeling like my friend Kathy at school whom we'd nicknamed the Lunger, with very good reason.

'Nothing, I—' He stopped again, and turned to me. 'I'm really sorry. I didn't want to – to make a pass like that.'

'You didn't!' I said. 'It was me. I lunged. I'm sorry. But—' I brushed some grass off my skirt.

Miles caught my hand, leaned in and kissed me again. 'I've wanted to do that before,' he said.

'Really?' I said.

'Yes, of course,' Miles said. 'For – well, it doesn't matter how long. But, yeah. I've always had a bit of a crush on you.'

I'm not the sort of person people have long crushes on, I thought. 'I'm not the sort of person people have long crushes on,' I said.

'Well, you are to me,' Miles said. He smiled, and my heart stopped. 'You always have been. Anyway, it doesn't matter. You're going away. And there's the David thing. I don't want to embarrass you, or put you on the spot. I shouldn't have done it.'

'You didn't do it!' I said, exasperated. 'Miles, shut up for a minute. We both wanted to do it. And this has got *nothing* to do with David.'

'Really?' said Miles.

'No – you're you, Miles. How could I look at you any other way?'

'Well, that's what I always thought,' Miles said. 'That's why I've never said anything before.'

'Well, something's changed,' I said. 'Everything's changing. Perhaps that's why . . . oh, I don't know.'

We were silent again.

'Lizzy,' Miles said. He took a deep breath. 'I know David broke your heart, but have you ever thought the reason things didn't work out between the two of you was because . . . well, maybe he was the wrong brother for you?'

'No,' I said truthfully. He flinched, as if I'd slapped him. 'Well, not really,' I amended. 'Because he hurt me a lot, you know. So perhaps that's why I never . . . But, Miles, this is weird. I'm sorry, it's just . . . it's hard to get my head round.'

'I know it is.' Miles tucked a strand of hair behind my ear. 'I know, darling Lizzy, I know. It is strange. And I don't know what we do now. Except . . . I don't want this to be it.'

I looked at him, really looked at him. 'Neither do I,' I said calmly. It seemed to make sense, all of a sudden, and I felt detached from it, as if I were merely a spectator, someone watching this scene from behind a tree, rather than the girl sitting on a blanket in the park with two empty glasses by her feet.

Miles was staring at me, quite white, with a fierce intensity. 'Lizzy?' he said, swallowing hard.

I saw that he was nervous, and my heart went out to him. 'Yes?' I said.

'What are you doing for the rest of the day?'

I met his eyes. 'Well . . .'

Miles moved closer, and kissed my neck. 'Why don't we just . . . why don't we stay here for a bit?'

'Yes?' I said softly.

He moved up my neck to my ear, put his hands on my hips. 'And then . . . why don't we just see?'

'OK,' I said.

'And then . . . tomorrow – we can just see again,' he murmured.

'We've got two months till I go,' I said.

'Two months till you go,' Miles said, kissing my collar bone.

'Yes,' I whispered.

'Definitely?' he said. He put his hand over mine on the grass. It was cold, clammy. He smiled, nothing like David now, bent forward and kissed me, gently at first, then more insistently, the pressure of his hand on mine now almost painful on the hard ground. I reached up to hold him and he pushed me down on to the rug, and as I lay there I felt dizzy. Everything seemed so strange, but the answers were right, and as Miles kissed me again, his hands running over my body, I gave up wondering and surrendered to it.

Summer

TWENTY-SIX

Early in the morning, long before anyone else was awake, I sat at my window and watched the soft mist hugging the lawn and the meadow behind. It was still cool, but the sun was already burning the mist away and shining with a warmth and crispness that signalled another beautiful May day. The trees in the orchard were still, heavy with new leaves. The flowers were unfurling and I could already hear the drone of a bee. In the background, a sweet-throated blackbird and a wood-pigeon gave a dawn chorus. It was my favourite time of day at Keeper House.

I sat in the old silk straight-backed chair by my window, my knees drawn up to my chin, T-shirt nightie tucked under my toes. I took a sip from the cup of tea I'd made oh-so-quietly in the kitchen. I love the secrets a house holds early in the morning, before anyone else is up. It sometimes seems to hum with the promise of the day ahead, as if it is readying itself for the people and things that will pass through it.

The chair was warm against my back. I hugged my knees and finished the tea, still looking out of the window, loving the feeling of being half-awake, cotton woolish and comfortable.

The marquee was already up at the back of the meadow. It was Thursday. In three days' time Chin and Gibbo would be married. In seven days' time the removal men would arrive. In eight days' time every sign that we had ever lived in this house would be gone. Apart from the scratchy initials carved into the newel-post at the top of the stairs, 'RFW ♥ HLW': Robert Francis Walter loves Hester Lena Walter. My grandparents. And in just over a month's time, I would be on the other side of the world, in a new city with a new life. I kept having to remind myself. It seemed utterly alien.

My room was bare, my books were in boxes, the clothes I hadn't worn for ten years were packed into suitcases, and my wardrobe door hung open and sad. The plastic bags full of girlish letters and cards, crammed in behind curled-up shoes and dusty boots, were gone. The top shelf, home to a couple of wilting straw hats and an old Burberry mac with a coffee stain on it, was bare now, except for torn shreds of old lining paper, flapping over the side.

My dressing-table, which had been Elise Walter's – an amazing contraption with a deep central space, tiny drawers rising up on either side, and three mirrored panels – was empty, the surfaces cleared of the dusty remains of my teenage beauty products, including a 1987 Body Shop gift basket of soap, Ice-Blue shampoo and Passionfruit shower gel. The wood was stained with circles that bore testimony to my vanity and that of my female forebears. The diamond-shaped mark to the left – had that been my grandmother's crystal scent bottle or a hallmark of my youthful obsession with Laura Ashley's Emma? The dull cloud-shape near the front was the result of an accident with nail-varnish remover, I knew that for sure.

The wardrobe and the dressing-table were staying behind. On one of her increasingly frequent visits, Simone Caldwell had been over the house and made a list of things she'd like to buy from Mum and Dad. Before I'd found out about Mike I would have been furious that they could sell them too, but what would have been the point? Keeper House was crammed with furniture, and the rented bungalow in Danby just wouldn't have room for it all. Mum also thought it would be nicer if some of it stayed in the house to keep it company. Kate didn't need any more furniture. Mum and Dad were taking what they needed. Tom, Jess and I had helped ourselves to things we wanted, but none of us felt able to deck out our homes in Keeper House regalia. I certainly couldn't imagine Tom's stark Clerkenwell loft, with its breakfast bar and ergonomically-designed red plastic and chrome barstools, playing natural host to the worn chintz sofa in the side-room, or my great-grandfather's rifle. We were going to see the new house on Sunday, after the bride and groom had left, and take with us some of Mum and Dad's stuff. We hadn't asked Mike if he wanted anything.

Kate had spoken to Mike a couple of times. He was arriving on Friday and I suppose if I'd been an outsider watching us, I'd have found our plans for his arrival pretty hilarious. Miles did. I'd arrived at Keeper House yesterday with Jess in the early evening, and as Mum, Dad, Kate, she and I were sitting with a drink before supper, we had the following conversation.

Mum: So Mike arrives on Friday – what time, John?

Dad: Er, not sure. I should think before lunch – his plane lands first thing in the morning.

Mum: So he'll be pretty tired, though they say with jet lag that you have to stay awake otherwise your body clock becomes terribly disruptive. Well, I'm at the surgery that day so we'll have to leave him a cold collation of some sort.

Kate: Mike loves ham, doesn't he?

Mum: You're quite right, Kate, he does. Or how about a

303

roast chicken? I could make that tomorrow. Darling, are you going to work on Friday?

Dad: No. I'll be at the solicitor's. Signing the completion papers.

Silence.

Mum: Right. Well, Chin'll be here, but of course *she* won't be much use. I think I'd better do a roast chicken *and* a ham, Kate, just in case – with potato salad and a green salad. That should be fine, shouldn't it? Then, Lizzy darling, all you need to do is whack it on the table.

Kate: Good idea, but of course the real question is, what do we eat on Friday evening?

Mum: I know. I suppose Mike'll be here for supper, and Mando is staying with us, Gibbo and Bozzer'll be here too then they'll go, so that's [counts on fingers] four, six – you and Tom will come over, won't you, Kate?

Kate: Yes, of course.

Mum: Eight, ten, eleven, including Mike – you think Rosalie's a definite no? I assume she's not coming although, of course, I've heard nothing about it from Mike. Typical.

Kate: Definite no.

Mum: You're sure?

Kate: Pretty much, yup.

Mum: Right. Eleven. Twelve, if we ask Gavin back after the rehearsal at the church. Chin, thirteen. Oh dear that's rather a lot, isn't it?

Me: Don't worry about me, I won't be there.

Mum: What?

Jess: What?

Me: I'm going out to dinner with Miles.

Mum: Darling, you must be there!

Me: I'm really sorry, I'll help beforehand and everything, and I'll be back first thing in the morning [trail off realizing terrible mistake] . . .

Mum: You'll *what*?

Me: I'm going to stay with him that night, but I'll be back at the house by ten a.m., I promise.

Mum: You – you and Miles? Miles Eliot?

Me: Yes.

Mum: David's brother? Is he your boyfriend?

Dad: More sherry, Kate?

Mum: You are *not* spending the night with Miles.

Me: It's a bit late for that.

Jess: What? Are you shagging Miles? Oh, my God, look at you, you are.

Me: Oh, God.

Jess: You're blushing. Oh, my God, you love him.

Me: I do not!

Mum: Darling, this is . . . well, wonderful. But . . .

Kate: Does David know?

Dad: Do I smell burning?

Mum: Be *quiet*, John. Does David know?

Me: Sort of. No one really knows. Please let's not mention this again – we're keeping it low-key and I don't know why I told you.

Mum: Well I never. Goodness gracious. But – but you're going to LA in a month's time – what will you do then?

Me: I honestly have no idea.

Silence.

Mum: I was thinking a huge fish pie for Friday evening.

Kate: Great idea. But isn't Mike allergic to haddock?

Mum: Quite right, of course he is. Back to the drawing-board.

It seemed that it was fine for Mum, Dad, Kate *et al* to rail against Mike, and quite right too, but now he was coming to the house and he was their relative, they had to suppress their feelings of murderous rage towards him

305

and worry about what to give him for lunch instead. Well, ha. He wouldn't get that treatment from *me*. If it was up to me he'd get the haddock. Would he be rubbing his hands with glee at having pulled the wool over our eyes or would he slink around contritely? When I was in London I always thought being at home was relaxing and cosy. It never had been, even before all of this, I saw now. In between Mike being allergic to haddock and when Mum was working at the surgery that week there was always a layer of confusion. At the moment, though, it was just pushed beneath the surface because of Other Events.

I'd conveyed all of this to Miles on the phone late last night when I was in bed.

'You know what I'm going to say,' he'd said, laughing.

'Yes,' I said.

'Vintage Walter situation.'

'I know,' I said. 'Change the record.'

'So I'll see you on Friday, then?'

'You will. I can't wait.'

'I can't wait either,' Miles had said, lowering his voice. 'I'm missing you so much already. I can't wait to . . .'

'Me too.' I shivered.

'Don't wear any panties.'

'"Panties" isn't a word, Miles.'

'Yes, it is.'

'It isn't a word girls use. Trust me.'

Miles laughed. 'Well, don't wear whatever they are.'

'Goodnight, Miles.'

'Goodnight, Lizzy. I love you.'

He'd said that before, and I didn't know what to say back. It was one of those things that made me worry, like I should be yelling, 'I love you more, Pumpkin!' back at him, but I couldn't. Or 'Hey, I love you too, but I'm not *in love* with you,' like an intensely groovy sixties film. It freaked me out a bit, as lots of things about this relationship did, late at night when I lay in bed, unable to sleep. In the morning it always seemed easier, more normal. But if Miles and I were going to be together, I'd have to accept that things like the David situation were weird, and that there was nothing I could do about them.

Anyway, I think I said something like 'Mmm, yes,' as I had the time before. Then I'd turned off the phone and put it on my bedside table, switched off the lamp and stared into the velvety darkness. It felt strange to be without Miles. It was one of the few nights we hadn't been together since Richmond Park. It was quite nice, actually, lying alone in bed, having freedom to think, to dream, to wiggle my toes without him turning over and asking if I was awake, rolling on to me, possessing me with a determination that made me wonder sometimes if it was me he was in love with, or if anyone else might have done.

In the last month Miles and I had been virtually insepa-rable, and I knew him so well, it was like going home. We had little in common apart from our misspent teenage years: he was flash, he liked accountancy, fine dining, clubs and observing the proprieties, but also got bladdered in pubs with his mates and shouted obscenities at the football. I liked *Pop Idol*, *Will & Grace*, old films and dancing to my old mix tapes in my flat. However, we were more than willing to meet each other half-way because the benefits were obvi-ous. We felt comfortable with each other, and I couldn't think about the future – that I'd have to leave him behind just when I'd found him. All that sort of thing. That was one of the other things that kept me awake at night, and I would lie staring into blackness, his arms wrapped around me, and wondering about what I should do.

Jaden had called one night while Miles was over to tell

me that the weather was great, he was centred and toned and that he'd seen Cameron Diaz having brunch the previous day. Miles was in the shower, and Jaden was not pleased when I told him what was going on. 'You're making a big mistake, Lizzy,' he said. 'Well, you're not if you're having fun, but if you let this guy stop you coming to LA you are.'

'I won't,' I said, nettled. 'Mind your own business.'

'Why are you with him? Why are you so keen on him?'

'I just am,' I said. How could I explain it to practical, efficient Jaden? 'It just feels . . . nice. Kind of like it should be right.'

'Yeah, but it doesn't *feel* right, does it?' Jaden said. 'Or does it?'

'Yes, it does,' I said emphatically. 'And keep out of it.'

'It doesn't feel like . . . oh, I don't know.' Jaden paused.

'Like what?' I prompted him.

'Like you're with him because he reminds you of where you grew up,' Jaden said, speaking quickly, 'and the guy who broke your heart and you can get both of those in one person so – hey presto! Let's get physical!'

'Absolutely not,' I said. I could hear Miles coming out of the shower. 'I've got to go, Jaden, I'll call you later.'

'Oh, you will,' said Jaden. 'Otherwise I'm calling you. To discuss your feelings. For a long, long time. Till you crack and beg for mercy. Thank you.'

'Oh, go away,' I said, as Miles put his arms round me, dripping all over the carpet.

'What did that idiot want?' Miles had asked.

I'd sighed. Clearly they were never going to be bosom buddies. In fact, Jaden's call and the conversation about LA had caused our only row so far. Miles didn't want me to go and made no effort to hide it from me. The making up had been worth it, though. That, and when, a week later, he'd asked about David.

We'd just got back from dinner. And were lying on the sofa in his flat, which was in a beautiful Victorian apartment block in Battersea. I'd taken Miles out to celebrate his pay rise, and we were rather drunk. Miles started to kiss me. 'I want you,' he said.

'Thanks,' I said lazily.

'I love you,' he said, stroking my hair.

'No, you don't,' I said, kissing him. 'Ridiculous boy.'

'I do,' Miles said passionately. 'I want everyone to know about us, Lizzy. When can we start telling people?'

'I told you, Miles. After the wedding. It's not the right time.'

Miles knelt on the sofa and took my hands. 'I want to tell David before, though.'

I shifted back on the leather cushions. 'Why?'

'He's going to realize something's up, Lizzy. We're not such good actors, you know.'

'Is he still coming to the wedding?' I asked, making a lightning bet with God that I would help the poor if he suddenly wasn't.

'Of course he is. Why wouldn't he?'

'Well, I don't know,' I said churlishly, cursing the Lord and all his Seraphim. 'He and Chin are friends but—'

'He's coming, Lizzy,' Miles said firmly. 'He wants to see Mum, in any case. Why do you care, anyway?'

'He doesn't have to find out, if we're really careful,' I said, pondering the situation and ignoring the question. 'We'll be careful. It'll be so embarrassing if he knows at the wedding. And he'll be – well, he might be upset.'

'Upset? Lizzy, I don't think he's going to mind that much. He'll find it a bit weird for a while but you guys – well, it was nearly a year ago.'

'I know,' I said.

'And, Lizzy, he . . . he kind of got over you, didn't he? He slept with someone else.'

309

'Yes.'

'So I can't think he'd mind that much. Honestly. And it's best he knows before the wedding so he has time to get used to it, yeah?'

'Yes,' I said slowly.

'We won't throw it in his face, will we? We'll be really discreet. But he should know before. He's my brother and I love him. I don't want to screw him around.'

'You're right.' I said. 'Tell him.'

'Good,' said Miles, moving closer. 'Good.'

Lying in bed on my own, I'd gone over this conversation again. I couldn't help it, really come on. They were brothers after all. Did David know by now? He was coming to the wedding: what would he say? Did he hate me and Miles, or was he pleased for us?

A fleeting movement on the lawn caught my eye, but the garden was empty. I sipped my tea staring into space, my mind drifting, thoughts crowding in one after the other. Miles and I were going on holiday next month to Portugal before I went, and Miles had already mentioned us moving in together in a few months' time. I'd pointed out, again, that I'd be in LA and so he'd have to move in with me there, but he simply smiled that nice smile at me and said 'It ain't over till it's over.' I knew the holiday I had with Miles would be planned out and correct to the last letter.

When David and I had been going out for a couple of months we went to Paris for the weekend. We had no money, we were staying in a horrible hotel with what I am sure was a cockroach in the bathroom, and it rained, rain like sheets of water when we arrived at the Gard du Nord on the Friday evening and trundled down to our hotel, laughing like drains, feeling like drains as rainwater drenched us through and through.

310

It was on that Paris trip with David that I'd found out David and Miles hadn't known each other very well when they were younger, how they spent a lot of time apart. Their parents had divorced when David was fourteen and Miles was eleven. Rupert Eliot moved to Spain with his new wife while the boys came with their mother to Wareham and took it in turns to go and see him in the holidays. We knew Miles but David was up at university in Edinburgh and spent a lot of time there.

So I'd never met David until the fateful summer's day when he ran over my bike outside The George in Wrentham. I always felt pathetic for finding this attractive, but the first thing he did was lift the front of his car almost to his knees and kick the crumpled remains of my beautiful blue bike out of the way. He bought me a Fab ice lolly and drove me to the bike shop. I dropped the lolly into the door pocket by mistake but said nothing out of embarrassment and, I suspect, secret rage about the bike.

We had a drink, then dinner, and then we ended up staying the night there. Both of us – we just knew. It was as simple as that. And so the next day, as we were leaving The George I opened the car door and a swarm of wasps flew out. I'd left my window open and they were all over the remains of the lolly, his really sad CD collection, a Great Britain road map and an old box of travel sweets. David just looked at me across the bonnet as I leaped around screaming, and then he laughed, and I did too, and when we stopped I looked at him again and fell irrevocably in love with him, in the car park of the pub in the next village to Wareham.

My tea was cold. I shook my head, ashamed that my mind, in its ill-disciplined way, had led me back along the same old routes. And then something, or someone, in the garden caught my eye again, and this time I heard a noise.

It was a voice. The lawn was empty and nothing was moving. Then it happened again: something moved, and someone yelled. I got up and craned out of the window. Yes, someone was creeping along by the walled garden. I stood up and banged my head on the eaves. The person in the garden spun round. He was tall, thin and angular, but I wasn't close enough to recognize him. He flattened himself against the wall and looked shiftily from side to side. On his arm he had a basket and in his hand a pair of what appeared to be secateurs. A woman's voice called in the distance, and the figure tensed, his head swivelling from side to side. He was looking for escape.

I waited no longer. I put my mug down on the floor, jumped into my slippers and ran downstairs, hair flying behind me. I ran into the sitting room and out through the french windows, across the terrace and through the door into the garden.

TWENTY-SEVEN

'Hey!' I yelled, running towards the intruder. 'Hey, you! What are you doing there?'

The man froze.

'Give me those roses,' I said, panting and sweating. I heard sounds from the house of people coming to find what all the fuss was about. 'Give them to me,' I said, snatching the basket.

'No!' said the man defiantly, looking at me with scorn. I looked down at myself and realised I was in my pyjamas and brandishing *Frederica* by Georgette Heyer as my weapon of choice.

'Go away, you horrible thief,' I said. 'My parents are coming – go away.' I stopped, realising I sounded like an eight-year-old.

'Oh dear,' he said. He had a nice face but with a curiously huge widow's peak. 'You have ruined it now – you realize that, don't you?'

A car door slammed in the driveway, then a door in the house. We turned at the same time and I considered my next move, although as I had never confronted a robber before, let alone one who stole roses and didn't run away, I had no idea what it should be.

Then I heard the voice again. 'Who's that?' I said suspiciously. 'Is someone calling you?'

'Mando!' the voice yelled. I could hear crunching on the gravel.

'Oh, my God,' I said suddenly recognising him. 'You're Mando, aren't you?'

The rose burglar bowed his head. 'Yes, I am,' he said sadly. 'I have brought Her with me. We have disagreed about flowers. Again.'

'Again?' I asked, in tones of no surprise, having heard enough about Chin's tempestuous relationship with every single person connected with the production of her wedding not to be shocked by this news.

'The roses are beautiful,' Mando said fervently, clutching the wicker basket to his chest and grimacing. 'But she cannot see it. I have almost had enough.'

'Tell me about it,' I said, feeling a pang of sympathy.

The wooden door of the walled garden banged and in strode my aunt, Hollywood film star to the life. She wore a red and orange gondoliers Prada scarf tied at a jaunty angle round her neck, black Capri pants, a slash-neck sleeveless black top, and red ballet pumps. When she reached us, she clicked her fingers imperiously at Mando. 'Here,' she said. 'Give them to me.'

'No,' said Mando, trembling.

I sat down on a bench with *Frederica*, still panting slightly at the drama just as Mum and Dad appeared.

'What on earth is going on?' said Dad, advancing up the path in his stripy pyjamas.

'Mando!' cried Mum, running towards him. 'How lovely to see you.' She flung her arms round his neck. 'I tried that pale pink Estée Lauder lipstick, Sea Shell Lady and you were right. Peach *isn't* my colour, is it? Thank you!' She threaded her arm through his.

Dad ran his hands through his hair. 'It's starting,' he said. 'Oh God.'

'Mando,' said Chin, in a quiet but terrifying voice. 'Give me those fucking roses. I told him,' she said to me and Dad, alarm written on her face, 'that they're the wrong pink. I've told him and Suzy about fifteen times. And does he listen? No? What does he do? Run out of the car while I'm trying to sodding park – honestly, John, you could have left some more space for me – and creep in here like a MENTALIST and start half-inching our bloody roses. Mando, listen to me. They're the WRONG PINK! Don't you understand?'

Her face crumpled and she started to cry.

Oh my god, I thought, they are all mad but finally a member of my family has actually gone stark bonkers in the back garden and I have completely witnessed it at first hand and it is *fascinating*.

'Chin,' said Dad firmly, 'this is no way to behave, shouting like a lunatic at nine in the morning. Mando, good morning. It's nice to see you again.'

'You too,' said Mando, fluttering his long Italian lashes at Dad and perking up somewhat. 'And you, Suzy.'

'Come inside and let's have some breakfast,' Dad said.

'I'm not having break—'

'I don't sodding care,' Dad said murderously. 'Come inside and stop behaving like a three-year-old. I know tensions are running high for all of us but I will not have people throwing themselves around like Ellen Terry among my peas. Oh, look,' he said, more cheerfully. 'There's Gibbo.'

Gibbo was loping along the path in a curious lord-of-the-manor get-up: a long checked shirt under a bright yellow corduroy jacket of seventies cut. 'Good morning, John,' he said. 'Suze, my girl, how are you?' He kissed Mum.

'Right, in we go,' said my father, like a major-domo. 'The

315

bride and groom have arrived. Let the festivities commence. Suzy, where's the sherry? I need a drink.'

'It's nine o'clock in the morning, darling,' said Mum, trotting behind him and beaming at Mando.

'I don't care. Gibbo, welcome to the beginning of the rest of your life. I'm so very sorry.'

'So,' said my mother, once we were all seated around the kitchen table, nursing coffee and eating toast, 'what do we have to do today, Mando?'

Mando was applying Marmite in a thick layer to his toast. '*Weeell*,' he said slowly, 'the flowers are arriving here at midday, Suzy, so you and I must start work then. When is Kate to be here?'

'Er . . . don't know. Midday?' said my mother, hopefully.

Mando held up his knife and ticked off each finger. 'Enamel jugs, I need, we must search for them. Old vases, glass ones, no disgusting china, these must come too. You have the glasses for the table decorations, yes?'

'Yes – there,' my mother said, pointing to the counter: an assortment of fifteen old glasses, some with patterns carved on the side, some chipped, some with painted flowers on them, stood on a tray.

'The ribbons are here now with me, polka dotty and plain. Lizzy, you will tie them where I say. And in the path through the garden to the meadow, we have the sticks with candles on. We tie flowers and ribbons to them, for the day, then light the candles for the evening. It will be so beautiful, very much like a *Midsummer's Dream*.' He stopped, and said, '*Night's Dream*. You see? So, I recap. Jessica, you will put the sticks in the ground on the path. They must be equal apart. Suzy, you will find the jugs and the implements.'

'Right,' we murmured.

'And on Saturday morning, all we must do is gather the

wild flowers for the table decorations, OK? Suzy and Chin, you and I will walk round the garden today and decide what will go in them. I *know*.' Mando turned to Chin, who was opening her mouth. 'No dog roses. They are the wrong pink. Well, you are wrong, and you will see you are wrong, but no matter. And, Suzy, you and I will go to the church with the flowers.'

'I've got to work,' said Mum. 'I'm so sorry, Mando, you'll have to do it alone.'

'I can come with you, Mando,' said Gibbo, looking up from his motorbike magazine. 'No sweat, I'd love to help. Flowers are great.'

Chin looked as if she was about to cry.

'I'll come too, if you need me to,' said Kate, who was standing at the door, staring at Mando with a look of deep scepticism in her face.

'No,' Mum said jealously. 'Lizzy can go. Oh, when are you off to meet Miles?'

'Your *loverrrrr*,' said Jess, unexpectedly, in the corner.

Mando turned towards me and raised his hands. 'Your boyfriend is coming to the wedding? Your beautiful boy-friend, how I long to see him again.' He smacked his lips. Kate stiffened in alarm.

'No, not that boyfriend any more,' I said.

'His brother,' my mother said, standing up to put some plates and cups in the dishwasher.

'You are not with David any more?' Mando said.

'No,' I said.

'But why?' Mando said, appealing to the wider group, except Dad who was in the larder looking for more Grape Nuts.

There was a pause: no one knew what to say.

'Ah,' said Dad, emerging from the larder with a packet in his hand. 'No Grape Nuts. Anyone in the mood for Alpen? Ho-hum.'

'More tea?' said Chin to Gibbo, who had returned to his motorbike magazine.

'Asparagus tart for lunch, Kate?' said Mum, brandishing a flan tin.

'So,' Mando pressed on, 'this boyfriend is not your lovely David. He is?'

'His brother,' Mum repeated, wiping the counter.

This was news to Chin and Gibbo, who stared, slack-jawed, at me.

'You're going out with Miles?' Chin said.

'Miles?' Gibbo said. 'Right. Good bloke.'

'Miles?' Chin repeated. 'Does David know?'

'Er, I think so by now,' I said, pushing the Marmite along the table with one finger.

Chin put down her mug and lowered her voice. 'Lizzy. Really? You and Miles?'

'Yes,' I said brightly. 'It's fantastic, and it's going really well.'

Chin looked searchingly at me. 'Is it? Really? Are you – are you serious?'

I met her stare. 'Yes,' I said. 'We are.'

'Can we have a proper catch-up later, Lizzy? Just the two of us?' Chin stroked the back of her smooth head still staring at me.

I'd known she'd have a problem with it. People outside a relationship always think they know better than the participants. I couldn't be bothered to explain why it was right, and I was sure she wouldn't believe me anyway, so I said, in a muffled voice, 'Sure, let's. That'd be great.'

'I haven't seen you properly for ages, have I?'

'Well, you know whose fault that is,' I said coldly.

She slid her palm flat along the table towards my hand. 'Yes,' she said, took my hand and held it. 'I'm sorry. I've been crap. But it's all been so hectic. And . . . there's lots going on. I want to talk to you properly, though.'

'Yep,' I said, only slightly mollified.

Chin got up and went out to her car to get her suitcase and some flowers she'd brought. Mum and Mando were in a huddle, Gibbo was still absorbed in his magazine, Dad was munching his cereal, and Jess and Kate had gone to unload chairs from Kate's car. It was strange that we should be bringing things in to the house when four days later everything would go out of it for ever.

After the dramatic start to the day, and overloading on Marmite, I was suddenly cast into gloom and impotent anger swept through me. I wanted to talk to Miles. I put my plate into the dishwasher, and went listlessly upstairs to get dressed. Perhaps I'd call him, I thought, then remembered he was in a deal-breaking meeting all day.

On the landing at the top of the stairs boxes had been filled with the contents of the bookcase outside my room, Mum's old Georgette Heyers, Jean Plaidys, Daphne du Mauriers and umpteen old book-club hardbacks with intriguing titles like *Without My Cloak* and *The Stars Look Down*. I'd read them all, along with most of *The Forsyte Saga* and *War and Peace*, one boiling hot summer of bored, sulking adolescence when I was sixteen and stayed in my room for eighteen hours out of twenty-four, convinced my best friend Jackie Poller hated me and that my parents were harsh and vile and that I had nine spots on my chin and nose because my sister had finished the Clearasil.

Tom had had a new bike that summer and was always out with Miles. Jess was at a holiday workshop organized by the vicar at Wareham, which meant she learned folksongs and put coloured paper fringing around lots of household items. I hated everyone and everyone hated me, I thought.

That summer I kissed Miles for the first time. We were outside the Neptune, sitting on a wooden bench, having been allowed a sneaky beer by Bill. It was late and warm, and the breeze was delicious on my shoulders. I was enjoying being out of the house and away from my horrible family, who repressed me and tried to thwart my every move, and – I can't remember how it happened, but it did. Then we were embarrassed, and then Tom appeared. Perhaps if he hadn't we wouldn't have wasted all the time we had.

I bent to look through the next box of books and found Mum's collection of *School Friend* annuals, pulled one out, took it into my room, threw myself on to the bed and opened it. In my mother's loopy, difficult handwriting (perfect for the indecipherable prescriptions she writes now) I read 'Suzanne Rodwell aged Ten'. I turned to the contents page, intrigued, and was overwhelmed. 'Celia and the Silver Ukulele', 'Jo's Amazing Maypole Ride', 'Well Done, Professor Sally!' – good grief, and people condemn *heat* magazine for sounding silly. I turned to page 91, 'A Parrot, A Plot – And Geraldine'. It was the absolute duffest of stories, about some half-witted girls at St Winifred's, and a madcap called Geraldine, who was always getting them into scrapes, but the heroine, Jane Watts, was a sensible girl, cheery, helpful and ready to take it on the chin even when all was at its worst. I threw it aside in disgust.

I lay on my bed, feeling sorry for myself and wanting to take out my mood on someone but I couldn't at a time like this. I should have been downstairs helping. Then I thought of plucky Jane Watts of 'A Parrot, A Plot – And Geraldine', and I thought well, if she can remain cheerful while all around her people are saying things like 'We won through in the end, didn't we, Matron?' and 'I say, that'll show those Fourth Year girls!' well then, I should take a leaf out of her book. Suddenly I saw the way forward. I swung my arm over the bed, picked up the *School Friend* annual, and started reading again. My sense of vocation increased at every sentence. I would be kind, helpful, with bright cheery eyes and a sparkling smile. I would load boxes and right wrongs and I would be nice to everyone in my loving family circle, and I would really think about whether I was going to let Miles persuade me not to go to LA, and when Saturday came and I saw David, I would be jolly and chirpy and he would say 'Madcap schemes are always afoot when Lizzy's around, but she always pulls it off!' and walk off with a spring in his step and no undertow of argh erk ouch, those things which characterised our previous meetings since our breakup. Yes. I leaped off the bed, flung the door open and skipped lightly downstairs, where I was met by the sight of Chin and Gibbo in a passionate clinch by the staircase. I slapped Gibbo on the back. 'Well done!' I cried heartily, and danced into the study.

'Dad,' I practically yelled. 'Can I help you with some packing?'

'Er . . . no,' said Dad, with alarm. 'I'm looking over the papers again. Stuart and Simone might drop by later, before completion tomorrow, and I don't want them springing anything on me.'

'Need me to check them for you?' I said.

'*You?*' Dad spluttered. 'No thanks, Lizzy. Tell you what though, Chin wants me to help her fold napkins in return for her giving me a lift to the solicitor's tomorrow. Maybe you could do it instead.'

'Why's she giving you a lift?'

'Car's packed up,' said Dad briefly. I sighed. His car was a twelve-year-old estate, called Dilys by her affectionate owner, and packed up at the most inconvenient moments. Need to get to the station in ten minutes flat? Dead engine. Dreaded family outing to visit Great Aunt Dahlia and Uncle Simon? Purring engine.

'Of course, Dad. Anything to help!' I trotted into the hall again. Chin and Gibbo were still there, having A Moment.

I lingered on the sidelines, unsure what Jane Watts would have done in a similar situation.

Thankfully the front door opened slowly and Tom came in, pulling a wheelie suitcase. A zip-up bag for his morning suit hung over one arm. Chin and Gibbo stepped apart and I walked forward nonchalantly, as if I'd been elsewhere doing important things.

'Tom!' I said, and went to kiss him. 'I thought you weren't coming down till teatime!'

'Hello, Tom,' said Chin. 'You're early!'

Kate's voice echoed from the kitchen. 'Tom? Is that you?'

'I stayed late last night to get a document ready for a client so I could be here early today,' said Tom, pleased with himself.

'Well, this is great,' said Chin, hugging him. 'You can go to pick up the glasses and cutlery! Suzy's got the address.'

'Uh?' said Tom.

She turned back to Gibbo. ''Bye, darling. I'll see you in a little while.'

'Where are you going?' I said.

'Manicure and pedicure,' said Chin, airily. 'And a massage.'

'Right,' said Tom, putting his suit on his case and his hands on his hips.

'Right!' I interjected hurriedly. 'Lovely. Where's that then?'

'You wouldn't have heard of it.' Chin put her bag over her shoulder and ran her fingers through her hair. 'Sophia Gunning recommended it. Dereham Spa'.

'Oh,' I said and I coughed and smiled inwardly to restore my schoolgirl equilibrium.

'Why aren't you going tomorrow?' Tom said. 'What if you chip the nail varnish?'

'I want to go today,' said Chin, smiling sweetly. 'Lizzy, your father's supposed to be folding the napkins. I've left a pattern specification on the table for him but I'm sure he'll get it wrong. You'll have to help him. Best do it now – there's loads to do this afternoon. And, Lizzy, find some gloves for picking the flowers this afternoon. I don't want people asking on Saturday why all my family are covered with scratches. Thanks. See you later.' She marched out.

'She's pushing her luck, she really is,' Tom said. 'God, I pity the fool— Hey! Gibbo! How are you, mate?'

'Good, thanks,' said Gibbo, the light of amusement in his eye.

By Thursday evening I was exhausted. There's nothing in the *School Friend Annual 1956* about jolly old Jane Watts having to take a rest cure for a month after setting up a wedding for a bloody control freak. While Chin was probably lying on a soft leather chair in a dressing-gown, with cucumber slices on her eyes, being attended to by soothing voices and velvety hands, back at the ranch her family worked themselves into a frenzy. We gathered, we polished, we picked things up, we dropped them off, we made phone calls, washed dishes, jugs and plates, we ran around the house packing the rest of our possessions into boxes and tidying up the essentials that remained. We wrote signs, we lugged crates of champagne, and Tom, Jess and I ruined pile after pile of napkins, until Gibbo, surveying the wreckage shooed us away and got to work. Ten minutes later – or so it seemed – two hundred napkins sat on the two tables nearest the door, deftly manipulated into the shape of a fleur-de-lis.

'How on earth did you know how to do that?' Tom asked.

'Y'know,' Gibbo said, pulling up his trousers, to which were attached an assorted variety of grass cuttings and bits of paper. 'Chin taught me. Pretty easy, really. I've been practising. Let's move these chairs into place, shall we?'

Mum and Kate appeared after seven, bearing a jug of Pimm's and some crisps. 'I thought we could have a drink out here. I've put a casserole in the oven and baked some potatoes,' said Mum. 'Here, have a glass.'

We all sat outside the marquee, on the grass that sloped down towards the house, and took in the view. Against a gun-metal sky, the golden grey of the lichen-covered stone house glowed in the early-evening sun, and the glass diamonds of the leaded windows flashed and shimmered. The budding lavender stretched towards us in mauve and grey rows, like spindly fingers reaching up to the meadow where we sat.

There was the sound of a car in the driveway and we looked up to see who it was but no one moved, as if we were reluctant to break the spell. Then I heard Chin's voice and her footsteps as she opened the gate that led from the lane by the side of the house into the garden. 'Here's Simone and Stuart come to say hello,' she called.

'Oh, hell,' muttered Mum, under her breath, as she scrambled up, brushing grass off her lap. 'Where's your father, Jess?'

'Don't know,' said Jess.

'Evening, all!' cried Stuart Caldwell, as he advanced towards us, his beefy torso crammed into a short-sleeved shirt. His face was aggressively tanned, his expression jovial. Chin and Simone followed him, the latter, hampered by her high-heeled clear plastic mules.

'Just enjoying the view, are you?' said Stuart. 'Making the most of it while you can, I expect.'

Simone screamed and clutched Chin's arm. 'Stuart!' she yelled. 'I'm, like, falling over in these bloody heels. It's hilarious. Hey, it's Lizzy! And is that Tom? Look, do you like them?'

We all stood up, and I looked down to examine the shoes in question.

'They're really nice,' I said, lying, because they were completely hideous, studded with glass stones around the heel and across the foot.

'Hi, Mrs – Suzy.' She waved at Mum. Every part of her – except her dodgy boobs – wobbled. 'We just wanted to come over and say hi. Is Mr – John around?'

'Stuart, would you like a drink?' said Mum.

Suddenly Kate materialized next to her, like the sinister Addams Family butler, and silently held out a glass. 'Pimm's, Sarah?' she said, to the incoming lady of the house.

'It's Simone, Mrs Walter,' Simone corrected her helpfully.

'Is it?' said Kate mutinously, but Mum elbowed her out of the way.

'Well, well!' Stuart repeated, taking the glass Mum offered him. 'Sorry to disturb. This time next week we'll be sitting here doing the same, I expect.' He smiled in a friendly way.

'The Caldwells just wanted to ask something,' Chin explained, in a neutral voice. 'I ran into them in town.' Her eyes were fixed on the ground.

'Oh, it's *so* lovely up here,' Simone said. Her heels were sinking into the ground. Stuart rubbed his hands together, then held out his stubby arms in an all-encompassing gesture. 'We were wondering what you think to something. I know this is a bit irregular, ahead of our moving in here. I mentioned it to Ginevra, seeing as how it's her wedding day on the Saturday. Simone and I, we've just got back from Thailand, see?'

'Lovely,' we murmured, not sure where this was going.

Simone nodded. 'We had a butler in our room all the time. And whatever DVDs we wanted, they'd order for us. CDs too! It was a six-star hotel – there's only, like, five in the world. I had to stay there one night on my own because Stuart had to go away. A meeting in Bangkok.' Stuart's eyes were boring into her like bullets, but Simone didn't notice.

'And I'm, like, well, what am I gonna do? So I went out, and there was this market, right outside the hotel, but I hadn't noticed it because we hadn't been out of the hotel before. Why would you? Seriously, it was that nice.'

'Anyway,' interrupted Stuart, tiring of this reminiscence, 'Simone buys this mini-temple thing, right? Well, four of them. And a huge, wooden door. It's almost eight foot high. Amazing they are, wood-carvings, totally authentic. The workmanship's genuine. It's not tat.'

The wind was picking up, providing respite from the heavy humidity of the evening. I looked up at the weathervane swinging gently in the breeze.

'Anyway,' he went on, 'we've just been to pick them up and we was wondering, you know.' He trumpeted a cough into his clenched fist. 'Seeing as how we're completing tomorrow, can we just pop them away here instead of taking them home and finding a place for them where the kids won't smash into them?'

Tom suddenly said. 'They're not those mini-temple things you put in your house to ward off evil spirits, are they?'

'Yeah, and they're lovely. I just had to have them, you know?' Simone said, clasping her hands in front of her. 'And,' her voice became serious, 'it's something a bit different. No one else has them, right, and they'll look great in my new house.'

'Are they ... Hm.' Tom bent his head, as if to access something buried deep in his mind. 'Are they like the ones Posh bought last year in Thailand?'

Tom's *heat* magazine knowledge is encyclopaedic.

'Yes, that's right.' Simone said, clearly nettled that she'd been rumbled. 'But, apart from her, no one else'll have them. I had to really beg the old man who was selling them to let me buy them. I thought he weren't gonna let me at first. But we came to, like, an agreement. I bargained with him.

326

Amazing that he was selling them right outside the hotel – it was really lucky.'

'That *is* amazing,' said Tom, beaming. 'Well, what a great idea. Do you want to put them—'

'Hang on a second, Tom,' Chin chipped in. 'I don't think there's room, is there?' Her eyes were clearly conveying a message that said, 'How dare they think they can start putting their stuff here?'

'Never mind. We'll find somewhere. The shed, maybe. It's pretty big and John cleared it out last week. How about that, Stuart?'

'No, Tom,' Chin said, through gritted teeth. 'I really don't think there's going to be room.'

'Oh, they won't do anyone any harm there, Chin, don't worry,' Mum said.

'That's not the point! They shouldn't be there – it's still our bloody house,' Chin said spikily, and stalked off towards the house.

'I'll go after her,' Gibbo said, as we all stood there, embarrassed. He followed her and a few seconds later we heard the kitchen door slam.

'Sorry about that,' Mum said. 'Wedding nerves.'

Stuart was unperturbed. 'Sure it is, sure,' he said, bobbing his head. 'It must be, erm, strange. This time next week and all that, eh? Well, it's a lovely house, and I promise you I'm going to take good care of it.'

Dad appeared from the house and the situation was explained to him. I noticed a bathroom catalogue poking out of Simone's pastel-lettered Louis Vuitton bag and my stomach churned.

Dad offered them the use of the shed, gave Simone his arm and set off with Mum and the Caldwells to their black Shogun with tinted windows. It looked like a huge shiny beetle, dark and smooth in the pretty rose-dappled lane.

'Twelve o'clock tomorrow, it has to be signed by, remember,' Stuart Caldwell said to Dad. 'Otherwise the deal's off.'

'Yes, I know,' said Dad. 'I understand, Stuart, don't worry. I'll be there at ten.'

'Good,' said Stuart, unsmiling, and climbed into the car. Then the mask fell back into place. ''Bye, all,' he cried, beaming like Tony Soprano. 'Good luck!'

'Yes, and good luck for Saturday,' Simone called, waving. 'We'll see you next week.'

'Why didn't you mind them putting the mini-temples in the shed?' I asked Tom as he, Jess and I sat on the ground again. Kate stood up, brushed down her skirt, and started to clear the glasses.

'Amusement factor, I suppose,' said Tom. 'But they do bring luck, those things. If you place them in a home they protect it. And as the Caldwells have got four I thought it was worth a chance.'

'Bit late for that now,' said Jess. 'Anyway, from what Dad says, if we don't sign tomorrow Mike misses some deadline to repay the money he owes.'

'How do you know?' I said.

'He keeps ringing to remind us,' Kate said, as she put the last glass on the tray. 'It has to get to him on time.'

'What happens if it doesn't?' I asked.

'I don't like to think,' said Kate. 'But I presume we're not talking about being fifty pounds in the red with one's current account.'

'So we need all the luck we can get, don't we?' said Tom, practically.

'Yes,' said Kate. 'We do. See you inside, then. Supper's nearly ready.'

A delicious smell wafted to us from the kitchen window. Above, Chin's room overlooked the garden and I could see her pacing up and down, while Gibbo stood with his arms outstretched, trying to catch her as she passed him, only to be slapped away. She was crying.

'It's just wedding nerves,' said Tom, following my eye.

'I'm almost past caring,' said Jess.

'Me too,' Tom said, as we stood up to go in. 'Still, if she wants something to take her mind off it, Uncle Mike's arriving tomorrow.'

I sighed into my glass and drained it. *The School Friend Annual* didn't have a section on Uncle Mike or indeed, the Caldwells. Let alone Miles and David. Its usefulness was limited.

TWENTY-EIGHT

Friday dawned humid again and overcast, and the atmosphere was ugly. Today was the day. It would overshadow Chin's wedding, no matter what we did to pretend otherwise. As I lay in bed I could hear Chin and Gibbo, down the corridor, bickering about something. My windows were wide open and the curtains hung limply. My phone buzzed again. I ignored it. Miles had left a series of phone and text messages, but he seemed to be from another world, a world unconnected with the weird, end-of-an-era gloom that hung over the house as thickly as the heavy clouds in the sky.

Downstairs Dad and Mum were packing the study, one of the last rooms that had to be sorted out. The low static of the radio floated up to me as I looked around my room. I didn't want to remember it like this, half-empty and forlorn.

I glanced at my watch. It was eight thirty. Mike's plane would be near England by now. Was it near us? Was he looking out of the window? What would it be like, to see him again? I couldn't bear the idea of having to hate him. Was he sorry for this? Miles had said I should forget about all of it, that it was in the past, but I couldn't – just as I couldn't forget about David sleeping with someone else, or how much I disliked Stuart Caldwell, or how awful Chin was being, or how nervous but relieved I was to be leaving next month for LA.

Chin's bedroom door slammed and I heard footsteps run down the stairs. She was giving Dad a lift to the solicitor's soon so that he could sign the papers – a gloomy way to spend the day before your wedding. Now that it was here, I felt no stab of pain. It was as if we were camouflaging the sale with the wedding. But everything I looked at in this house held some kind of memory connected with me, my family, our lives and those of our relatives before us. And from Wednesday it would be the Caldwells' home. I dug my fingers into the palms of my hands, feeling the sharp crescents of nail press painfully into my skin. I stayed like that for a while, then got up, dressed and went downstairs.

Through the kitchen window I could see Mando kneeling in front of a bench on the lawn, with a tarpaulin on which rested flowers, jugs and ribbons, all of which he was dividing up and sorting out. It was hot, but the sky was a murky sea-green-grey. I poured myself some coffee, grateful for the relative cool of the kitchen.

Kate staggered in with a box of plates in her arms. 'There we are,' she said, as she deposited it on the table. 'God, it's a vile day. You can feel the humidity on your skin.'

'Have Dad and Chin gone?' I said.

'Not yet. Your father's still in the study. Budge over, Lizzy. I need to get that pie-dish out of the cupboard.'

'When's Mike getting here?' I asked, as Kate knelt on the floor, her floral skirt flaring out about her.

'Lunchtime.'

'You spoke to him last week, didn't you?'

'Yes,' Kate said, shutting the cupboard.

'How was he?'

'Fine,' said Kate. She stood up with the pie-dish. 'Where's the butter?'

'Here,' I said. 'What did he say?'

'Mike? He said . . .' Kate gave a tiny sigh. 'He just said he was arriving at lunchtime today. I don't think he's looking forward to it. To be honest, he's . . . well, he's terrified.'

It was so unlike Kate to venture information of this nature voluntarily that I was unsure how to continue. She stared vacantly at the butter, twisting her wedding and engagement rings, then grimaced suddenly. 'That's salted, Lizzy. Get the other butter from the larder.'

Kate and Mike. What I wouldn't give to know what was going on there? I mused, as I went into the larder, where jars of chutney and pickles stood on the deep shelves with trays of fruit and vegetables. I picked up an apple and rubbed it on my jeans.

'Hello, John. Nearly ready to go?' I heard Kate say.

When I came out, Dad was standing there in his suit, his wallet-style leather briefcase under his arm. He looked smart, like a little boy on his first day at school. The sharp juice of the apple stung the back of my throat.

Mum appeared behind him, her hands in her pockets. Her eyes were red and her face was blotchy. She had been crying. It was such a miserable scene, so stupid that my mum was crying about this, that I felt a new wave of rage against Mike.

'Have you got everything?' asked Mum, wiping her nose on the back of her hand.

'Here,' said Kate, and handed her a kitchen towel.

'Thanks.'

'It's hot,' Dad said.

'Boiling,' said Mum. 'I'm afraid you're going to swelter in that suit, John.' Then she tried to put a positive spin on the conversation: 'Chin'll bring you back in time for lunch and you'll have a nice glass of beer and a nap and you'll be relieved it's over. We all will.'

'Yes,' said Dad doubtfully.

'Where's Chin?' said Mum.

'Don't know,' said Dad. He went out into the corridor. 'Chin! I'm ready when you are.'

There was a silence, broken only by the sound of Mando gabbling to himself on the lawn.

'Chin?' Dad called again.

'She's around somewhere,' said Mum. 'I saw her first thing and she bit my head off. Said the dried flowers in the downstairs loo reminded her of something from a retirement home and couldn't I make them look less repellent?'

'Oh, *honestly*,' Kate said impatiently. 'She *is* the limit. I know it's her big day tomorrow but, really . . .'

'Chin!' Dad called, advancing further into the corridor. 'I can't be late. Mike needs the money to go out today, and Caldwell has some tax issue he's worried about.'

'Really?' Kate said.

'Oh, yes,' said Dad. 'Their solicitor's a terrifying woman. If it doesn't get signed and completed today, aside from the mess that'd leave Mike in, the Caldwells can pull out. We'd have to pay them compensation.'

'Ridiculous man,' said Kate in disgust. She strode out and stood at the back door. '*Ginevra*!' she boomed, so loudly that the birds scattered out of the mulberry tree.

'Mando, have you seen Chin?' Mum called out of the window.

'Chinevra? No,' said Mando, standing up and brushing off his trousers. 'Well, not since one hour ago when she left in the car.'

Kate stomped up the path towards him as Mum and I leaned out of the window.

'She left an hour ago?' I said.

'Mando, are you sure? In the car?' Mum said.

'Why didn't we hear it?' Kate demanded suspiciously.

'Yes, in the car. In her car,' Mando said, waving a branch of Chin-approved pink roses at us. 'She parked it round the corner last night – do you not remember? – because of the Caldwells.'

'What's all the shouting about?' asked Tom, as he came into the kitchen.

'Chin's gone and she's supposed to be giving John a lift to the solicitor's now,' Kate said succinctly.

'I'll take him,' said Tom. 'Let me get my keys.'

'That's not the point, though,' I said. 'She said she'd give Dad a lift – she made a big deal about it, how out of her way it was and everything. What's she playing at?'

'Morning, everyone,' said Gibbo, ambling into the kitchen.

We rounded on him.

'Where's Chin?' Mum screeched.

'Gibbo!' Kate boomed from outside, where she and Mando were peering into the kitchen. 'Where's Chin?'

Gibbo looked tired, and who could blame him? 'I don't know,' he said, looking around at all of us. 'She was . . . well, we had words last night. And first thing this morning. Then she didn't sleep at all. Then she just stormed out. Mate, it was strange,' he said, appealing to Tom.

'But did she say where she was going?' Tom asked.

'She said she had to go into town . . . with John.' He spotted my dad and smiled at him. 'Hey, John, there you are! So where's Chin?'

'We don't know,' said Kate, through gritted teeth.

'Oh,' said Gibbo. He drooped a bit.

'What did you argue about?' Tom demanded. 'Was it – was it a *serious* argument?'

'No, not really. Well . . . sort of . . .' Gibbo scratched his head.

Dad ran his finger around the back of his collar.

'To be honest, I'm not sure,' Gibbo said, his voice quieter. 'The last month or so . . . she's been in a right state. Snappy. Nothing's right.'

'About wedding stuff?' I asked.

Gibbo thought for a moment. 'No, not really. She knows what she wants there.'

'What, then?' Mum said.

'I don't really know. I think it's to do with the house. And that Sophia Gunning. She's always off meeting her and her friends.'

I remembered Sophia's flaxen hair and perfect white teeth, her patronizing manner. Why on earth was Chin so keen on her?

'Hey. What's this?' Mum said sharply, and picked up a folded piece of notepaper that was propped against the breadbin. It said *John* on the front. She opened it, her hands shaking a little. ' *"Dear John,"* ' she read. ' *"I can't take you in today. Something important's come up. Don't sign the contracts, don't go to the solicitor's. I'll be back as soon as I can. Love C XX PS Tell Gibbo I'm sorry."* '

There was a silence.

As if by unspoken consensus, Mum, Tom and I took a step towards Gibbo and patted his arm.

'Well, well,' Mum said, refolding the note. ' "Don't go to the solicitor's." Honestly, what's she playing at?'

I looked at the clock. It was nearly ten. 'Dad, you're supposed to be there soon. Shouldn't you give them a call?'

'I'm going to,' said Dad, heading for the study.

'Someone else can give you a lift,' said Mum. 'I've got to go to the surgery now. Kate?'

'Of course,' said Kate.

'Right,' said Mum. 'Well . . . I suppose I'd better go. This is all very strange. See you later. Lizzy, remember the pie's in—'

335

'Yes, Mum,' I said. 'Don't worry about any of that. See you later.'

Mum hurried out, jacket over her arm, handbag swinging from her shoulder. I turned to Tom, who crammed some bread into his mouth and raised his eyebrows at me. 'It's not her failing to give Dad a lift that pisses me off,' I said. 'It's just – sorry, Gibbo – that she's been such a bitch lately. It was the one thing she had to do for Dad, and she can't even do that.'

'I'm with you, honest I am,' said Gibbo, his brows knitting, 'but there's something about it I don't understand. It's just not like her.'

'Well . . .' Tom and I began, but Kate flashed us a warning glance.

Dad came back into the kitchen, still on the phone. I could hear Stuart Caldwell's voice in a trickle of tinny noise. 'Yes, Stuart. I know . . . Yes, I know. Look, I really don't see— Yes. I've said I'm sorry. I'm on my way now . . . Yes, of course I want this to go ahead! I've said so . . . Yes, I appreciate that was one of the conditions . . . Yes . . . Yes, I know . . . Look, we can have this conversation when I get there.'

Dad stood next to me and picked up a wooden spoon. His face was like thunder.

I could hear Stuart Caldwell saying, 'I'm not happy, John. Not happy.'

'Yes, I can appreciate that, but it's not the end of the world. I'll see you in twenty minutes.'

'This money has to go out of my account today or I'm fucked.'

'You've said that,' said Dad. 'Goodbye, Stuart. See you in a little while.'

'John, you'd better—'

Dad switched the phone off.

'Something dodgy going on there,' he said slowly. 'He says he has a financial commitment and has to move this money out today for tax reasons. If we don't have the papers signed by twelve it won't and some deal of his'll fall through.'

'He sounded pretty cross.'

'He was,' said Dad briefly. 'Nasty piece of work. I wish it was anyone but him. She's a sweet girl, but he's a thug. Still, I'm going to have to go, no matter what Chin's note says. If she gets back, give her a short sharp shock from me.'

'Come on, John,' said Kate, jangling her car keys.

We walked with them to the hall, then Tom, Gibbo and I stood in the courtyard and watched Dad flick through his papers one last time. Not a leaf stirred in the trees.

'See you later,' Dad said. He raised his arm and turned away.

At that moment, an extraordinarily loud noise rang out from behind us, like a roaring wave heading towards us from the road away from the house. It sounded almost like a jet plane. Tom jumped, and we all swivelled round, in time to see a sleek silver car screech round the corner and come to a ferociously abrupt halt.

'Fuck!' yelled Kate, all composure gone.

I giggled, more out of shock than anything else.

'What the hell—' Tom said simultaneously.

'*Stop!* Stop!' someone screamed, and through the gate, looking like a bedraggled water rat, ran Chin, crying, one arm waving at us, the other dragging behind her a beautifully presented, beaming Sophia Gunning.

'Hello, John, hello, Kate,' she panted, as we lined up to greet her. 'Do you remember my friend from school, Sophia?'

'Yes,' said Dad.

'Hello,' said Kate.

337

'Eh?' said Tom.

'Ssh,' I hissed.

Chin brushed her hair out of her eyes. She looked about nineteen again. 'Thank God I caught you in time,' she said. 'I'm so sorry about all of this. Hello, gorgeous,' she said, and blew a kiss at Gibbo.

''Lo,' said Gibbo, looking as if he'd swallowed a gobstopper.

'Oh, it's so lovely to be here again,' Sophia said, in her calm, silvery voice. 'It's going to be just great.'

'It is,' Chin said. They grinned at each other.

What's going to be great? I wondered idly, as I do in moments of drama rather than simply saying, 'What on earth are you talking about?'

'What the hell is all this about, Chin?' said Dad. 'I'm so furious with you I'm seriously considering – I have to walk up that aisle with you tomorrow and give you away, and apart from relief at having you off my hands, I'll feel a huge sense of disappointment at you and your behaviour lately. First Mike, now you. I'm sorry. You've let us all down. Now, if you don't mind . . .' He gazed at her coolly and put his hand on the car door.

'I'm not explaining very well,' Chin said, unperturbed by my father's uncharacteristic anger. She took his hand. 'Oh, John, you're going to love me. I love me. You don't have to sell the house.'

'What?'

'You don't have to! Sophia works for Lizzy's company. She wants to hire it! For a film! And she'll pay us rent for the orchard and the meadow, so there can be production offices and catering vans and things there too! They want to film entirely on location for three months, all here, at Keeper House. Here! It's a vast amount of money! You can get the rest to pay Mike by remortgaging – we all can. I've done the sums and I'll explain, but the main thing is you don't need to sell the house.'

'It's true,' Sophia said quickly, before any of us could say anything. 'Chin and I met up for a drink about a month ago – we hadn't seen each other for years.' She coughed, tactfully, and Chin looked at her feet. 'I've been in the UK working with our location people, trying to find the right place to film this wonderful script – it's been driving us up the wall.'

'*The Diary of Lady Mary Chartley*,' I said, as if in a dream.

'Yes, of course, Lizzy. I can't believe you didn't think of it yourself.'

'I—' I began lamely.

Sophia turned to Dad. 'I came down here with Chin a couple of weeks ago, John, when you were away for the day. You'd gone to see your aunt.'

Dad nodded, clearly unable to speak.

'I brought a couple of people down with me. Paul, Jaden—'

'Jaden was here?' I said.

Kate cleared her throat and spoke for the first time. She looked at Chin. 'Is this true?' she said. 'Is this the real thing?'

Chin nodded. 'I promise you it is. I couldn't tell you because I didn't want to raise your hopes till it was definite. That's where I was yesterday afternoon, sorting out the rest of it. See?' She held out her hands. 'No manicure. Do you believe me now?' She turned to Dad. 'John, you'll have to move out next month for the summer but – hey – you're all packed up anyway, aren't you? I've got all the sums here. We don't have to sell. I promise you, *we don't have to sell*.'

The phone rang inside the house.

'I think I know who that is,' said Dad, turning towards the front door.

'Who?' Chin said.

'The bloke who was going to buy the house. We need to sit down so you can explain it all to me, Sophia. But right now I'd better break the bad news to him. Blimey.' He stepped forward. 'You're absolutely sure, aren't you?' he said to Chin. 'I'm about to burn my boats. Just say it once again.'

'You don't have to sell. I promise,' said Chin. Dad gave Chin a hug, then disappeared into the house.

Tom yelled and jumped up in the air. 'You gorgeous, gorgeous woman!'

Chin seemed bashful. She glanced up at Gibbo. 'I'm sorry for being such a cow,' she said.

''S all right,' said Gibbo, smiling.

'I thought if I told anyone it might jinx it. And I wanted to do it by myself. I didn't want it to be anyone else's fault if it went wrong. God, I was dying to say something earlier – especially yesterday when those bloody Caldwells turned up. That vile man groped me in the lane.'

'In the where?' said Tom, smirking.

'Anyway,' Chin went on, ignoring him, 'I know I've been a total bitch lately. I'm really sorry. But it's been getting to me, not knowing – Sophia only got the final call this morning from the director so she drove down straight away. John has to agree, you see.'

'I can't see that he won't,' I said, but thought that actually Mike was the one who had to agree, and if he didn't I would chop him up into small bits and sauté him in butter. With haddock.

Gibbo stepped forward and gripped Chin's shoulders. 'I'm proud of you, doll,' he said, and hugged her. Chin looked almost girlish.

As we were all hugging each other – even Sophia Gunning,

to whom Gibbo gave a big smacker on the cheek – a shadow appeared at the doorway. 'Hello,' called Jess. Her curly hair was like a halo round her head. 'What's been going on? Have you all had breakfast yet?'

TWENTY-NINE

I am ashamed to say we all got knee-walking drunk at lunchtime. Dad opened a case of the wedding champagne, which had arrived that morning. We were too excited to eat the pie Mum had made. Instead we munched bread and grapes, but mostly we talked, asking Chin and Sophia questions, congratulating ourselves, getting pleasurably maudlin about what might have been, explaining the situation over and over again to Jess and Mando, drinking toast after toast to:

1 Chin
2 Sophia Gunning
3 Monumental Films
4 My big boss from New York Paul's wife, Julie who had walked out on him earlier that year for her yoga instructor (I personally don't remember that being one of the central principles of yoga, shagging your rich Tribeca-based clients), sending Paul into a spiral of drink-and-drugs hell, which culminated in him being flown over here to dry out at an exclusive clinic where the only book in his room apart from Mills & Boons and The Complete

Works of Shakespeare was *The Diary of Lady Mary Chartley*, which was why the film was being made in the first place. Thank you, Julie! Hope all's working out with the yoga instructor.

I tried to call Jaden in LA, to ask him what the hell he'd been playing at, coming to my house and not telling me, but I couldn't get hold of him so left an emotional message saying how great everything was and how I loved him, Sophia, Monumental, the world and the universe.

We rang Mum at the surgery and told her what had happened, and she put a pin through Mrs Weedon's bandage into her knee. Dad had several unpleasant conversations with Stuart Caldwell and his solicitor, then with Paul, our bank, our solicitor Rupert, and Monumental's lawyers, but emerged looking happier and reassured.

Sophia got the office to email the contracts they'd drawn up so that Dad could print them out and sign them.

Some time during the afternoon as we were sitting at the long wooden table by the kitchen garden, my phone shook with a text message. I saw that it was from Miles, and my heart sank. I opened it. 'Three messages and no answer. I'm starting to think you've died or you've dumped me. Are we still on for tonight? Have you been speaking to David? Please just let me know. I love you, love Miles.'

I ran into the house to call him from the landline.

'Miles, it's me,' I said, when he answered.

'Hello.' He sounded a bit cold.

'Listen,' I said, 'I'm sorry I didn't call you yesterday evening but –'

'Or today,' Miles interrupted.

'– but something amazing's happened. I still can't believe it.'

'What?' said Miles.

'It's a long story. I know it's not what you want to hear but you'll be pleased. I thought it was all over. I'll explain later.'

'What?' said Miles again. 'You can't – what? Tell me. Is it David? You've been speaking to him, haven't you?'

I was sitting on the rickety old table where we kept the phone. 'What?' I said. 'David? No, why would I? What's David got to do with anything?'

'I thought . . .' Miles trailed off, sounding miserable.

'Miles, oh, my God, you're mad. Of course I haven't,' I said. 'Forget about David, OK? This is – God the house has been saved! We don't have to move. I'll explain it all later.'

'What?' said Miles.

'We don't have to move! It's all OK!'

'Well, that's great,' Miles said. 'You can tell me about it tonight.'

I'd forgotten about the Oak Grange, the fantastically expensive hotel Miles had booked us into for the weekend. It was our special treat – and it meant we could have some time to ourselves over the weekend. But suddenly I wanted to stay at home, to be with everyone here, on this legendary Walter weekend.

'Lizzy?' Miles said, as I was silent.

'Yes,' I said, pulling myself together. 'What time are you picking me up? It's been the most amazing morning! We don't have to sell the house! We're not moving! Hurrah!'

'I know, darling,' said Miles, his voice softening. 'I can't wait to hear all about it. I'll pick you up at seven. Is that going to be OK? I don't want to barge in or anything.'

'Of course,' I said, (though cravenly I had already planned to myself that I'd listen out for him and dash out before he drew in, so he couldn't get out of the car and have some massive Walter inquisition from my assembled relatives).

344

I put the phone down and wandered through to the sitting room. On my way through the hall I passed the box Kate had been packing that morning. Resting on the top was the photograph of my grandparents on their wedding day in 1942. Grandmother was in a beautiful tailored white suit, with one of those hats that frothed and spilled over the side of her head. My great-uncle, Charles, was next to them, smiling broadly. It had been taken outside the church at Wareham – you could see the gate that led to the meadow and the path home in the corner of the picture. The next year Charles had died in France on D-Day.

I lifted the photo, and put it back on the dresser next to the hall table, where it had always stood, then went into the sitting room. As I reached up to undo the bolt on the french windows, a shadow appeared on the other side. I yelped and jumped back.

The prodigal son had returned. There, clutching the arm of his estranged wife in one hand and a battered old suitcase in the other, was Mike.

'Well, look who's here,' I said, as we passed through the garden and reached the others.

Mike and Rosalie's arrival had the effect of pouring cold water over everyone. Dad jumped up. Gibbo and Chin stared at them. Tom and Jess narrowed their eyes and Kate froze, napkin in one hand, glass in the other. This vignette lasted only two seconds, and then *en masse* their instincts kicked in: they all smiled and jumped up.

'Mike,' Dad said. 'Hello there.' He did that hilarious man-greeting, shaking his hand and half hugging him. 'And Rosalie. Hello, my dear, it's so lovely to see you. We didn't hear you arrive.'

'No, we've been enjoying the sunshine, as you see,' said

Chin. 'Hello, Mike, how lovely to see you.' She kissed her brother as if she had seen him yesterday.

'Ah, hello,' Mike cleared his throat and shuffled along the table. 'Bride-to-be looking . . . lovely. Hello, Jess, Tom – Gibbo.'

I stole a glance at him. His head was bowed and his clothes hung off him. He looked much older. He kissed Jess, Tom too, shook Gibbo's hand, was introduced to Mando, who'd been texting someone behind a tree, then stood rubbing his bald spot and gazing round him, blinking like a mole who'd just emerged into broad daylight after months underground.

Rosalie, dazzling in acid green and huge black sunglasses, looked a bit shell-shocked, but she was nothing if not a pro at this kind of situation. She was making small-talk to Dad about the flight. It was Christmas all over again, I thought, wanting to bang my head slowly but hard on the table. And what was she doing here?

Mando disappeared back into the marquee, taking Jess with him. I could hear them giggling as they retreated and wished I was with them.

'Hello, Mike,' said Kate, eventually, putting down the plates she'd been stacking and looking up at him.

'Hello, Kate,' said Mike. Then he pulled himself together. 'Kate, my girl, how are you?' He walked round the table. 'Darling thing.' He pulled her into his arms and gave her a hug, and that was stranger than anything else, because it was real emotion, pure and simple.

As if embracing Kate had been symbolic of something, Mike turned to the rest of us, rejuvenated. 'Suzy said there'd be a pie waiting for the hungry travellers. I brought some . . . Where is it?' He rifled through his pockets. 'Aha, here's the fella. I picked up some Colman's mustard on the way. Can't have one of Suzy's pies without *la moutarde*, oh, no. And

346

here's some chutney. Bought them on our way to the airport. Store downtown, sells English things. So let's tuck in, shall we?'

It was so like Mike to be carrying around in his coat a selection of condiments that any fool could buy in any corner shop but which he had selected at some overpriced deli in SoHo that I smiled. He put them on the table, and, despite myself, I felt a pang of affection for him.

Kate went in to fetch the pie. Mike watched her go, then looked round at his surroundings. I followed his gaze, saw him take in the side of the house, the corner of the L where we were sitting, the lawn and the walled garden, which led up to the meadow at the back where the marquee stood at the top of the hill.

Everyone sat down again, with Tom, Chin and Gibbo in a row, crossing their arms like a particularly unwelcoming audience at the Comedy Store.

Rosalie swung a toned leg over the side of the bench and sat down next to Dad. Mike continued to stand, obviously working himself up to say something. In ordinary circumstances this would have been uncomfortable, but somehow, knowing what we all did, I think we wanted to make him suffer a bit longer. God knows, he deserved it.

'Look,' he mumbled indistinctly.

'What was that, Mike?' Chin said brightly.

'I said look.' He turned round. 'I want to say sorry. I know what I've done. I know you all hate me. If you don't, you bloody should. I've caused you so much pain, a lot of misery, through my own stupidity. And I'm sorry. I don't know what else to say.'

We all looked at him politely, as if he were apologizing for being a trifle late, or for breaking wind, not for lying to us all and trying to make his own family homeless. As climactic family moments go, it was a bit of a let-down,

347

but in real life these things never happen the way you've imagined them. We don't do long family confessionals. Even Mike's was pretty out of character and that I am sure is because he's been living in America for so long. All those TV movies finally got to him.

Added to which there was the extra detail of Rosalie, never less than confusing. The only two things of which I was sure were that a) Mike was uncomfortable, and looking like he'd rather be in jail than here and b) Rosalie was gazing at him with a look of rapt adoration that showed, I am sorry to say, that she had learnt absolutely nothing from her brief marriage to him, the status of which was still as clear to me as a muddy puddle on a cloudy night. Dad and Chin looked at each other.

'It doesn't matter,' Dad said quickly. 'I'll explain why in a minute. But it really doesn't. We're just glad you're here.'

'And don't do it again,' Chin said quietly.

Rosalie stood up. 'I might just go and get our bags out of the car,' she said.

'I'll do it,' said Mike, automatically. 'Sit down, darling.'

'Hey, do it after lunch,' Gibbo said, waving his knife at him. 'We're celebrating and having some pie. Have a glass of wine.'

Rosalie looked at Mike and raised her eyebrows in a mute question. He looked back at her. They nodded. Somehow, watching that one brief exchange, I knew they were back together. It wasn't a declaration of love, or a new wedding ring, it was much tinier than that, but much more fundamental.

Suddenly Sophia, the heroine of the day, appeared from the house. She'd been checking her emails in the study and speaking to the film's location manager. She stood at the edge of the lawn, her hand above her eyes to shield them from the sun. 'Hey, guys,' she called. 'There's just a couple of things I need you to sign. Can we have a quick chat now, before you get stuck in?'

Dad darted a look at Chin. 'Sure. Can you give us a minute?'

'This is my friend Sophia from school, Mike. D'you remember her?' said Chin, waving her hand negligently at her brother. 'Everything OK, Sophia?'

'Absolutely fine,' Sophia said, approaching us and smiling her perfect smile. 'Hi, Mike. It's nice to see you again.'

'And you, Sophia,' said Mike, twiddling his glass. 'I curse the day I forgot your beautiful face, and now here it is in front of me again.'

'You last saw her when she was thirteen, don't be a perv,' Tom pointed out.

'I'll be in the study,' Sophia said.

Dad stood up. 'Come on, Chin,' he said.

'What? Oh, yes, of course,' said Chin, kissing the top of Gibbo's head. 'We'll be back in a few minutes. Mike, we need to have a chat with you before you get settled in. Can you come with us, please?'

Her tone was businesslike. Mike leaped up. 'Of course,' he said uneasily. 'Anything wrong?'

Dad and Chin smiled, like a couple of schoolkids who have planned a devastating prank on their teacher.

'No,' said Dad. 'You'll like it. Come on.'

They walked off in single file, Mike bringing up the rear.

'Rosalie, a glass of wine?' said Gibbo, patting her hand as she gazed after them.

'What's that?' she said distractedly. 'Yes. That'd be great. Thank you so much, Gibbo.'

'You hungry?' Gibbo asked.

'A little,' she admitted. 'I haven't had any breakfast – airplane food is so gross. And my dried apricots are in my suitcase.'

'I'll get you some pie,' I said.

'Thank you, Lizzy. Gosh, it's nice to be back here. Sad day, though.'

'Yes,' I said, smiling. 'But wait and see.'

'What do you mean?' said Rosalie.

'Nothing,' I said, walking away. 'Just wait and see.'

'What do you mean, you've *done a deal*?' Mike was saying in agitated tones as I walked past the sitting room.

'We don't have to sell the house,' Dad said patiently. They were standing by the fireplace. Chin was in the armchair, hugging her knees. I stood still and listened.

'John, I've got to have this money, you do understand that, don't you?' Mike said, pacing around the room. ''Scuse me,' he said, brushing past me as he walked out on to the patio.

Chin got up, and she and Dad followed him out.

'We'll have the money for you,' Dad said. 'Calm down. But we don't have to sell the house. We'll have to remortgage – but I don't mind that. With what the film company's giving us, we'll be fine. It'll just be a couple of months before you get your money. That's all.'

As if the balance of power had shifted, Mike whirled round and hissed, 'No, it's not fine! For fuck's sake, John, I need that money *now*. I *told you* – the penalty clause – it has to go out today or I'm screwed. I'm already late with it.'

'And you will,' Dad said soothingly. 'That's loads of time. Oh, Mike, I do wish you'd understand how good this is—'

'You don't know what these guys are like,' Mike said.

'Whoever they are,' Dad said suddenly, showing a steeliness he usually kept hidden, 'and believe me, I don't *want* to know, they're businessmen, aren't they? They'd rather

350

have the money than not. We've got the contract from Monumental and you can show it to them. They're paying us almost immediately. It's a delay of a week, no more.'

'Who the hell is Sophia Gunning, anyway?' Mike growled. 'I've never met her before. How the fuck do you know she's not pulling the wool over your eyes? Taking you for everything you've got?'

'She's not,' Dad said. Chin still said nothing, but was standing there squinting up at her brother, the sun shining in her eyes.

'But how do you *know*?' Mike repeated. 'I don't like this, John. I'm not saying what I've done's right but, as head of the family, I have the controlling share and you ought to have—'

He got no further. With a scream like a steam train, Chin launched herself on him, pummelling him, slapping him, shouting at him so loudly that I could barely make out what she was saying.

'You MONSTER! How DARE YOU? Have you seen what you've done? Have you been here to see it? No, you wanker! You're there in New York fucking hiding from all your problems, breaking that poor woman's heart, and then you fucking SWAN IN HERE the day before my – my wedding, and when we present you with the perfect solution to this total FUCK-UP of yours, what do you say? How DARE YOU? God, every day I ask myself . . .' she came up close to him, still breathing heavily. I thought I'd misheard what she said, but I hadn't. 'Why did Tony have to die, and why is Mike still here? That's what I ask myself every day. Every. Single. Day.'

'Chin, that's enough,' said my father, grabbing her shoulder and pulling her away. She was shaking. 'Don't ever mention Tony like that again. It was a horrible thing to say.'

'I don't care!' Chin said, sobbing now. 'After everything

351

I've done today, to be questioned like this by him – I don't believe it.'

Dad put his arms round her. 'I know, darling,' he said softly, into her hair. 'But none of us could be prouder of you than we are now. It doesn't matter about Mike. Don't worry about him.'

'You're pathetic, Mike,' Chin said, eyes ringed with mascara. '*Pathetic*. This dream you have that Keeper House is the magical happy place you remember when you were little Master Mike and you didn't have to run away from it to preserve it in aspic, you can't get over it, can you? You can't move on. You're like an antique.' She hiccuped. 'Like an antique Just William, pretending he's still a boy, wanting everything to be the same as you remember it. Well, it wasn't like that then, and it isn't like that now. And you know why? Because of *you*. You're the one who's done this. Grow up.'

Mike was still standing there, looking totally shell-shocked. I hurried through to the kitchen.

'What's all the yelling about?' Rosalie called.

'Practising speech-making for tomorrow,' I muttered. 'Loosening the vocal cords. Gavin the vicar told them to.' Stupid woman, what did she think it would be about?

'Right,' said Rosalie.

Sophia picked up her mobile phone.

Rosalie looked at her, then at me. She swung herself off the bench and came over to the kitchen window, leaned on the window-sill and took off her glasses.

'Hi,' she said.

'Hi,' I said.

'All OK?' Rosalie asked. Her long nails beat a tattoo on the sill.

'Yup, fine, thanks. You?' I said.

'I'm really well.'

352

'Me too,' I said, reminded of the scene in *Annie Hall* where Woody Allen and Diane Keaton have one rather boring conversation and a separate conversation in subtitles beneath.

'It's great to be back,' Rosalie said.

I am not a crook.

'Well, it's fantastic you could come.'

Are you and my uncle back together again?

'Yes, I'm so glad I was able to get the time off.'

Yes, I'm so glad I took him back. You see, I'm stupid.

'How come?'

Why on earth did you do that? What if he just breaks your heart again?

'I finished one big project and I've got a few days before I start another. Isn't that good luck?'

It's a risk I'm willing to take. And in any case he thinks he needs me more than I need him. It's actually the other way round, you know, but don't ever tell him that.

'It is good luck.'

I won't. Trust me. I've enjoyed this little chat.

Rosalie grasped my hand through the window and winked at me. 'You're a good girl, Lizzy. What's this I hear about you and Miles, then?'

'How on earth do you know that?'

'Young David told me. He's been amazing in all this, you know. Practically tied your uncle up and forced him to talk to me and sort it all out. God bless him, he's great. But whatever.' She shook her head. 'So, you and Miles – it's going well, is it?' She looked like a bright little bird, her head on one side.

'Yes, it really is,' I told her. 'So – so David knows about us, does he?' I'd not had the courage to ask Miles again if he'd talked to his brother.

'Honey,' Rosalie said, 'he knows. I think he's fine with it.

That's what he told me, anyway. Why shouldn't he be? It's a little weird for him, sure, but it's no big deal, is it?'

'No,' I said. 'Couldn't agree more.' I couldn't work out why I felt rather deflated after she said this; after all, it wasn't a big deal.

'I'm coming through. Stay there,' said Rosalie. 'I need a drink.'

'Yes,' I said, gazing past her into the garden. 'So do I.'

THIRTY

By the time Miles arrived to pick me up, I was glad to be getting out of the house – and who could have predicted that a few hours earlier when we had been crying with joy that the house was saved. The atmosphere was as thick as pea-soup and we were no longer dancing around with joy. The reason, of course, was Mike. And it wasn't really his fault, more that all the stress of the last forty-eight hours, or perhaps the last five months, was finally catching up with all of us. Anyway, as is usually the way with large family gatherings, I'd changed my mind about wanting to spend as much time as possible in the bosom of my family and was practically standing by the side of the road with a sign saying 'Take me Away from Here' when Miles zoomed, too fast, round the corner in his zippy Mercedes at precisely one minute to seven, I was sitting on the grass verge with my case under my feet. Thankfully, the others were still at the wedding rehearsal.

'Hello, beautiful,' he said, as he screeched to a halt.

'Hello,' I said, jumped in and kissed him.

His dark hair was sticking up in peaks because of the

wind, his face was flushed, and he looked so pleased to see me that I was infected by his enthusiasm.

'Don't you want me to come in and meet the family?' he said, teasingly.

'No. I just want to get out of here and be with you,' I said, trying to sound like an exotic Soviet spy, but instead sounding rather desperate, like a sex-starved librarian who couldn't give it away.

'God, you're gorgeous,' said Miles, and as we kissed again, I felt all my cares disappear. He was a great kisser. The house wasn't being sold. Chin's wedding was tomorrow. The weather forecast was for twenty-five degrees and sunny. And I was going out on this lovely evening to be a proper grown-up. I would have sex, which is always a great prospect at the start of an evening.

'Mm,' Miles said, shifting in his seat. He brought me closer to him, and I relaxed even more. 'Mm,' he repeated.

'Mm,' I said back, then saw that Mum, Dad, Chin and Gibbo were staring at us from the other end of the bonnet. They must have walked back across the field from the church.

'Oh, my God,' I said, leaping away from Miles and pushing him away as if I were being assaulted by a complete stranger.

'Hi there,' said Gibbo, smiling broadly.

'Hello,' said Miles, confidently. 'I won't keep you. Lovely to see you, Mr Walter, Dr Walter, Chin, Gibbo. Good luck for tomorrow. We'll see you then. We're off.' He put the car into gear and shot off, before we could enter into any further conversation. I turned and waved as my family disappeared into the distance.

'So,' said Miles, as the sommelier retreated, leaving us to enjoy an insouciant little dessert wine from the company of Overpriced and Curlicues. 'Is this really all OK? Are you enjoying yourself?'

356

It's always about me when I'm with Miles. Am I happy? Am I enjoying myself? Is Miles pleasing me? I found it odd at first but relationships are all about balance, aren't they, and if both of you are content why fight it? It's like when people say, 'If I had all the money in the world, I still wouldn't want to do nothing all day, I'd soon get bored.' Rubbish, you'd like to try it for a while, wouldn't you?

Before David, most of my previous relationships had been characterized by me running to catch up with men who didn't like to be seen in public with me. My ex-boyfriend after university, Jim, whom I went out with for three years on and off, was a nice man – but we drifted apart. I was pretty upset when it ended, but a couple of months later I was relieved. I should have known it was on the skids when I agreed to cater for a dinner party he was having for five other friends *to which I wasn't invited*. I went, I cooked, I laid the table. We even had sex in the bathroom before the guests arrived. Then I left, having angled desperately for an invitation to stay. Jim dumped me a couple of weeks later and I don't blame him. I'd have dumped myself after that.

Anyway, my point is that I was used to being a table-laying geisha-style girlfriend, rather than the stroppy princess who has to be placated with mini-breaks, expensive meals, flowers and jewellery. Part of me worried about why Miles did this. Perhaps he felt guilty about David. I did. Perhaps we should have talked about it, but Miles didn't like talking about it, and neither did I.

Secretly, I didn't really like the imbalance it created between us – like I was the girly girl and he was the cash-heavy man who took his lady out and threw money around. Once in a while I wished I could take him out, or cook him a meal, or do more normal things, like see a film, but we didn't and over the last couple of months I had got used to living this rather glamorous life.

357

The Oak Grange was very nice. Plush, dimly lit, all mod cons and very tasteful, with some of the charm of the original sixteenth-century house but brought fully up to date. We were by the window in the dining room, which was wide, low-ceilinged, with the doors flung open on to the flagstoned patio. Actually, it was all a little bit Crossroads: the gerberas on each table were fake, in those tiny jars with clear gel to hold them up, and the music drifting over from the 'lounge area' was distinctly Dion-esque. I couldn't have cared less, but Miles was anxious: he'd thought we'd signed up for the last word in exclusivity, and the plastic gerberas were a big disappointment to him. Several long discussions with the head waiter about the sea bream, the white wine and the Reblochon had soothed him, though, and he was now more relaxed, no doubt helped by the copious amounts of wine we'd drunk.

'I'm having a wonderful time. What about you?' I said.

'Me too,' said Miles seriously. 'I'm sorry to be fussing.'

'You're not.'

'I just feel guilty about being such a plonker this morning on the phone.'

'You weren't. I'm sorry I didn't reply to your texts. I should have done – you understand now?'

'Of course I do. I was just worried all of a sudden, that's all.'

'Don't be,' I said.

'I can't help it.'

I finished my wine and wished I could help myself to more.

A few other people were dotted about the dining room, mostly couples. I wondered if any were staying there for the wedding. A couple near us, a few years older than us, were sitting in total silence. The man looked bored and boring, the woman cross. She had one of those sinewy, grasping

358

faces and pale blue eyes. I let my gaze drift over the others. Were they all having similar conversations? Were they arguing? Would they go upstairs and laugh like drains, were they happy?

Miles took my hand and kissed it. 'Thank you so much,' he said.

'Why?' I said, touched.

'It's so great of you to come when you could have stayed at home with your family and had a celebration.'

'Honestly,' I said, thinking of Chin screaming and crying, 'I'd rather be here, you know.'

'Really?' Miles said eagerly.

I could be truthful about it because it was a fact: I'd rather be in this nice hotel with this lovely man than in the House of the Rising Tempers fifteen miles down the road. 'Absolutely,' I said. 'Of course. I feel . . .' I tried to work out what to say. 'I feel . . . well, like I've been clinging to all of that for too long. To the past. Lots of things. Well, I've been stupid.' Suddenly I experienced the liberating rush that comes when you know you're saying what someone else wants to hear. 'I'm sick of the house, and I want to be with you. I'm so lucky, I can't believe it. I keep thinking you'll change your mind.'

'I won't,' said Miles, smiling. 'I want you to change your mind, though.'

'About what?'

'About lots of things. About not supporting QPR. About moving to LA. About coming to live with me. About . . .' he leaned forward, smiling wickedly, and lowered his voice '. . . about doing that thing I want you to do.'

I laughed. The couple at the table nearest to us looked over, and the woman gave us one of those typically female appraising glances that mean, 'I'm jealous of you, but I'll hide it by staring rudely at you.' I do it all the time.

'It's getting late,' Miles observed. He put his hand on my knee and slid it slowly higher.

'Yes,' I said.

'Time for bed?' Miles said.

'That would be nice,' I said.

We got up and left. As I walked out of the room I threw a glance over my shoulder at the woman with the pale blue eyes. But she wasn't looking jealously at me any more: she was laughing with the man opposite, looking at the pudding menu, her necklace glowing in the twilight. She looked quite different, and as Miles put his arm round my waist and drew me towards the lift I felt a little jealous of her.

We had had sex, and Miles got up to get a glass of water. He came back into the bedroom and sat down beside me, slipping his hand between my thighs and kissing me. 'Was that good?' he murmured enquiringly.

'Yes,' I whispered.

Miles sat back on the sofa. 'Can I ask you something?'

It's surprising how little one likes the question that follows that one. 'Of course,' I said.

He bent his head over me, stroked my hair and nuzzled my neck. He murmured something. I caught his head in my hands and he smoothed my hair away from my face, section by section, lifting it behind my shoulders. He kissed the hollow at the base of my neck. 'Better than David?' he said.

I opened my eyes. 'What?'

'You must have known I'd be curious. Am I better than David?'

'Fuck off, Miles,' I said, and stood up, smiling to show I wasn't pissed off, although I was. David.

Miles flung one arm across the headboard. With the other he reached out and grabbed my arm. He said, in the same maddeningly calm tone, 'Come on, Lizzy, it's kind of natural

I'd want to know. How did he fuck you? Was it better than this? What else did he do? What did you do to him that you won't do to me? Anything I should know about?'

I tried to walk away but he was still holding my arm. 'Get off, Miles,' I said.

'No.'

'I mean it. Get off,' I said, trying to walk away. But he was stronger than me and he wouldn't move. He was pulled along the sofa and on to his knees on the floor. He laughed, like it was all a big joke.

'Don't be cross, Lizzy,' he wheedled.

'Miles! Get a fucking grip. You look ridiculous.'

Suddenly I felt nothing but contempt for him. I looked at his face, so like David's yet so different, and felt sick.

'I just want to know,' he said, sounding totally unlike himself. 'Did he make you come every time? Did you fake it with him?'

'I don't fake it,' I said.

'Liar.'

'OK, I did once, maybe twice. But—'

'Why?' Miles stood up. 'Why? Don't I – don't you—'

He put his hands on my face. I could smell the wine on his breath. It isn't in my nature to demand to know what's going on, or to cause a fuss. I wanted to smooth this over, make us both believe everything was OK. So I tried to laugh it off. 'Well, you know, brothers,' I said. 'You're very much alike, sometimes it's hard to tell. Oh, I'm joking, Miles, calm down. Let's just go back to bed.' I stroked his cheek.

But he stayed where he was, staring at me, and his grip tightened. 'You never loved me,' he said, after a moment.

'Miles! I've never said I did,' I wrenched my head from his grip.

'Are you thinking of him when you're with me?' he said.

'No, of course not!' I said, aghast. 'God, no, never.'

'Why not?' Miles said, backing away. 'David told me what you liked. I've been doing what you liked. I thought it might remind you of my big brother. I thought it might make you like me better.'

I felt dizzy. 'Stop it, Miles,' I said.

'I'm sorry, Lizzy. I shouldn't have said it.'

'It doesn't matter.'

'Yes, it does. I'm a twat.'

'You're not, just forget it.'

So we had sex again, and I faked it much more convincingly this time, and as we lay there afterwards, Miles breathing heavily, his arm weighing down hard on my ribs, I bit my lip and stared up at the ceiling. I could have been at home. I should have been at home. David had told Miles about our sex life (not very successfully, though – if he was going to betray our deepest secrets I wish he'd been more specific in his descriptions to Miles) and Miles was – what? I didn't know this side of him and I didn't like it.

The difference between Miles and David was that when I found out something new about Miles it always alarmed me. Nothing David could have told me about himself, short of him being a UKIP MP or president of a golf club, would have worried me. I'd wanted to know everything about him, what he liked, what he hated, what made him sad, when he'd been most scared, what made him happy and what might make him happy.

Miles rolled over in his sleep and wrapped his arm round me, pulling me towards him. I felt his chest against my back, his breath on my neck, his twitch as something in his dream disturbed him. After a while my thoughts started overlapping and spooling together, and I slept the sleep of the dead, so heavily I dreamed of nothing and no one, until Miles woke me the next morning, and it started again.

THIRTY-ONE

Despite all the palaver, weddings don't vary that much in the essential details, do they? A group of people gathers at a church or somewhere similarly picturesque. They watch their friend/relative/enemy/colleague/secret lover get married. They drink champagne. They eat. The cake is cut. The speeches are made. People circulate. They get drunk. They dance until the wedding is over. Within that framework there are different kinds of flowers, bridesmaids' dresses, waistcoats, speeches, food, photos, music and snogs. But it's like there's a Venn diagram of about six basic weddings and all of them overlap at certain points. For the person attending the wedding there is only one point at which they all meet: it's much better to go with someone than to go alone.

Chin's wedding was Wedding Variation Number Four: Notting Hill Boho Relaxed Shabby Chic (but God forbid that any of the Portaloos don't have Cologne and Cotton hand-towels and Molton Brown liquid soap). I was going to wear a dress I'd bought in an amazing shop in Bloomsbury. It was 1930s, soft apple-green silk, empire line, with a chocolate brown trim, and a plunging neckline, which, with the empire line, hoicked my boobs up to my neck. I was pleased with the result: it made me look like Simone Caldwell. I had some chocolate brown suede kitten heels and a matching wrap. Early in the morning I had my hair blow-dried in the beauty salon at the Oak Grange while Miles was in his bath, singing James Brown at the top of his voice.

I didn't want to talk about the previous night. So I didn't. And I was glad when I went back to our room to get my bag and make sure Miles was ready. He was standing in the middle of the room, fiddling with his buttonhole, trying to pin it on. 'It's weird that I'm an usher and you don't have anything to do when she's your flipping aunt,' he said, swearing as the safety-pin pricked his thumb.

'I'll do it,' I said, putting my bag and wrap on the bed and going over to him.

'Hello,' he said, kissing me. 'You look beautiful.'

'Thanks,' I said. 'So do you.'

'Let's not make a big deal of this, Lizzy,' he said.

'It's done now,' I said, having pinned the rose into place. 'All fine.'

'I meant last night.'

'Oh,' I said, and took a step back. 'Forget it.'

'Yes, let's,' said Miles, easily. 'I was drunk, I was a wanker. It was nothing. I don't want it to ruin today, OK?'

'Right,' I said lightly. I wanted to say something more, but I didn't know what. 'Let's go then.'

'Great,' said Miles. 'You really do look beautiful.'

He picked up my overnight bag as I checked myself in the mirror. Suddenly I knew what I wanted to say. But it was too late then, and we left the room.

Miles dropped me off at Keeper House fairly early. It was only ten o'clock and already obvious that it was going to be yet another hot day. It was a record-breaker for May, according to the news that morning. The sky was almost white, and the mulberry tree in the courtyard was totally still. He had wanted to come in to help, but I wasn't sure of the status quo. Too many cooks spoil the broth? Or many hands make light work? Whichever, I didn't want to risk exposing Miles to the ugly atmosphere of yesterday, especially with the added factor of bridal Chin. And I wanted to be on my own for a little while.

I'd forgotten my keys, so I had to ring the doorbell. I felt like a visitor, standing on the doorstep, and I realized my night away had given me a sense of perspective. As I gazed up at the front of the house, so peaceful and golden in the morning sun, I couldn't believe it was only yesterday that Dad had been standing in his best suit in the kitchen, prepared to sign it all away. It was a miracle. It made all the arguments, the petty family issues and crises, seem irrelevant. None of it mattered.

There was a long silence, so I rang again, and eventually I heard Mike's muffled voice coming towards the door. 'It's Lizzy,' I heard someone else say – Mum, I think.

The door swung open, and there was Mike, in a crumpled old morning suit, with a piece of toast in his mouth, and next to him, David.

I felt cold, standing on the doorstep in the bright sunshine. My hands and feet had turned to water, and my stomach churned. I leaned against the doorframe for support, and stared up at him. Then I pulled myself together. 'Hello,' I said, stepping over the threshold.

'Morning, Titch,' Mike exclaimed. He kissed my cheek. 'Well, we're all very grown-up here, aren't we? David – Lizzy. Lizzy, this is my friend David. I believe you two know each other.'

'Hello, Lizzy,' said David, shaking my hand mock-formally.

Thank God Miles hadn't come in. Now I was inside, I

realized how lovely it was to see David. It was the first time since I'd put the phone down on him. And since I'd started going out with Miles. But it was fine. Because of the water being all under the bridge. I smiled back at him, until I realized he was directing his warmth towards Mike, and not me. His hand was cold, heavy in mine, and he didn't even meet my eyes as I stared at him. I couldn't help it. I had always thought Miles looked like him but now it dawned on me that they were quite different. He was tanned. Where had he been?

He released his hand from mine and I felt something rasp against my palm. There was a plaster on his middle finger. What had he done? Was it just a papercut or something.

Mike turned to me and put his arm round me. David put his hands into his pockets.

'Lizzy,' Mike said, 'I think your mother needs you. There's some kind of horticultural crisis unfolding up at the marquee. Chin – well, she's on edge already, but your mother's worried she's about to go nuclear. Other than that, all's fine.' He turned to David. 'Chin and I had a bit of a dust-up yesterday. Anyway, all in the past. Atonement, I'm all for it. Look at me, atoning away, left, right and centre. So, David old thing, I've done you now. Are we square? Lizzy, you still here?' He removed his arm from my shoulders. 'Go away now, old girl. I want to talk to David.'

'I don't see why,' I said, nettled.

'Mike and I need a quick chat,' said David. He turned to my uncle and said quickly, 'Honestly, Mike, I know you're sorry. I'm sorry too. I think we both fucked up.'

'Well,' said Mike, 'the boot's significantly more on my foot than yours old thing, but decent of you to say it. Hallelujah. Hang on a sec. Let me go and see if the light of my life is up yet. She'll want to see you, I know. Two shakes.'

He bounded upstairs, singing 'All People That On Earth Do Dwell'.

'I'd better go outside and find Mum,' I said. 'Golly, it's ten thirty already. We've got lots to do.'

'Yes, you have,' said David. 'Sorry about this.' He gestured around him, as if to explain his presence.

'Not at all,' I said politely.

'Mike called me yesterday evening. He's got a bout of penitence he needs to get off his chest. He just wanted to apologize, clear the air, all that kind of thing. He – well.'

'He was crap. I'm sorry,' I said. 'I'm glad he's apologized. What about Rosalie?'

'He owes her more than an apology,' said David, briskly. 'I'm fine – he just messed me around. A lot of crap happened because of him. You know.'

He stopped. Oho, I knew. But, I reminded myself, these were the waters that were now way under and past the bridge.

David rocked on the balls of his feet, his hands still in his pockets. 'Anyway, I had to bring over some more cutlery from Mum, so I thought I'd kill two birds with one stone.' He looked down at the floor, then at me and said ruefully, 'I'm the mummy's boy who gets up early to run her errands. I'm going to the bottle bank next.'

'Right,' I said, not sure what his point was.

'And Miles,' said David, sounding his name like it was a rock dropping into water, 'Miles swans off to luxury hotels with his new girlfriend for the night.'

'Yes,' I said.

David patted his breast pocket. 'Where are my car keys? Look, Lizzy, it's OK, all right? I've got to go. I haven't time to say hello to Rosalie.'

'Oh, right,' I said, realizing suddenly that it was hard for him, hating the thought that he was miserable – and also, intensely, not wanting him to leave. 'Look, I'm sorry, you don't have to rush off because of me. It is weird, I know, but we're just going to have to get used to it. Stay a little while. I'm going to the garden.'

'I didn't mean that,' David said. 'Thanks for the sympathy, Lizzy. Very kind of you.'

My face was burning. He opened the door and held its edge lightly. 'I just meant there's no time left. I can't stay. Give my love to Rosalie. See you later, Lizzy. Hope it all goes well. You look great.'

The door slammed behind him, and I patted my flaming cheeks. How dare he? But how stupid of me.

Gibbo and Bozzer left for the church at about a quarter past eleven. Thirty minutes later we all congregated in the hall, waiting for Chin to appear. It was like the gathering of the clan in a Walter Scott novel, minus the kilts. Jess, Tom and I. Jess had on an SJP-style jacket with a flared silk skirt, and looked like a doll, with her curls bobbing round her head. Tom was sleek and shiny in a beautifully tailored new morning suit and plump blue tie. Mum and Dad, Kate, Mike and Rosalie. Mum, already crying, was in a diaphanous Ghost-style creation with a matching pale green hat, while Kate was regal in one of those dresses one finds advertised in the back of the *Telegraph* Saturday magazine made of what they call fine lawn cotton: puffed sleeves, elasticated waist, button-through, crazily floral. Next to Kate, the fashion *yang* to her *yin*, Rosalie wore an extraordinary rose-pink taffeta suit. It had a long tulip-shaped skirt, a creamy, low-cut separate bodice, and a jacket tailored to within an inch of its life, making her waist look like a hand-span. She looked like the Fairy Godmother from *Shrek* 2. I assumed it must be the kind of thing rich people wear on cruises or to benefits when they're not quite sure of the dress code but don't want to be accused of not making an effort. Standing beside her, Mike looked like an old shoe in his beaten-up morning suit, which had been Tony's and was slightly too big for him. Nevertheless, there was something reassuringly real about him next to Rosalie.

A door upstairs slammed and Mando shouted down, 'She's coming!' We all bristled with excitement.

She was lovely, in my grandmother's veil, with the prettiest tracery pattern of flowers scattered across it, a simple cream silk sheath dress, plain and beautifully made. Her hair shone, her eyes shone, her face was aglow with happiness and excitement, and she fitted the bill perfectly. Some people aren't naturally bridal and others are. I hadn't thought Chin would be but she just was. She was the most beautiful bride I'd ever seen. At the sight of her coming down the staircase, clutching the carved banister, tears filled my eyes and I bent over to shake them on to the floor rather than let them run in mascara stripes down my face and dress.

Mando came down after her, fussing with his tie, his buttonhole and his hair, waving his arms as Chin stepped across the threshold towards the waiting car. 'Careful!' he breathed. 'Oh, the dirt . . . Oh dear.'

'Coming, John?' Chin said, as Dad waited for Mum to pin on his buttonhole. He stepped forward and gave her his arm. She raised herself on tiptoe and kissed his cheek. 'Thank you so much,' she said.

They set off for the car and we all followed them, led by Mike. 'See you there,' Chin said, smiling at him.

'Yup, sis. You're beautiful,' said Mike, holding the door open for her. 'Come on, you lot, we've got to go. Don't want to arrive after the bride. Rosalie, where are you? There. Marvellous.'

Dad smiled and got into the car.

Mike turned to us. 'Tom, you're taking your mother, yes?'

'Yes,' Tom said, swinging his car keys in his hand. 'Right. Let's go. Lizzy, are you ready?'

It's funny how the mind stores certain events and gives them a significance they don't appear to have when they're happening. When I look back now I find it strange that I remember sitting in the church. Miles next to me, his hand in mine – in fact all of the wedding ceremony so clearly. The sound of Chin's voice and Gibbo's. The heavy scent of lilies. The promise Gibbo had made to us at Christmas in the pub, that if he married Chin we would find out Norman Gibson's middle name: Tom, Jess, Miles and I stood bristling with repressed hysteria as Ginevra Mary Walter took Norman Lorenzo Gibson to be her lawfully married husband. (His grandmother was Italian.) And I remembered Mike reading from the Song of Solomon, then Kate reading a Shakespearian sonnet, in her clear, beautiful voice, something about true love and impediments, and I remember thinking it made such sense and that it was heartbreakingly sad, coming from her. 'The marriage of true minds'. I liked that.

And I remember standing outside the church with all my family. We were all a bit embarrassed, as if we were on display and didn't want to be. Jess took photos of us standing around before the official photographer started snapping away – Mum, fussing; Chin, stunning but mutinous; Tom, licking his finger and smoothing his hair down; Mike and Rosalie standing stiffly side by side, looking like pioneers in an early daguerreotype. Gibbo, tilting alternately left to right, which none of us could understand till the official photos came back and we worked out he'd just been swaying ecstatically from side to side all day, like a very long tall Weeble.

When we were finally allowed to disperse, Chin took Kate

and Tom by the hand, whispered something, and they walked over to Tony's grave; Chin put her bouquet of lily-of-the-valley next to the headstone. I found myself trying to picture him. How different would our family have been if he hadn't died? I suspected he had been the favourite, the pacifier. I suspected that when Kate met him she wasn't a cross, inscrutable woman who stomped and huffed, but beautiful, graceful, quiet, which was why Tony had fallen in love with her. Perhaps Mike too. Would he have turned out differently if his brother hadn't died? I don't know – but I couldn't help thinking, as I watched my uncle's wife and son standing by his grave, that to understand a family you have to know more about them than who's still in the room.

'Back to the house!' Gibbo yelled, after this interlude was over.

It was Chin's idea to walk back across the fields to Keeper House, and I'm sure it had seemed like a good idea at the planning stage. Surely one of the essential components of the Notting Hill Boho Relaxed Shabby Chic wedding must be the bridal party, followed by the guests, rambling in a delightfully relaxed way across a meadow to the family home for the reception.

In practice, though, it's a dead silly idea. (1) Who, apart from Kate, wears shoes to a wedding that they can walk more than ten yards in? (2) Who is screaming? It's the bride, getting delightful May mud and grass stains on her Alice Temperley dress. (3) What was that soft thud? Great-aunt Dahlia has got her walking-stick stuck in the ground and pitched herself head first into the ditch.

The whole wedding party started off through the church-yard, holding hands and looking all understated and lovely, laughing in a carefree way in case a photographer from *Country Living* should appear (to take some black-and-white shots, grainy and ethereal). But the path across the meadow was still damp enough from the recent rain for heels to sink into the ground and long enough for shoes to start rubbing, and the sun was so hot that after about four minutes the whole party looked less like Kate Moss and her friends on a boho field trip than Moses leading the Israelites out of Egypt – the tail end of the procession, when they were all exhausted.

'Are you OK?' Miles asked, as I strode along confidently, trying not to convey the agony of my lovely but treacherous shoes.

'Fine, thanks.'

'Really?' Miles said, hands in his pockets.

Someone moaned.

I could see the house in the distance, a shimmering palace of promise containing my comfy flip-flops.

'Go down . . . Moses . . . Way down in Egypt-land . . . Tell old Pharaoh . . . Let my people go . . .' I sang to myself, trying to get some rhythm going.

'What are you grumbling about?' Miles said.

'I'm not grumbling,' I said. 'I'm singing to take my mind off my blisters.'

'Oh, good grief,' Miles said. 'Stop.' He crouched to look at my foot. 'Ouch,' he said, when I showed him the raw red patch that clashed with my beautiful iridescent lilac nail polish. 'Come on,' he said, straightening. 'Here you go.'

In a lightning quick movement, he hoicked me on to his back, jiggled me around until he was comfortable, and set off. I screamed with shock, then delight. He waved to those we passed, like a merry French farmer. It started a bit of a craze. Chin turned round, saw what was happening and started to laugh. Then she took off her shoes, waving people to walk past her, and went the rest of the way barefoot, laughing as she winced over the pebbly path.

As we reached the lane and the entrance to the house, the wedding car drew up. Out stepped Rosalie and Sophia Gunning.

'Oh, sorry,' I said, as Miles staggered beneath me. 'We all walked – we should have told you we were setting off.'

'Yes, I know,' said Rosalie, gazing at me as if I had two heads. 'We got the car, honey.' We were in the courtyard and Miles let me slide off his back. 'You British,' she added, and advanced towards a waiter proffering a tray of champagne, 'you perplex me.'

Mike and Kate appeared through the gate. 'Rosalie, darling, there you are,' Mike said, going over to her. 'I missed you. Where did you get to?'

'Came in the car, darlin',' Rosalie said, handing him a glass and smiling mistily up at him. 'I missed you too. Shall we go in?'

'Good idea,' Mike said, kissing the top of her head. 'My job's over so I can relax.'

'What job?' I said. 'What have you done today?'

'Well,' Mike looked hurt, 'the reading.'

'Oh, sorry,' I said. 'It was very nice. Very nice indeed.'

'Solomon knew what he was about, didn't he? Marvellous stuff,' Mike said. ' "Behold, thou art fair, my love," ' he declaimed to Rosalie. ' "Thy hair is as a flock of goats, that appear from Mount Gilead." '

'Thanks a lot,' Rosalie said, stroking hers. 'Lizzy, see you later. Good luck for the speech, honey.'

'Thanks,' I said, turning to Miles. He handed me my bag. 'Thanks for the ride,' I said, as Jess limped through the gate, followed by the bride and groom. Chin stopped to put her shoes on, and Sophia Gunning stepped in, with David at her side, their heads together, deep in conversation. Then Bill from the Neptune appeared, helping Aunt Dahlia, with Mum, Dad and the rest of the motley crew.

'Good luck with the speech, Elizabeth,' Bill bellowed.

'What?' Miles said, releasing me. 'That's the . . . What speech?'

'What?' I said dreamily, watching David disappear through the gate, glass in hand.

Chin had reached the gate to the garden, but she heard this and turned round. She tripped back to me. 'Oh, Lizzy, darling, I forgot to ask you. We only decided last night.'

'What?' I said, a cold, clammy fear clamping my stomach.

'It's *not* a big deal.'

As these words always presage something that *is* a big deal, I gritted my teeth.

'I don't want Mike to make a speech. Obviously.' Chin laughed, girlishly.

'Obviously!' I agreed.

'And John's done enough. Besides, you know him – he'll happily blather on to us for half an hour at Christmas but getting up in front of a marquee full of people . . . he hates that sort of thing. But we all thought you'd be perfect. It doesn't have to be that long, I don't want any formal shit or toasts or any of that. Just a few . . . words. About me, Gibbo, life. What love is, what it means, why we're all here, you know. No big deal.'

'What?' I said, in a strangled tone.

'Is that OK?' Chin asked solicitously, making to leave.

'No!' I croaked. 'Chin, please. Please don't make me.'

'But you're the only person. Your dad can't.'

'I'm his daughter!' I cried. 'Who do you think he passed it on to? Get Tom to do it!'

'No,' said Chin, stubbornly. 'I want you. Come on. I meant to ask you ages ago, but I couldn't. Because of the hen night. I knew you hated me. And I was so busy . . . you know. Because of saving the house.'

Foreseeing that the excuse of Saving the House was going to come up again and again over the years with monotonous regularity, I sighed. She had a point – and I owed her. We all did.

'What love is, what it means, and why we're all here. And about you and Gibbo,' I said weakly.

'Yep!' Chin touched the arm of an arriving guest. 'Hi, see you in there!'

'But, Chin,' I said, '*Aristotle* and – people like that couldn't work that stuff out. What makes you think—'

'Great. You're on after Gibbo,' said Chin, cutting off any further discussion by walking off.

I must remember that, it is an excellent tactic.

THIRTY-TWO

No matter that the sun was shining, Mike was back in the bosom of the family, the house was ours again and it was Chin's wedding day. The making of the speech hung over me throughout the reception, as if I was one of those cartoon characters who walks about with a small grey raincloud above their head. We stood in and outside the marquee for drinks as the sun beat down. People around me laughed, and I shot them looks of loathing that they could be so carefree.

As I was muttering to myself and pacing around the outside of the marquee, trying out jokes like 'Funny thing. Opal Fruits are now called Starburst. What's that all about?' and then banging my head quietly against a pole. Tom appeared.

'Tom,' I said urgently, gripping his arm. 'Please help me, I've got to make a speech and I don't know what to say.'

'*You?*' Tom said, looking outraged.

'Yes,' I said. 'You were an usher. Help me. I don't have time for this. What shall I say?'

'God, you poor thing,' said Tom solicitously. 'I can't imagine anything worse.'

'Thanks a bundle,' I said. 'How are you, anyway?'

'Good,' said Tom.

'See anyone you like the look of?'

'Don't try and pimp me out, Lizzy. I'm not a carton of milk that's about to go off, you know.'

'I know,' I said. 'I'm just asking, that's all. Pulling at weddings used to be my speciality. I wanted to pass my gift on to you.'

'Yes,' said Tom. 'I remember your 2001 season with particular fondness. You were on fire that year. Five weddings – and was it three or four pulls?'

'Four,' I said, with pride. 'That was the summer of the Good Haircut, though.'

'I remember it well,' said Tom. 'Isn't that why we had to go on holiday to Cyprus the following year, to find where that hairdresser had gone back to?'

'We found him, though, didn't we?' I said. 'It was worth it. Lovely Pavlos. He was gorgeous.'

'He was,' said Tom.

'I think he was gay, you know,' I said subtly.

'He was,' said Tom. 'Oh, look, here's Miles, your stalker boyfriend.'

'Shut up,' I said. 'Don't change the subject. Very quickly, you and Pavlos? Seriously? Right under my nose!'

'I'm saying nothing,' said Tom, looking pleased with himself. 'And it wasn't right under your nose. All I will say is, I left knowing the Greek for "Meet me where they keep the mops in five minutes."'

'Hello, you two,' said Miles, gliding over and putting his arm round me. 'Tom, are you being perverted again?'

'Pretty much all the time, yes,' said Tom, coolly. 'And now I'm off to get another drink.'

'Oh, don't go,' I said. 'You're supposed to be helping me with the speech.'

377

'You'll be fine, Lizzy,' Tom said. 'Just talk about why you think they're a great couple. All that kind of thing. What love is all about, blah blah. It's true in their case,' he added, flicking a speck off his jacket, 'so it won't sound fake.'

'Is Tom OK?' Miles asked, as he wandered off to chat to the group next to us, which included Sophia Gunning and David. I'd thought David was on the other side of the lawn – not that I'd been looking out for him.

'He's been rather off with me lately. Since you and I started going out, actually. Have you talked to him about it?' Miles went on.

'No,' I said. 'I know what you mean, though. Hold my glass – my strap's rubbing again.'

'I'll have a chat with him later,' said Miles.

I saw David glance at us, then turn away.

'God, I wish I could take this bloody jacket off.' Miles groaned. 'It's so hot. Look, I don't want him to think . . . well, you know . . .'

'I know what?' I said. I straightened up and took my glass back.

'That . . . Well, that this is just a fling. That it's not something we're taking seriously. We are. He should know that. People should understand that.' He put his hand on the back of my neck and kissed me.

I suddenly thought of Jaden, as if he was from a past life, or a character in a film I'd seen ages ago. Without warning, I found myself remembering what he'd said to me in March on the steps of the V&A; it seemed so long ago. *Take it seriously*. He'd told me to take the LA job seriously, and it struck me, like a bolt from the bright blue May sky, that what he'd really been saying was, Take your own life seriously. Have more faith in yourself. And even though Jaden was so unlike me, so easy for me to mock, there was something good and comforting about him. Why did all *this* feel so unreal, then? Was it the day itself, or was it more than that? Uncertainty bloomed inside me, then spasmed as I remembered the speech. 'Shit, Miles,' I said, promising myself I'd think about it later when I had it straight in my head. 'The speech. I've got to sort out what I'm going to say.'

A *ting* from the marquee made me swivel round. Miles put his hand on my back. Dad was tapping a glass nervously with a fork. 'Ladies and gentlemen, would you take your seats, please?'

I sent Miles in and hung back, waiting for Tom. He came over, with Sophia Gunning and David following.

'OK, Lizzy?' Tom said. 'Thought about what you're going to say yet?'

'No,' I said.

'Say what?' David asked.

'I've got to make a speech,' I said, as Miles reappeared by my side.

'Seriously?' said Sophia Gunning, as if she wanted to ask for her money back.

David looked amused. 'You?' he said.

'Yes,' I snapped.

'But you hate making speeches,' David said.

'I'm aware of that,' I said, doom settling in my guts.

'She'll be great,' said Miles, proprietorially. 'Don't worry, Lizzy. Tell them about Gibbo proposing to Chin while she was cleaning her teeth.'

'Quote from the order of service,' said David. 'Just pick a bit of one of the readings and read it out again in an authoritative voice. It works a charm. They'll think you're being symbolic, Lizzy. They'll love it.'

'I've lost mine,' I said.

'Here,' he said. 'Have mine. In case you dry up.'

'Or draw on your own experiences,' said Tom, evilly.

The Eliot brothers glanced at each other, then at me. A

379

silence fell as a waiter poured champagne into our glasses and we scanned the table plan.

'Where are we?' Miles said. 'Here – come on. See you later, guys.'

'Good luck, Lizzy,' said David.

I turned to look at him. 'Draw on your own experiences,' he said. 'Tom's right.'

And he walked off.

The wedding breakfast passed for me in an agony of appre-hension, the raincloud still perched above my head. The thought of food made me feel sick. It was Chin's wedding, though, so there was no salmon, smoked or poached, or chicken or new potatoes: this was Wedding Variation Number Four, Notting Hill Boho Relaxed Shabby Chic wedding, remember. There was a Moroccan mezze-style starter on huge platters, then organic bangers from the farm up the road with mash, lots of it. I perked up: surely there is no nicer dinner than bangers and mash. In fact I had quite recovered from (a) being annoyed with Miles (b) being annoyed with David and (c) the looming speech, when scarcely was the last morsel of potato in my mouth than the plates were whipped away, the glasses were refilled, and people were listening to Gibbo explain confusedly why he fell in love with Chin and what today meant to him. I'm sure it was all lovely, but I don't remember any of it. Then Bozzer told lots of stories about Gibbo, including the time he fell asleep in a wheelie-bin, the time he got mistaken for a homeless person, and the time he went to the loo and tried to get past a stranger in the bar. He stood face to face with the man for about three minutes, saying, 'Ahm, excuse me, mate?' before it occurred to him that he was talking and gesticulating to a reflection of himself in a mirror. How we all laughed. Some of us laughed louder than others – this was the famous incident that had taken place at Gibbo's Friends and soon-to be Relatives Wish Him *Bon Voyage* evening, otherwise known as the world's most spurious stag night.

'And now,' Gibbo said, waving in a friendly manner at me, as if he wasn't just about to throw me to the lions, 'please welcome Lizzy, Chin's niece, who'd like to say a few words.'

I stood up. Someone handed me the microphone and I looked around the marquee. Two hundred faces, silent, watching me expectantly, the waiters standing against the wall, like ballboys at Wimbledon, their hands behind their backs. Through the open side of the marquee, Keeper House looked friendly and welcoming in the early-evening sun.

I took a deep breath and looked at Chin. 'Hello, everyone,' I began. I thought suddenly of my friend James, who had started his best man's speech at a smart London wedding by yelling, 'Hellooooo, Mayfair!' and this put me off a bit.

'Hello, everyone,' I said again. I didn't know how to go on. What did I want to tell Chin and Gibbo? I felt a wave of suppressed British panic from my audience. Oh, no, she's nervous. Oh, no, she's insane. She's going to try to persuade us to become Jehovah's Witnesses. 'I really won't go on for very long,' I said carefully. People smiled. I was encouraged, and ploughed on. 'Because I don't think there's very much to say.'

Chin looked at me dangerously from under her fringe.

'Er . . .' I said, 'not much to say – because I think I speak for everyone here today when I say that we're all hugely happy to be celebrating with you.'

There was some nodding. OK, I was on the right lines. I cleared my throat.

'Chin and Gibbo . . .' There they were, on the top table, holding hands, looking so pleased and so right together that my nerves left me and I knew exactly what I wanted to say. 'Well,' I said, 'I don't know about any of the rest of you, but I knew Chin and Gibbo were right when I first saw them together. It's obvious to anyone with a blind bit of sense.'

Someone laughed, but I ignored them.

'We spend all our lives looking for love, looking for the right person, and so often we get it wrong, and our hearts are broken, or we get it wrong and don't realize till it's almost too late.'

I looked round the marquee for the face in the crowd that I was really saying this to. 'And I bet when all of you were getting ready this morning, none of you were thinking, Good God, what are they doing, this is a terrible mistake. I bet all of you were thinking, Well this is going to be a brilliant day, and I can't wait to see those two get married. Because they belong together.'

My legs were shaking, so I stood on one and put the other knee on a chair, like a stork.

'I want to say something else, too. Today is a great day for our family. Chin is lots of things. She's an amazing aunt, a wonderful sister, a great friend, and her family has always loved her and been so proud of everything she does. But never more so than today, and she knows why. I think being with Gibbo helped her, though, so much. So I want to thank him on behalf of my family, and his wife, for letting us be here today with them. It's been a strange year for us in lots of ways, but it's all OK now. And what I said before, about making mistakes, well, we do. All of us. And that's what makes us human.'

My gaze roamed around the marquee, was looking for Mike, but found myself staring straight into David's eyes. I knew with a white-hot certainty that he was looking only at me, thinking only about us, that he was trying to tell me something. Suddenly I didn't care how many people were

382

there, what I said, if I was nervous. I just wanted him to know. To talk to him, no matter if it was in front of all these people. I stood stock still for a few seconds, until a murmur of discomfort reached me, and I came to with a start. 'I – I can't remember what I wanted to say,' I whispered to myself, under my breath, staring at David. I stumbled on. 'We – we are here for them . . . so . . . we should raise—' I looked back at him once more. He picked up something from his neighbour's plate and held it up. An order of service.

My fingers flew to the table, I picked up the thick card and cleared my throat authoritatively. 'I'm reminded of one of the readings we heard today,' I said. David nodded encouragingly. I opened the page. ' "Let me not to the marriage of true minds admit impediments." '

A couple of people gave me an approving nod. He was still smiling, in the way that I loved. Only at me. ' "It is an ever fixed mark," ' I read, and saw I'd missed out a few lines, but it was probably for the best. I paused. Then I said, as if it was obvious, 'Um – well. There we go. That says all that needs to be said, doesn't it?'

Most people nodded, and the more pseudo-intellectual among the crowd did deep head-bobbing and lip-pursing, though I'm sure they'd had no idea what I was talking about – as, indeed, neither did I.

'So,' I concluded, 'if you'd like to stand up, will you all please join me in raising your glasses to the happy couple, and wish them a wonderful marriage and a happy life together. To Mr and Mrs Gibson.'

Everyone stood up. The sound of chairs scraping filled the tent like a hurricane. 'Mr and Mrs Gibson,' came the booming response, and then there was applause.

Chin blew me a kiss. 'Thank you,' she mouthed.

I didn't look anywhere else. With a sigh of relief I drained my glass.

I clutched the table and sat down. Instantly my right leg started to shake. The stunning girl next to Miles poured him another drink and tapped his shoulder to indicate it was there. Miles smiled at her, then turned to me. 'That was fantastic, darling. Are you all right?' he whispered, putting his hand on mine surreptitiously.

My teeth were chattering. 'I'm fine.'

'Have a glass of champagne,' he said solicitously.

'Thanks,' I said, grabbed it and took a gulp. Great Aunt Dahlia appeared behind me as Miles turned to Jacquetta and asked her about her career as an underwear designer.

'Well done, dear girl,' Aunt Dahlia said, slapping me heartily on the back. 'Wonderful speech. Unusual to hear from you, but a break in tradition is always welcome when it's done with such grace and poise.' She banged her stick on the ground for emphasis.

'Thank you, Aunt Dahlia,' I said, chuffed.

'Poise,' Tom scoffed from my other side, pouring another glass of wine. 'I don't call bursting into tears and wiping your nose on the back of your hand poise.'

'I didn't do that!' I said.

'Hm,' said Tom, drinking deeply. 'Whatever.' Aunt Dahlia moved off, smiling uncertainly, and I took a sip of champagne. 'It was a nice speech though, Lizzy. Well done,' he added.

'Thanks,' I said.

I was starting to feel slightly better, but I sat quietly and observed the scene in front of me as the setting sun cast long shadows across the crowd in the marquee. It was that stage of a wedding where the rhythm of the day is clearly established, the food has been eaten, love has been distributed by the giving of the speeches, and people sitting next to each other have worked out if they're going to snog or not. I watched Gibbo feed Chin a slice of cake and they chatted quietly, absorbed in each other. ('Cut the cake in front of everyone? Standing there like a page-three girl while some mad old cousins take photos of you with a knife in your hand smiling gormlessly? Do get a grip, Lizzy. The caterers can earn their crust and cut it up themselves.')

Mike was chatting to Kate, his hand on the back of her chair. She had turned to face him and was looking right at him. They were obviously having one of those conversations where it is not OK to mooch up and sigh, 'Hi! How're you? Can I join you!' Mike looked sad; Kate looked sad. They both looked vulnerable, like real people, rather than my relatives from a different generation. Mike brushed something out of his eyes and smiled at something Kate said, then moved his chair closer to hers. I looked at Tom to see if he was taking this in. He was. 'What's going on there, do you think?' I said softly.

'Don't know,' said Tom warily.

At that moment Miles, still talking to Jacquetta on his other side, put his hand on my thigh and moved it in search of my hand. When he found it, he squeezed it. A sixth sense made me look up and there, standing behind him, was David. I slid my hand out of Miles's, and nodded at him.

'Are you having a good time?' I said.

'Yes,' said David shortly, looking at Miles. 'Are you OK?'

'Oh, fine, thanks, just superb. [*Superb?* Good grief.] Thanks, by the way.'

'What for?' David said.

'This.' I raised the order of service. I looked away, back up at him. 'How's your table?'

'Good. Mando. Some Australian cousins of Gibbo's. Rosalie and Mike. Kate. They're chatting so I thought I'd go for a stroll. You know, see how you all are.'

I realised he was slightly drunk. His eyes were glittering and his jaw was set.

Miles turned easily to his brother and said, 'You staying, mate? Or do you think you'll leave before the band starts?'

'Is that what you want me to do, mate?' David said, with a tight smile. 'Of course, if that's what's most convenient for you two, I certainly don't . . .' He trailed off, swallowed as if he would say more, but stopped himself. 'Yep, I think I'll head off soon.'

'Oh right,' I said.

David looked at me. 'There's nothing I need to stay for now, is there?' He inclined his head, as if he was making a tiny bow, and walked off.

'Oh, God,' said Miles, reaching for another cigarette and sliding his arm round me. 'He'll be fine, don't worry about it. He's always been a bit of a drama queen, hasn't he?'

He pulled me to him and kissed the top of my head. I swivelled round in time to catch David at the edge of the marquee, still watching us.

'Sorry,' Miles said. 'I thought he'd gone.'

Jacquetta of the underwear leaned forward again, her lace top slack against her bony shoulders and collarbone. 'So, Miles, what do you do?' she said, lighting a cigarette and smiling at him.

'Well,' said Miles, purring like a cat, 'I'm afraid it's not a very interesting answer, but . . . I'm an accountant.' He smiled self-deprecatingly.

Jacquetta purred back at him: 'No, not at all. I think accountancy's really intriguing.'

Suddenly a thought came into my head: was Miles always like this, or was he doing it to make David or me jealous? Would I always be watching out for the gorgeous girl on the other side of him at a wedding? And if I was, why didn't I mind?

Tom caught my eye and raised an eyebrow. 'Yeurch,' he said, which was comforting somehow, as if Miles was our old friend again, not my other half. He held out a hand to me. 'Let's get out of here – go and have a walk in the garden.'

So we set off hand in hand, as if we were Tom and Lizzy aged six again, and walked out of the marquee on to the lawn, which sloped down to the gardens and the house. I could hear the soft murmur of conversation from other people outside and felt the delicious cool of the evening on my bare skin. Tom stopped to light a cigarette and I gazed down at the house.

'I can't believe we don't have to leave,' I said, feeling rather emotional but not wanting to make a song and dance about it.

'Me either,' said Tom. 'It seemed so wrong, but now that it's all been sorted out I keep thinking it's a dream and we'll wake up and have to leave again.'

Dad appeared behind us, a glass in his hand. He was tootling a tune under his breath. 'Hello there,' he said, rocking on the balls of his feet. 'Pretty nice, isn't it?'

'Yes,' I said, nudging him. 'You happy?'

'Bloody delirious,' said Dad, throwing his arms round us and squeezing. 'Hurrah, hurrah, for your awful, nightmarish aunt and her wonderful Mary Poppins ways.'

'Hear hear,' said Tom.

I felt something wet on my arm and looked down. Dad, in his expansive moment of joy, had flung red wine in a long thin streak down my dress. 'Oh, Dad, you mallet,' I wailed. 'My lovely dress! I'll have to go and get a cloth.'

'Sorry,' said Dad, contrite. 'I'll look after your glass.'

I hurried down the path that led past the lavender and the walled garden, round the side of the house, past the shed with the battle-wagon in it, grabbed a towel from the collection that resided by the back door with the wellies and the recycling, wet it with water from the outside tap and dabbed

387

my dress. Then I took off my shoes and walked back up the path, listening to the voices, trying to recognise from the moans who was snogging whom in the garden, and trying not to feel annoyed with Miles. A burly drummer from the band who were to play squeezed past me clutching a sheaf of music and his sticks as I did tiny pigeon-steps up the path, feeling the cold, soft, muddy grass beneath my poor tired feet.

I could hear Dad and Tom chatting companionably in the way men do, and stopped to admire them in their natural habitat.

'Good solid wall that, always has been,' Dad said ruminatively.

'Yup.' Tom did a head bob in agreement. I walked a little closer, smiling broadly.

'Band sound good. I expect people'll enjoy that too,' Dad went on.

'I'm sure they will,' Tom said.

'Hello, David,' said Dad. 'Haven't seen you yet today, how are you?'

I stepped back and did a tiny slide, then a tiny shriek, and ended up gently hugging a rose bush with my bottom. 'Ark grr sss,' I said softly to myself, trying to stand up and hoping I wasn't horribly drunk. So much for saving the dress.

I turned to go back down the path but there, at the bottom, were Mike and Kate, by the entrance to the back door where I'd just come from. She was crying. He had his arm round her and reached up to brush a tear away from her nose. The honeysuckle growing over the wooden posts by the kitchen garden framed them in the dusk. I prayed David, Dad and Tom would take a manly stroll round the garden.

Tom said, 'You OK, David?'

There was silence. I looked up towards the rose bush and leant against the kitchen wall to see if I could see David's face, but all I could make out was a quarter-profile, impossible to read.

'Well,' Dad said, 'it's lovely to see you. I know Chin's glad you could come. Have you spoken to Suzy yet? She'll want a word, I'm sure, to see how you are.'

David laughed, a nice laugh. 'That's very kind of her. I'll go and find her in a minute.'

'Well, it's good to see you again,' Dad said again. He sounded a bit stiff. 'Yes, we liked having you around. Old Suzy misses that, you know. It's a shame things didn't go according to plan with – with Lizzy.' He paused and coughed. 'Harrumph. But I suppose that's the way – that's the way it happens, isn't it. Is it?'

I bit my lip and flattened my palms against the brick of the wall. It was scratchy, sharp against my skin.

'I know.' It was David. I couldn't see his expression. He was silent, and then I heard him say, almost in a rush, 'I've thought about it a lot. Things just don't go according to plan, and that's the only way I can explain it. I – I wish it had been different, though. I still don't understand it.'

I held my breath. Come on, Tom, say something. Don't let him get away with it for the millionth time. 'Well, I don't see why,' Tom's voice rang out clear like a bell in the night air.

'You're the one who slept with someone else, David. You were having an affair behind her back.'

There was a short silence. I could feel Dad's embarrassment even from where I was lurking.

'What?' David said.

'Come on, no point in raking all this up again,' Dad said.

'What did you say?' David said. He stepped forward and I could see his face more clearly, harsh, angular in the dark.

'You were having an affair. With the girl who was your colleague,' Tom repeated.

'Me?' David said. I could hardly hear him. 'I was having an affair? When?'

Tom sounded belligerent. 'Whatever, David. Let's get another drink, shall we? Forget about it.'

David grabbed Tom's arm. 'Sorry, but I don't know what you're talking about,' he said, as my father, who had turned away, spun back. 'I haven't had an affair. When I was with Lizzy? Are you mad?'

'You slept with that bitch Lisa Garratt,' Tom reeled off, parrot fashion.

The brick wall was painful now against my shoulder-blades but, in a strange way, I liked it: there was something almost reassuring about it.

David drew himself up to his full height. 'John, I'm sorry about this. Look, Tom, you're mad. She kissed me at a party – Lizzy knows that. She literally came up to me and stuck her tongue down my throat. I never slept with her and I certainly wasn't having an affair with her. I don't—' he put his hand out, as if he was trying to hold on to something invisible. He sounded hoarse. 'We – Look, this is mad. I'm not going through the reasons why, but we split up because Lizzy – well, she just fell out of love with me. I thought she loved me and then she just changed. Once I was away in New York, she lost interest. She suddenly told me it was over and I—' He stopped. 'I'm going.'

Tom isn't a lawyer for nothing. He wasted no time in gawping and going, 'Oh, my God!' which was what I would have done. He said quickly, 'David, get back here. Stop. Stand here, listen to me. You were caught – come on, David! You were caught at the photocopying machine at work a week later. Miles told her! Are you saying Lizzy made it all up?'

Miles.

'What?' David said. I could see his chest rising and falling.

Dad said, suddenly, 'I'm afraid we know about it all, David. Not very nice.'

'No!' David said, and there was fury in his voice. 'Is that what Lizzy thinks? Do you know what I went— Where is she? You think – you all think I *slept with someone*?' His head fell forward. And then he looked up and into the distance, just where I was standing. He looked almost right at me, and I crouched down even further, he couldn't find me there then, I couldn't bear it. He said, 'Miles. Where's Miles?'

'David,' said Tom, uneasily, 'I know you're not happy about Miles and Lizzy but . . . just get over it, OK? He's mad about her.'

'Ah, John!' said a fruity voice. 'Marvellous to see you, old boy. Wonderful day. Y'sister never looked better. Stunning gel. I was wondering, would it be possible to take a look at the Edwin Walters? Rather a speciality of mine, you know.'

'Of course, Sebastian,' Dad said. 'My pleasure. Come with me. David, Tom, I'll see you in a minute.'

Oh, my God, I thought, they're about to come down the path. I braced myself to shrink further into the bush until I realized it'd never work. Thankfully, my father said, 'Let's go through the garden. It's quite nice at this time of year, even at night.'

'Wonderful idea. Beautiful pointing,' said Sebastian, whoever he was.

Thank you, Lord, I muttered to myself, as Tom and David stood alone, staring at each other.

'I mean it, David,' Tom said again. 'Don't cause a scene. I know you want to. It's all in the past. He loves her. He really does.'

'He . . . he loves her.' David stopped. 'And you think I don't? You think I wanted to split up with her? That it's OK she's . . . Miles! Where is he? I need to talk to him.'

He started to walk away, Tom running after him. 'Why?' Tom said urgently. David stopped and turned to him.

'Miles did this,' he said, his voice carrying on the night air. 'He must have told Lizzy. Getting caught in the photo-copying room shagging someone? You really think I'd do that to Lizzy? Anyway, that's how I know.'

'Know what?' said Tom.

David spoke slowly: 'How I know it must have been Miles. He was cautioned at work last year for doing the same thing. My God.' He passed a hand across his forehead. 'My own brother. Come on.'

From the marquee a microphoned voice rang out: 'Come on! Laydeez-n-gennlemen, there'll be no first dance tonight, so instead get ready to rock around the clock as the Frank Walden Band gets this party started with some Stevie Wonder! "Superstition", coming right up!'

I stood up and stared after them as they disappeared, David striding ahead, Tom trotting behind him. I looked at my hand. It was covered in little red blood spots. The red wine stain on my dress had dried. It was funny to think that ten minutes ago it hadn't been there.

THIRTY-THREE

I scurried up the path and ran towards the marquee, my shoes in my hand, heart pounding. The band was in full swing: Rosalie and Gibbo were doing synchronized disco movements together. ('First dance? Stumble around the floor with two-left-feet Gibbo? While everyone watches and laughs and points? You must be joking.') But I was too late. David and Miles were outside, flanked by Tom and Jess. David wasn't shouting, but his voice sent a chill through me.

'What do you mean, it was just a bit of fun?' he was saying.

I couldn't see Miles's face. 'Look, mate,' he said, putting up his hands in a gesture of self-defence. 'It's all in the past now, isn't it? Let's forget about it, OK?'

'No, I fucking won't forget about it,' David said. 'Listen to me, you little shit. What did you tell Lizzy last year? It was you, wasn't it? She thinks I had a fucking affair with someone and you told her that, didn't you?' He grabbed the lapels of Miles's jacket and pulled him up so they were face to face.

'David, stop it,' I yelled. 'Stop it now, put him down. What are you doing?'

'Lizzy, you fool,' David said, and let go of Miles so suddenly that he staggered and almost fell over. He came over to me. 'Is that what you've been thinking? Is that what he told you? God, all this time I've been trying to understand why you ended it, and it was *because of this*?'

'Yes,' I said, as the song finished and the crowd in the marquee whooped loudly. 'But you admitted it. You told me you were sleeping with someone else.'

'What? *What*?' He turned back to Miles. 'Miles?' His voice was slow, broken. 'Do you realize what you've done?'

'I didn't do anything,' Miles's hair was wild in the moonlight. 'I must have got the wrong end of the stick, mate. Right? Honestly. I thought you were shagging someone else. That you just weren't keen on her any more.'

'*No!*' David shouted. I jumped. 'For God's sake, no! You've lied to her all along and now you're lying to me. Lizzy, do you really not understand? It's all a lie. And you believe it. My God—' He broke off and collected himself as I stared at him, trying to re-evaluate the events of the last year.

'Look,' said Miles, smoothing his hair. 'You need to calm down, David. It's all in the past now. Lizzy's with me, and we're in love. You weren't the right one for her – was he, Lizzy? – and we're happy. So it's all worked out anyway, even if I did help it along. To get what I wanted. Just once.' He put his arm round me and pulled me towards him.

I pushed him away. 'Get off me.'

Miles looked at me with amusement, but there was fear in his eyes too, and desperation, as if he was trying to walk a tight-rope. 'Come on, Lizzy. I know I shouldn't have lied, but . . . hasn't this all worked out for the best?'

'I don't love you.' I said. David was breathing heavily as if he had been running.

'I know,' Miles said soothingly. 'I know you don't just

394

yet, but you will. I'm here to look after you, to take care of things. Like this. Look, shall we . . .' He glanced around. 'Tom, do you think it'd be OK if we slipped off a little early? I'll take Lizzy back to the hotel.'

'I don't love you,' I said again.

'Yes, I know,' Miles said, a little impatiently.

'But I was in love with him,' I said.

'Right,' said Miles. I don't think he was even listening properly.

'Miles,' I said slowly, 'I was in love with him. Don't you understand?'

'No, you weren't,' said Miles.

'She was,' David said, and I jumped at the sound of his voice so close to mine. 'She was,' he repeated conversationally. 'I loved her too, if that matters to you at all. You know. No big deal. But it's too late now.' He turned to face me, and said quietly, only to me, 'Lizzy, how could you have believed him? How could you think I'd do that to you?'

'I don't know.' I couldn't bear to see his face. I closed my eyes.

'Look at me, Lizzy. How could you think that? Didn't you know how much I loved you?'

It was heartbreaking. 'I didn't want to believe him,' I said, my voice breaking, 'but it was so weird after you went away, and you were fine, and I didn't want to show you how much I missed you.' The words were tumbling out. I couldn't stop them. 'And I thought I was fine because I knew you loved me, but when I thought you didn't, that I'd got it all wrong – oh, I don't know. I can't do this any more.' There were tears running down my cheeks and I wiped them off with the back of my hand. I didn't feel cross or angry, I just felt tired.

I stared up into his dark brown eyes, searching for something to hold on to, a small piece of hope.

'I can't believe you thought I'd do that. To you. To you, Lizzy. I can't believe you're that weak. It's too late. I'm sorry.'

He turned and walked away. I watched him stoop to go under the honeysuckle and then he disappeared. He would walk through the courtyard, past the mulberry tree in full flower, with the windows of the house watching him. He would walk out of the gate, down the lane, where the lacy white cow parsley and the elderflowers gleamed eerily in the moonlight, and the light green of the oak trees shone luminously in the dark. He would walk down that path, over the tiny bridge across the river, in the moonlight back to his mother's cottage and I knew I might never see him again.

I understood everything now. And there was almost nothing I could do about it. Almost nothing.

A voice spoke behind me. 'Come on, Lizzy. Come and have a drink. Let's talk about it,' said Miles, stroking my shoulder.

I grabbed his lapel, just as David had, and kept my voice steady, although I wanted to scream. 'Miles,' I said, 'I'm trying to understand you. I know you're jealous of David. I know you wanted what he had. Just tell me one thing. Do you really think you're in love with me, or do you think you've got one over on your big brother for once?'

'What do you mean?' said Miles, slowly.

'I mean,' I said, 'if you think you're in love with me, then I'm afraid you're about to get your heart broken just like you did with me and David. If you wanted to get one over on your brother, well, you've failed. Because you'll never, ever be half the man he is.'

'That's got nothing to do with it.'

'I'm giving you a taste of your own medicine, Miles,' I said, trying not to shout at him, pull his hair, scratch the complacent smile off his face.

'You're overreacting,' Miles said. I gaped. 'Let's—'

'No, let's not,' said Tom suddenly. 'Just go, Miles.'

'Yes,' said Jess, anxiously. I hadn't even noticed she was there. 'Honestly Miles. Go away. We don't want you here, I'm sorry.'

'OK, OK,' said Miles, as if he hadn't heard them. 'Listen, chaps, I think I'll go now. Lizzy, are you sure—'

'God, Miles, you're pathetic!' Tom said. 'You really are. Have some self-respect! Go away!'

I looked at Miles again, and he reminded me of the chubby twelve-year-old he'd been when we first knew him, not the devious, sad man he'd become. I felt sorry for him – and so glad that I didn't have to be with him any more that, momentarily, it dulled the pain I was feeling about David, a pain that had faded over the last year but was fresh again, stabbing me in the side, like a kind of stitch.

'Don't hate me, Lizzy. I do really love you,' he said. 'It wasn't just about David. It's about you. I – I love you.'

'Oh, Miles,' I said. 'No, you don't. You'll see.'

'You're wrong,' Miles said. He inhaled deeply and drew himself up to his full height. I could tell he was trying to stay cool. 'Well, 'bye then.'

''Bye,' I said shortly, as if we were delegates on a paper-clip conference. I thought of him going back to our room at the Oak Grange, sitting on the edge of the bed, watching the cricket highlights with his tie loosened and a beer in his hand. Would he be OK? Of course he would. Would he do something like this again? I didn't know, and the deadening feeling I had inside swelled into something else.

'Miles,' I called, and ran to catch up with him. The wind had picked up: the trees were rustling and the door to the marquee was flapping, almost in time to the music.

Miles turned eagerly.

'Do you hate him?' I said.

'No,' he said, with a small sigh.

'Well, I don't get it,' I said, as the anger I'd struggled to control rose again. 'You must understand what you've done, Miles. He's your brother.'

'It's families, Lizzy,' Miles said, brushing something out of his eye with an impatient gesture. 'It's complicated. I don't hate him, I love him. But sometimes he's the person I'd most like to trample all over. I want to beat him. To be better than him. And he does too.'

'No, he doesn't,' I said. 'That's just you.'

'Forget it,' Miles said, and walked away.

'No,' I said, catching up with him and grabbing his shoulder so he had to face me. 'I can't. You've done something terrible to me and I don't think you understand.'

'I really do,' said Miles. 'Trust me.'

'You don't,' I said furiously. 'You lied to me. I was missing David desperately. I thought he didn't love me any more, and you lied to me. You looked me in the eyes and told me he'd slept with someone else. Then you rang him up and told him – what? The same thing? Something similar?'

Miles said nothing.

'That bit doesn't matter,' I said, though it did: I wanted desperately to know. 'It's what you did that matters. You didn't want your brother to be happy so you took it away. You wanted me for yourself so you broke my heart. That's not love, Miles. That's – that's horrible.'

I put my hand on my collarbone to calm myself down.

'David and me . . . You don't understand it,' Miles said suddenly. 'He didn't understand how I felt about you. He always thinks it's just him. Who deserves everything.'

'He didn't *deserve* me,' I said, my voice rising. 'We were together, that's all. I didn't pick him over you. There wasn't a competition!'

'Yes, there was!' Miles cried. 'There fucking was. You don't understand it, Lizzy. It's not about you. We were friends for ages and I've always wanted you, wanted to be with you. Ever since . . . years ago. I promised myself that when I grew up I'd do what I could to make you want me, and then—'

I tried to contain the fury and hatred that flared up inside me. His voice broke. He covered his mouth with a fist, then said, 'And I get back from holiday and there's David in the kitchen, telling Mum all about how he'd just met you, how he'd *had* you, how you were going out. Just like that. And Mum's all pleased and grinning. Oh, well done, David, ooh, how exciting. Oh, hello, Miles, what are you doing there skulking around in the background?' His eyes flashed in the evening gloom. 'I hated him then, and I promised myself I wouldn't let it get to me, but it did. And I won in the end, you could say.' His smile was twisted. He touched my arm. 'You wouldn't understand.'

Then the dam broke, and I was in the grip of an uncontrollable rage. 'Wouldn't understand?' I shouted, clutching my skirt as I staggered up the slope towards him. 'You stupid. Fucking. Idiot.' I was yelling, spitting almost, inches away from his face. '*Wouldn't understand?* Do you have any idea how much I understand? I'm the one who's been at the centre of *all* of this – this *crap* – for the last year. You selfish, selfish . . . I can't even begin to tell you the damage you've done. It was none of your business, me and David. And you, with your sad little fantasies, your weird fucked-up way of seeing things, do you know how awful you made me feel? How can you say you loved me all that time you watched me crying over him? You knew how much I loved him, you knew how good we were – how can you say that what you did was from true love?' My throat was aching. 'You've ruined everything! I – I—'

I couldn't breathe. I actually couldn't breathe, and I stood back and gulped air in long, shuddering breaths that hurt with the force of my anger. I remembered suddenly what it was like to be little, to have no command of yourself, to feel hysterical, out of control.

Miles's white face swam in front of me, looking like Miles, looking like David, I couldn't tell. I gritted my teeth to stop myself crying, and took another deep breath. Suddenly, all those things I'd been wanting to say for ages were tumbling out, and I couldn't stop them. In the distance I could see people watching. I didn't care. Now it wasn't just Miles I was so angry with. 'All this year, I've been trying to be so good, to be a good daughter, not to let the sale get us all down, worrying about Tom, wondering what's up with Mike, and Rosalie, and – and Mum and Dad. All this year I've kept all these things to myself, that I kept wanting to stop remembering, and I couldn't. And we've all been through so much, and do you understand, Miles, what it would have been like if I'd had David with me through all of that?'

'Stop it, Lizzy,' Miles said. He looked beaten.

I stood up straight, feeling as if I'd stretched my legs and arms after I'd been asleep for a long time. He backed away, as if breaking the thread between us. After all, he had nothing to lose by going.

'I'm sorry, OK? One of these days I hope you'll forgive me. But that's enough now. I'm not listening to any more. I'll – just, well, take care. Don't – just stop worrying about everything. It's over now. 'Bye.'

My gaze followed his retreating figure. He seemed unfamiliar to me. In my mind I'd tried to make him into something he wasn't, and I'd been wrong. I couldn't think of a joke we'd both liked, or a film we'd loved together. He just adored me. He was safe. He wouldn't ever hurt me. I had thought that was enough, but I'd got it wrong.

As a thousand thoughts like these crowded into my mind, a picture came into my head of me and David on my sofa, watching *Robin Hood: Prince of Thieves* late on a wintry Saturday afternoon. I was pretending to be really into it and David was pretending to hate it and doing a brilliant Kevin Costner impression. Both of us were laughing like drains, so much so that I spilt my tea over him. I don't think I'd laughed once like that with Miles.

Tears filled my eyes. That was what I'd lost and it was a stupid thing to remember but to me, at that very moment, it was heartbreaking.

I walked towards the house, not bothering to acknowledge Miles as I overtook him on the gravel path. I went to my room, my comforting old room, and all of a sudden I saw what Mum and Chin had been hinting at: that it had been less vital to save Keeper House than I'd thought. Humans and relationships are more important than homes, and while I couldn't have been happier that the house was ours again, I saw how much time and energy I'd spent living in a dreamworld about it when I should have hunted David down, begged him to talk to me about what had gone wrong. We were stupid, both of us, the way Mike was stupid; we had put our heads in the sand and hoped everything bad would go away; we blamed ourselves but took no action. I'd spent hours wishing and hoping we could avoid the sale of the house, praying it wouldn't happen, mooning over old napkins, dusty books and fond memories. Well, Keeper House had been saved in the end, but by Chin, whose outlook on life was different from mine. I sat on the bed. It was too late for anyone to do anything about me and David, and the person I was now was too different from the girl I'd been then for the gap to be breached.

The band were still in full swing: no one would notice that I wasn't there and I knew Tom would make any excuses. I shut the window, brushed my teeth, put on my nightie and curled up in the chair. I didn't want to go to bed: I just wanted to be by myself. I stayed in that chair for what seemed like hours, looking at nothing, thinking about everything.

I'm ashamed to say I felt rather sorry for myself and cried myself to sleep. Happily no one noticed I wasn't there. Jess snogged a waiter, Rosalie led the demand for a band encore, and Chin and Gibbo danced in each other's arms until the sun came up and the house cast its long, friendly shadow across the marquee.

THIRTY-FOUR

When I woke up, the sun was shining through the gap in the curtains. The diamond-shaped leading in the windows cast distorted patterns on the floorboards. I shut my eyes again. I felt as if I had been hit over the head with a hammer, made to run a marathon, then put forward for eyelid testing, which involved my eyelids being puffed-up with a syringe to nine times their normal size and weight. It was a hangover, of course, but often you can drink all night and wake up feeling relatively fresh because you have had a hilarious, raucous evening. I reopened one eyelid. The sun patterns on the floor were dancing. I groaned.

I opened both eyes carefully, and rolled my gaze out across the floor. There were some brown kitten heels, lying askew under the chair. Suddenly, like Bobbie's daddy appearing through the swirling mist at the end of *The Railway Children*, a picture of the previous day emerged. The shoe strap that hurt on the way back from Chin's wedding. The house – saved. My speech. Rosalie's rose-pink taffeta outfit. Miles – God, Miles: I wasn't going out with him any more. And then I remembered. David hadn't slept with anyone else.

David hadn't slept with anyone else!

I sat bolt upright in bed, which sent me into a relapse. My arms ached, my ribcage hurt, my legs felt lumpen and bloated, so I lay down again. I hadn't dreamed it, had I? Miles had lied to me. And David had said he loved me. We shouldn't have broken up. Hope glared in my heart. Ouch, my head was aching again, as if I was thinking clearly for the first time in months and I'd forgotten how to do it.

Whatever had happened yesterday, I felt as though something had changed irrevocably. As if I'd look out of the window and find the house had blown out of Kansas and into Munchkinland. I couldn't face sitting up but I wanted to get up. I wrapped myself in my duvet, like a sausage roll, and got completely tangled in it. How long I would have stayed there I have no idea, because at that moment I heard a tentative knock on the door.

'Lizzy?'

'Tom!'

The door opened a crack. I wriggled and managed to free an arm. 'Help me, I'm stuck,' I said pathetically.

Tom crouched and moved his head to one side so I could see his face.

'Hello,' he said, rather stiffly. 'Are you OK now?'

'I can't unravel myself,' I said. 'I'm hiding.'

Tom coughed politely. 'Well, after your performance last night, I'm not bloody surprised. Who are you hiding from?' he asked, turning me over like a Swiss roll and freeing the edge of the duvet. 'Has Miles reappeared? David? Or even Jaden? Or some other, as yet unknown to me, paramour?'

'No.' I sat up. 'Thanks. I'll come down in five minutes.'

'Good. Chin and Gibbo are going. I came to see if you wanted to say goodbye.' He patted my arm. 'You look terrible. Did you get any sleep?'

'Yes. No. Not really.'

'Well, this sounds trite but—'

'At least it's all sorted out now,' I finished.

Tom stared. 'That's what I was about to say.'

'That's why I said it.' I got out of bed. 'I'll be down in five, I promise.'

'Are you—' Tom began.

'I'm fine,' I said coolly. 'I'm not going to repeat my behaviour of last night, don't worry. That's all finished.'

'Right,' Tom said. 'See you downstairs, then?'

'Absolutely,' I said. The door slammed behind him.

'Lizzy!' Chin called as Tom and I trotted feebly down the stairs. 'Darling, I didn't want to get you up.' As I descended the final two steps she jumped up to kiss me. She looked fantastic – clear-skinned, bright-eyed, incredibly happy. She was dressed in a beautiful kaftan, embroidered with gold thread, and some loose trousers, like an advert for a bride off on holiday to a boutique hotel in Marrakech – which was, of course, the case.

'Morning, you two,' said Mum, from the bottom of the stairs. She had no makeup on and her fluffy hair was sticking up on end, making her look like a surprised cockatoo.

'Morning,' Tom and I muttered.

There was an air of anticlimax in the hall, a bit like New Year's Day. Dad and Jess looked tired but chirpy. Mike had apparently gone ten rounds with Lennox Lewis and was using his eye pouches to store loose change. Rosalie, of course, was as fresh as a daisy, succulent as roast chicken, with her arm threaded through Mike's, smiling at everyone.

'Is Mum here?' Tom said.

'No,' my mother told him. 'She's coming over for lunch. Right, you two, are you ready to go?'

'I think we are,' Chin said, as Gibbo appeared from the car where he'd been stowing the last of the luggage, as any married man should. 'Oh, Suzy,' she said, hugging Mum hard, 'thank you so much, for everything.'

'Well, you too,' said Mum. 'Darling Chin.' She sniffed surreptitiously.

'You all right, Lizzy?' Chin said. 'I didn't see much of you last night. What happened? Did you and Miles go off somewhere?'

'They left early,' said Tom, truthfully.

'You two, eh?' said Gibbo, as if Miles and I were a well-known, long-established couple who were notorious for sneaking out of events ahead of schedule.

'Yes,' I said. 'Have you got everything?'

Gibbo hugged me, then shook hands with Tom. 'See you soon, mate. I'll give you a call when we're back, yeah?' Tom and I stepped back gratefully as Gibbo moved along the line to Rosalie and Mike. 'Hey, Mike, take care of this gorgeous gal, won't you? Let's go dancing when you're next in the country, Rozzer. Throw some shapes down.'

'Sure thing,' Rosalie said, laughing. 'Bless you both. G'bye, Chin,' she added.

Chin kissed her. ''Bye,' she said, and paused in front of Mike. ''Bye, bro,' she said softly.

Mike had been standing there in a light doze, his chin in his hand, but at the sound of his sister's voice he started awake. 'Ah, Chin! You off, then?'

'Yes,' said Chin. There was a clattering sound from upstairs, and a scream followed by a wail.

'Mando's still here?' I said.

'He's coming with us,' Chin said. 'I'm putting him in the back and if he says a word he's going in the boot.'

'Don't go!' Mando yelled, from upstairs. 'Give me time!'

'For God's sake,' Chin muttered. She turned back to Mike. 'Well, 'bye, then. See you . . . at Christmas, I suppose.'

'Yup,' Mike said. Rosalie nudged him. He stood up a bit

straighter. 'Why don't you and Gibbo come over for a bit, though? Stay with us. We'd love that. Show you the sights. All that sort of thing.'

'We'll think about it,' Chin said solemnly. ''Bye Mike.'

Mike stepped forward suddenly. ''Bye, sis. Lots of love.' He threw his arms round her and lifted her a foot off the ground. Then he carried her outside, put her into the car, as if she weighed no more than a bag of feathers, bent down and kissed her. 'Sorry,' I heard him mumble. Chin caught his head as he leaned into the car and they stayed like that for a while, till Mum and Mando appeared and we all went outside.

'Oh, Mando, goodbye,' Mum said.

'Suzy, oh, Suzy,' Mando said tragically. He was wearing a tight pink polo shirt and checked golfing trousers. 'I will see you next month, yes?'

'What for?' asked Dad, with interest.

'The sales,' Mum said severely. 'You wouldn't like it. Oh bye, Mando, do take care, thank you for everything.'

'No, thank you,' said Mando simply. 'It has been wonderful. You are a lovely family.'

Mike stood up and joined Rosalie. Tom, Jess and I stood along the hedgerow, in the shade.

'Goodbye,' Mando said, disentangling himself from my mother. 'Good luck with things,' he said to us. 'Tom, you are an excellent *omosessuale*. Jess, you are an excellent painting. Painter. *Bene*. Lizzy, you are excellent – I am sure at many things.'

'Come on, M,' Gibbo said, like somebody's dad. 'We're leaving now. OK? Get in.'

Chin leaned out of the window. 'Thank you so much, everyone. See you in a couple of weeks!'

'Have a wonderful time,' we chorused, as Gibbo started the car.

''Bye,' Chin called, as they drove away. ''Bye – love you all.'

As they drove off, Mando yelled something, then threw out all the left-over rose petals. They gusted up into the air, and floated down on us as we stood and waved.

'Typical Mando,' said Jess. 'I've never met someone who had no other use except being decorative. But who'll clear this all up, may I ask?' she said, pointing to the petals.

'I will,' Mum said quietly. 'I miss him already. My new best friend.' She sighed as the car rounded the corner and disappeared.

I felt melancholy all of a sudden. 'When were you thinking of going back, Tom?' I said, as we went into the side-room, where breakfast was ready.

'I wanted to get back before lunch.' He sat down, then poured himself and me some coffee. 'Do you want a lift?'

'Why before lunch?' I said.

'I'm going out tonight and I need to do some work before then,' Tom said.

'Where are you going?' I said nosily.

'Just out,' Tom replied.

I was sure it must be a date but I said nothing: I reminded myself that from now on I was a mature, discreet person who did not prod for vulgar details.

'Mike and I were planning on leaving after tea,' Rosalie said, 'so I guess we can both say goodbye to Kate.' She reached for the jam.

Mike looked up at his wife, an unreadable glance, then gazed back at his lap.

'Can't we, Mike?' Rosalie continued.

'Sure,' he said, and reached for the paper.

She knows, I thought. That's why she wants him to say goodbye to Kate. He needs to.

'Then I want to go to the airport via Stonehenge,' Rosalie

continued. 'My gosh, it'll probably be the oldest thing I've ever seen.' She took a bite of toast.

'What about your first husband?' Mike said, a faint glimmer in his eyes.

'What about my third husband?' Rosalie countered, munching toast, glinting back at him. 'I'm going to finish our packing,' she said after a pause, standing up and collecting her things together.

'I'll come and give you a hand,' Mike said. 'I'll get the pictures and put them in the car.'

He was taking a couple back with him for their apartment. He said he wanted something to remind him of home. Rosalie had examined them on Friday afternoon with her portable magnifying-glass – for all the good it'd do her: they were Edwin Walter's London print series and not up to much. I could see her in her apartment, waving her hand at them in a *faux*-casual manner as she ushered guests past them into the lounge that overlooked Central Park. 'Those? Yes, they are beautiful, aren't they? They're from my husband's family home in England. Edwin Walter was his ancestor. Yes. I know. It's a beautiful place, quite old. Queen Elizabeth the First. We're hoping to go back for Christmas again this year.'

They went out, and Mike put his arm round Rosalie's shoulders as they receded into the corridor.

'Lizzy,' said my mother suddenly, from the other end of the table, 'I meant to say yesterday but I couldn't find you. Well, your father and I wanted to say it, really.'

Dad looked alarmed. He picked up a spoon and bashed his boiled egg with unusual vehemence.

'What?' I said.

'Well, about Miles. Darling, I'm sorry.'

'Thanks, Mum,' I said.

'We think he's great.'

'Thanks,' I said, grabbing more toast.

Tom said, 'Suzy . . .'

'Well, he is,' Mum continued. 'And I wanted to tell you. Because you know we weren't very supportive when you told us on Wednesday. I suppose it was a bit of a shock. And because of David – we did love him, you know. But Daddy says he was behaving most oddly last night. Swearing and – well . . .'

'Thanks a lot, Mum,' I said, because I appreciated the gesture. Jess was knitting her figures together helplessly. 'Actually,' I said, 'Miles and I split up last night, I'm afraid, so don't worry about it too much.'

'What?' said my mother. 'You split up? What does that mean?'

I glared at her. 'It means . . . we're not together any more.'

'Oh,' said Mum, discomfited. 'Oh, darling.'

'Really, don't worry about it, Mum,' I said. 'I'm fine, honestly. They're both mad. And weird. And not for me.'

'So you're sure neither of them will do for you?' said Mum, hopefully.

'Nope,' I said, reaching for the Marmite. 'Yes, I mean. I'm safe, sane and single, and I'm staying that way. For the moment, anyway. Roll on LA and m' future husband George Clooney.'

'Well,' said Dad, from behind his *Observer*, 'she's certainly given it her best shot with each of them. We can't expect any more from her, can we? Any cousins of theirs we should know about? What's their father up to, these days? He should watch out. I might have to have a word with him to warn him off.'

'Dad!' Jess and I yelled.

'John,' Mum murmured reproachfully. 'Well, that's that, then. But you'll still be friends, won't you?'

'No,' I said. 'Absolutely no.'

'No way,' Tom and Jess chorused.

410

'Dear me,' Mum said. She looked at each of us in alarm. 'What did they do?'

'Well,' I said. My brain started to hum confusedly. Dad had put down the paper. Mum was looking on expectantly. Tom jumped in helpfully.

'Miles has always had the horn for Lizzy. I mean, he thinks he's in love with her. He lied to her to get her to break up with David, he did the same to David, then he was all "Oh, Lizzy, I understand what you're going through. Let me take you out for expensive meals and make you laugh and soothe away your problems, so you'll think you like me, and then I'll pounce and have my own way and get to shag you."' He assumed a high falsetto: 'And Lizzy's all "Oh, Miles, you are a bit like David. I'm all confused, go on, shag me, and at least I'll have a boyfriend for Chin's wedding, and David will be pissed off, ha, ooh, it's all so complicated."'

'Tom, don't be vile,' Jess said warmly. 'That's not how it was.'

'Really?' said Mum, turning sunken eyes on her younger daughter.

Dad coughed, and stroked the table.

'No,' Jess said. 'It wasn't like that at all.'

'Thanks, Jess,' I said. 'I love you.'

'It was more "Ooh, David, I love you, I love you, I love you! Ooh, David, I hate you now, oh, you're so mean, I'm going to cry all the time and get nothing done for months and months. Ooh, David! You're horrid! Oh, no, you're not, you're great!"'

'It's really not about me most of the time,' I said, embarrassed, blushing in what I hoped was a flatteringly modest way.

'Hm,' said Jess severely, and went back to her tea in silence.

'Well, I don't know,' Mum said. 'La, la. Hum. Should I

invite Alice Eliot to our mulled-wine party this year then, or would it be too embarrassing? Poor woman. Imagine having sons like that. They sound mad, both of them. How funny. I always thought they were quite normal.'

'And then they met Lizzy,' Tom chimed in. 'Ask yourself, Suzy. Which came first, the chicken or the egg?'

'Tom, I'm going to deck you in a minute,' I hissed.

'It all seems perfectly clear to me,' said Dad, unexpectedly. I turned to look at him. 'Does it?'

'Yes,' said Mum, as Dad got up and went out. 'Me too. Perfectly. But you have to see it clearly yourself. And you don't.'

'I—' I began.

'So,' Mum said, changing the subject, 'did you see that Sophia Gunning girl snogging the trumpet player from the band?'

'No!' Tom said.

'Yes,' Mum said gleefully. 'Our saviour was rather the worse for wear. She disappeared with him behind his kit for a good ten minutes, I'd say.'

'Mum!' Jess said. 'You are awful. Talking of awful, though, did you see what Eliza Baker was wearing? A cut-off denim skirt. With stilettos.'

We spent the next forty minutes in this manner. Tom ate ten pieces of toast, Jess eight, me seven. Mum made another pot of tea. Jess went back to bed. The marquee men arrived to – you guessed it – take down the marquee. Mike appeared and gave them a hand. Rosalie went into the study with Dad, and showed him how to use Excel spreadsheets. I helped Mum with the rest of the clearing up. We picked some lavender for me to take back. We persuaded Tom to leave after lunch. Mum did some more packing and unpacking – the film crew were coming in ten days' time, meaning some nifty forward planning was called for in terms of what Mum and

Dad would need over the next few days. Dad and Mike set up the barbecue, amid much arguing and abuse, and did the leftover sausages from the wedding breakfast. Kate appeared, with a potato salad and some ice-cream. We sat about, drinking beer and eating. The sun shone. Mike put a hanky over his head and went to sleep. Our cat, Collins, rolled around on his back on the lawn. I could smell lavender on my fingers every time I took a bite of my sausage sandwich. The barbecue and the flowers, an insect droning nearby – I felt calm for the first time in I didn't know how long.

As the first summer's haze hung over the garden, and evening approached, Tom, Jess and I stuffed our bags into the boot of Tom's little car, with the others gathered round. The sun was sinking, and in the east the sky was a deep blue. A couple of early stars had appeared.

'Goodbye, darling,' Kate said, hugging Tom. 'See you next week.'

''Bye, you two,' Mike said, enfolding me and Jess in a hug. 'We might catch you up on the motorway.'

'Stonehenge, remember, Mikey,' Rosalie said, behind him.

'Yes, of course. Sorry. We won't catch you up on the motorway, as we'll be on a completely different one, dawdling around some bloody stones,' Mike said amiably. 'See you at Christmas, girls. Or come and stay. We'd love to have you, wouldn't we?'

'God, yes. Now everything's . . .' Rosalie trailed off. 'Well, we'd love it. Think about it, won't you?'

'Thanks,' we said.

''Bye, Lizzy,' Dad said, as Mum was kissing Jess. 'We'll see you soon. Let us know when you'll be down next, won't you?'

'Of course. 'Bye, Dad. Thanks. 'Bye, Mum,' I said, turning to her.

She hugged me, hard. 'Think about what I said,' she

whispered. 'Look at things clearly. I'm so proud of you, Lizzy. So proud of you.'

'Why—' I began, but Tom pulled me away, pushed me and my sister into the car. Before we knew it the engine had started, the others were standing in the road, waving madly, and we were flying down the lane in the twilight, away from our home, and back to London, back to normality. I turned in my seat as we raced away, and watched them all, waving and smiling. They disappeared around the corner as the sky in front of us changed, becoming indigo, then an inky blue. We sat in happy silence as Tom let the roof down, feeling the rush of warm summer air on our arms and faces.

THIRTY-FIVE

Going into work on the Monday after a big weekend is always strange, but much more so when during that stage you have undergone a sea change. By Monday morning I was feeling better, but I still had a vaguely weird feeling, not exactly a headache, but the sensation that a headache might start at any moment.

Being on the top floor, my flat is always sunny and bright in summer. I woke early on Monday morning, before six, and did unlikely things like squeezing myself some fresh orange juice and putting my shoes back in their boxes. I even labelled them. I ironed all my summer clothes, which had lain in a crumpled pile since last September, finding something therapeutically about the smooth crunch of the steam and metal on fabric.

It was already hot when I left for work and it was a relief to come out of the Tube, stuffy even at eight thirty, and turn into the cool, shadowy streets behind Oxford Circus. There weren't many people about. As I crossed the road I walked through a shaft of sunlight and shivered in the sudden flash of heat. It felt as if the pavements were warming up, the city was shedding its usual Edwardian grey feeling and turning

Bolognese, Sevillian, Parisian. The baker was opening, and in the little French bistro a waiter was tying his apron round his waist as he stood in the doorway with his face to the sun. Across the road someone was rolling up the blinds in Luigi's and Luigi was putting a blackboard out on the street, with the legend 'Special Summer Salads' chalked in red and green. I waved at him, and clattered up the tiled stairs that led to Monumental's front door, leaning against the swipecard lock to let myself into the air-conditioned lobby.

'Woah!' Ash said, as he slid into my room. 'Eow! It's Lady Elizabeth of the grand stately home! Good morning, Your Highness. Can I get you some emeralds while the ghastly film crew runs amok in your beautiful house?'

'Shut up, Ash,' I said automatically, depositing my bag on my keyboard. 'Did you know about it?'

'No idea,' Ash said, handing me a coffee (we took it in turns to go to Prêt each morning). 'Only found out on Friday. So did Lily. It's not my project, is it?'

I crouched under my desk to turn on my computer.

'So,' Ash continued, sitting down in my chair, 'you live in some big mansion, then?'

'No, I bloody don't,' I said.

'Liar,' he said. 'I always thought you were a nice normal girl, and now I find out you're some posh bird with a butler and a swimming-pool.'

'I am none of those things,' I said. 'I mean, I don't have a butler or a swimming-pool. It's just an old house. And we don't have to sell it now.'

'That's great,' said Ash. 'Really pleased for you, ma'am. We should go out for drinks tonight to celebrate.'

'I'm meeting Georgy, I can't,' I said.

'I know,' Ash said. 'I saw her on Saturday.'

'No!' I said, impressed. 'I thought she'd threatened to call the police if you carried on bothering her?'

'I wore her down,' Ash said.

I looked out at the children in the playground below my window: they were running around yelling in the sunshine, and I reflected on how blokes always get the women they want by chasing them until they give in. I'm always amazed that so many men – usually the ugly ones – are convinced they could pull Claudia Schiffer if they were given the chance, while someone gorgeous, like my friend Victoria, is always convinced blokes don't fancy her. It rarely happens the other way round.

'You and Georgy, eh?' I said. 'Well, that's great.'

'It *is*,' Ash said. 'This weekend, man. It was amazing. She . . .' He was lost in a reverie.

I wasn't in the mood to discuss the first flush of young love, so I changed the subject, while Ash played with his shirt cuffs, a memory-laden smile playing about his lips in a smug, annoying way.

'So,' he said finally, looking lasciviously at me, 'how's love's young dream? And his brother?'

'If you mean Miles and me, it's all off,' I said. I pushed him out of my chair, sat down and started scrolling through my inbox. 'One hundred and four emails. How can I possibly have that many? I don't even *know* a hundred and four people,' I said, pressing the delete button smartly.

'What do you mean, off?' Ash said, sitting on my desk. 'You and Miles have split up?'

'Yup,' I said, and carried on deleting.

'Oh, Lizzy,' Ash said, with feeling. 'That's awful. I'm so sorry. When did he do it? I mean, how did it happen?'

I stopped clicking. 'Why are you assuming he dumped me?' I said.

'I didn't. I just thought . . .' Ash trailed off. 'Well, good, if you ended it,' he said firmly. 'Or not. What happened? Spill the beans.' He shuffled about on the end of the desk to make himself comfortable, and settled in for the long haul.

'Oh, God, I've been such an idiot,' I said, getting ready to launch into the story. And then I stopped. Before I do this, I thought, I need to think it all through. The trouble with a big story that you have to retell many times is that after a while you reel it off so glibly you forget what actually happened. You lose the truth of it, the essence, somewhere along the line. It becomes The Story. All right, it was over, once and for all, but while I could keep what he'd said close to me I stood a chance some day of being able to rationalize it. I didn't want it to become part of my past. I knew it was, but I wanted to keep it to myself for the moment.

Lily walked past, and looked briefly into the office, recalling me to my senses. "Lo, Lizzy,' she said. 'I'm coming back in a minute. Great news about the house. We need to talk about *Dreams* when you've got a moment.'

'Sure,' I said.

'So?' Ash pressed. 'What happened?'

'Who told you about it?' I said, taking a sip of my coffee.

'What?' Ash was still caught in a moment.

'About the house, I mean that *Mary Chartley* was being shot there.'

'Oh.' Ash nodded briefly. 'Jaden.'

'What?' I said. 'He called you?'

'No,' Ash said casually. 'He's here again. Oh, here he is.'

And into the sunlit room strolled the man himself, grinning from ear to ear and looking even more like a catalogue model than he usually did. I jumped up, ran over to him and flung my arms round him. I wanted to cry, but I settled for shouting, 'Jaden! Jaden!'

Jaden is a great hugger. He held me tight, then pulled back and looked at me, smiling. 'You look great, Lizzy,' he said, kissing me again. He smelt of citrus and fresh laundry.

'So do you,' I said. 'What are you doing here? This is such a lovely surprise.'

'I'm over for some meetings about *Dreams Can Come True*.'

'Oh,' I said, trying not to show I was miffed to have known nothing about it.

'It all happened on Thursday,' Ash interjected, standing by the door to which he had slunk, smirking, as Jaden entered. 'Paul doesn't like the Iranian boy. He thinks he should be a cute Irish kid instead. Well, you've got lots to discuss, so I'll leave you alone.' He resumed slinking and slunk off. I could tell he was already thinking, in his simplistic, any-relation-ship-is-better-than-none way, Fantastic, that's those two sorted. She's warm for his form and he for hers.

'No big deal,' Jaden said. 'He'll change his mind back, I promise. Paul's just been a nightmare since he got out of rehab. Keeps altering things for the sake of it. The yoga-instructor thing hit him real hard.'

'Idiot,' I muttered. 'Get over it.'

'Hey, Lizzy,' Jaden said. 'What's this I'm getting from you?'

'Nothing,' I said. 'All back to normal. It's nice to see you, it really is. I can't believe it's only been six weeks. It feels . . . well, it feels like ages.'

'How's that Miles guy?'

'Oh,' I said. 'Actually, we split up. On Saturday.'

'Seriously?' Jaden said, his forehead puckering.

'Yes,' I said.

'He dumped you?'

'No, he bloody did not,' I said heatedly.

Jaden nodded. 'So you're single again?' he asked.

'Yes,' I repeated.

Jaden looked at me as if he would say more. I tensed, waiting for the onslaught of milk-thistle tea recipes. Then he rocked on the balls of his feet. 'What are you doing for lunch?' he said, quietly.

419

'Nothing,' I said.

'I'll take you out. We can talk about the film and catch up. There's things we need to discuss.'

Outside, the whistle for the playground blew. 'That'd be lovely,' I said. 'Listen, Jaden, I've got loads to do . . . I'll see you later, OK? Meet you outside at one?'

'Sure,' Jaden said, and he left with a smile as my phone rang.

'Lizzy? Is it true? Have you and Miles split up?'

'Hello, Georgy,' I said, watching Jaden's retreating form. 'That was quick. You've spoken to Ash.'

'Ash has nothing to do with this. I've just been talking to Tom. What happened?'

'It's a long story,' I said, sitting down again. 'Hey, are you still on for this evening? We'll talk about it then. And about you and Ash, Georgy? What are you doing?'

'Yes, yes,' Georgy said impatiently. 'Are you OK, though? God, I've got to go. But look, before I do, Lizzy, another thing, v. quickly. I've got to try out our new hotel somewhere in Corfu. Dead posh. In about a month. Think you can swing a week's holiday then? All expenses paid, you'd just have to get a flight.'

Sea. Sun. Drinks with little umbrellas. Lying around for a week in a luxury hotel. I said, 'Are you serious?'

'Yes, of course,' Georgy said. 'Come on, you'll really be saving my bacon. It's all booked for a week and I don't want to have to go on my own.'

'Someone else ditched you, have they?' I asked resignedly. I know her so well.

'I thought I was supposed to be asking you that.' Georgy's throaty cackle crackled over the phone.

'Oi!' I said, banging my fist on my desk. 'I was not ditched! I ditched him!'

'So what happened? Oh, my God, I can't believe it. I've got to go! But, hey, how was the wedding?'

420

'Great, it was great.'

'Was the tulle OK in the end?'

'Fine. The buckle on my shoe was a right pain.'

'I *said* they'd be too tight.'

'I know,' I said grimly. 'I should have listened.'

'Yep,' Georgy said, with sad satisfaction. 'And the pants?'

'You were right there too. They well showed through. I wore the blue ones instead. I think it was OK.'

'Good, good. Listen to me next time. And Miles is history then? Well, I can't say I'm—'

I could have carried on this conversation happily for the next couple of hours, but I became aware of a movement below my right shoulder. Lily was making 'get off the phone' gestures and rolling her eyes. 'Got to go now, Georgy,' I said regretfully.

'See you later. And don't worry, I'm about to call Ash and deliver the blow. He won't be there, I promise.'

After dealing with Lily, who was incandescent with rage about Paul's latest meddling, and comforting a sobbing Ash in the men's loos, which took some explaining to Simon from IT who walked in on us there, the morning raced by and I was happily lost in the world of work again, the dramas, the emails, the gossip and the coffee machines. I had to tear myself away for lunch and run round the corner so I wasn't late for Jaden. We went to Carluccio's in Market Place and we sat outside and pretended to be Italian. I had a glass of wine. Jaden had an organic pineapple and orange juice.

There was something strange about sitting outside with Jaden in the summer heat. He felt like a part of my past, someone who existed only in the rainy days of last winter. 'It's great you're having a holiday,' he said, after I'd told him about Corfu with Georgy. 'You need one. Some you-time.'

'I can't wait,' I said. 'Only four weeks to go. How about you?'

'I'm taking a week off in late August. Hiking in the hills with some friends. Camping, doing a nature trail. Should be cool. If you're over by then, you should come. What's happening with that, by the way?' he added casually.

'Don't know,' I answered, equally casually. 'I still want to go . . . for six months, maybe a year.'

Jaden popped a cherry tomato into his mouth. 'In other words, you're not planning on staying.'

'I didn't say that,' I said, because in fact I wasn't.

'But you're not. I can tell from your body language. Something else is up, isn't it? It's the cast of your shoulders. You're like an open book.'

I remembered one summer at home, when I was about fourteen, Tom bought an old paperback at the Wareham fête called *Understanding Body Language*. We devoured it, and became obsessed with it over the next few weeks. When Mum or Kate told us to do the washing-up, we'd cross our arms to let them know we were aggressively opposed to the idea. When Mark Lenham, the boy from the next village whom everyone fancied, was sitting on the green at the same time as Jess and I, we lay down on our jumpers and pointed our feet subtly at him, to let him know we were subconsciously attracted to him. 'What do you mean?'

'Why don't you tell me?' Jaden said. 'Starting with the house. It's a beautiful home, Lizzy. I really enjoyed going there. I'm just sorry I couldn't tell you about it.'

'Not at all,' I replied, as the waiter arrived to clear away our plates. 'You and Sophia Gunning are the heroes of the hour down my way.'

'That is one talented girl,' Jaden mused. 'We've had a lot of very interesting conversations since then about this *Lady Mary* project. I think it's going to be very special.'

'Oh, come on,' I scoffed. 'You fancy her, you massive liar.'

'I do not!' Jaden exclaimed.

'You bloody do,' I said, laughing as he blushed.

Jaden caught my hands. 'I'm going to go a little crazy and have a coffee. And so are you. Why don't you tell me about this weekend? I think you're fine, Lizzy. You look better than I've seen you for ages. Perhaps being single finally agrees with you.'

So I told him everything. About Miles, and how blind and stupid I'd been. About home, and having to deal with packing up and getting ready to leave. About the Caldwells, and Chin, her brilliant last-minute save. About Miles and David, and how fucked-up Miles really was, about what he'd done, about the wedding. I'd forgotten how fascinated Jaden was by my family, and now he'd seen the house he had a context for it all so it was easy to tell him everything and he was a great listener.

When I'd woken up that morning I'd had a funny feeling about today, as if normal service was suspended in some way, like when you get sent home from school early because of a power cut: the regime by which you normally live your life suddenly seems flimsy, as if anything could blow it away. I realized as I talked that that was the cumulative effect of the weekend: I wasn't worried about anything any more. But neither was I convincing myself that everything was perfect when it clearly wasn't, which was what I'd been doing when I was going out with Miles.

As I drained my second coffee I looked at my watch. It was a quarter past two. 'We should be getting back,' I said.

'In a minute,' Jaden said. 'There's time.'

'How's Alina?' I said. Alina was Jaden's sister, chief services executive with a globally recognized brand of computer printers. She lived in Houston and was unlike her brother, from what I had gleaned.

423

'She got a haircut,' Jaden said. 'Are you going to call David, then?'

'What about – what was her boyfriend called? Pete? Paul? Did he make tenure?'

'Yes,' said Jaden. 'Another coffee, please. My gut is going to be shot to hell. Thank you,' he said, to the alarmed-looking waiter. 'So, are you going to call David?'

'That's great,' I said. 'About Paul. Pete.'

'Lizzy . . .'

I gazed around Market Place, the merry lunchtime drinkers, the gorgeous clothes happily hovering in the windows of Reiss opposite. 'Why would I?' I said.

'Because you're still in love with him.'

'Oh, for God's sake.' My stomach lurched at the thought of having conveyed the situation so inadequately. 'No, I'm not. And that's not the point . . . The point is that it's all over, and it's sad, but I know it's for the best.'

'What a load of bull!' Jaden said. 'Don't sit there and tell me what happened on Saturday and then say you're not going to call him.'

'I'm not.'

'The guy calls your house Christmas to try and sort it out. He comes round to your place in March and has to watch you behave like a total bitch – I'm sorry, forgive me – while you flirt with his brother, then kiss him, then flirt with me. He calls you to tell you he's still interested, and you brush him off. You hook up with his freaking brother and he has to stand by and watch! Jeez, Lizzy!'

So this was why Jaden didn't drink coffee. 'I'm not stubborn,' I said, equally heatedly. 'I'm not – listen to me,' for I could see he was about to interrupt again. 'I know all that. But I was angry with him then. I thought he'd . . . I'm not like you. Neither's David. I don't like talking about it, when there's nothing to talk about. That's not what either of us wants.'

'But!' Jaden smacked his head with his palm. 'Listen to yourself! You're talking about him as if you're a couple! If you know he thinks that and you know you think that then do something about it!'

I set my jaw. 'I'm not like that,' I said firmly. 'I've spent nearly a year getting over him. I'm not letting myself in for all that again.'

Jaden was more worked up than I'd ever seen him. He glared at me. 'Lizzy.'

'Yes?' I said.

Jaden said, 'I have three things to say to you, in a calm, rational way, and then we won't talk about it again. And I want you to listen to these three things and confirm them with me as I say each one. Because I'm right about them.'

'OK,' I said, looking anxiously at his fresh coffee.

'One. You and David were in love with each other when he went to New York, right?'

'Yes, but—'

'Yipbibibibi – no interrupting. Yes or no?'

'Yes.'

'Two. Basically, you guys split up because someone else tried to break you up. OK, you were both totally useless about the whole thing and kinda rolled over like sheep at the first sign of trouble, but you were told he'd slept with someone else and he was told you didn't love him any more. Right?'

'Well . . .' I began.

'Lizzy,' Jaden said again, dangerously.

'Yes,' I said.

'Three, and this is really important. Can you imagine feeling that way about anyone else?'

I was silent.

'Can you, Lizzy?' Jaden said quietly. 'Do you think he was the one?'

'It's—' I tried to speak.

'You do, don't you?' he said softly.

'Yes,' I whispered.

'Right,' Jaden said, sitting back in his chair. 'How many other people out there do you estimate there are for you?' I shook my head at him, bewildered. 'Exactly. So what are you gonna do about it?'

'I . . .'

'Come on, Lizzy!' Jaden barked.

'I'm going to . . . write to him,' I said, suddenly brave, feeling like I was in a revivalist meeting.

'Yes!' Jaden punched the air. 'Why don't you call him instead?'

'No, it's too weird,' I said, feeling momentum surging through my body at the idea of this course of action. 'He's in New York. I'll write to him. I want to put it all down so it's there in black and white. Everything, so he knows.'

'Great,' Jaden was standing up, carefully removing coins and notes from his man-bag and depositing them on the table. 'Let's get back. My work here is done.'

'Why are you doing all this for me, Jaden?' I said, as we walked back to the office.

'I'm the scriptwriter,' he said. 'Put it this way. I like being the *deus ex machina* once in a while.'

That night I went out with Georgy, and she said the same thing as Jaden, except we drank a lot more and she screamed a lot more and waved more cigarettes in the air. So when I got home late on Monday night, fired up by all of this, I sat on my sofa and thought about what I wanted to say. In the end I decided I couldn't put it *all* down. It was too complicated. So I took the photo of us in front of the Eiffel Tower, found an envelope, and wrote David's address on it very neatly. I wasn't going to take the risk of this being one of those 'And she addressed the envelope whilst drunk, and put the wrong street number on, and he never got her letter and he died a broken man six months later' things.

The windows in my little flat were wide open as I sat there chewing my pen. The contents of my bag sprawled on the floor where I'd thrown it down in my eagerness to complete my task. I could hear the late-night sounds of the city outside. In David's apartment the portable aircon had whirred all night, I remembered.

I stretched my legs and glanced at the window-sill, where my geraniums were poking their heads up, searching for the sun. I loved my flat. It was my home, and only I had the responsibility for making sure I was happy there. The one thing the last year had taught me was that your home had to be where you live, where you put down roots, not where ghosts of past lives and emotions flit about. While Keeper House would always be my favourite place in the world, I knew now that I also belonged here, in my tiny flat off the Edgware Road, near the joke shop, the market and the canal, where photos of Georgy and Tom were on the fridge and, on the noticeboard, the efficient list of tasks to do that I'd drawn up that morning. Renew the insurance. Get the front-door lock checked. Glue together the mug I'd broken. Get the photos of Chin's wedding developed.

I thought about Rosalie and Mike, safely back in their home, unpacking the bubble-wrapped pictures and hanging them on the wall. Rosalie would probably be the one with a hammer and tack in position, Mike advising her, a glass of wine in his hand, as the lights of Manhattan gleamed through the window. I thought of Kate, sitting outside her cottage with a cup of tea, listening to Radio Four, watching the stars. Was she thinking of what might have been with Mike? Was she remembering Tony? Did she look up to the sky and search for a sign of him? And I thought of Mum and Dad, labelling boxes, walking around our home, where Mum had stroked our hair and sung us to sleep, where Tony had slept on the night before he died, where Edwin Walter had stood one spring morning a hundred years ago and decided he was going to build a family.

Inaction was the thing to fear. I picked up the photo again, and looked at it. And on the back I wrote,

David,
I'm sorry for everything that's happened. What a mess.
I just thought you should know, I love you. I always will. I never stopped, even though I tried to pretend I had.
It's no big deal if you don't feel the same way, and I wouldn't be surprised. Just ring me up and tell me to go away if you want, and then at least it's sorted out, once and for all.
Lxxx

I posted it the next day. A week went by, and I heard nothing. Then two weeks. Then three, and I went on holiday knowing by then that it was all over.

THIRTY-SIX

The stuffy trains were taking people to the leafy, lawn-filled suburbs and towns outside London: Hanwell, Windsor, Henley, Oxford. The hot weather gave the station a festive, holiday feeling. Gone were the black accountants' suits, women in sensible court shoes, people hurrying with newspapers under their arms. Instead, as the heat of the day rose from the ground and the setting sun cast beams of light across the huge iron-and-glass tunnel of the station, the mood was relaxed, happy, friendly. Girls in flip-flops with pastel flowers on them, little tops, flowery skirts. Boys, who are always less sure of themselves in this temperature, in trendy long shorts, baggy shirts and designer shades. Above the concourse rose a babble of sound, the happy murmur of conversation and purpose, as passengers disappeared towards their trains.

I waited for Georgy under the huge electric timetable, sitting on the hard shell of my suitcase. She was late and we were about to miss the first Heathrow Express, but I was relaxed: we had time. I spread my hands and idly examined my forearms – the sun of recent weeks had turned them a light honey brown, the soft hairs on them white-blond. I wiggled my toes, painted a bright new pink for the holiday ahead. In my suitcase I had an assortment of clothing, lots of glittery makeup and sandals, books I'd probably never read. In my handbag I had a travel guide to Corfu and the book I'd picked to start first, then cast aside in favour of magazines. Suddenly my phone rang. I idly plucked it out of my bag.

'Where are you?' Tom's voice demanded.

'At Paddington,' I replied. 'Why?'

'The station?' he said, sounding almost cross. 'You're on the main bit? The concourse?'

'Yes,' I said. 'I'm waiting for Georgy. Why, what's up?'

'Oh, nothing,' Tom said. 'I just wanted to know how you were getting to the airport.'

'Eh?' I said. 'Why?'

'Are you sure that's the quickest way? Oh, well, it's your decision, better go now. Whereabouts are you waiting? I like it outside Dixon's.'

'What?' I said, confused. 'Tom, are you drunk? Why do you care where I'm waiting?'

'Oh, you know. Ergonomics. There should be benches.' He sounded less and less sure. 'So, where are you?'

'I'm underneath the main sign, right in the middle,' I said. 'By the tourist bureau. That way, I can see the trains and spot Georgy in case she comes off the Tube. Does that make ergonomic sense to you?'

'Great, thanks. 'Bye,' said Tom, and simply put the phone down. I was astonished yet again by the eccentricity of my family, which revealed itself to me on a near-daily basis. I swivelled round to lean against the upright handle of my suitcase and watch the scene in front of me.

The sounds and smells of an early summer's evening washed over me, the bustle and hurry of people on their way, smiling, frowning, the station guards chatting lugubriously

430

at the gates, train drivers wandering around. I yawned and stretched. A booming voice reminded me that the seven forty-five train to Exeter departing platform nine prevented me from dozing into a light sleep and possibly sliding onto the floor.

A movement out of the corner of my left eye caught my attention. Someone was skidding through the crowds, running for a train, and had bumped into an old lady. I closed my eyes again, listening to the footsteps hurry past her. They were coming in my direction. I opened my eyes.

David was standing in front of me. I blinked and looked again. Yes, it was definitely him.

'Hello?' I said, uncertainly.

'Hello,' he said, pausing for breath. He'd obviously been running for some time. His T-shirt clung to him and he was flushed. He swallowed, and looked down at me. 'Lizzy,' he said blankly. He was holding his phone. I stood up, determined to be friendly.

'Hello again.' I leaned on my suitcase, surprised to discover my legs were shaking. 'Off anywhere nice?' I asked politely. 'Had any interesting post lately?' I said in my head. 'Any letters from people telling you they're still in love with you? Yes?'

David brushed his hair off his forehead. 'Yes, I'm off on holiday, actually,' he said, more calmly.

'Lovely,' I said. 'Where?'

'Corfu.'

My heart sank at the sheer bad luck that bedevilled my every waking move. 'Oh . . . that's nice,' I said, rooting around nonchalantly in my bag, as I tried to stop my stupid legs from shaking. Then I looked at him properly. 'Why haven't you got any bags or anything?'

'I – I had to leave in a bit of a hurry,' he said. 'All my stuff's at the airport – I've just landed. You see—'

431

'I've got to go,' I interrupted. 'Sorry, David. Great to see you. I'm waiting for Georgy' – why did I still want him to know I wasn't going on holiday with a love rival? – 'and I've just seen her going into WH Smith's.'

'No, you haven't,' said David calmly.

'Yes, I have,' I said, raising my arm. 'Over there, in the blue dress.'

David caught my arm. 'You haven't. She's not there. She's not coming.'

'She is,' I said, wrenching my arm away. 'We're going on holiday together, as if it's any business of yours.'

David took my hand and held it, stroking my palm. 'Georgy's not coming. She's in her flat, getting ready to go out – or she was when I spoke to her five minutes ago. I'm coming with you. We're going to Corfu together, and then I'm moving back to London, and we're going to live together, and in the future – well, who knows? Well, I know one thing for sure.'

'What's that?' I said, hardly daring to breathe.

David moved closer towards me. 'I made the mistake of not coming to find you before, Lizzy,' he said, and I could feel his warm breath on my cheek, 'and I'm not doing it again. No matter how brave you pretend to be. I want to be with you. I always have. Since the moment I first met you.'

'What are you talking about?' I said, feeling as if I'd been winded. People were walking past and staring at us as we stood a few inches apart, eyes locked. I stepped back a little, David still holding my hand. He was here. He was standing in front of me and he was in love with me. I'd spent so long thinking I'd seen him at the pub, at a party, in a post office, and now he was actually here, and I knew without a doubt that the most natural thing in the whole world was for me to be with him.

'I got your letter last week, Lizzy. But I'd already decided I was going to come and find you. After the wedding – I was being stupid. Proud. I dialled your number a thousand times, but I was too chicken. I thought it was too late. I thought you were over me. Or that it was just too complicated.'

'Me too,' I said, moving closer to him. 'I thought it was just me, and I'd have to get over it.'

'I rang Tom when I got back to New York. I didn't know what to do. And he arranged it all.'

'Tom,' I said, comprehension dawning. 'He just rang me.'

'I couldn't find you,' David said. 'I was running around looking everywhere so he called you to make sure you were still here.'

'God, I'm going to kill him,' I said. Then I thought about it. 'No, I'm not. I'm going to buy him a huge bar of Toblerone in Duty Free.'

David held my hands to his chest. I could feel his heart beating. 'I haven't stopped thinking about you, Lizzy,' he said, as the noise around us faded. 'Not once since the day I met you. Even after we split up. It was hell. I didn't know what had happened. I couldn't understand why you'd suddenly changed your tune, and I was so angry with you for being weak and throwing it away.'

'But I wasn't—' I'd had this conversation in my head countless times and I couldn't believe it was really taking place. I looked around me, to remind myself of where I was. I was still in the station, with the same noises, bustle, purpose around me, but everything had changed. David put a finger to my lips. 'I want to say this. I've thought about saying it so many times. Oh, Lizzy,' he said softly, 'when I think about it, what we went through, how miserable I must have made you, and that – that stupid, *stupid* brother of mine.'

'It was other things too. I was stupid. All these different

bits and pieces, like Mike, the house and all that, Miles . . .'
I took a deep breath. 'Well, Miles being a total wacko. And
what my family was on about and stuff – and you most of
all. I've been blind. But not any more.'

David smiled. 'Really?' he said.

'I'm wise now,' I said. And I meant it. 'Even without you.
Those things can't hurt me any more. It's just . . . the idea I
hurt you so much. I hate that.'

I cupped his chin and kissed him. 'I'm so sorry,' I said.

David pulled me to him, and said, almost angrily, 'It's not
you, darling Lizzy. It was never you. I hate what I did to
you. The idea of anyone hurting you makes me so angry. So
full of – of rage, I don't know what to do. So when I think
about how much I must have upset you, how vicious I was
to you . . .' He trailed off, then said seriously, in a much
quieter voice, 'And all the time I was furious with you, I
couldn't stop thinking about you. And you were there, whatever I did. I could hear your voice, the funny things you say,
the way you look curled up on my sofa, in my bed, walking
through the park. You were everywhere. I couldn't get you
out of my mind. Never have been able to.' He paused. 'We
should *be* together, Lizzy. We always should have been. It
was my fault – it was your fault too, but it was my fault. I
shouldn't have gone to New York.'

'Yes, you should. I just shouldn't have been so pathetic
about it.'

'I was scared, you know. I loved you so much but I thought
if I go away and we stay together that means it's marriage
and babies and everything – and I didn't know what you
wanted. You were a bit distant. I was on my own so much,
I had too much time to think about stuff. I started to think
you – perhaps you . . . Well, that it was me who felt more,
and you weren't missing me . . .' He coughed. 'And I was
so angry with you at Christmas when I saw you. I really

434

thought I hated you. For ending it, for not loving me enough. I couldn't understand it, or why it had gone wrong, so I just assumed it was something you hated about me and never asked you to talk about it properly. It was my fault.'

'God, no – that was my fault too,' I said. 'I was thinking the same thing. I hated you – at least, I thought I did. I never worried about anything till you weren't there . . . I should never have believed Miles. I should have trusted you.'

'Well, I did snog Lisa,' said David, reasonably. 'Sort of. She snogged me.'

'I know . . . but how about we let that one slide, eh?' I said, equally reasonably. I put my hands on his chest and he pulled me to him. It felt like coming home. I could feel the warmth and hardness of his body, his fingers digging into my back. He bent his head and kissed me, and I forgot where I was or what had happened over the last year. It was as if we'd never been apart. Tears ran down my cheeks.

'I love you,' David said, and kissed me again. 'Fuck, this is strange.'

'Don't swear,' I said, patting my pockets for a tissue.

'Here,' said David, handing me one and taking my suitcase. 'Now we should go or we'll be late.'

'Right, sir,' I said, and slung my handbag over my shoulder. I grabbed his hand as we walked towards the Heathrow Express. David stopped and kissed me again. 'God, Lizzy, I can't believe I'm here with you. If you knew how much I'd missed you—'

'Don't,' I said, squeezing his hand. 'I do know, remember?'

'And there's no crazy cousins or brothers or friends to get in the way and screw things up. We can do it all by ourselves.'

'But I don't think we will,' I said, and rested my head on his shoulder as we walked towards the train.

Acknowledgements

Thank you so much to the following people for their support and advice and much more besides: Rebecca Folland and Pippa Wright – I don't know what I would have done without you two, and I thank you from the bottom of my heart. You are beautiful. Thanks also to Clare Betteridge, Jake Poller, Rob Williams, Auriol Bishop, Mary Mount, Liz Iveson and Air Commodore Rowland White. Shout out to Lindsey Jordan for being such a bez for eight years. Charlotte Robertson, thank you for telling me to do it in the first place. Big thanks to my best friend Sophie Linton for her wise ways, her property info and plot rehearsals over wine. And especially to Man Friday Thomas Wilson for being a great friend and computer technician (not in that order). And a special thanks to the gorgeous girls in Puccini's Caff: Hannah the beautiful bride and the lovely landlady, Caroline, Taissa and Claudia.

To all my lovely friends and colleagues on the Euston Road, in particular Jane Morpeth, Marion Donaldson, Charlotte Mendelson, Clare Foss and Catherine Cobain – thank you.

To the fantastic team at HarperCollins, who have made this such a great experience – thank you so much. In particular to Amanda Ridout, Lee Motley, Damon Greeney, Karen Davies, Kate Elliott, Carl Newbrook, Karen-Maree Griffiths and Shona Martyn with a massive thank you to the great and talented Maxine Hitchcock and the equally great and talented Helen Johnstone – big love to you both, ladies. Thanks also to Hazel Orme.

My biggest thanks go to Mark Lucas and Lynne Drew. I owe all of this to you. Mark, thanks for believing in me right from the start and for your great advice and wisdom (incredible in one so young). You truly are, as Raj said, God's Creation. Lynne – what can I say? You are the greatest publisher, as well as the greatest friend. I wish you a lifetime's happy shopping at Anthropologie and much more.

And last of all thanks to my family, my beautiful sister Caroline (big hug) and my parents, Phil and Linda, who are the best parents in the whole world and my inspiration.